THE SWISS ACCOUNT

The
Swiss Account

Paul Erdman

ANDRE DEUTSCH

First published 1991 by
André Deutsch Limited
105-106 Great Russell Street London WC1B 3LJ

British Library Cataloguing in Publication Data
Erdman, Paul *1932-*
    The Swiss account.
    I. Title
    813.54 [F]

    ISBN 0 233 98604 9

Printed in Great Britain by
Billing & Sons Ltd, Worcester

Preface

This is a novel, but it is a novel that leans very heavily on historical events and personae. In order to help the reader separate real events from those I have made up, I decided to provide a running guide in the form of footnotes, citing the original sources of the factual material in all cases.

Regarding the characters, the 'real' ones include such a diverse group as Allen Dulles, who headed the American espionage efforts in Switzerland in World War II; Karl Barth, probably the leading Christian theologian of the twentieth century; General Walter Schellenberg, who was in charge of the foreign intelligence operations of the Nazi SS during the war; and the Swede, Per Jacobsson, of the Bank for International Settlements, the central bank of the world's central banks. The two tarts who travel with Schellenberg are fictional (I think), as are the three protagonists in this novel, all young (i.e. thirty and younger): two are Swiss, Peter and Felicitas Burckhardt, who are brother and sister, and one is an American, Nancy Reichman, who represents the United States as vice-consul in Basel, Switzerland, between 1940 and 1945.

Having said this, I hope that when you now read on you will forget all of the above and enjoy this book for what it was intended to be: a story of intrigue and romance set in the unique atmosphere of neutral Switzerland during World War II.

Prologue

On 29 April 1944, a prototype of an advanced version of one of Nazi Germany's fighter aircraft, a Messerschmitt 110 Cg + EN, which had been engaged in an air battle over southern Germany, landed by mistake at Dübendorf airport outside Zurich, Switzerland. It was powered by radically new engines and was equipped with highly secret and extremely advanced instrumentation which gave the plane a unique capability in night operations. The pilot tried to take off again when he realized where he was, but was prevented from doing so by the Swiss military.

When Adolf Hitler was told this he immediately summoned General Walter Schellenberg, who headed the intelligence operations of the SS, as well as Schellenberg's right-hand man, Rittmeister Hans Wilhelm Eggen. His instructions were very precise: if a deal for the return of the Me 110 could not be worked out within forty-eight hours, SS Intelligence should immediately determine the exact location of the aircraft. Then it was to be destroyed either by a bombing attack on Dübendorf airport by the German Luftwaffe, or by the dropping of a unit of German paratroopers which would include a demolition squad.[1]

One hour later Schellenberg telephoned his intelligence counterpart in Switzerland, Colonel Roger Masson, the head of Section 5 of the General Staff of the High Command of the Swiss

---

1 This information was revealed in a secret deposition given by Eggen in Switzerland on 10 August 1945. See the Swiss Federal Archives, *BAr 2809/1.4.*

vii

army in Lucerne: 'You have surely heard about the Messerschmitt which landed last night in Dübendorf,' he began. Then: 'We must have that plane back, Herr Oberst. We are acting under direct instructions from the Führer. He has told us that he expects us to resolve this matter within two days. To that end I have already arranged for my adjutant, Rittmeister Eggen, to come to Switzerland to work out the details. He will arrive at the Badische Bahnhof in Basel at nine o'clock this evening.'

'One of my adjutants, Lieutenant Peter Burckhardt, will be there to meet him,' the Swiss colonel replied. 'I'm sure we can work something out, Herr General.'

The German with many titles – Rittmeister, Sturmbannführer, Major – arrived at the Badische Bahnhof at 21.07 that evening, and was met by Lieutenant Peter Burckhardt as soon as he had cleared Swiss customs. Burckhardt came equipped with the outline of a deal which had been relayed to him by telex just one hour earlier. The telex had also contained orders, issued by no less than the commander-in-chief of the Swiss army, General Guisan himself, authorizing him to negotiate the details of the deal for the Messerschmitt 110 with Eggen on his behalf. But he should only proceed if Eggen came equipped with a similar authorization, in writing, signed by someone in an obvious position of authority in the upper hierarchy of the Nazi regime.

Eggen had booked a room at the Three Kings Hotel overlooking the Rhine in the centre of Basel. Burckhardt, who had driven him there in his Mercedes, rather than join him in his room as Eggen had insisted, suggested that the German take his time to unpack and get refreshed. He would be waiting for him in the bar. Burckhardt sat there alone at a corner table for ten minutes. Then the German reappeared, carrying his briefcase. He had no sooner sat down than he extracted a sheet of paper and handed it to Burckhardt. It contained the exact authorization that Burckhardt required, and carried two signatures: that of Marshal Hermann Göring, the head of the Luftwaffe whose prize plane had gone astray, and that of General Walter Schellenberg, the head of SS Intelligence and the man whom Hitler had charged with getting it back. Burckhardt read it and then withdrew from the breast pocket of his jacket that portion of the telex he had received earlier that evening which contained General Guisan's orders to himself. Eggen read it and nodded.

'It looks like it will be up to the two of us, doesn't it?'

'At least for the moment,' Burckhardt replied.

'So why not get right to it? The issue is very simple. We want that plane back. You will want something in return for doing us that favour. What is it?'

All the cloying charm of the German had disappeared. He was now all SS . . . brutal and arrogant.

'The plane will not be returned. That decision has already been taken by the general and the Federal Council and it is irrevocable,' was Burckhardt's response, and from the expression it evoked on the face of the SS major, it was totally unexpected.

'Are you Swiss crazy?' he now hissed at Burckhardt. 'Don't you realize that it is Adolf Hitler you are dealing with?'

'We are not dealing with Hitler. We are dealing with you, Herr Eggen.'

'But you just said that there can be no deal. That . . .'

Burckhardt interrupted. 'I said no such thing. I just said that we will not be returning the Messerschmitt. Doing so would be totally incompatible with the generally recognized rules governing the conduct of neutral nations during times of armed conflict.'

'I can tell you right now, Herr Leutnant, that this will be totally unacceptable to the Führer. He will not tolerate a situation in which there would be even the slightest chance that the British or Americans might gain access to this plane.'

'We fully understand that.'

Now Eggen looked puzzled. 'But how in the world could you guarantee that?'

'By destroying the plane. In the presence of whomever you choose to witness its destruction.'

Now the suave Rittmeister Eggen resurfaced. 'How ingenious, Herr Doktor! And how very typical of you Swiss. You always find a way. If need be, I am sure you would even find a way to square the circle. Yes, I like it.' Then: 'When?'

'As soon as the details of the *quid pro quo* are worked out.'

'Aha. And what might these details involve?'

'In exchange for the destruction of the Me 110, we want twelve of your standard fighter aircraft, Me 109Gs, for our air force. We would expect them to be delivered within two days of the demolition of your prototype night fighter, and flown in to the same airport where the Me 110 landed: Dübendorf.'

'I assume the 110 is still there?' Eggen interjected, slyly he thought.

'I doubt it,' Burckhardt replied, although he didn't have the slightest idea of whether it was still there or not.

'There is one more detail,' Burckhardt added. 'We are fully prepared to pay for these Me 109s. Full price. Cash. In Swiss francs. On delivery.'

'Aha. This is becoming very interesting,' the German said, and Burckhardt could almost hear the wheels spinning in his head. 'What price did you have in mind?'

'A half million francs per plane.'

'Five hundred thousand francs each,' Eggen repeated, savouring the words. 'And cash, you said.'

'Cash.'

'I think, Herr Doktor Burckhardt, that we already have the essential elements of a deal, at least as far as I am concerned. I am sure that Herr General Schellenberg will second me in this. The problem will be Marshal Göring. To convince him that his Luftwaffe must give up twelve fighter planes under the current circumstances will not be easy.' Then he hastened to add: 'But do not misunderstand me. Difficult it will be. But not impossible.' Then: 'Might *I* now make a suggestion, Herr Burckhardt?'

The Swiss braced himself. 'Certainly.'

'That we drink a nicely chilled bottle of Dom Perignon. Agreed?'

It took longer than either the Germans or the Swiss had anticipated, but on 18 May 1944 — Ascension Day! — the Me 110 Cg + EN was blown to smithereens on the tarmac of Dübendorf airport outside Zurich (using German explosives which had been brought in by Eggen), and just to make sure, gasoline was poured over the fragments and set ablaze. There were six official witnesses: from the German side SS Major Eggen and Captain Brandt of the Luftwaffe (the personal delegate of Marshal Hermann Göring, who, upon direct orders from Hitler, had signed off on this deal); from the Swiss side, two brigadiers from the Swiss High Command, Rihner and Wattenwyl, as well as Colonel Masson and Lieutenant Burckhardt of Section 5 of the General Staff of the Swiss High Command.[2]

Exactly two days later, on 20 May, twelve German Me 109s were flown into Dübendorf and turned over to the Swiss air force.

This was typical of the cynical deals which were being cut during World War II in Switzerland, where the espionage services of all of the major warring nations were seeking to take advantage of the unique freedom of action allowed them . . . for a price, of course . . . by the host country. But in terms of importance for the outcome of the war, none of the many such episodes were even remotely worthy of comparison with the one which was approaching its culmination point just over half a year later, in January of 1945.

---

2 For full details of this incident, see Willi Gautschi, *General Henri Guisan: Die Schweizerische Armeeführung im Zweiten Weltkrieg* (Zurich, 1989), pp. 563–7.

PART ONE

Chapter 1

The fog which enveloped the train rose from the River Rhine, and it was exceptionally heavy in early January of 1945. The frozen bodies of thousands of American GIs who were dying in the Ardennes forest as a result of the unexpected and savage counteroffensive which the German Wehrmacht had launched just before Christmas represented a further ghastly testimony to the record cold which had descended upon the dying continent of Europe that year. It was death, in its all-pervasive presence, which was on the mind of the Swede, Per Jacobsson, as he sat in solitude in the darkened compartment of the night train from Frankfurt as it worked its way through the dense night toward Lörrach, the last stop before the Swiss frontier.

Everybody but Jacobsson and the heavy contingent of German military guards left the train in Lörrach before it once again began moving, very slowly, across the border into neutral Switzerland. Ten minutes later it came to a second halt at the Badische Bahnhof, the German railway station which was an extraterritorial enclave within the ancient Swiss city of Basel. This extraterritoriality was attested to by the Nazi uniforms of the guards who watched the Swede as he descended from the train onto the cold concrete of Bahnsteig 3. There were no porters there. In fact none had been there for well over five years — since 3 September 1939 to be precise, the day World War II had begun.

After walking fifty metres through the eerie empty vastness of the Badische Bahnhof he came to a barrier in the form of a high fence made of steel mesh. The gate which led through it was closed. To the left of the gate stood a long wooden table. He put his black leather suitcase on top of it, and waited. After less than a minute the door to the room behind the table opened and three officials emerged. One of them was an Oberst in the SS. He remained five steps behind the other two as they moved into position on the other side of the table.

'Geben Sie mir bitte Ihren Pass,' came the order.

The Swede handed over his passport.

'Sie sind ja sehr weit weg von zu Hause, Herr Jacobsson. Warum?'

Before the Swede could even begin to explain his presence so far from his native land, the man with the skull and cross bones insignia on his black uniform stepped forward.

'We have been expecting you, sehr geehrte Herr Jacobsson. I trust your journey from Berlin was uneventful?'

The Swede nodded. And then motioned toward his still unopened suitcase. 'Nicht nötig,' said the SS colonel, and indicated that he could proceed through the gate, suitcase still unopened.

The colonel pressed a button mounted below the wooden table. A loud buzzer sounded and the gate through the steel mesh fence swung open. On the other side of the gate there was another wooden table, a small one. Behind it stood a single Swiss official, a corporal in the ugly green uniform of the Swiss military. When Jacobsson once again handed over his passport, it was very carefully examined. Then a huge book that lay on the table was opened and pages turned to the section which dealt with Swedish nationals. The passport was again examined, numbers compared, and the passport returned without comment, but this time the suitcase was not only opened but thoroughly inspected.

'In Ordnung,' said the Swiss corporal finally.

It was almost exactly midnight when Per Jacobsson finally emerged from the train station and stepped onto Swiss soil.

Two people were standing on the other side of the Resenthalstrasse watching him as he emerged from the Badische Bahnhof – the man a Swiss, the woman an American. They stood together

4

in front of the restaurant 'Kleinbasler Weinstube', which served a lot more beer than wine since it was located in the middle of the working-class quarter of Basel. A fourth man sat silently in an old black Fiat parked directly in front of the station, apparently waiting to pick up an arriving passenger. In fact, the fourth man had no intention of picking up anybody: his job was to observe and to interfere only if the national security interests of Switzerland were at risk. His name: Dr Wilhelm Lützelschwab, the head of the political police of the canton of Baselstadt, the unit responsible for all counter-intelligence in the northwestern part of Switzerland. Swiss counter-intelligence had had a busy war so far: 1,389 people had been arrested on espionage charges, 813 had been tried and convicted; of these, thirty-three had received the death sentence for committing treason. Not bad for a country with a population of less than five million.

Lützelschwab watched as Jacobsson crossed the Resenthalstrasse and approached the two people standing in front of the Kleinbasler Weinstube. Seconds later all three of them — the Swede, the Swiss, and the American woman — disappeared inside the restaurant. Then, apparently satisfied with what he had seen, Dr Lützelschwab drove off.

After they sat down at a table and ordered a carafe of Dôle, the heavy Swiss red wine which was fully appropriate on this icy winter night, the American woman was the first to speak. 'Mr Dulles was unable to come over from Bern this evening. His presence was urgently required in Paris. So he asked me to come instead.'

The Swede just nodded. He knew that the American woman worked with Dulles. In fact, the three of them had even dined together in Basel on one occasion.

'Were you able to find out where Heisenberg is?'

'No,' answered the Swede. 'Mr Dulles' information was correct. Heisenberg, Hahn, von Weizsäcker, they have all disappeared from Berlin. And all the equipment they were using at the Kaiser Wilhelm Institute has likewise disappeared.'

'Did you get any indication of how close they were before they disappeared?'

'Yes.' Jacobsson paused, and then went on. 'Close. Very close. I don't understand exactly what it means, but I was told that it was no longer a matter of design but just the lack of heavy water and uranium. That final problem was expected to be corrected in February.'

'You are sure about it no longer being a matter of design?'

'Positive.'

'Mr Dulles will want to hear about this immediately.'

'He and you must handle this information with the utmost discretion. It was only at enormous risk that Herr Dr Puhl could find this out. We both are mere economists and bankers and hardly concern ourselves with matters which involve advanced physics. Peter knows this of course, but for your information, Miss Reichman, Dr Puhl is the director of the Reichsbank in Berlin and also one of the directors of my bank, the Bank for International Settlements here in Basel. Over the years we have become quite close. When Mr Dulles asked me to help him in this matter, it was natural that I turn to Puhl for assistance, since he travels in the highest circles in Berlin, both financial and academic. One of Puhl's closest friends is a chemist who also works at the Kaiser Wilhelm Institute. At times the physicists seek out his advice. That is why he was able to give Puhl the information that I have just passed along to you. But if any of this gets back to the Gestapo . . .'

'We fully understand that, Herr Jacobsson,' the American woman replied.

Then Peter Burckhardt, the young Swiss man, intervened. 'Speaking of Gestapo, they have people all over Basel, so I don't think that the three of us should be seen together any longer than necessary.'

'You're right,' the American woman said, and then added: 'Would you mind dropping me off first? I know it might be out of the way, but . . .'

The two men immediately agreed. Peter Burckhardt motioned to the waiter and paid the bill. His Mercedes was parked immediately in front of the restaurant, and all three climbed in.

Once inside, Peter Burckhardt turned to his boss at the Bank for International Settlements and said: 'I was just reflecting on your last words. About the Gestapo. How were you able to justify your visit to Berlin, if I may ask, sir?'

'Puhl asked me to act as an intermediary for one last shipment of gold from Berlin to the Swiss National Bank. Since he is no longer able to leave Germany, in order to work out the documentation for the payment arrangements – which will be done through the BIS – I went to him. All this is totally repugnant to me. But Mr Dulles convinced me that so much is at stake here . . .'[1]

Then all three fell silent. After a five-minute ride they crossed the Rhine over the Mittlerebrücke, the eleventh-century bridge which connected the two parts of the city of Basel – Kleinbasel, which lay north of the river, and Grossbasel to the south, contiguous to the rest of Switzerland. From there Burckhardt drove to the Marktplatz, the centre of the city where each morning since the Middle Ages the Baslers came to buy their fresh produce in the open-air market. There the American woman suggested that he let her out. After doing so, she checked to see if anyone was watching – in fact the square was totally deserted – and then waved goodbye to the two men who had remained silent and watching in the car. After the Mercedes had moved on she walked briskly up a steep narrow passageway, the Martinsgasse, leading to an ancient cobbled street, the Augustinergasse. The houses on the north side, all dating back to the thirteenth and fourteenth centuries, looked down on the Rhine. Nancy Reichman lived in a small apartment on the third floor, the top floor, of Augustinergasse 11.

After climbing the stairs, and letting herself in, she flung her coat on the sofa, and picked up the phone. Despite the hour,

---

1 According to a Swiss journalist who stumbled upon this previously secret information in the Swiss National Archives in the early 1980s, this last wartime shipment of gold from Berlin to Bern took place in April of 1945. As he notes, sarcastically, in his book on this subject, it occurred three weeks before Hitler committed suicide. See Werner Rings, *Raubgold aus Deutschland: Die 'Goldscheibe' Schweiz im Zweiten Weltkrieg* (Zurich and Munich, 1985), p. 162.

somebody at the American embassy in Bern immediately answered.

'This is Nancy Reichman, the vice-consul in Basel. Please let Mr Dulles know I will be calling him at eight o'clock tomorrow morning.'

'Will do,' said a cheerful voice on the other end. 'And sleep well, Miss Reichman.'

She did not sleep well. In fact she barely slept at all. For she was one of the few people in the world in January of 1945 who had ever heard the adjective 'atomic' applied to the noun 'bomb'. Not even Harry Truman, the Vice-President of the United States, had been brought into the know. She was also among the few people in the world who knew that Herr Professor Dr Werner Heisenberg was thought to be, in the words of the Swedish banker, 'close, very close' to manufacturing one that would work.

Allen Dulles was having breakfast in his apartment, which was situated in Bern high above the ravine formed by the River Aare, when Nancy Reichman's call came through. After he had thanked her and suggested that she make no plans for the immediate future which could not easily be cancelled, he hung up. He already had the germ of an idea as to what to do next . . . provided he could cut yet another deal with the Swiss. Which would meet with heavy opposition in some circles back in Washington where patience with the Swiss had just about run out in view of their continuing economic and financial cooperation with Nazi Germany. When they found out that he, Dulles, had essentially talked the head of the Bank for International Settlements into arranging for yet another deal involving the swapping of looted Nazi gold for American dollars in Switzerland, God knows how they would react. Which made everything he was about to undertake all the more dangerous, more delicate: almost tantamount to consorting with the enemy. Yet there was no choice. Somebody had to find out where Heisenberg was and how far he had gotten before it was too late. If Dulles were to do so, he desperately needed the help of the Swiss. Yet again.

8

And if he found out what he feared he might, he might very well have to arrange for some people to be killed, and quickly, cost what it may in terms of the lives of those who would have to act as the executioners. Yes, even if it meant putting the life of a nice young American girl like Nancy Reichman on the line, he had no choice. Where Peter Burckhardt was concerned he had fewer qualms. For Dulles knew that the young Swiss, in addition to being a banker, was also a lieutenant attached to Section 5 of the General Staff of the Swiss High Command, and as such one of the most responsible officers in Swiss Intelligence. Running high risks went with the job.

Callous thoughts for an American diplomat in the official service of his country!

Their explanations could be found in the fact that Allen Dulles lived and worked in a world which was really totally new for Americans − the underworld of intelligence, of active intelligence, where the rules of diplomacy did not apply and where, in fact, moral and ethical principles were often ignored because, it was reasoned, they had to be ignored if the Western democracies were to survive in the face of both Fascism and Communism. For Allen Dulles and all his colleagues in the Office of Strategic Services, the OSS, the first real national intelligence agency ever put into the field by the United States of America and the forerunner of the CIA (that feared and often unjustly maligned agency which Allen Dulles was destined to head), regarded the Nazis and the Soviets as being in the same class: mortal enemies of the United States. If *either* were about to produce an atomic bomb, they had to be stopped. From the very beginning, he had been fighting a two-front war against both the Nazis and the Soviets from his post in Bern from which he directed all OSS activities on the continent of Europe, and if he needed the help of the Swiss, or the devil himself, to win that war, he had no qualms whatsoever about seeking that help.

He and the Swiss had already used each other on quite a few occasions . . . to their mutual profit. In fact, were the truth to ever come out, it was Dulles' highly secret connection with Swiss Intelligence − a secret often kept from both of their superiors −

9

that had made the difference between his success and failure. Their highly unorthodox cooperation had already started just three months after he had assumed his post as the OSS's 'man in Bern'.

Chapter 2

The origins of the OSS, and Allen Dulles' association with it, dated back to June of 1942, when 'Wild Bill' Donovan, who was the only American soldier to emerge from the fighting in France during World War I with more medals and fame than General MacArthur and who had later gone on to run unsuccessfully for governor of New York in 1933 on the Republican ticket, convinced President Roosevelt that the United States needed an organization that could not only gather intelligence but also conduct 'unconventional' wartime operations.[2] One of Donovan's first recruits had been Allen Dulles, a Princeton graduate and a professional diplomat, which was fitting since he was also the nephew of former Secretary of State Robert Lansing. Dulles had been associated with the Foreign Service in one capacity or another since World War I and had served in various European countries, including Switzerland. In his Swiss post in the final years of World War I, his real activity had been providing Washington with intelligence about what was happening in Germany, Austria and the Balkans. Dulles was, therefore, perfectly qualified to run the OSS's operations in central Europe, and Switzerland, neutral Switzerland, which he knew well, was the obvious place from which to do it.

So on 2 November 1942, Donovan had sent Dulles off to

---

2 See Richard Dunlop, *Donovan: America's Master Spy* (New York, 1982), for the definitive history of the OSS and the role played by Allen Dulles.

Switzerland, and he followed exactly the same route that the Swiss were later to use as their last-ditch supply line from the extra-European world. He had flown into Lisbon on a Pan Am Clipper via Bermuda, and had then proceeded by train to Barcelona and finally to the Spanish—French frontier at Port Bou, where he had boarded yet another train that had taken him through Vichy France to the border outside Geneva, where he arrived on 7 November. There his career with the OSS and subsequently the CIA almost ended before it really got started. The reason according to Dulles: 'I found that a person in civilian dress, obviously a German, was supervising the work of the French border officials. I had been told in Washington that there would probably be a Gestapo agent at this frontier. I was the only one among the passengers who failed to pass muster. The Gestapo man carefully put down in his notebook the particulars of my passport and a few minutes later a French gendarme explained to me that an order had just come down from Vichy to retain all Americans presenting themselves at the frontier and to report each case directly to Marshal Pétain.' While Dulles protested at length, suggesting that the Marshal probably had many other things to worry about, since the Americans had just landed in North Africa, noontime arrived and the Gestapo man had disappeared. It seemed that, with his fixed Germanic habits, promptly at noon he always went down the street to the nearest pub and had his first beer of the day. The gendarme immediately interrupted Dulles, and motioned him back onto the train, whispering: 'Allez passez vite. Vous voyez que notre collaboration n'est que symbolique.' (Go ahead quickly. You see our cooperation is only symbolic.) Minutes later Dulles had crossed the French border into Switzerland legally. He was one of the last to do so until after the liberation of France.[3]

Immediately Dulles began recruiting aides, hampered by the fact that, right after his arrival in Switzerland, the Nazis had occupied Vichy France, countering the threat to France's Mediterranean coast which had now arisen with the Allied

---

3 Allen Dulles, *The Secret Surrender* (New York, 1966), pp. 12ff.

presence in North Africa, meaning that now all Swiss borders were closed by zones of Nazi or Fascist occupiers. Among those recruited were a few aides already stationed in Switzerland whose original assignments had become outdated now that Switzerland was isolated: men and women from various departments of the American government dealing with commercial matters, or those involved with consular activities − providing visas for Swiss businessmen intending to visit the United States, or giving aid to American tourists visiting Switzerland.[4] One of the first to be signed up was the American vice-consul in Basel, Nancy Reichman.

The consulate in Basel could not have been more strategically placed from the standpoint of the OSS, located as it was in the centre of that Swiss city which bordered on both Germany and France, a city which furthermore was one of central Europe's most important transportation hubs. The problem was that it had been staffed with only two Foreign Service officers, and one of them, the consul, had just retired and not been replaced. Nor could he be replaced now that Switzerland was sealed off. There was a 'problem' also where the vice-consul was concerned: she was a woman. Not only that, she was a Jewish woman.

But Dulles was desperate. So exactly thirty days after he had arrived in Bern he invited her to visit him − not at the embassy itself, where his clandestine activities were not always appreciated by the old-line State Department types, especially the chief of the American Legation in Switzerland, Leland Harrison, but at his apartment on the Herrengasse in Bern.

When he opened the door to greet her he was stunned by her appearance. She was a petite dark-haired beauty, extremely well dressed, a woman who had more than a passing resemblance to Gene Tierney, the young actress whose Hollywood career was just beginning. Dulles' first irreverent thought was that his boss, the head of the OSS, Wild Bill Donovan, who had an eye for

---

4 Ibid., p.16.

13

young women, would have recruited her on the spot without a further word.

But that thought was quickly submerged since Dulles, in contrast to the Irish Catholic Donovan, was quite puritanical and in fact served as a Presbyterian elder, with the sad result that he never mixed hanky-panky with the business at hand or, for that matter, anything else.

'May I take your coat?' were his first words to Nancy Reichman, and when she handed it to him, Presbyterian elder or not, he could hardly help but notice that she was a very well-endowed young lady.

'Coffee?'

She hesitated.

'It's real American coffee, not the ersatz stuff,' Dulles immediately added. 'I brought some with me on the Clipper. And let's sit over there by the window while we drink it.'

The window looked out over the ravine which had been formed by the River Aare below, and behond that the Alps of the Bernese Oberland.

'Beautiful, isn't it?'

She agreed.

'And an added feature is that vineyard that you see down there growing between my house and the river below. It provides an ideal cover for any visitors who might not wish to be seen entering the front door on the Herrengasse.'[5]

Nancy Reichman said nothing.

'I mentioned that because of the nature of the business I am in and the reason I have asked you to come here today. Have you been informed about me by Minister Harrison here at the Legation, or by anybody else in the Department?'

'No, sir,' replied Nancy Reichman. 'Although I did read in the *Neue Zürcher Zeitung* that you are regarded by the Swiss as the personal representative of President Roosevelt.'[6]

Allen Dulles laughed.

---

5 Ibid., p.15. In this autobiographical book, it is obvious that Allen Dulles relished the role of being a 'spy'.

'That's not quite true, but I'm the last person who's going to deny it. What I really am is an intelligence officer attached to an organization in our government which goes under the name of the Office of Strategic Services. President Roosevelt signed the order creating the OSS just over a half a year ago. We've been around for a while before this in a sort of informal way under the leadership of William Donovan, whom President Roosevelt appointed as Coordinator of Information in July of 1941 reporting directly to himself. Now we report both to the President and the Joint Chiefs of Staff. So we are a relatively new organization, and brand new where Switzerland is concerned. We're looking for help here, and that's why I asked you to come over from Basel to see me.'

Dulles then added: 'I must impress on you from the very outset, however, that all that I am about to tell you is highly secret. You understand?'

'Yes, sir.'

She answered in a voice that was slightly shaky. For the man sitting opposite her was one who, by his very presence, inevitably made others uneasy. He was a man in his fifties, of medium build, and dressed rather informally. To be sure he wore a tie, but rather than the blue suit so prevalent in diplomatic circles, Dulles had on a brown sports jacket and tan slacks. Nothing unusual there. It was his head and eyes that commanded respect . . . mixed with an element of fear. His grey hair was impeccably groomed, his head squarer and larger than normal. But it was his steel-grey eyes, behind the rimless glasses, that set him apart from mere mortals. They did not just see: they penetrated. And those eyes were firmly fixed on the eyes of Nancy Reichman as he continued.

'Now one thing just struck me. You said that you read about me in the Swiss newspapers. Are you that fluent in German?'

'Yes. Also in Schwyzerdeutsch, the Swiss dialect.'

'How come German?'

---

6 Ibid. Dulles notes here that he had no idea as to how this false rumour was started.

'My parents emigrated from Germany, and we still speak German at home.'

'Where is home?'

'Palo Alto, California.'

'Why Palo Alto?'

'My father teaches economics, the history of economic thought to be more precise, at Stanford. He studied under Max Weber at Heidelberg.'

Allen Dulles nodded approvingly. He was getting more interested by the minute.

'And how come you're fluent in the Swiss dialect?'

'After I finished my undergraduate work at Stanford in the spring of 1937 I came to Switzerland to do postgraduate studies at the university of Basel — in fact, last year I resumed taking lectures and seminars there, part-time of course — and made a deliberate effort to learn Schwyzerdeutsch. You see the Swiss students always hated the Germans who came to Basel to study before the war. They were arrogant, stand-offish, and they kept to themselves. They made no secret of the fact that they regarded the Swiss as a bunch of provincials, as cultural inferiors. I guess we would use the word "hicks". And the more successful Hitler became, the more superior their attitude. As a result the Swiss started referring to Germans as "chaibe Schwobe".'

'Translation?'

Nancy Reichman blushed. 'I guess a very loose translation would be "Kraut bastards".' She blushed again.

Dulles loved it. And tried it out. 'Chaibe Schwobe. Did I say it right?' His pronunciation was abominable, but Nancy Reichman nodded eagerly.

'And when did you join the Foreign Service?'

'In the summer of 1939, just before the war started. My father insisted I break off my studies here and return home. So I did. I took the Foreign Service exams, passed, and after an initial stint in Washington at the State Department was sent to Basel in August of 1940 as vice-consul. I guess for obvious reasons.'

'Who do you know in Basel?' Dulles then asked.

'You mean Swiss?'

Dulles waved his hand. 'In general. Important people, Swiss or foreign.'

'The Swiss keep to themselves, as I am sure you know, sir. But still, through the university, especially through Professor Edgar Salin, I have been unusually fortunate in being able to meet, in fact more than just meet, some quite unusual people.'

'Such as?'

'Lawyers. People active in the arts. Also bankers − from the Bank for International Settlements, for example.'

'Such as?'

'You mean from the BIS?'

'Yes.'

'Per Jacobsson. And his personal assistant, who is a young Swiss who studied with me at the university before the war started, Dr Peter Burckhardt.' Dulles thought he detected another faint blush when Nancy Reichman mentioned the name of the young Swiss man.

'Who else?'

'A lot of other students, or, better said, former students who have taken positions with the chemical companies in Basel, such as CIBA-Geigy, Hoffman La Roche, Sandoz. They all have operations throughout Europe and around the world. Or with commercial banks like the Swiss Bank Corporation, which is Switzerland's largest and has its headquarters in Basel. And with ex-students who live in other cities like Zurich. They are among Switzerland's elite, since they came to Basel to study under professors who are among the greatest thinkers of our time. Men like Professor Karl Barth, the Protestant theologian, and Professor Jaspers, the German existentialist philosopher who couldn't stand to live in Nazi Germany; and Professor Carl Gustav Jung, the psychiatrist. He comes over from Zurich twice a month to lecture, as does Wolfgang Pauli, the physicist. Then there is Professor Edgar Bonjour, the Swiss historian who is chronicling the history of Swiss neutrality, and . . .'

Dulles interrupted: 'And your Professor . . . what was his name again?'

'Salin. Edgar Salin.'

17

'Who is he exactly?'

'He is German, from Frankfurt am Main. He also studied under the Webers at Heidelberg. He knows my father from there. They were part of a group who at that time were "disciples", I guess you would call them, of Stefan George, a very influential poet who was resident there. In the early 1930s both Salin and my father left Germany. Like Jaspers, and so many other German academics, they could see what was happening. A lot went to America, especially to Princeton, including, as you know, Albert Einstein. My father went to Stanford, as I already mentioned. Others like Jaspers and Salin, wanted to stay in Europe, in German-speaking Europe if possible, and so when Salin was invited to head the economics department at the university of Basel, he immediately accepted. He seems to know everybody in Europe but especially Germans: émigrés like my father or like Siegmund Warburg, the Hamburg banker who now lives in London but who somehow gets to Switzerland even now, or the Seligman family who have a bank in Basel. But Professor Salin also maintains close contacts with a lot of people still in Germany, former students now often in high places in that country, or academics who have remained in Germany and still teach there. When these people come to Basel he usually puts on private dinner parties for them and invites some of the local bankers or businessmen, like Jacobsson or Seligman, as well as a few of his favourite students, or ex-students like Peter Burckhardt, and there they discuss everything from economics to philosophy to art to politics.'

'And you are usually included?'

'Yes. No doubt because of my father.'

Dulles liked that last statement. It was unusual, in his experience, to find beautiful young women who were also modest.

He'd already heard and seen enough. 'Miss Reichman, I would like it very much if you would come to work for me. It would be a part-time job. You would, of course, continue with your duties as vice-consul in Basel. From our point of view, your setup and location could not be better. I can think of no one who is better qualified to help us with some of the missions I have in mind. But

18

before you answer,' and Dulles could already tell from her facial reaction that her answer would be enthusiastically positive, 'I must warn you that our work can, at times, become extremely dangerous. Which leads me to a question which I am embarrassed to have to ask, but which I must.'

He paused.

'You are Jewish, are you not?'

She looked Dulles straight in the eye and said, 'I am. And very proud of it.'

'Working for me may, I stress may, require, though only under the most extreme of circumstances, that you cross the border into Germany, clandestinely of course, but involving a risk, a high risk maybe, of being caught. Which would be bad enough for any American, but could be even worse for a Jewish American.'

She appeared to be about to say something, but Dulles held up his hand. 'Let me finish. There are consistent rumours swirling about concerning what Hitler is doing to the Jews. They are being systematically removed from Holland and Belgium and France and deported chiefly to Poland, to work camps. No one knows for sure, but I feel it my duty, Miss Reichman, to point these things out to you before you make a decision. After all, you also have a duty towards your family. You may want to take a few days to think about it, although I am afraid that I must insist that you consult no one, absolutely no one, including your father or your Professor Salin. If you decline, both you and I will forget we ever had this discussion. And that loss of memory will be permanent. Understood?' Now it was not the voice of the diplomat Allen Dulles which the young American woman heard, but rather that of the spymaster Dulles, still a subdued voice but now one with harsh, even threatening, overtones.

'Yes sir, I do understand, and you have my word,' she replied solemnly, and then continued: 'But if you don't mind, I would prefer not to wait. I have no reservations whatsoever about working for you and fully understand the personal risks it might entail. And I am absolutely sure that my family would fully concur, were it possible for them to know. You see, America has been good to us. Germany has not.'

19

Even the tough diplomat and spymaster Dulles was touched by her last words, but he tried his damnedest not to show it. 'All right.' He rose from his chair, and, after she had done the same, extended his hand to her. 'Welcome aboard, Miss Reichman.' He was surprised at the firmness of her handshake. He concluded that he had just got hold of not only a very smart young lady, but also a tough and determined one.

Dulles then looked at his watch. 'It's four o'clock. When were you planning on returning to Basel?'

'At six o'clock, but . . .'

'That gives us ample time to work out some of the details, the first of which is going to have to be what we tell, or don't tell, the people at the State Department, especially the chief of mission here in Switzerland, Minister Harrison. Now let me tell you right at the outset that Leland Harrison and I don't see eye to eye on a lot of things. He belongs to that school of thought in the State Department which feels that gentlemen do not read other people's mail. Needless to say, that's the only kind of mail I like to read.'

It was agreed that Dulles would work matters out directly and immediately with the head of the American legation. She would continue with her normal functions as vice-consul, on the understanding that on OSS matters she would report exclusively to Dulles. If there ever appeared to be a conflict of interest arising out of her now serving two masters, he, Dulles, and he alone would adjudicate the matter.

When Minister Harrison was told all this the next day, he balked at the last condition, prompting Dulles to remind him that his mandate in Switzerland came directly from President Roosevelt, and that if Harrison wanted to argue the matter further – one which Dulles considered a matter of principle – then he, Dulles, would have no alternative but to take it up with the White House. Since Leland Harrison was a man who avoided making waves at almost any cost, that proved to be the end of that, at least for the time being.

Chapter 3

Nancy Reichman had made the six o'clock train back to Basel on that early December night in 1942, and in the weeks that followed began her first 'mission' on behalf of the OSS: to cultivate those contacts in Basel who could provide direct, first-hand information about what was happening in the country which lay immediately to the north of that city, a country almost totally sealed off, with access impossible for all but a few. It was those few that Nancy Reichman was to seek out.

Dulles' confidence in her ability to do just that was fully justified almost immediately. Two weeks after their first meeting in Bern, Nancy Reichman came up with information so startling that even Dulles, though accepting her information as valid, was hesitant to pass it along to Washington without further confirmation from other sources.

It had come to her after one of those dinners which Professor Edgar Salin, her mentor at the university of Basel, put on for visiting firemen, usually in a private room of one of the finest restaurants in Basel, in this case the 'Zum Sternen' on the Sankt Alban Vorstadt. Attendance was small, due to the Christmas break at the university which had just begun. In fact, Nancy Reichman was the only one of two ex-students who had been asked to join the men who met at eight that evening of 22 December 1942. All but one were residents of Basel: the professor, Salin; the private banker, Seligman; a local lawyer, Karl Meyer, whose clientele was chiefly German, particularly German industrialists, and who was also a major in the Swiss army. Nancy Reichman later learned from Dulles that the lawyer had close connections with the Swiss Foreign Ministry. Then there was Dr Peter Burckhardt, former student of Salin and now assistant to Per Jacobsson. The fifth man was Professor Arthur Sommer, who, like the lawyer, was a member of the wartime army, but in his case it was the German army, where he served as an officer with the General Staff in Berlin. He had a third job which brought him to Switzerland regularly. He was a member of the permanent Swiss–German economic commission, that body which regulated those immensely – and mutually – important trade and financial flows between Nazi Germany and neutral Switzerland. The commission met often, almost always in Switzerland, so Sommer crossed back and forth across the Swiss–German border at Basel almost every other week.

During the dinner itself nothing unusual had come up. In this December of 1942, the main subjects of discussion were the battles raging on Germany's Eastern front in Russia, as well as the success of the Americans in North Africa after their landing there on 8 November. Salin was of the opinion that the tide had turned against the Nazis. It was now just a matter of time. Professor Sommer was less optimistic. Though anti-Nazi to the core, he was highly critical of the Allies' failure to begin establishing a second front on the continent of Europe. Despite some of the recent setbacks which the German army had taken, the Nazis still considered themselves invincible and, in fact, were embarking on some new programmes that he had just learned about, ones of a truly frightening nature. Sommer had suddenly backed off. The presence of the Swiss lawyer, with his known German connections, might have been the reason. In any case, the discussion had moved on to other matters.

But afterwards, on the way home, Salin had persisted. Salin, as was his custom, had offered to drop Nancy Reichman off on the Marktplatz before proceeding to his house on the Hardstrasse. But first he brought his guest to the Hotel Euler, located directly opposite Basel's central railroad station. The two professors sat in the front seat of Salin's massive BMW; Nancy Reichman alone in the back. Despite the fact that the German, Sommer, spoke in a soft voice, she heard every word, words which were to remain indelibly imprinted on her memory.

'Die Entscheidung war am 20 Januar dieses Jahres getroffen worden,' he had begun. The decision had been taken on 20 January of the current year, 1942. It had been taken at a meeting held in Wannsee, a suburb of Berlin, which had been convened by Reinhard Heydrich, the Number 2 man in the SS. The problem that had prompted Heydrich to arrange for the meeting had been that of methodology . . . of how to most efficiently kill Jews. By the end of 1941, 500,000 Jews in Nazi-occupied Russia had already been murdered by special SS death squads under Heydrich's supervision. They were shot, and then buried in mass graves dug by the next batch scheduled to be shot. The process, however, was simply too slow, too cumbersome, Heydrich had explained to his SS colleagues gathered in Wannsee. A better 'Lösung', solution, to the Jewish problem was required. And that is when Heydrich had first used the word that would go down in eternal infamy:

'Endlösung'. The Final Solution.

Nancy Reichman would never forget that first time she heard that word. Even Professor Salin, a German Jew himself, who had become accustomed to horror stories concerning his former countrymen of similar religious beliefs and background, seemed to recoil at the word.

'Was soll das bedeuten? Endlösung?'

What it meant, Sommer then explained, was the total elimination of all Jews in all of Europe, a colossal project which required a vastly improved 'methodology'. Heydrich's proposal: the construction of gas chambers, principally in Poland, which fell under Heydrich's supervision. The place he had especially in mind was a small town called Auschwitz. The gas, a highly efficient one called Zyklon B, was available to order from I.G. Farben. Everybody attending the Wannsee meeting thought the idea was brilliant. A man by the name of Adolf Eichmann, Heydrich's 'Jewish expert', had kept the minutes of the meeting. Sommer had seen a copy.

In mid-July of 1942, Heinrich Himmler, head of the SS and thus Heydrich's immediate boss, had personally witnessed the gassing of 449 Dutch Jews in the 'experimental plant' in the Auschwitz complex known as 'Bunker 2'. He liked what he saw. Thereafter the implementation of the Final Solution went into top gear.[7]

'How many are being killed?'

Professor Sommer answered Salin's question with the ultimate in 'Galgenhumor' – gallows humour, for which the Germans are known. 'The rail traffic to the camp has reached enormous proportions. Which has led to the sick joke now making the rounds in the innermost circles in Berlin to the effect that Auschwitz must have developed into one of the biggest cities in Europe since so many people enter it and no one ever leaves.'

In the last few minutes before the BMW stopped in front of the Hotel Euler, the two men sat in silence. Salin left the car running as he stepped out to say goodbye to the German visitor, and they exchanged their final words.

'Aber haben Sie Beweis?' Salin had asked. Did the German have evidence?

'Leider nein,' came the answer. Regretfully, no.[8]

'But could you at least repeat what you have told me in writing?' Salin then asked.

Sommer hesitated. Then: 'I will write you a letter this evening,

---

7 See Callum MacDonald, *The Killing of SS Obergruppenfuehrer Reinhard Heydrich* (New York, 1989), pp. 40ff. Also Walter Laqueur and Richard Breitman, *Breaking the Silence* (New York, 1986), pp. 14ff and 138ff.

8 Ibid., pp. 264–5. In *Breaking the Silence* Laqueur and Breitman tell the story of a German industrialist, Eduard Schulte. He was, they claim, the heretofore 'unknown man' who, to use their words, 'first passed on to the outside world the unbelievable news that Hitler's extermination of the Jews had begun'. These historians determined that Minister Leland Harrison, Chief of Mission in Switzerland, was the initial recipient of this information. When Harrison passed it on to the State Department in late 1942, they relayed it further to the OSS in Washington, terming the legation's message a 'wild rumor inspired by Jewish fears'. Later, in early 1943, after Schulte established contact with Dulles, he convinced him, the OSS, and President Roosevelt of the awful truth.

However, there are other historians who dispute that it was Schulte alone who

Edgar, and hand-deliver it to you at your home on the Hard-strasse tomorrow morning.'

The two professors had then shaken hands, and Salin had returned to the car and taken Nancy Reichman home.

*

---

first informed the Allies of the nature and scope of the Final Solution, suggesting that its origins could be found rather in the Sommer/Salin connection. The dispute arose due to the fact that Schulte's name was never mentioned in the cables sent from Switzerland transmitting the information passed on by the German informant: only the letter 'S'. In fact it was the mystery of the identity of the man behind that letter 'S' which Walter Laqueur set out to solve, and which led to his co-authoring the book on Schulte under the title *Breaking the Silence*. In a Postscript to that book, Laqueur wrote the following:

> Through an accident I established that the man's name began with the letter 'S'. At the time this did not help very much, for 'S' is the most common initial for German last names. A great many Schmidts, Schöllers, Strausses, and Stumms had been in Basel, Zurich, and Bern during the war. I inquired among surviving German and Swiss industrialists whether they could give me any clues. I wrote dozens of letters and made scores of phone calls but without success.
>
> Meanwhile some other historians had reached the conclusion that Arthur Sommer was the mysterious messenger. Sommer was a German economist who had belonged to the circle of admirers of the German poet Stefan George. Another member of this circle was Count Claus von Stauffenberg, the brave officer who almost killed Hitler on July 20, 1944 . . . Sommer was not a Nazi, and from time to time he met with Jewish friends in Switzerland, including Professor Edgar Salin, a native of Frankfurt, who taught economics in Basel. According to postwar evidence provided by Salin, Sommer sent Salin a letter in 1942 to the effect that extermination camps had been established in Eastern Europe to kill all the European Jews (and also most Russian prisoners) by means of poison gas.

Laqueur then goes on to point out that according to Dr Haim Pazner, a historian who had studied under Salin, Salin got the word to the Americans in Bern, who then disseminated the information to Washington and the Allies. Laqueur says this thesis is 'interesting but wrong'. I had the privilege of studying under Professor Edgar Salin, and, in fact, it was he who was my 'Doktor Vater' (roughly, thesis supervisor) when I received a Ph.D. in economics at the university of Basel in 1958. I personally heard this story from him, but I have no way of knowing whether or not his information ever reached Washington, or, if it did, whether it was believed.

Nancy Reichman had called Dulles in Bern immediately the following morning, explaining that she had something of extreme importance, but would prefer to discuss it in person. Dulles concurred. So she took the next train to Bern, and a taxi to Dulles' apartment.

He listened intently as she repeated word for word the conversation she had overheard from the back seat of the BMW the prior evening in Basel.

His comment was: 'You have a remarkable memory.'

'Yes I do.'

'You also believe every word of what you overheard, don't you?'

'Yes.'

'So do I. If you recall, in our first conversation in this apartment I mentioned the fact that all kinds of rumours are floating around about what is happening to Europe's Jews. But like the German professor, Sommer, we, the OSS, also have no evidence. I repeat: strong suspicions, yes; proof, no.

'And there is also another problem. If I were to transmit this information to Washington, there is a strong possibility that your sources, and you yourself, would be totally compromised. You see, we have just found out that the Nazis have cracked the code our legation here is using for both their radio and telephone transmissions. We are working on it, to be sure. But until we have corrected that situation . . .'

She was obviously terribly disappointed.

'But believe me, Nancy,' he continued, 'this is a matter which I will now pursue with the highest priority. And you will too. But remember, there are many people in Washington who don't want to believe these things. They feel that they are being presented with misinformation, intended to pressure the United States into opening its doors to unlimited Jewish immigration. The Swiss attitude is the same, in fact even more crass. They are literally tossing Jews right back across the border into both Germany and Austria. "Das Boot ist voll," they have said. The Swiss lifeboat is full. So we must have absolute, definite proof before information like yours will be believed anywhere.'

'I understand,' she said, but her face said she didn't.

'You feel let down, I know. It won't be the last time,' Dulles then added. 'Now how about a good glass of Swiss white wine while I discuss another matter about which some of our people in Washington are becoming increasingly disturbed?'

While he got a bottle of Aigle from the refrigerator and opened it he kept talking. 'We have just heard a rumour that there has been a tremendous increase in the amount of gold Germany is shipping into Switzerland. What we, particularly our Secretary of the Treasury, Morgenthau, want to get is confirmation of this. If it is true, the Bank for International Settlements is bound to know about it, since the BIS is usually right in the middle of Europe's gold transactions. So cultivate your contacts there — carefully, since this matter is not particularly urgent — and see what develops. It's just a fishing expedition, but you never know what you'll catch unless you put a line in the water.'

Chapter 4

Nancy Reichman made slow progress until mid-February when, shortly after she got home from the consulate, she received a phone call from Peter Burckhardt. She had tried to get hold of him in January but had been told that he was on full-time military service. He told her how much he had enjoyed seeing her at Professor Salin's dinner in December, and suggested that they might get together again, maybe for a coffee. She agreed immediately but, she hoped, not too eagerly.

After she had hung up the phone, she began to wonder what had brought this on. For although they had known each other since 1938 when both had studied at the university, it was just the passing relationship of students who were studying under the same professor. Burckhardt, she knew, had gone on to finish his dissertation, and after receiving his doctorate in 1939 had joined the Bank for International Settlements as a junior staff member in their economics research department. There, it was said, he had caught the attention of Per Jacobsson, the Swede who was not only chief economist at the BIS, but also one of its chief policy makers and spokesman for the institution. She knew enough about the BIS to know that if Dulles wanted her to sniff around about intergovernmental financial matters, that was the place to do it.

The origins of the BIS dated back to World War I, and the billions of dollars of reparations which the victorious Allies had forced Germany into agreeing to pay. The problem was that post-war Germany had never really recovered, lurching from near-revolution to hyperinflation to massive unemployment, with the result that by the end of the 1920s it was experiencing such great financial difficulties that it had to suspend any further payments to its international creditors. Germany's position then was much the same as that in which Brazil, Argentina, Mexico and a host of other Latin American countries found themselves involved by the 1980s: heavily indebted to the United States and the other financially powerful nations of the West, but unable to earn enough dollars to meet even the interest payments. The solution: they borrowed yet more so that payments could be resumed.

The 'solution' to the German reparations payment problem was very similar and came in the form of the Young Plan in 1929 (named after the president of General Electric, Owen D. Young), under which the Allies arranged for Germany to borrow enough money, through the issue of bonds, to resume payments. The establishment of the Bank for International Settlements was part and parcel of the plan, aimed at 'depoliticizing' the reparations process: it would replace the old Reparations Committee and take over the administration of the flow of funds into and out of Germany. The apolitical nature of the new institution would be reinforced by the fact that it would be based in neutral Switzerland in the traditional financial centre, Basel.[9]

Almost immediately after its founding in 1930, however, it become obvious that the importance of the Bank for International Settlements would go far beyond the technical function of overseeing monetary 'settlements' between the former warring powers. This had, in fact, been foreshadowed by the unique nature of the ownership of the BIS: the controlling shareholders (and the 200,000 shares were also unique in that their nominal value was defined in terms of a physical quantity of gold –

---

9 For a history of the founding and early years of the BIS see Paul Einzig, *The Bank for International Settlements* (London, 1930). Also Eleanor Lansing Dulles, *The Bank for International Settlements at Work* (New York, 1932). Note that the author was the sister of Allen and John Foster Dulles, showing that the links between the Dulles family and the BIS go back to its very beginnings.

145,161,290.32 grams to be exact — which represented the paid-in capital of the bank) were the leading central banks of the world, initially those of Belgium, England, France, Italy, Germany and Japan.[10] The American participation came from a consortium of American commercial banks — J.P. Morgan, the National Bank of New York, and the First National Bank of Chicago — with the Federal Reserve Bank staying in the background in order to avoid any possible political interference by its supervisor, the American Congress. Gradually the list of participating nations was expanded to include Sweden, Romania, Poland, Holland and Switzerland. Since the men who ran these central banks were also responsible, ultimately, for the running of the BIS, they were now obligated to gather regularly in Basel. Net result: the BIS became the Club of Clubs, the Central Bankers Club, a place where they could secretly confide in one another, cut deals, and often involve the BIS in the execution of these deals. As a result the BIS almost immediately developed into the central bank of central banks, a powerful link between the most important financial systems of the world.

Although all of the above was true, and was the generally accepted description of the BIS and its function, this account masked the fact that from the very beginning the BIS had been to a large degree a German creation and an instrument of German policy. For at least in part, its founding had been inspired by the notorious Hjalmar Horace Greely Schacht who a few years later was to become Hitler's Minister of Economics and president of Germany's central bank, the Reichsbank. He acted in consort with Emil Puhl, who, after Schacht was dumped by Hitler, co-ran the Reichsbank under the regime of Schacht's successor, Dr Walther Funk.

During the war, there can be little doubt that the BIS was essentially under Nazi control. Among its most important directors were Hermann Schmitz, head of Germany's largest industrial trust, I.G. Farben; Baron Kurt von Schröder, head of the J.H.

---

10 The First National City Bank, *Bank for International Settlements — Documents* (Chicago, 1930).

Stein Bank of Cologne and a leading officer and financier of the Gestapo; and both Dr Walther Funk and Emil Puhl of the Reichsbank. The last two were Hitler's personal appointees to the board of the BIS and their brief was to make sure that this institution would continue to function as a back door to international finance even in the event of a major armed conflict. It was ideally located for such a function, being in neutral Switzerland but located in Basel, directly on the German border, and operating under a charter, agreed to by all of the world's major powers except the Soviet Union, which stipulated that the BIS would be immune from seizure, closure, or censure, whether or not its owners were at war with each other.

In all of this they were undoubtedly aided and abetted by both the chairman and the president of that bank. The chairman was a Swiss with a German bent who was also chairman of the Swiss National Bank, Emil Meyer, and its president an American, Thomas McKittrick, who undoubtedly sympathized with the Nazi crowd.

Not that the Germans had everybody at the BIS in their hip pocket. The glaring exception was a Swede who had been a key force in and for the BIS from the very outset. Per Jacobsson was the man in charge of the bank's economic policy, and it was he who had single-handedly made the BIS and Basel the place where the most powerful financial men on earth regularly gathered to coordinate their control of the world's money and finance. Jacobsson was staunchly anti-Nazi and pro Anglo-Saxon. In fact his sister was married to a key figure in Britain's military establishment, Sir Archibald Nye, who during World War II held the post of Vice-Chief of the Imperial General Staff. But Jacobsson kept his views to himself, especially because he felt it his obligation to do so in light of the fact that he was a 'guest' of neutral Switzerland. So in spite of the war which separated their nations, he encouraged his staff — the Germans and British, the Italians and Americans, the Poles and the Czechs — who worked there to continue to work together, and to lunch together, though unfortunately they were no longer able to play golf together, since Basel's only golf course was located across the border in

France (where land was plentiful and cheap), a border which had been sealed since September of 1939.[11]

The bank was physically located in a most unassuming building, formerly a small hotel, opposite Basel's main railroad station and immediately next door to one of the city's famous coffee houses, Frey. It was known that the staff of the BIS came to Frey's regularly for either morning coffee (known in Swiss German as 'Znueni', or 'at nine o'clock') or afternoon tea (known as 'Zvieri', or 'at four o'clock'). And so it was here that Peter Burckhardt suggested he and Nancy Reichman meet for coffee in the late afternoon of that Tuesday, February 16, 1943.

She got there first, and took a table looking out on the Centralbahnstrasse, ordering tea and some chocolate pâtisserie. Minutes later Peter Burckhardt walked in, deep in thought, and carrying the afternoon edition of the *Basler Nachrichten*. Then he saw her, and the seriousness was replaced by a broad smile as he came directly over to her table.

'Salut, Nancy,' he said, as she stood up to shake his hand. 'Das isch aber nett dass Du ko bisch.' He used the familiar 'Du', as was customary in Switzerland where former fellow students, or 'Kommilitonen' as they were known there, were concerned.

She decided to switch to English. 'It was a nice surprise when you called, Peter. Would you like to share some of my tea?'

'No thanks,' he said with a grimace. 'Can't stand the stuff.' He got the waitress's attention right away, and ordered coffee and Kirschwasser, explaining the latter with the words, 'It's cold out there.'

Then: 'I noticed in the telephone book that you live on the Augustinergasse, Nancy. Wie schön,' he added, reverting momentarily to Swiss German, and then, catching himself at it, 'Sorry, but somehow it seems more natural talking to you in dialect. At the Uni we Swiss always admired you for how quickly you picked it up.'

'You know why I made the effort,' she replied, adding: 'And it

---

11 See Erin E. Jacobsson, *A Life for Sound Money: Per Jacobsson, His Biography* (Oxford, 1979), where she describes her father's passion for golf.

sure turned out that the Germans were as bad as we all thought them to be.'

Peter Burckhardt at first said nothing. 'But not quite all. For example, the man at Professor Salin's dinner.'

She noticed that he did not mention the man's name. Interesting, she thought. And then went right at it.

'Have you seen him since?'

'No. But I hear that he will be back in Switzerland next week. For a meeting of the German–Swiss economic committee. In Bern, though, not here. Why? Do you want to meet him?'

'No, no. At least not now. I don't think it would be healthy for him to be seen together with an American Foreign Service officer, even though I am but a lowly vice-consul.' She paused. 'But you've aroused my curiosity. You implied that you could arrange a meeting. How does the BIS fit in with the gentleman we're talking about?'

'It doesn't, at least in any direct sense. His connection is with the Swiss government. And now, so is mine. You see, since October I've assumed a new job at the BIS which grew out of the fact that I'm one of the few Swiss who work there – I mean of the professional staff, not the secretaries and all that. Actually Professor Salin helped me get the job in the first place. Anyway, I'm now responsible for overseeing the relationship between the BIS and the Swiss National Bank. So I am a lot better informed about a lot of things that are going on in this country than I used to be.'

He then added: 'I guess I really shouldn't be telling you all this, Nancy. You know how paranoid we Swiss are these days. Nobody is supposed to know anything, or, if they do, to ever talk about it. Especially with foreigners.'

'Like that poster tells you,' Nancy Reichman interjected, pointing out of the window at the wall of the railway station where a poster depicted the huge shadow of a Swiss soldier in his battle helmet with his index finger in front of his lips, looking down on three obviously working-class Swiss. The warning was clear. Keep your mouth shut. Or else. And the authority behind that warning was equally clear: another reminder that Switzerland was a state under martial law. Its citizens did what the military told them to 'do, or they would disappear behind barbed wire.

Peter Burckhardt suddenly looked at his watch.

'It's four-thirty,' he said, 'and it's already getting dark out there. Look, I've got an idea. Let's go and see a movie. There's a new Jean Gabin thriller playing at the Rex, and I think the first showing starts at five. Do you want to go?'

'I'd love to!'

Five minutes later they paid separately, donned their coats, put on their scarfs, and left the warmth of the coffee house. As they stepped onto the Centralbahnstrasse it began to snow ever so lightly.

'We could take the tram, or we could walk. It's only about ten minutes.'

'Let's walk,' she replied.

And they did. To the Margarethenstrasse, then downhill to the Heuwaage and across the small square to the Steinenvorstadt, the street where Basel's first-run movie houses were all situated.

'You know what I used to call this street when we were students?' she asked. 'Broadway. When all the movie houses were lit up with their neon lights it looked just like the downtown of an American city. And they even played the same movies.'

'They still do,' Peter said, 'although it now takes longer for the American films to get here. But it hardly looks like Broadway any more, does it?'

'No. It's too bad. But I guess necessary.'

The reason was that, like everything else, electricity was in very short supply in Switzerland. Where meat or bread was concerned, it was because it was very difficult now to get supplies to Switzerland from its traditional sources of supply — Argentina for beef, Canada and the United States for grain. In regard to electricity, however, the shortage had another reason. Switzerland had ample domestic supplies of hydroelectricity from huge generating facilities below Alpine dams or those located on the River Rhine. But it now exported immense amounts to Germany where the electricity supplied by Switzerland was critical for the

34

production of the aluminium which, in turn, was essential for the Nazi production of fighter aircraft and bombers. Such exports were 'necessary' in that they represented one of many similar reasons why it was beneficial for Nazi Germany to leave Switzerland alone rather than attempting to incorporate it into the Third Reich by force and thereby risk destroying the golden goose — Swiss armaments factories, hydroelectric facilities, chemical and machine tool plants — which was supplying the exports so strategic to the Nazi war effort. But Peter Burckhardt did not expand upon this. Like so many of his fellow countrymen, he thoroughly disapproved, but to say so publicly would mean running the risk of denunciation by other countrymen who kow-towed to the Swiss government's insistence on total silence in such matters lest the Nazis be provoked.

It was only ten to five when they arrived in front of the Rex, but already there was a long line-up for tickets. And not just at the Rex. Across the street in front of the Capitol it was the same. Where else could the Swiss turn for a little escape from the grim reality in which they found themselves? For over three years now, they had been locked up in their tiny country, the borders sealed in all directions. Their only window on the outside world was the screen in their movie theatres. But there, despite the war, the whole world was still open: they could see Clark Gable and Betty Grable in American movies made on Hollywood sets, or British films starring the young Laurence Olivier made in studios located in rural Buckinghamshire, films that came into Switzerland via the Lisbon/Genoa/Geneva link. German movies starring the likes and deep voice of Zara Leander and made in Berlin were equally available: they came in directly to Switzerland via the regular rail freight service that still linked Basel with all of Germany, films that not only earned much-needed Swiss francs for the Nazi regime, but also had great propaganda value relative to the German-speaking Swiss in the eyes of Goebbels' ministry. The Paris/Basel railroad link was also intact, and that was how the French films of the type known in Switzerland as 'Krimi's' usually got there. They were movies which were extremely popular during the war, probably because they were purely escapist in content. This movie, *Moontide*, was typical of the genre and had Jean Gabin playing the role of a tough sailor who woke up after a drinking spree to find himself accused of murder.[12] Once the screen lit up in one of the theatres on the Steinenvorstadt it was possible to forget that just three miles away lay the evil empire of Nazi Germany. So the theatres were packed every night of the week.

At seven the movie was over, and, as Peter Burckhardt and Nancy Reichman left, they found themselves faced with another long line which was standing outside on the Steinenvorstadt, despite the snow and growing cold, waiting to get in for the second showing. Burckhardt took her arm for the first time as they pushed their way down the sidewalk.

'Now I've got another idea. Do you know the Witwe Hunziger's place?'

'No.'

'It's a tiny little restaurant in the old city, owned and run by a little old lady known as "the Widow Hunziger". All she serves is wine, dark bread, and for special clients, but only for them, the best entrecôte in town. Are you game?'

She was. But asked: 'Don't you need a reservation?'

'Not really. Frau Hunziger knows us.'

She glanced at him rather sharply. But there was no arrogance to be detected, although that trait was all too common among the 'us' that Peter Burckhardt had referred to. They were members of the elite society of the city and canton of Baselstadt known throughout Switzerland for their haughtiness, and commonly referred to in Swiss dialect as the 'Daig', in high German, the 'Teig' . . . the 'crust', the upper crust. They were members of the families who controlled the city's private banks, its legal establishments – including both the leading law firms and the judiciary – families which, over centuries, had accumulated the choice real estate both in the city and in the countryside surrounding it. The

---

12 What was not typical of this Jean Gabin film was that it had been produced in the United States by 20th Century Fox. It was the first movie Gabin made there. It had come in through Lisbon.

power of the families even extended to the military establish-ment. Their sons were expected to go beyond the usual obligatory time in the military by volunteering for officers' training school, with the result that they inevitably ended up holding the highest ranks in the Swiss army — an army which had very few full-time soldiers and was composed almost entirely of citizen-militia under a system of universal compulsory service where every Swiss male was subject to a periodic call-up into active service in the army from the age of twenty to that of fifty, whether he wanted to or not. Conscientious objectors were not tolerated. They were simply put in jail.

One other peculiarity of this Basel aristocracy was their names. For instance, there were lots of Burkharts in Switzerland, but only those few families whose surnames were spelled with a 'ck' and ended with 'dt' — Burckhardt — were members of the elite. The same applied to the Fischers. There were hundreds of families with this surname, but only those who spelled it with a 'V' — Vischer — belonged to the aristocracy.

Then there were the Bernoullis — a clan which had produced one of Europe's most famous mathematicians in the seventeenth century — and the Merians, of sixteenth-century cartography fame. The Von der Mühlls were another family, and in fact Peter Burckhardt's mother had been one, while his grandmother was a Sarasin, yet another family which belong to Basel's 'Daig'. This upper crust stuck together, they protected each other, and intermarriage had been the rule among these families for centuries.

They were, however, elitist also in the positive sense. The opera — one of the best provincial operas in Europe — was their creation, as was the ballet. Chamber music flourished in Basel as in few other cities. The art museum was superb. And the university of Basel was one of the world's oldest, founded in 1456 and ranking, in age, just behind those in Bologna, Prague, Oxford, Cambridge and the Sorbonne. Yet the 'Daig' which supported all this numbered barely into the thousands in a city which had a quarter of a million population.

Nancy Reichman knew all this. And on this evening of 27

37

December 1942 she could not help but wonder what a Peter Burckhardt was doing taking an American woman, no, an American-Jewish woman, and furthermore officially attached to the government of one of the chief protagonists in a war of which Switzerland was having no part, out to dinner in a restaurant which the 'Daig' regarded as more or less their own.

The answer − or at least some of it − came shortly after they had entered the little restaurant located on the Spalenberg. And it related to two other characteristics of the 'Daig': they were staunch Protestants and they were Anglophiles.

The black bread and a carafe of Dôle, the heavy Swiss red wine, had been placed automatically on their table, which was situated right beside the iron coal-burning stove that was almost red-hot. Both Nancy Reichman and Peter Burckhardt wore heavy sweaters like everybody else in Switzerland, since by law, to conserve energy, temperatures in homes, offices and even theatres were not allowed to exceed 68 degrees. Almost immediately both decided to take them off. Nancy could not help but notice that her companion took full notice of her figure when she did so. He was well worth looking at himself, she thought. In contrast to most Swiss, he was tall − at least six feet − slim yet muscular, had blond slightly curly hair, and a bearing that reflected his patrician status. During her undergraduate years at Stanford, if she had been seen dating a guy like this, when she got back to the dorm the girls would have called him a 'dish', and then giggled. That was one of the problems about living in Switzerland: nobody seemed to ever giggle. The other problem was dates: not a single one since she had returned to Basel as vice-consul. During the two years she had studied there, dates had hardly been a problem, since she was a 'dish' in her own right, and knew it. So why all of a sudden, Peter Burckhardt?

'Nancy, could I ask you something that has to do with your present job here?'

'Sure.' Here it comes, she thought. 'Are you in regular contact with the leading people in your embassy in Bern?'

She thought it over.

'No. Not really. Unless something unusual requires it.'

'Like what?'

'Arranging a visa for some local bigwig who needs it in a hurry. Or if some unusual information comes to my attention.'

'Like a visit of —' and this time, in the privacy of Widow Hunziger's restaurant which was practically home turf, he named the name — 'Herr Doktor Sommer?'

'Maybe.' Now she was afraid of getting into dangerous territory. 'In fact,' she then added, 'I wondered why Professor Salin invited me to that dinner.'

'I know why. Because we have no channel of communications with either the British or the Americans. We are much more isolated here in Basel than you might think.'

She thought that one over.

'You know as well as I do where our embassies are, Peter,' she then stated, and it came out rather sarcastically. So she quickly added: 'I hope that didn't sound like I think it did.'

Peter grinned. 'It sounded American. But I will answer the question very bluntly. If a Swiss like me, or, for that matter even Professor Salin, were seen entering the British or American embassies we would soon have people asking why.'

'Well, what about being seen together with me?'

'You're different. After all . . .'

And then he stopped.

So she continued his sentence for him. 'After all, I'm just a woman. Right?'

He now appeared extremely embarrassed. 'You know us by this time, Nancy. I mean the Swiss men. We do not even allow our women to vote. A woman's place in Switzerland is still in the home, and at home, by law, a Swiss wife must obey her husband in all matters. If not, he has the perfect right, under law, to punish her. She is expected to be seen and not heard. Like children in your country. So they are not taken seriously where political matters are concerned. I guess the best word to describe how we regard women in our society would be "harmlos".'

'And although I'm an American, I am regarded as being just as "harmless" as any other woman?'

'I'm afraid so.'

'Thanks a lot! I'll warn you right now, Peter Burckhardt, I'm not!'

'I know that.' Then, abruptly changing the course of the conversation, he asked: 'Do you know Mr Allen Dulles? Personally?'

It came as such a shock that she knew that her facial and body reaction must have been a dead giveaway.

'How do you know about Allen Dulles?'

'We read about him in the newspaper, just like everybody else. To explain why I brought up his name, let me begin by saying that there are some of us who are not happy about Switzerland's behaviour in this war. We know about things that the rest of the world should also know. Yet we are forced to remain silent. Forced by a government that is heavily under the influence of men who have been ambivalent about Fascism from the beginning. You surely know who they are. To name just two, Marcel Pilet, our foreign minister, and Otto Rottemund, the head of our national police force, the Fremdenpolizei. My family, and most of our family's friends, consider this attitude immoral. Despicable. Some on purely theological grounds, the rest because their attitude stands in total contrast to our political heritage. After all, we are a democracy — at least until this war broke out — and have been one long before even the Anglo-Saxons got around to it.'

All of a sudden Burckhardt stopped talking, realizing that his voice had been rising. He looked around the small room. Nobody was taking any notice of them. So he continued, but now in a voice that was barely above a whisper.

'I'm sorry if I got a bit carried away. I'll come right to the point. Some of us have information about what's happening in Germany, because we maintain relationships, personal and otherwise, with some men who have key positions there. Some of that information, some of those men, could potentially be helpful in bringing closer the defeat of Fascism, provided we can get that information and introduce those contacts to the Allies. We have decided that you may be exactly the conduit we have been searching for.'

Conduit. She had never been called that before.

'And who more specifically are "we"?' she asked.

After a slight pause, he continued. 'As you may or may not know, in Switzerland intelligence is the responsibility of the army. The army shares the responsibility for counter-intelligence with the various political police units in the country. These tasks have been specifically assigned to Section 5 of the General Staff. It's a very small group. Not even a hundred men are involved. Some — not all — of them do not like how our government is behaving. They want to align themselves with the cause of the Allies, with the British and the Americans, and help where they can, but with the understanding that their first and foremost loyalty is to Switzerland, to maintaining her democratic traditions, her Christian ethics, and her basic neutrality. They want this purely on principle, but as a side benefit — not a condition — they hope that this will be remembered. Especially if the Russians try to stir up trouble for our country either during this war, or after it is finally over. You understand?'

She nodded. This was serious.

'I work for them, sometimes full-time, sometimes part-time. They approached me about a year ago, since they know my beliefs and attitude and they trust me. And they thought my position inside the BIS might be helpful. You can be sure that they will protect us — and you — as best they can should we now continue beyond this evening's conversation. Now back to where I began — your Mr Dulles. We — especially the two officers in charge of our intelligence, Colonel Masson and Captain Waibel, who is my immediate superior — want to get into direct contact with him. As soon as possible. But they must do it very, very carefully. A direct approach by my superiors in Bern was considered, but rejected. If our foreign minister, Pilet, found out that the top men in our intelligence had made a direct approach to Dulles in Bern, he might disband the entire organization and start over with his own people. Bern is like a village. So we thought it better to make an *indirect* approach to him via *Basel*.'

'Enter Nancy Reichman.'

'Exactly. You might represent the beginning of the solution we've been searching for, depending on how well you know Mr Dulles.'

'I know him well enough.'

Peter Burckhardt let this sink in. 'So you are both able and willing to help?'

'Of course.' Should she tell him how ironic this all was? That it was *she* who had intended to use *him*? No, she decided.

But then she asked: 'Were you and Professor Salin by any chance looking me over at dinner with this in mind?'

'I was. Not Salin. He is not connected with us. He helps, but he is not connected.'

'But Peter, couldn't you get into very serious trouble doing this sort of thing?'

'Maybe. That is not the issue.'

'Do you trust me that much?'

'I certainly trust *you* that much. About those behind you, or above you, well, we will just have to hope, won't we?' Then he added with a grin: 'I guess there's a lot more to little Nancy Reichman than we thought.'

He looked at his watch. 'Let's order two big entrecôtes. Then I'm going to walk you home. And after that, I'm going to be on the phone with my superiors in Bern. I trust you will be doing the same.'

'Yes I will.'

'Anything else we should discuss?' Burckhardt then asked.

'One small thing that I've been asked to check out. We've heard some disturbing stories about the Nazis making huge gold shipments to Switzerland, perhaps with the help of the BIS. Can that somehow be verified?'

Burckhardt obviously did not like what he had just heard.

'That's a very tough one. Because it goes right to the heart of the dilemma we find ourselves in: how to help you without in any way hurting Switzerland.'

'I assume, however, you mean the real Switzerland. Not that of the ruling clique in Bern,' she responded.

'Touché.' He nodded grimly. 'All right. I'll look into it. Now let's forget about all this for a while.'

He walked her home an hour later, kissing her ever so lightly on the cheek when he left.

Five minutes later Nancy Reichman was on the phone, leaving a message for Allen Dulles. When she hung up, she could not help but wonder about who was manipulating whom. Had Dulles, somehow, known about the desire of Swiss Intelligence to get into contact with him? And had he somehow set all this up? No, maybe both he *and* they had come up with the idea of the Basel connection. Leading to Burckhardt's 'vetting' her at the Salin dinner, and then the phone call, and now the proposal. And had Dulles' interest in gold and the BIS been designed, from the very beginning, as an excuse, knowing that she would be approached by one of 'their' men who worked there?

At dawn the next morning she received a phone call telling her that Mr Dulles was unavailable, that he would be out of town until the beginning of the following week, and that she would be expected on Tuesday, 23 February, at the usual time and at the usual place.

Chapter 5

Nancy Reichman called Peter Burckhardt that afternoon, this time inviting him to meet her for coffee — at her favourite place, Spielman's, the coffee house situated on the Rhine next to the Middle Bridge. Just as Frey's was a 'hangout' for the BIS people, Spielman's was the place where the ladies who belonged to Basel society gathered for afternoon coffee or tea. Oddly, it was also the place regularly frequented by Basel's wealthier Jewish women — which appealed to Nancy Reichman for various reasons, one of which was that it was about the last place that those who sympathized with the Nazis would ever be found.

This time it was Burckhardt who arrived first. In fact, Nancy Reichman arrived a full half-hour late, despite the fact that the American consulate was located just two blocks away, in a modern building at the corner of the Spiegelgasse and Blumenrain, by coincidence right next door to the building that housed the infamous Fremdenpolizei, the Swiss national police charged with the control and surveillance of all foreigners in Switzerland. And it was these police who had caused the delay. They had in custody a Jewish woman who had managed to cross the border from Austria, and had somehow ended up in Basel. She had been staying with a local Jewish family, apparently for months, concealed most of the time in their attic, only leaving the house for an occasional nocturnal walk. A neighbour had seen her 'sneaking in and out of the house' on two different occasions, and 'because she did not look or dress like a Swiss' had tipped off the police.

The woman refugee obviously knew what the Swiss would do with her: throw her right back across the border into Austria. So in desperation she had claimed to have American relatives who would sponsor her emigration to the United States if only the Swiss authorities gave her time to work it out. The Fremden-polizei, not out of sympathy but merely following the rules, had informed the American vice-consul of the situation that after-noon by phone.

Nancy Reichman had personally gone next door to the Swiss police, suggesting that if she were given all the particulars, the names and addresses of the American relatives, she would see what could be done. It was purely to buy time: she knew full well that it was hopeless. The American government had shut the door to Jewish immigration almost as brutally as had the Swiss. The woman would eventually, probably within weeks, be handed over to the Austrian authorities at the border, and after overhear-ing that conversation in the back of Professor Salin's BMW, Nancy Reichman knew what would happen next.

It was, therefore, a highly depressed American vice-consul who arrived late at Spielman's.

'Problems?' Burckhardt asked, as soon as she sat down.

She just shook her head, but he could notice her brown eyes welling with tears.

'If I can help . . .' he continued.

Again she shook her head. But he did reach over to touch her hand. And then the waitress came to take their order.

'About that gold matter,' he began, once she had disappeared. 'This is very touchy stuff.'

'Not to worry,' she immediately said. 'I left a message for Mr Dulles last night as I promised to do. He's out of town right now, but I will be going to Bern next Tuesday to meet him. I thought you should know this — that's why I called you.'

'I'll pass that along right away,' he replied. Then, very hesi-tantly: 'I have another meeting that I would like to arrange.'

Nancy Reichman's face indicated that she had not expected

this. And Peter Burckhardt immediately noticed her concern.

'No. It has absolutely nothing to do with business. I would like you to meet my parents.'

This left Nancy Reichman literally speechless. In Switzerland *nobody* ever asked *anybody* to meet their parents!

He then handed her a small piece of paper. 'That's a map showing you how to get to our family's place in Riehen.' Riehen was a small suburb of Basel where the estates of many of the 'Daig' were located.

'In fact, it was my parents' idea. They would like to invite you to join us for dinner next Monday.'

And then, as embarrassed as she, he changed the subject. They stayed together at Spielman's for another forty-five minutes, discussing skiing, what it was like living in California, the latest novel by Remarque — anything but the war. A casual observer of the pair could see that what kept them lingering was their obvious pleasure in being together — two young people starting to fall in love in the middle of a world which seemed to have forgotten the meaning of that word.

The Burckhardt estate was comprised of six acres. In addition to the main house, there were stables, servants' quarters, a tennis court, and, very unusual for Switzerland, a swimming pool.

When Nancy Reichman arrived at 7.30 on the evening of Monday, 22 February 1943, in her tiny Fiat Topolino bearing the CC licence plates which designated the owner as a member of the consular corps, she was a rather nervous young lady.

'Guten Abend, Fräulein. Darf ich Ihren Mantel nehmen.' The maid who had opened the door spoke high German with difficulty. As she took Nancy Reichman's coat, an extremely elegant woman in her mid-fifties appeared. Her clothes could have come from nowhere else than a pre-1940 Paris boutique; her hair was exquisitely coiffured; the pearl necklace which swooped into her rather deep décolletage was perfection itself.

'How very nice of you to come,' the woman said, in impeccable Oxford English. 'I'm Peter's mother. He said you were a beautiful young woman, and you are. May I call you Nancy?' Then without waiting for an answer she continued: 'Good. Now,' and she actually took Nancy's arm, 'let's have something to drink.'

Together they crossed the marble floor of the entrance hall, and entered the salon. The two men who had been sitting in front of the fireplace rose immediately. Peter greeted her formally with a handshake, and then said: 'Nancy, I would like to introduce you to my father.'

Herr Doktor Maximilian Burckhardt-Von der Mühll, tall like his son and perfectly tailored as befitted the chairman of Switzerland's largest commercial bank, the Swiss Bank Corporation – the pinstriped suit must have been made in Savile Row, the dark red silk tie was no doubt Italian – gave her a thorough examination from top almost to bottom. Then he stepped forward, extended his hand, and said: 'We are honoured to have an American in our home.' His handshake was firm, and his grey eyes warm.

'Now,' he said, 'in celebration of having you in our presence, I propose we all indulge in a dry Martini. Are you game?'

'I'd love one,' Nancy answered.

Peter's father then picked up a small silver bell from one of the end tables, and rang it. Almost immediately a male servant appeared, the butler that Nancy had been anticipating with such trepidation before her arrival. But now those fears had totally disappeared, and when Peter suggested she join him on the sofa she took her place beside him with confidence.

Peter's mother now took over. 'Peter has told us that your family lives in Palo Alto. We visited there in what year was it, dear?' she asked her husband. Then without waiting for a reply, she continued: 'Nineteen thirty-eight. We were staying at the Mark Hopkins in San Francisco in September and drove down. We loved the campus at Stanford. Peter tells us that your father teaches there.'

'He does. Economics. More precisely, the History of Economic Thought.'

And so it went through cocktails and then through a magnificent dinner which began with smoked trout, continued through venison – both coming from a hunting estate which the family maintained in the Jura mountains – and was accompanied by, first, a 1939 Meursault, and then a 1933 Lynch Bages. It ended with a Grand Marnier soufflé.

They all went to the library for coffee and cognac, and in the case of father and son, Cuban cigars. Then, precisely at nine o'clock, pleading a long day at the bank, Peter's father rose, the signal for his mother to do the same. They said good-night to Nancy, graciously expressing their hope that this evening would only be the first of many. Peter and Nancy were finally alone in front of the fireplace which had just been attended to by one of the maids.

'Your parents are absolutely wonderful.'

'They liked you immensely, from the first moment on,' Peter replied.

Then the door to the library swung open once more, and in plunged a young woman in her mid-twenties, still dressed in a ski parka. Peter Burckhardt looked up in surprise and, with the grin which had already so endeared him to Nancy Reichman, rose to introduce the intruder. 'My sister, Felicitas. And this, dear sister, is Nancy Reichman.'

'I didn't want to interrupt, Peter,' she said, 'but I did have to . . . have to see what your mysterious American woman friend looked like. She's smashing!'

That would have been the correct word to describe Felicitas Burckhardt as well. In contrast to the dark petite beauty of the 'American woman', Peter's sister was tall, blonde and blue-eyed – just as he was – and exuded a warmth and enthusiasm which were rare in subdued, controlled Switzerland.

'Would you have lunch with me one day?' she asked.

'I'd love to,' Nancy replied, taking an immediate liking to the young woman.

'Then I can tell you all of Peter's secrets,' Felicitas said. And with that, blowing Peter a kiss, she disappeared.

'I didn't know you had a sister,' Nancy said, as soon as the door to the library had closed again. 'What does she do?'

'She is studying at the Uni. Physics,' Peter replied. 'But I have the feeling that it bores her. I think she wishes she could do things like you are able to do. But this is Switzerland . . .'

'You like her a lot, don't you?'

'I do. Maybe you could help cheer her up.'

That surprised Nancy. 'She doesn't look like she needs cheering up.'

Peter shrugged. 'Have lunch with her soon. She'd appreciate it. Now, how about us having another cognac?'

Nancy Reichman looked at her watch. 'I'd love to, Peter, but it's getting late. And as you know the blackout starts at ten. Furthermore, I have to take an early train to Bern.'

There was no mistaking his disappointment, but he dutifully went to get her coat.

As he helped her into it he said: 'By the way, when you see Mr Dulles you might tell him that we know about the back-door approach to his apartment through the vineyard, so it's hardly worth the trouble.'

'I will,' she replied, noting that they were back to business.

'You're coming back from Bern tomorrow, I assume?'

'Yes.'

'Then shall I call you at, say, seven tomorrow evening? At your apartment?' he asked, as he opened the car door for her.

'Yes. And now, Peter, I'd better go.'

He escorted her to her car, and after he had opened the door for her the good-night kiss he gave her was on the cheek and barely perceptible. As she drove slowly back to Basel along the dark deserted road, she could not help but say to herself: 'Maybe it's time, girl, to stop mixing business and pleasure. Next time stick to pleasure.'

She went to bed that night thinking of Peter Burckhardt.

In Bern the next morning it took Nancy Reichman less than twenty minutes to describe the conversation that had taken place at the Witwe Hunziger's a week earlier. Allen Dulles did not interrupt her once.

'Excellent,' he said when she finally fell silent. 'I trust you

49

understand how extremely delicate this is. If some people in the government here in Bern find out about this, you will be declared persona non grata and kicked out of Switzerland within a matter of days. Which could well mean the end of your career in the Foreign Service.'

'I understand that, sir.'

'Good. Now what Burckhardt told you about Section 5 all checks out. I have exactly the same information from other sources. Colonel Masson and Captain Waibel run the show. Waibel and Burckhardt are especially important to us since they are attached to the unit within Section 5 which runs all operations directed at Germany. So tell Burckhardt that I am prepared to meet Masson at any time that is convenient to him and at any place of his choosing, since he might have more of a problem there than I do. And suggest that Waibel and your Peter Burckhardt join us. I'd especially like to meet Burckhardt.'

Then Dulles looked at his watch.

'I have another appointment in a few minutes. As soon as Burckhardt gets back to you, let me know right away. Should I call you a taxi?'

'No. I think I'll walk.'

'Before you leave, let me tell you this, young lady: you have done one great job!'

Then she told Dulles that the Swiss were onto the back-door approach to his apartment through the vineyard, and, rather pleased with herself, left by the front door which led onto the Herrengasse. She might have been less pleased had she known that her coming and going had been observed by *two* men, only one of whom worked for Colonel Masson. The other was a member of an organization which was known to Swiss Intelligence as the 'Rote Kapelle', the Red Orchestra. The head of that organization in Switzerland was also an officer, also a colonel. In the NKGB.[13]

---

13 We know this organization today as the KGB. Originally its name had been Cheka, then GPU, then NKVD. That was changed to NKGB in 1943 and finally shortened to KGB in 1953.

PART TWO

Chapter 6

That evening, at precisely 7 pm, Peter Burckhardt called.

'Have you eaten?' he immediately asked.

She said yes for some reason, although she had not.

'Then let's go to the Three Kings. We can talk there, have a drink, and maybe dance. Lothar Löffler's orchestra plays there every evening but Sunday, and he's the best we've got in Basel.'

She hesitated.

'All right,' adding: 'But not too late.'

'I'll pick you up at eight sharp and have you home by eleven. OK?'

'I'll be waiting downstairs. It's Augustinergasse 11, by the way.'

'I know.'

As she shed her vice-consul's uniform, which consisted of a white blouse, grey skirt and blue jacket, she began to weigh the merits of the only two frocks she owned that she considered suitable for dancing. And as she did so, she realized that she was as nervous as a sophomore before the first high school dance.

'Pull yourself together, girl,' she said to the full-length mirror as she stood in front of it in her bra and panties – the body that was reflected there was definitely not that of a high school sophomore – as she began to work seriously on her makeup.

Peter Burckhardt arrived as the bells of the ancient cathedral, the Basler Münster, which was located just 200 metres away, finished chiming eight. He was driving a black Mercedes. When he stepped out of the car, his greeting was in the form of a firm Swiss handshake. No kiss this time.

As they drove away she thought, if this evening is obviously going to be all business yet again, why not get right down to it?

'As long as we're in the car, let me tell you what I was able to accomplish today. I went to Bern this morning as I told you I would, and spent a short time with Mr Dulles.'

'We know. Twenty-three minutes.'

Which really startled her. Then she remembered.

'Right. You know about the back-door approach to Herrengasse 23.'

'I seriously doubt whether we always keep an eye on it, but in this case Colonel Masson was anxious to know how serious you were. You and Mr Dulles.'

She didn't particularly care for that remark, and it was reflected in the new tone of her voice. 'Then for openers you can tell your Colonel Masson that Mr Dulles is *very* serious, and that he is prepared to meet him, in his own words, "at his earliest convenience".'

'Where?'

'He will leave that up to your people, since, as he put it, Masson no doubt has more problems with that than he does. But Mr Dulles had a further request. He said it was not critical, but if you could accede to it it might be helpful . . . in the longer run.'

'And that is?'

'That Captain Waibel also be present. And you.'

Now it was Peter Burckhardt's turn to be startled.

So Nancy Reichman added: 'I think maybe he would like to look you over just like . . .'

'Like we looked you over last month. Fine with me. But you should tell him that this will be up to Colonel Masson.'

By this time they had pulled up in front of the Three Kings, Basel's premier hotel, located in the centre of the city on the southern bank of the River Rhine. Statues of the biblical Three Kings were mounted above the main entrance on the Blumenrain.

They were no sooner inside the lobby than a huge bear of a man approached them.

'Peter,' he said. 'Was für eine nette Überraschung!' Then he noticed Nancy Reichman at Peter Burckhardt's side and switched immediately to English, to be sure a heavily acented English. 'You are the pretty American vice-consul, aren't you? Perhaps you remember me from one of Professor Salin's dinners. Per Jacobsson is my name.'

'Of course I remember you, sir. My name is Nancy Reichman.'

He took her hand, and bowing slightly, said: 'How very nice to see you again.'

Peter Burckhardt, watching all this, appeared flustered, not quite knowing what the next move should be. His boss at the Bank for International Settlements immediately resolved the problem.

'Now don't worry,' Jacobsson continued, 'I'm not going to bother you any further. I'm going to bed, since I have to take the early morning train to Berlin, as you know, Peter. Otherwise,' and now he turned back to Nancy, 'I certainly would have asked for a dance. Perhaps some other time?'

'I would love to,' Nancy replied.

'Maybe that occasion will arise after I return from this trip,' Jacobsson added, and he glanced at Burckhardt as he said it. Then he said good-night and disappeared up the hotel stairway.

Peter Burckhardt noticed the somewhat puzzled look on Nancy's face. 'Something's bothering you,' he said as they started to move in the direction of the bar located off to the left of the lobby.

'Two things. What is he doing here, and what was the meaning of that last remark?'

'He lives in the hotel now. He felt that his family would be safer in Sweden, and, after they left, he closed up his apartment and moved into the Three Kings.'

'When did all that happen?'

'Ten days ago.'

'Isn't that rather strange?' she asked.

'What do you mean, "strange"?'

'Why would he feel that his family is threatened here? And why now?'

'Let's get a drink first. Then I'll explain.'

55

They left their coats at the cloakroom and when the maître d' asked Peter whether he preferred to sit at a table or the bar Burckhardt suggested a table by the window, overlooking the Rhine. A waiter appeared immediately and took his drink order: a bottle of Veuve Clicquot.

Only then did he return to Nancy's questions. And when he did so he leaned far across the table and spoke in a very low voice. 'No doubt for the same reason that Colonel Masson wants to see your friend in Bern as soon as possible. Rumours indicate that they may be planning something.'

She said nothing, waiting for Peter Burckhardt to explain further.

'We have heard that Hitler himself has approved a plan to invade Switzerland in March. In other words, it is now just a matter of weeks.'

'From whom have you heard this?' she asked, knowing that she could hardly expect an answer. And she was right.

'That doesn't matter. Suffice it to say that it comes from a source very close to the top in Berlin.'

'Why should the Germans invade Switzerland now?'

'Because the whole strategic situation has changed where the Germans are concerned. As late as last September it appeared that Germany was on the verge of winning the war. Their Sixth Army had just crossed the Don River and was moving into the suburbs of Stalingrad. After that Moscow and Hitler would have totally controlled Europe from the Atlantic to the Urals. The last holdout in Europe, Switzerland, under those circumstances would have just been a detail, one that could be taken care of any time, almost at leisure.

'But then came the landing of the Americans and British in North Africa on November 8th, one that completely surprised the Germans according to our sources in Berlin. The knee-jerk type of countermove by the Germans followed immediately, on November 11th, when they occupied Vichy France to cover the newly exposed southern flank of Europe on the Mediterranean coast.

'But now Hitler has experienced his first severe military

setback. His entire German Sixth Army had no choice but to surrender to the Russians at Stalingrad at the end of January. As a result the whole dynamics of the war has been drastically changed, the role of the chief combatants reversed. For it will now be the Russian army in Eastern Europe and the Americans and the British in North Africa who will be on the offensive. And it will mean that the German army will, for the first time since September of 1939, be on the *defensive*. This has already forced the German high command to formulate a new overall military strategy, and, according to our informants, they already have a name for it: "Festung Europa" – "Fortress Europe". Within that context, the strategic importance of Switzerland has suddenly been moved front and centre. If the Allies invade Sicily or Sardinia, as will inevitably happen soon, all of Italy will eventually become a war zone. Today the only direct transportation link between Germany and Italy that is controlled by the Nazis is Austria's Brenner Pass. It is extremely vulnerable to bombing attack, and could easily be put out of business as part of an overall coordinated Allied invasion of Italy proper. This could "force" Hitler to make a preemptive strike against Switzerland to gain control of our two north–south railroad tunnels, the Gotthard and Simplon, as well as our Alpine passes and the roads which go through them, and thus ensure that the German troops fighting in Italy would not be cut off from their only source of supply, Germany proper. We are told that this is now under serious consideration in the Führer's command headquarters in East Prussia.'

'And how does this relate to Mr Dulles?'

'We want his help.'

'Can you be more specific?'

'Very specific. We are interested in troop movements within Germany. Anything that points to an increasing concentration of military forces in the south of that country would tend to confirm these rumours. What we are specifically watching out for are unusual movements of troop trains and of freight trains moving large numbers of camouflaged flat cars – that's how they transport their tanks and armoured personnel carriers to the front. If they suddenly get diverted south, instead of going east to the Russian front, we will know that serious trouble lies ahead for Switzerland. The Americans and British are constantly monitoring such movements from the air. We, of course, are unable to conduct aerial surveillance of Germany. But we still do rather well from the ground, in fact maybe better than you do, since most of these types of movements take place at night when aerial cameras are useless. So although your help here would be extremely valuable, it is not of critical importance to us yet.

'What is critical, extremely critical, is a very specific piece of information, information which we need to receive as soon as possible. But first let me back up just slightly to explain why. If intelligence, especially military intelligence, has one key function it is to help prevent military surprises. Like what happened to the Russians on June 22nd of 1941 when Stalin was taken completely by surprise when Hitler attacked. Or like what happened to you Americans on December 7th of the same year when the Japanese bombed Pearl Harbor.

'To prevent such a thing from happening to us – and the future dates being mentioned for our big surprise are either March 6th or March 25th – we in Swiss Intelligence have come up with what we consider to be the best possible single early warning of an impending German attack on our country. We are convinced that if there is one prime indicator of Nazi military intentions vis-à-vis Switzerland it is the location of the special units of their army which have been specifically trained for mountain warfare. Quite obviously, they will be an essential component of any invasion of our country. For the Nazis know full well, just as you must also know, that should they attack us from the north, the basic military response of our commander-in-chief, General Guisan, will be to fall back across the relative flatlands south of the Rhine to our redoubt, our mountain fortress, in the Alps which is centred on and beneath the Gotthard Pass. From there our military forces will take their stand and fight, literally, to the death. Believe me.'

Burckhardt paused, and briefly looked around the room. More

people, mostly young people, were arriving, but nobody as yet had occupied any of the adjacent tables.

'Now back to my boss, Per Jacobsson. He heard from his sources in Stockholm a week ago that it is rumoured that a significant number of these troops which were concentrated on the Finnish/Russian front have "disappeared". This now has the Swedes worried that they might well be moving in their direction. The Wehrmacht unit in question is the 20th Alpine Army under the command of General Eduard Dietl. Where is it? It is the answer to that question which we are now so desperately seeking. Please ask Mr Dulles if he can help us. My boss, Colonel Masson, would have preferred to put this request to Mr Dulles in person, but time is now of the essence. So we're depending on you, Nancy. If you could . . .'

As he spoke, Lothar Löffler and his orchestra had taken their places on the podium in front of the restaurant's dance floor, and they now began to play a Glenn Miller piece in the Glenn Miller style.

She could not help herself. 'That's "Moonlight Serenade"!' she exclaimed. It was the twenty-seven-year-old American girl in her best frock, one who was 6,000 miles from home and alone, who said it. When the American vice-consul then apologized with the words, 'Oh, I'm sorry, I interrupted,' it was to Peter Burckhardt's great credit that he immediately stood up and extended his hand to her. They were the first and for a time the only couple to approach the dance floor.

It took a few seconds for them to adjust to each other, but thereafter it was to the graceful movements of the tall, blond aristocratic Swiss and the dark, sultry American girl that all eyes were drawn, even those of the bandleader. And as he moved his orchestra into 'String of Pearls', 'In the Mood' and then 'Tuxedo Junction' it seemed like the whole room poured onto the dance floor. And as they did, Peter Burckhardt and Nancy Reichman slipped ever closer into each other's embrace. He became aware of the thinness of her waist and the fullness of her breasts. She knew it. And pressed even closer. By now Lothar Löffler's orchestra was playing 'At Last', and Nancy hoped he would never stop.

But then, suddenly, Peter Burckhardt stiffened and drew back, and when the orchestra finally paused he steered her back to their table.

'What is it?' she asked when they were once again seated.

'The two men who just sat down at the bar. Don't look now.' She didn't.

'Who are they?'

'I just recognize one of them and he's German, in fact a major in the Waffen SS. His name is Hans Wilhelm Eggen. He's watching us, and I don't like it.'

'Maybe it's just a coincidence.'

'Maybe. And maybe not.'

'What's an SS major doing in Basel?'

'He's a big wheel in the "Beschaffungsamt", the procurement agency, of the Waffen SS. They operate under the cover of a company which they secretly own — the "Warenvertriebs G.m.b.H. Berlin". Eggen is its managing director. He first came here in 1940 to try to negotiate a deal for a huge quantity of our new Swiss-made machine guns. In the end he failed and had to settle for just 250 guns in exchange for 200,000 litres of gasoline. The next deal involved military barracks. Two years ago Eggen signed a contract with a Swiss company located here in Basel, Extroc S.A., providing for the delivery over a two-year period of two thousand wooden barracks, made in Switzerland, for the German Wehrmacht.[1] Eggen comes here regularly to make sure that everything is proceeding on schedule. We're also told that he is currently negotiating for another thousand units. But nobody believes that's all he does when he visits Switzerland. There was an attempt to kill the British ambassador to Switzerland eighteen months ago. Eggen was in Basel the night it happened.'

Then all of a sudden he smiled. 'Another new arrival at the bar. And this time it's good news. One of ours. From Lucerne.'

Now, despite his warning, Nancy Reichman looked directly at the bar.

---

1 See Pierre-Th. Braunschweig, *Geheimer Draht nach Berlin* (Zurich, 1989), pp. 179ff.

'Unless I've got the wrong men, it looks to me as if they just said something to each other,' she said.

Five minutes later the Germans got up and left the bar. The Lothar Löffler orchestra began to play again, and the interlude had apparently ended.

But then Peter Burckhardt spoke. 'Strange,' he said. 'Now our man has also left.'

'Isn't that what he's supposed to do?'

'Yes.' Then he continued: 'But he's hardly supposed to talk to them first, is he?'

'Perhaps there's a special reason.'

'Such as?'

'The same one that has us talking together.'

The shocked look on Burckhardt's face indicated that her remark had struck home.

'I think we had better call it a night, Nancy,' he then said. After paying the bill, they went to the cloakroom to collect their coats.

As they waited a man approached Burckhardt from the rear and took a firm grip on his right arm. 'If you will please excuse us for a moment,' he said to Nancy Reichman, in English.

The two men then walked to the far corner of the lobby, and began to exchange what were obviously heated words. After no more than three minutes their conversation ended and the intruder turned to leave. But before he did so he directed one last verbal salvo at Burckhardt, while wagging his index finger directly in his face.

When Burckhardt returned, his face was red with anger. 'Let's get the hell out of here,' he said, now taking Nancy's left arm in a tight grip.

'Who . . .' she began to ask as he steered her out of the door of the hotel.

'The police,' he answered. 'The head of the political police of the canton of Basel. Can you believe it! He wanted to know what "we" are doing secretly consorting with the Nazis on Swiss soil. And, while he was at it, he asked about you. And he wants to see me at eight o'clock sharp in his office, and expects a full explanation. Or else it is going to be my head.'

61

'What did you tell him?'

'To bugger off!' He paused. 'Sorry. It just slipped out.'

Then he continued: 'He said one additional thing just before he left. He has people who have infiltrated the various groups of local Nazi sympathizers. They have heard questions being raised about you during the past couple of days. He warned me that if something happens to you all hell could break out with the American government, and I would be held directly responsible. Eggen's presence in Switzerland, he said, is very bad news, as the British ambassador nearly found out a year and a half ago.'

By this time they had reached his Mercedes. Five minutes later they were back in front of her apartment building. He got out, leaving the engine running.

'I'll see you up.'

She did not protest. After she had unlocked her door, he entered the apartment with her. As she turned on the lights, he scanned the room. 'Let's check the rest of it,' he said. First the bedroom, then the bathroom.

'Everything's fine, Peter,' she finally said.

'All right. But Nancy, be careful. Tell Mr Dulles about this right away.'

'I will. And I will also tell him about the rest of our conversation first thing in the morning.'

She saw him to the door, and as he turned to say good-night she knew that this time it would be with neither a handshake nor a peck on the cheek. They kissed first tentatively, then deeply. When he finally withdrew and started down the stairs, Nancy Reichman discovered that she was trembling from head to toe.

A man watched all of this through binoculars from the attic of a house directly across the Rhine from Augustinergasse 11. He also watched her undress a few minutes later. Until she suddenly remembered that the blackout had been in effect for at least an hour, and drew the curtains.

Chapter 7

Despite his words of bravado the previous evening, Peter Burckhardt showed up five minutes before the 8 am deadline that had been put to him by the chief of the political section of the police department of the city and canton of Baselstadt. Dr Wilhelm Lützelschwab, who held this position as well as that of prosecuting attorney, received him immediately.

'Herr Doktor, nehmen Sie bitte Platz,' were Lützelschwab's opening words of greeting to Burckhardt.

'Danke, Herr Doktor,' was Burckhardt's reply. Both had studied at the university at the same time and had got their doctorates in the same year, Lützelschwab in law, Burckhardt in economics.

'I'll come directly to the heart of the matter. What are you idiots in the D Bureau doing consorting with a man who reports directly to the criminal who runs the SS, Heinrich Himmler, and who is reputed to be the right-hand man of Walter Schellenberg, who is, for God's sake, the head of SS Intelligence?'

The D (for Deutschland) Bureau which he referred to was the Swiss intelligence unit, run chiefly out of Basel, from which all espionage directed at Germany originated.[2] Intelligence acquisition was the responsibility of Captain Waibel, Burckhardt's immediate superior, who reported to the head of all Swiss

---

2 For a detailed description of the activities of Bureau D, see Braunschweig, *Geheimer Draht nach Berlin*, pp. 101–50.

espionage operations, Colonel Masson, operating out of the Hotel Schweizerhof in Lucerne under the codename 'Rigi'.

'Have you all gone mad? And on *my* territory! I should have ordered that you all be put in jail right then and there in the Three Kings.' The primary function of the political section of the local police — which included over 100 special agents — was counterespionage.

'And what in God's name was that young American woman doing there? She's the vice-consul of the United States! Need I point out to you that the consulate in question is located on *my* territory and that *I* am responsible for keeping her alive? That's difficult enough in a city which seems, at times, to be full of goddamn Germans and Communist sympathizers, which is bad enough. But not bad enough for you guys. No, you've got to bring in a major in the Waffen SS so he can watch you two waltzing around the dance floor. Are you setting her up or what? I thought that the Americans were supposed to be our friends and the Germans our enemies. Or have I somehow got things mixed up?'

Finally Peter Burckhardt spoke: 'Enough. I had absolutely nothing to do with Eggen's presence at the bar last night. Furthermore, that was not one of our men in the narrow sense of the word. He works out of Lucerne and, as far as I know, reports directly to Colonel Masson.'

'Are you suggesting that the left hand here in Basel doesn't know what the right hand is up to in Lucerne?'

'It's been known to happen.'

'Did you know that the three of them met later in a room at the Euler Hotel?'

'No. By the way, who was the man with Eggen?'

'A local lawyer by the name of Rudolph Widmer. Really bad news, in our opinion. And our opinion is based on telephone taps which we maintain on his lines, both in his opulent office downtown and his fancy apartment in the Gellertquartier.'

'Is he German or Swiss?'

'Swiss. He's purportedly Eggen's lawyer here. Advises him on contracts, like the one under which they've been buying military barracks from us. Are you people familiar with that?'

'With the barracks stuff, yes. With this Widmer fellow, no. Should we be?'

Lützelschwab shrugged. Then: 'Leave him to us. We want to know what's going on with Eggen. So that we can determine whether or not to arrest him. And I want you to pass those exact words on to Lucerne. Immediately. Have I made myself clear?'

'I'll see what I can do. But in the meantime, if I were you, Herr Doktor, I would keep all this to myself. I would like to suggest that perhaps something has come up which involves our national interests. Maybe that's why the Lucerne man was here. So my suggestion is that you lay off, especially lay off Eggen, until you hear from somebody who knows exactly what's going on.'

The two Herr Doktors then just stared at each other, until Peter Burckhardt rose from his chair.

'Does your father have any idea what you're into these days?' Lützelschwab asked, as Burckhardt headed for the exit. Instead of answering, he just kept walking.

After Burckhardt left the Spiegelhof, where the political branch of the Basel police was located, he was at first uncertain as to what to do next. Then he made up his mind and walked rapidly down the hill to the market square where he headed directly for the phone booth located there. His boss, Captain Waibel, answered immediately, and Burckhardt explained what had just happened. Waibel said he would talk to Lucerne right away, and then take care of Lützelschwab. But he did not sound totally convincing. After leaving the phone booth, Burckhardt, who had intended to board a tram which would have taken him up to the Bank for International Settlements, changed his mind and instead kept walking up the Frei Strasse. A few minutes later he stood in front of the world headquarters of the Swiss Bank Corporation. Lützelschwab's last remark had given him an idea.

After announcing himself to the porter at the entrance, he took the private elevator to the fourth floor where he was met by another uniformed porter who ushered him into his father's office, the office of the Chairman of the Board. His father rose to greet him and they shook hands.

'What a pleasant surprise! Come, sit down over there. I'll get us some coffee.' His father went back to his desk and, after saying a few words on the intercom to his secretary, joined his son at the coffee table.

'I can only stay a minute,' Peter said. 'I've got two favours to ask of you.'

'Just name them.'

'First, could you call Lützelschwab over at the police department? Tell him we've just talked, and you would appreciate it if he would just let things be for the moment.' This request grew out of the son's knowing that his father had a lot of political clout in Basel not only due to his position at the bank, but also because he was a member of a group made up of a dozen of Switzerland's most prominent and powerful bankers and industrialists who unofficially advised and often helped Swiss Intelligence. All of them had contacts on the highest level in Berlin, Rome, Paris, London and New York and used them both to gather information and to constantly reassure *both sides* that Switzerland intended to remain strictly neutral, and to defend that neutrality with its armed forces, if necessary. Since they were regularly briefed by both the Swiss Foreign Office and the military they were normally as well informed as anybody in the country.

But they had obviously been kept in the dark on this one. Which prompted Herr Doktor Maximilian Burckhardt-Von der Mühll to ask his son: 'May I inquire as to what you mean by "things"?'

'That's all you will have to tell him.'

His father smiled, but said: 'All right. But can you tell me?'

'Yes. And that relates to the second request. Could we use our place in Benken for a very private meeting, either tomorrow or the next day?' The 'place' Peter Burckhardt referred to was a medieval Schloss near the Swiss village of Benken, located ten kilometres outside Basel close to the French border, a castle which the Burckhardts had bought and restored forty years earlier.

'Certainly. I'll send some people up this morning to make sure that everything is ship-shape. And to light some of the fireplaces.

It's cold up there this time of year. Will anybody be staying overnight?'

'I'm not sure. But just in case, why not prepare four or five bedrooms. Especially the master suite in the tower.'

'And for whom will that be?'

'Allen Dulles, if everything works out.'

Burckhardt Senior let out a low whistle.

'What's the occasion?'

'We've heard, from an excellent source, that Hitler may be planning to attack us in March. We want the Americans to help us find out if it's true.'

His father's face turned grim, but he said nothing.

'One other thing, come to think of it,' Peter then said. 'Can you find out who's involved with a company by the name of Extroc S.A.?'

'What do they do?'

'Make wooden barracks and sell them to the German army.'

Again his father whistled softly. 'You're full of news this morning, aren't you Peter? If they bank with us, I can tell you within minutes.'

He went back to his desk, picked up the phone, and gave his instructions. Minutes later a man knocked on the door, and then entered, carrying a dossier which he handed to Peter's father, and then left again without saying a word. The banker Burckhardt glanced through it rapidly.

'They bank with us. Sales this year are 12 million Swiss francs. Decent profit. It says that they are involved in the manufacture of prefabricated wooden structures, but nowhere does it say that they are selling them to the Nazis.' He spoke as he read. Then, abruptly, he stopped reading.

'If you were looking for trouble, you've found it, son. Guess who's on the board of directors? The son of our commander-in-chief, General Guisan . . . the man who is in charge of keeping the Nazis at bay. Jesus, if this comes out, this country could be dumped into one hell of a political crisis.' Then: 'Is this why the phone call to Lützelschwab?'

'Yes. Because the man who is in charge of *buying* those barracks, a major in the Waffen SS by the name of Eggen, was in town last night. And Lützelschwab caught one of our men meeting him in the bar of the Three Kings.'

'How do you know all this?'

'Because I happened to be in the Three Kings last night too. Dancing, for God's sake. Which led Lützelschwab, who is now threatening to throw everybody in jail, to call me on the carpet earlier this morning.'

'Don't worry, I'll take care of him as soon as we're done.' Then: 'But what the hell is going on here?'

'I don't know for sure yet, but I'm increasingly reaching the conclusion that our people in Lucerne, with the help of Guisan's son and the backing of the general himself, are in the process of setting up a direct line to some top-level Nazis, and I mean top-level.'

'Such as?'

'My guess would be the SS major's boss, Heinrich Himmler.'

'Do you mean that the general might actually *meet* with *Himmler*?'

Peter Burckhardt shrugged. 'All things considered, that's where things seem to be heading.'

'But where?'

'Maybe somewhere in Switzerland. I don't think our people, or the general, are dumb enough to meet them on their turf.'

Now his father's face turned even grimmer. 'And that puritan Lützelschwab has got wind of it and is trying to stop it. And he's probably right. Christ. They're all playing with fire! If the general is serious . . .' He paused. 'No, it can't be. He isn't trying to work out a deal, surely. Especially now that the German army has finally been stopped.'

'Au contraire, dear father. That, paradoxically, might be precisely *why* Masson and the general are running this risk. To get someone who has direct access to that maniac Hitler to carry the message that if he tries to "consolidate" central Europe by invading Switzerland he's going to face one hell of a battle.'

Peter's father thought that one over, and then said: 'If the general is taking those invasion rumours *that* seriously maybe I should get your mother and sister out of here.'

'They would never go, and you know it,' Peter said.

At this juncture his father's secretary peeked into the room, prompting him to look at his watch, and Peter to get up. After making sure that the secretary had firmly closed the door behind her, the banker said a final word.

'Before you leave, I've got a suggestion. Tell your people that if they need a very private venue for that other meeting, one which even Lützelschwab and his hounddogs won't be able to penetrate, they can have the Schloss in Benken any time they want, even at very short notice. Although I'm not sure that it would be advisable to have both Dulles and Himmler there on the same weekend.'

'I'll pass it along today. And thanks, Dad.'

When Peter Burckhardt got to his office at the Bank for International Settlements shortly after 9 am there were two messages for him. One asked that he call his aunt . . . the prearranged signal that he call Captain Waibel. The other came from Nancy Reichman. He called her first.

'About that meeting,' she began immediately, after they had got by the hellos. 'Our suggestion is tomorrow night. Seven o'clock. You should name the place. And I've passed on the word about the other matter.'

Burckhardt immediately phoned his superior in Bureau D, Captain Waibel, with this information, adding to it his suggestion that they use his family's place in Benken as the meeting place. Waibel said he would contact Colonel Masson right away. He also suggested that Burckhardt drop by his office later that morning. So around eleven o'clock Burckhardt told his secretary that he would be out for the next hour or so: a dentist appointment.

The Basel operations of Bureau D of Swiss Intelligence were housed in rather luxurious surroundings – an eighteenth-century patrician mansion located on the Petersplatz, across the park from the new building which now housed the lecture halls of the university. It was less than half a block from the university library, which was one of the reasons for its being located there. Peter Burckhardt drove there in his Mercedes and Captain Waibel received him almost immediately.

'You've managed to disturb a wasps' nest,' were his first words, but he said them with a grin. He was a good-looking man, in his late thirties, and despite his captain's rank had a very easygoing, non-military way about him. He was destined, in later years, to be Switzerland's military attaché in Washington, where he was regarded as very 'non-Swiss', which didn't hurt him a bit. This later appointment was in no small way related to the events of early 1943, just now beginning to unfold. 'But before I get into that, I want to officially inform you that Colonel Masson has agreed to meet with Mr Allen Dulles tomorrow evening at the venue you suggested.'

Peter Burckhardt looked at his watch.

'Then I will confirm that to the American vice-consul right away, if I may use your phone.'

After talking to Nancy Reichman for all of twenty seconds he hung up and dialled again. 'My father,' he explained to Waibel.

'It's on for seven tomorrow night,' he said, the moment his father answered. Then: 'I'll ask. Hold on a minute.'

'How many from our side? And how many total will spend the night?'

'I don't know for sure,' Waibel answered, 'but I assume that there will be just three of us, including you. My guess is that Masson will probably not want to spend the night. But I will. It's not every day that I get invited to your family's Schloss. Where the Americans are concerned, that's your call.'

Burckhardt returned to the phone. 'Three of us of which two will stay the night. Two of them, Dulles and Nancy, and both will stay over.' He listened for a few seconds, and hung up.

'Does anybody need travel arrangements?' Waibel then asked.

'I'll take care of the Americans, if you agree,' Burckhardt answered.

'All right. I'm sure Masson will arrange to be driven directly to

Benken from Lucerne. And I'll drive myself. So we'll all meet there tomorrow night at seven.'

'Done.'

'All right. Now Topic Number Two,' said Waibel. 'Heikel, sehr, sehr heikel,' he continued. 'In fact, it is so difficult I'm not even sure I should be discussing any of the details with you. But I will anyway.' And he grinned.

'Waffen SS Major Eggen, whom you spotted in the Three Kings last night and were unfortunately spotted doing so by our friend Lützelschwab, delivered a request to one of our men from Lucerne during a subsequent meeting at the Euler Hotel: Heinrich Himmler would like to meet with General Guisan in Switzerland and as soon as possible.'

Peter Burckhardt said nothing.

'You don't look very surprised.'

'I'm not,' Burckhardt answered. 'And what was our reply?'

'Himmler? No way. Our man simply told them that it would be suicidal for our general if it ever came out. He sensed that Eggen anticipated this answer, since he immediately came up with an alternative suggestion: General Walter Schellenberg, Himmler's deputy and the head of their intelligence operations. It was made clear that the Germans would be very put out if this request was refused. So it wasn't . . . in view of the rumours that have been swirling around.'

'When?'

'That has yet to be determined.'

'Where?'

'The Germans suggested Arosa. Or Davos. Apparently the good General Schellenberg likes to ski. We nixed that, since the last thing we want is any public knowledge of this. The Swiss press would kill us. When I called Masson this morning, right after you called me, we talked at considerable length. He explained that he felt obliged to keep me fully informed since, after all, Germany was primarily my responsibility, which I thought was rather generous of him. Be that as it may — when the question of venue came up for a potential meeting with Schellenberg, and we are talking here about a *preliminary* meeting, without General Guisan, I suggested that Masson might consider using your family's place in Benken again. He said he would want to check it out first. Which he will do tomorrow evening.'

'What about Lützelschwab? He'll go up the goddamn wall if he finds out that an SS *general* is now about to set foot on Basel soil. A *major* like Eggen was bad enough. But now a Schellenberg?'

'Look, Peter, I'm basically on Lützelschwab's side. And so are you, I'm sure.'

Burckhardt nodded.

'I also talked to Lützelschwab this morning and made it crystal clear that all the goings-on last night were instigated by Lucerne, not us. I think he also got the message that the people in Bureau D, meaning specifically you and me, think that Masson and the general are being led down the garden path. By the way, he brought up the subject of the American girl, and asked what you were up to with her at the Three Kings last night.'

'What did you tell him?'

'That it had nothing to do with us. That it was a date, pure and simple.'

'Did he believe you?'

'I doubt it. Which reminds me: did she pass on our request to Dulles?'

'Yes.'

'I'll relay that immediately to Masson. You've done all right with her, Peter, and we're all grateful. She could develop into one of the most important assets we've got.'

'Then we'd better have our people keep an eye on her, especially at night and over weekends when she's not inside the consulate.'

'I've already thought of that, Peter. Arrangements are being made.'

Chapter 8

In fact, such arrangements had already been made. But not by the Swiss. Other eyes had been watching Nancy for weeks from the top floor of a house that was located almost directly opposite her apartment on the Augustinergasse, although not across the street but rather across the Rhine. The house that was being used was Rheingasse 37. It was a three-storey house, built in the fifteenth century, a building that would have been worth a lot of money had it been located on the other side of the Rhine in Grossbasel. The side on which it *was* situated, Kleinbasel, was home to the city's bars and nightclubs; its restaurants served Wurst, not entrecôte, and specialized in Warteck beer, not wines of the Bourgogne. It was, in other words, where Basel's working class lived. Or, as the man who lived in that house would have put it, where the proletariat were kept — out of view of the rich people who lived on the other side of the river. For at that point in the flow of that river, which took it from its origins in an Alpine glacier to its final destination, the North Sea, the Rhine was perhaps 400 metres wide, just wide enough to make it difficult for the naked eye to bridge it.

But eyes assisted by Zeiss binoculars could observe objects or happenings across the water in the most minute detail, day and night. Were an observer interested primarily in religion or architecture, those binoculars would no doubt have been focused on the Basel Münster, the medieval cathedral built of red sandstone. It was only of interest from the outside, since the

Basel Bürgers who had taken it over in the sixteenth century had stripped its interior to the bare bones in a show of Protestant piety, or hypocrisy, a point of view which, of course, would depend upon the religious affiliation of the observer. In the case of the people who were handling those binoculars in the winter of 1943, neither religion nor architecture played a role in their choice of objects. They scorned religion, regarding it as the opiate of the masses, and they knew nothing about architecture, as was thoroughly demonstrated by the type of buildings favoured by their supreme leader, Joseph Stalin. For Rheingasse 37 was the clandestine Basel headquarters of the Rote Kapelle, the Red Orchestra, the espionage network which the Soviets had installed throughout central Europe in the decade prior to the outbreak of World War II. The man who owned that building represented one of the last remnants of that network, since most of his colleagues had been hunted down and put out of business by the counterespionage unit of the SS — under the leadership of General Walter Schellenberg.[3]

The name of the owner of Rheingasse 37 was Werner Lentz. He had come to Basel in 1929, a returnee from Russia where his Swiss parents, who were in the watch repair business, had taken him as a boy. They had opted to stay in Leningrad after the revolution despite the increasingly hard times that had come down upon their adopted homeland — although for them the times were not that hard, since, despite the fact that very few new Swiss watches had entered Russia since 1919, everybody who already had one treasured it and thus kept it in good repair. Two years after both of his parents were killed in a train accident in 1927, the boy, by now a young man, had chosen to take advantage of his Swiss passport and return to his native land. He had learned the skills of watch repair from his father, and had no trouble finding a job with Basel's premier jeweller, Seiler's, on

---

3 For the best histories of the Red Orchestra, see Gilles Perrault, *Auf den Spuren der roten Kapelle* (Zurich, 1956); W.F. Flicke, *Spionagegruppe Rote Kapelle* (Kreuzlingen, 1954); Heinz Hoehne, *Codeword: Direktor* (New York, 1971); Leopold Trepper, *The Great Game: Memoirs of the Spy Hitler Couldn't Silence* (New York, 1977).

the Barfüsserplatz. In 1935, Lentz had opened his own small jewellery shop in Kleinbasel. In 1939, shortly before the war broke out, he had bought that house on the Rhine for the then princely sum of 8,000 Swiss francs.

In reality, Werner Lentz was a full colonel in the NKGB who had been assigned the 'operational alias' of Igor Scitovsky, and whom the Soviets had planted in Switzerland under deep cover, as they had done in many other cases throughout Europe in the late 1920s and early 1930s. Scitovsky got the job because, like the original Werner Lentz, he too had been an apprentice to a watchmaker, also German-speaking, in a small town located directly on the Volga River 300 kilometres northeast of Stalingrad. Everybody in that town, and in the entire surrounding area, spoke German, since they were all descendants of the German and Swiss colonists whom Catherine the Great had enticed to settle in this region of Russia in the 1760s. By the early twentieth century their numbers had grown to almost half a million, and their contribution to the development of Russia had been so great that, despite the fact that they had remained separate from the rest of the land, maintaining their own language, customs and even religion, Lenin had granted their region the status of republic within his newly founded Union of Soviet Socialist Republics – the Volga Republic. Igor's mother's ancestors had come to Russia from eastern Switzerland along with 153 other Swiss in 1767, and in August of that year had founded a new village on the Volga and named it Schaffhausen, after the city on Lake Constance which they all knew so well. Much to the chagrin of her relatives, she had married 'outside' the community, her husband being a Russian stationed with the local military command, Captain Vladimir Derzhavin. Their chagrin would have been even greater had they known that he was also attached to the NKVD. Their son Nikolai grew up almost perfectly bilingual thanks to his mother, but also 100 per cent loyal to the Communist regime in Moscow, thanks to his father. With such qualifications, it had not been difficult for his father to arrange his recruitment by the Soviet secret police following completion of his apprenticeship. When the 'opening' had developed as a result of that train accident outside Leningrad, son Nikolai — who was a natural for the job — had undergone intensive training aimed at further developing his ability to handle the 'Alemannische' dialect, the dialect spoken by his mother, and one which was common not only to the majority of Swiss cantons but also to parts of southern Germany as well as the Alsatian region of France. By the time he arrived in Switzerland bearing the doctored passport of the only offspring of the now dead Swiss watchmaker, he was immediately able to pass for a native son. As for the real Werner Lentz, he was as dead as his parents, although in his case it was not a train wreck which had finished him, but rather a bullet in the back of his head, one that had been fired fifteen years earlier.

The prime job of Igor Scitovsky, alias Werner Lentz, was military espionage, and the prime target was Germany. For the most part it was extremely mundane. He — or, more often one of his three men, all Swiss Communists, one a bartender at the Three Kings Hotel, one a room clerk at the Schweizerhof Hotel, and the third an assistant in the jewellery store in Kleinbasel owned by Lentz/Scitovsky who doubled as the radio man — monitored Nazi military shipments through Switzerland, using those Zeiss binoculars, usually night glasses, to observe and count the number and types of rail cars coming from Germany and passing through the Badische Bahnhof, the German railroad station located in Basel just ten blocks from where Lentz lived. They knew that this almost endless string of trains transported war materials (his men regularly broke into the cars to determine their exact contents) destined for deployment in Italy or North Africa. Why such monitoring? Because the more war materials that headed south through Switzerland, the less, his bosses at Moscow Centre reasoned, would be available to resupply the German armies fighting the Soviets on the Eastern front.

That type of information was easy to come by and involved little risk. Much more important, and by 1943 much harder to come by, was accurate information about military movements — troops, armour, and other materials — inside Germany proper. As a result of the decimation of their agents by Schellenberg's men, in early 1943 the Soviets had few 'assets' on the ground in Germany and they were being caught and killed at an accelerating rate. Which was forcing the Soviets to seek out alternative sources of information. Someone in Moscow had come up with the bright idea of infiltrating one or more of the other intelligence services operating in Switzerland which still had a good number of agents intact and on the ground inside Germany, as was the case with both Swiss and British intelligence, and, perhaps much more promising, the new network that Allen Dulles had just begun to build up from his operational base in Bern. Slipping a double agent inside his fold might be relatively easy to accomplish in the opinion of Moscow Centre (which considered Dulles a crass amateur), one that had been relayed to Scitovsky as soon as the Soviets had caught on to what Dulles was up to in Switzerland, which they had just weeks after his arrival there. Or even more promising: turning one of Dulles's recruits into a Soviet informant. But first they had to be identified. Thus the surveillance by the Red Orchestra of the comings and goings to and from Dulles' apartment; and thus, subsequently, the surveillance of Dulles' 'man' in Basel, a regular visitor to the building Dulles occupied at Herrengasse 23 in Bern, a 'man' who, it had turned out, was a woman by the name of Nancy Reichman.

The trouble was that while the surveillance of Dulles (conducted by agents chiefly operating out of the Red Orchestra's base in Lausanne, although Scitovsky's men were occasionally brought in) was proving to be very productive, at least in terms of the number of prospective candidates, since the traffic in and out of Herrengasse 23 was heavy, so far the surveillance on Nancy Reichman's apartment by the Scitovsky crew had turned up nobody, except for a young Swiss aristocrat who worked for the Bank for International Settlements and who thus was about as likely a candidate for recruitment by the Soviets as the American vice-consul herself. But, it was reasoned, somebody, something, was bound to turn up inside Augustinergasse 11. So the surveillance was maintained. And at 5.30 on the evening of 25 February it produced a winner, in the person of no less than Allen Dulles himself.

It set the machinery of the Red Orchestra in full motion for the second night in a row. And it would lead to another flurry of radio traffic between Basel and Moscow, traffic already at a dangerously high level that week as a result of Colonel Scitovsky's decision to immediately relay to his superiors what his agents, planted years ago in strategic listening posts in Basel's two premier hotels, the Three Kings and the Schweizerhof, had reported after coming off work the previous night, namely the presence of an SS major in Basel in the company of what were obviously agents or representatives of the Swiss government – either top-ranking military staff or intelligence. For after the bartender at the Three Kings had overheard elements of a brief conversation at his bar, he had alerted the room clerk at the Schweizerhof that some special guests were headed his way. After they had arrived fifteen minutes later and collected the key, the Red Orchestra's man inside the Schweizerhof had determined that the room reservation had come from no less a place than the headquarters of General Guisan himself.

The issue that now had to be resolved: Were these events interconnected? And if so, was something under way – such as complicity between the Americans, the Swiss and the Nazis – which could undermine the strategic objectives of the Soviet Union?

Allen Dulles had arrived at the Bahnhof in Basel at 5.07 that evening and had been met there by both Nancy Reichman and Peter Burckhardt. After Nancy had introduced the two men, they walked to Burckhardt's car which he had parked directly across from the station in front of the Bank for International Settlements. Dulles had come with a small black overnight bag which he insisted on carrying himself.

'Would you like me to put that in the trunk for you, sir?' Burckhardt asked when they had arrived at his Mercedes.

'Please.' And as Burckhardt did so Dulles stood back to look at the building that housed the bank. 'Did you know that my sister Eleanor wrote a book about the BIS?' Dulles asked Burckhardt, as the young man closed the trunk and then proceeded to open the doors of his car. 'In fact, it was really her dissertation. At Radcliffe.'[4]

'No, sir. I was unaware of that.'

'You might look it up some time and give me your opinion. By the way, I understand that you work directly under Per Jacobsson.'

'Yes, sir. I do.'

'I'd be most interested in meeting him. Is he here?'

'No, sir. He's in Stockholm right now . . . after stopping off briefly in Berlin. But he's planning on returning to Basel next Monday.'

'Could you perhaps let him know that I will be calling him right after his return?'

'I will. I'm sure he will be very eager to meet you.'

'Good. Then I'll suggest that we dine together. What's his favourite restaurant here in Basel?'

'Unquestionably the Schützenhaus. It was formerly a hunting lodge, but is now the city's premier restaurant.'

Dulles turned to Nancy, who had been standing silent, listening as the two men became acquainted. 'Could you arrange that?'

'Certainly.'

'Let's tentatively aim for next Tuesday or Wednesday.' Then back to Burckhardt. 'Now what's the drill for this evening?'

'We are scheduled to meet Colonel Masson at seven. At our family's country home outside Basel.'

'So Nancy told me. How long will it take us to get there?'

'Thirty minutes.'

Dulles looked at his watch. 'So we have time to spare.'

'How about a coffee at my apartment?' Nancy interjected.

'Splendid idea,' Dulles replied. 'I need a little warming up.'

*

---

4 Her book was published in 1933 by Macmillan under the title, *The Bank for International Settlements at Work.*

Once they were inside Nancy's apartment and had shed their overcoats, Nancy went into the kitchen to prepare the coffee, and the two men stood in front of the french doors which led out to the terrace overlooking the Rhine. Darkness had already fallen, and the lights of the city — the pre-blackout lights — were reflected in the swiftly flowing water below. Then, gradually, a huge very dimly lit barge came into view, followed immediately by another, and then yet another.

Dulles watched in silence, obviously fascinated, and then asked: 'What are they carrying?'

'No doubt coal.'

'This happens every night?'

'Yes, sir.'

'Where does the coal originate?'

'Germany. The Ruhr. The barges you see down there were probably loaded at Duisburg four or five nights ago. They only move at night, and only run with lights when travelling this very short distance through Basel where both banks of the Rhine are in neutral Switzerland. As you can imagine, with their size, and at the speed they move, they are easy targets for any Allied aircraft in the area, bombers or fighters. So they move at night, and at dawn they pull up to preselected spots on the banks of the Rhine, out in the countryside, and spend the daylight hours there under heavy camouflage.'

'But what harbour are they headed for in south Germany?' Dulles asked, obviously puzzled.

Peter Burckhardt appeared similarly puzzled — by the question.

'Actually, sir, they are Swiss barges — Swiss registered, Swiss owned, and flying the Swiss flag — and they are headed for Swiss harbours. Most offload downstream at the Rhine harbour here in Basel, but some, like the ones you are now watching, proceed further up the Rhine to Augst or Schaffhausen.'

Dulles did not show the slightest sign of embarrassment. 'I should have realized that, shouldn't I? The coal is obviously part of the compensation agreements your government periodically enters into with the Germans, isn't it? Coal for . . .' He left the sentence unfinished lest he, in turn, embarrass the young Swiss.

His politeness was unnecessary, as was evident when Peter Burckhardt finished the sentence for him. 'Coal for use of our rail transit facilities,' adding, 'under a trade agreement which is just about to run out.'

'Really.' Dulles paused. 'How interesting.' He was obviously trying to draw the Swiss out further, but Burckhardt remained silent. So Dulles tried again. 'Has that got anything to do with what we will be discussing this evening with Colonel Masson?'

'Perhaps.'

Dulles just nodded. 'Tell me something else if you can, Dr Burckhardt, or may I call you Peter?'

'By all means, sir.'

'Good. These barges. Do they return empty?'

'Usually. Although sometimes they carry back some Swiss exports. Bulk cargoes. Like cement.'

'But they also move by night and hide by day regardless?'

'Yes, sir.'

'I see. And what about checkpoints?'

'Normally the barges are kept clear of all harbour facilities in between, because such ports are prone to bomber attack at any time.'

'Makes sense.'

Nancy had arrived back in the living-room minutes earlier, with a tray bearing coffee, but had said nothing. Now she did. 'It's getting late, sir. Perhaps . . .'

'Of course,' Dulles replied. 'How impolite of us.' And they immediately joined her at the coffee table as she poured.

Twenty minutes later they were on their way once again. Nancy Reichman was the last to leave, turning out the lights before she closed and then carefully double-locked the door. The man across the Rhine who had been watching the whole time checked his watch. It would be a close call but most probably Colonel Scitovsky, whom he had alerted by phone at the jewellery shop the instant he had recognized the face of Allen Dulles, would have had time to get over there before they left.

In fact, he had.

81

Chapter 9

The Augustinergasse was a dead-end for automobiles, since it narrowed to a pedestrian passage just fifty metres down the street from Nancy Reichman's apartment. So Peter Burckhardt had to go through a series of manoeuvres to turn his Mercedes around before being able to head back out to the square in front of the cathedral 100 metres up the street. Thus by the time he drove past the Opel van which had been parked, though very briefly, in the cathedral square, the van's driver had been fully alerted that something was starting to happen. The darkness made it impossible for Colonel Scitovsky to be sure that the car was the one transporting Allen Dulles from the apartment of the American vice-consul to his next rendezvous, the meeting that was no doubt the reason for his excursion to Basel on this dark, inhospitable February night. But since there had been no other movements, cars or otherwise, on the Augustinergasse or for that matter on the cathedral square itself since he had arrived five minutes earlier, he felt that the odds were definitely in favour of the Mercedes. He pulled immediately behind it, feeling that he could follow fairly closely without arousing any undue suspicions, since full blackout restrictions first went into effect at ten o'clock and thus there would still be a good deal of traffic, at least by Swiss wartime standards, on the streets of the city.

But ten minutes later he was less confident, and as they went further and further into the outskirts of Basel he dropped further and further behind, even letting first one, and then another vehicle, the second with military markings, come in between. He also became increasingly sure that he was tailing the right car. By the time they had passed outside the city limits he had dropped so far behind the Mercedes that its tail-lights were barely visible. Fortunately it was a fog-free night. Equally fortunately, the moon was but a sliver in the night sky, meaning that his van would be all but invisible in the rear-view mirror of the cars ahead.

Now in the suburbs, they first passed through the village of Binningen, then Bottmingen, followed three kilometres further by Oberwil. One of the cars between Scitovsky's van and the Mercedes had turned off in Bottmingen; the second, the military vehicle, had pulled to the side in Oberwil. The Swiss countryside took over after Oberwil, and during the next seven kilometres the only lights to be seen were those of the two remaining vehicles, both moving fast despite the fact that the road was now becoming increasingly narrow, the terrain more hilly, and the curves more frequent. Then came the road sign indicating that they were entering the next small farming community, the twin villages of Biel and Benken, always referred to locally as Biel/Benken. Suddenly the brake lights of the Mercedes lit up, causing Scitovsky, a full half-kilometre behind, to slam on the brakes and pull to the side of the road while simultaneously switching off the Opel's lights. From his vantage point he could easily follow the further progress of the Mercedes as it turned right off the main road and began to climb a road leading up and up into the dark hills to the west of Biel/Benken. Scitovsky now got out of the van – there was a crisp layer of snow beside the road, and it cracked beneath his boots – and raised the Zeiss night glasses to his eyes, scanning the western horizon. And there, at an elevation of probably 400 metres and directly in line with the direction the Mercedes was taking, was light. Minutes later the two light sources appeared to merge.

Mr Allen Dulles, it seemed, had reached his destination.

Colonel Scitovsky had no sooner got back into his van than the headlights of another vehicle appeared in his rear-view mirror. Just as it passed the van it began to slow. It was the same vehicle with military markings which had stopped at the side of the road two villages back, probably to allow the driver to check his bearings. A half-kilometre further down the road, its brake lights lit up and the vehicle appeared to have once again pulled over to the side of the road, its lights remaining on. Three minutes later it began to move again, turning right off the main road, and then moving up the hill to the west, following the exact same route the Mercedes had taken. So that was the 'other' party. But were there still more to come? Scitovsky remained in his van in the darkness for another twenty minutes. Not a single vehicle passed him in either direction.

He started up the Opel, turned on his lights, and proceeded, slowly, into the village of first Biel, then Benken. In the centre of Benken there was an intersection and at the near corner of that crossing, on the right, was a restaurant − 'Zum Ochsen' according to the very dimly lit sign which hung above its entrance and bore the image of a huge ox. Scitovsky pulled up right in front of it and looked at his watch: 7.22. Plenty of time before the blackout would be enforced.

It was a typical Swiss village inn, with ancient beams crisscrossing the ceiling, wooden floors, and pewter plates and mugs mounted on the walls as decoration. In the front of the room stood a dozen tables covered with red and white table-cloths and immaculately set for dinner. But only one was occupied. To the rear were another five tables − no table-cloths there − with the one at the very rear, up against the wall, large enough to seat at least a dozen. It was no doubt the village 'Stammtisch'. Every country restaurant in Switzerland had one: the table where the locals, men only of course, gathered evening after evening to have their beer or perhaps a glass of the local wine, to discuss politics and local events and, when that wore thin, to begin the card game − the same card game, evening after evening, 'Jass'. It was the game, a version of euchre, that was regarded, and not even so jokingly, as the Swiss national sport. Just as Scitovsky walked in one of the seven men back there slammed down a card triumphantly. The game had ended; the cards were gathered in, shuffled, and re-dealt, the pipes and cigars relit. The next Jass was about to begin. But not before all seven men had carefully sized up the stranger who had just walked in. As they watched he sat down at one of the tables in the rear, nodding to them as he did so. None nodded back. The waitress, clad in the peasant costume known as a 'Tracht' — each Swiss canton had its own version, hers, blue and white, being that of the rural half-canton of Baselland — immediately approached his table.

'Guten Obe, Fräulein,' the stranger began. 'Ich haette gern e Bier und e Paar Würstli.' It was now Werner Lentz who was speaking. He spoke in the dialect of the urban half-canton of Baselstadt, and he spoke it impeccably. Nothing new about such visitors at 'Zum Ochsen' in Biel/Benken, since the city folk from Basel had been coming there to get some real country food for centuries. The pause at the Stammtisch ended. The next Jass began. And so did the running conversation among the players. The stranger was forgotten.

The waitress returned immediately with the beer Scitovsky/ Lentz had ordered, and delivered it with a smile, an inviting smile. For Scitovsky was a good-looking man in his late thirties, and a quick glance at his left hand had confirmed the absence of a wedding band.

'I'll be back with the wieners in about five minutes,' she said, adding, 'if that's all right.'

'Of course. I'm in no hurry at all.' And he smiled right back at her. 'After all, it's nice and warm in here. It must be ten below freezing outside.'

'I just looked at the thermometer a few minutes ago. It's actually twelve below,' she said. 'I'm not looking forward to walking home tonight.'

'I hope you don't live too far away.'

'No, no. It's just a few hundred metres. Benken is not Basel, you know.'

'Be happy it isn't.'

'They all say that. But since the war started it has been very quiet here. Even on weekends. Because of the gasoline rationing, you know.'

'I can understand that. It must get to be very lonely at times. Although I did notice at least two cars ahead of me on the road from Basel. And both turned off here.'

'Ja. But that's because of the Schloss. And those people up there have nothing to do with us.'

'Really. Who owns it?'

'One of those families in Basel. You know, the "Daig".'

'A Sarasin? Or perhaps a Von der Mühll?' And he spoke imitating the haughty form of the Basel dialect used by that city's aristocrats.

She giggled. 'You don't like them either.'

'Not too many do.'

'Well, these are Burckhardts.'

'Which ones?'

'He — the older one — is the big banker. You must know of him.'

'Of course. He runs, or some say he rules, the Swiss Bank Corporation.'

'That's the one.' Then: 'You know, it's really quite odd. This is the second time this evening that this subject has come up. Right before you arrived somebody else came in to ask how to get to the Burckhardts' Schloss. A bigshot in the army. A colonel, I think. Something's obviously going on. Probably a big dinner party. I saw two of the maids shopping for food in the Migros store this morning. Which is also rather unusual. Normally nobody is up there in the winter months. Now I've got to go and see after your wieners.'

The wieners came with potato salad, hard rolls, and a tube — like those used to dispense toothpaste in other countries — of mustard.

When he was through, Scitovsky looked directly at the waitress, who had been watching him most of the time from her perch behind the bar. She immediately came over.

'You know, I think I'll switch to a glass of wine. After all, "Wein nach Bier, das rat ich Dir." What would you suggest?'

'Something local?'

'Yes. And why don't you bring a glass for yourself? It doesn't look like you're going to be busy tonight. That is, if the landlord allows it.'

'He's not here tonight.' She looked over at the Stammtisch. 'And they're taken care of for a while. Sure. Why not?'

During the next half hour, over a slightly sour though quite drinkable Baselbieter Riesling, he learned that her name was Liselotte. That she was twenty-seven. That her family were farmers and had owned and worked several parcels of land outside Benken for generations. They had cows and chickens and some cherry trees – her father made Kirschwasser from them every spring – and that not only did she work as a waitress at 'Zum Ochsen' six days a week, with Sundays off, but she was also expected to help out at home, including taking her turn milking those stupid cows and even cleaning out the disgusting chicken pen.

He also learned, as she bent over increasingly close to him, talking all the time, that she not only had a very pretty face – he had spotted that immediately upon entering the restaurant, since he had an eye for such things – but beneath the peasant costume, there was a very full peasant body, one that seemed ready for some robust animal activity that had nothing to do with either cows or chickens.

The first glass of wine was followed by a second, and now as she continued to talk – about her brother who was a lazy bum, her three sisters, all still in school, about how she just loved Basel and would move there in a second if only she could find some kind of job there – she punctuated her remarks by reaching over to touch the hand of Werner Lentz. And it was an increasingly hot little hand that did so . . . especially after he revealed that he owned a small jewellery store in Basel and maybe, just maybe, might need some more help there. Nothing fancy, at least to begin with. Maybe to help out at the counter, to clean up in the evening, that sort of thing. Maybe.

By nine o'clock, the place had completely emptied out. A couple of the men from the Stammtisch glared at Lentz as they left, looks that indicated that they knew what he was up to and thoroughly disapproved. But then they were alone. Lentz looked at his watch.

'You know, I've got to get back to Basel before the blackout starts, Liselotte.' And he looked into her eyes as he said it. 'So as much as I hate to do so, I'm afraid I'm going to have to ask you for the check.'

When she came back he laid two ten-franc notes on top of the check and rose to collect his coat which he had hung on the rack beside the door which led into the kitchen. When she returned with his change — nine francs — he waved it aside.

'Will I hear from you again?' she asked, as he began struggling into his overcoat. 'Soon?'

'Definitely,' he said, thinking that this was too good to pass up in any case. 'Maybe we could take in a movie together. In Basel. I could pick you up. On a Sunday. Maybe this Sunday?'

'Oh, I'd love that, Mr Lentz.'

'Werner, please.'

They walked to the door together, and when he stepped outside into the darkness she followed him.

'But you'll catch cold!' he protested.

'I just want to thank you for the wine. And to tell you how much I am looking forward to Sunday . . . Werner.'

He stepped toward her and, very hesitantly, kissed her on the cheek. She moved into him — all the way. And now he kissed her fully on the lips. And she responded by pressing even closer. His hand moved over her back. And then to her breasts.

Liselotte was ready. Scitovsky's guess was that with very little further encouragement, they could end up as bedfellows — rather strange bedfellows — immediately after the Sunday matinee.

And, as a bonus, Colonel Igor Scitovsky now had yet another 'man' in place . . . just down the hill from the Burckhardts' Schloss, where some even stranger bedfellows were probably about to sit down to dinner.

Chapter 10

The Benkener Schloss, as it was known locally, dated back to 1513 when it was built by a local who had risen to power and riches as a mercenary in the employ of King Louis XII of France. It was not unusual for Swiss to hire themselves out to foreign powers as warriors: the practice has survived to this day in the form of the Swiss Papal Guards in the Vatican. The men who protect the Pope were and still are always recruited from the canton of Wallis, which borders on Italy, and where the Catholic Church is controlled by extremely conservative priests and bishops, clergymen who have always been able to convince the local youth that it was better to serve God than Mammon. The soldier from Benken, which is located barely five kilometres from the French border, was definitely on the side of Mammon, however, and came home from the wars a rich man – rich enough to build a monument to himself in the form of the Schloss.

By the eighteenth century the founder's family had become impoverished and had fallen back into obscurity. The Schloss remained abandoned thereafter, right up to 1903, when the Burckhardt family – in the person of Peter's great-grandfather – had gained control of the castle, and, parcel by parcel, the land surrounding it, land which now extended right up to the Swiss frontier with France. Most of the land had been kept as a hunting reserve, although a small section, about twenty hectares, was planted in grapes, Riesling grapes, just as it had been centuries earlier. In fact the house wine of the local inn 'Zum Ochsen', the

Baselbieter Riesling, was made from grapes grown on the Burckhardt estate.

It had taken almost ten years for the castle to be fully restored.
But thereafter, since the beginning of World War I, it had served
as the summer home of the Burckhardt family. It was therefore
the place where Peter Burckhardt had spent much of his childhood and youth.

'How I envy you for that,' said Nancy Reichman, as they
finished the castle tour during which Peter had given her and
Allen Dulles a brief history of the place.

When they returned to the main living room, formerly the
entrance hall which was dominated by a fireplace in which huge
logs were burning furiously, the two Swiss army officers who had
been sitting before the fire, talking very seriously it seemed, rose
from their chairs. The greeting formalities had been already
taken care of twenty minutes earlier, when both parties − the
Swiss and the Americans − had arrived within five minutes of
each other.

Peter Burckhardt continued his duties as host. 'If you all agree,
I would like to suggest that we sit down to dinner.'

The dining-room was right out of a museum. An immense oak
table was the centrepiece, but upon entering the room the eye
was immediately drawn to the Gobelin tapestries which adorned
the walls, and the medieval arms − from crossbows to pikes −
which seemed to be there for a purpose rather than just mere
display. It was as if one were stepping back into the fifteenth or
even fourteenth century.

There were five places set in the middle of the huge table, and
Peter Burckhardt immediately took charge of the seating, putting
Allen Dulles between himself and Nancy Reichman, with her to
his right, of course, and placing the two Swiss army officers,
Colonel Roger Masson and Captain Max Waibel, facing them.
They were no sooner seated than a man-servant appeared and
poured white wine into one of the four Baccarat crystal glasses
that accompanied the blue Meissen china atop the pewter under-
plates and the Jetzler silverware at each setting. He was immediately followed by two serving girls bearing smoked trout and

Alsatian goose liver pâté. There was no doubt that all of the guests at the Burckhardt castle wondered how all this was possible in wartime Switzerland, with the borders to the rest of Europe closed to normal traffic in all directions, yet no one dared ask − not even Allen Dulles.

But after the murmurings of pleasure which the arrival of the first course had evoked, it was he who broke the ice with his counterpart in the world of intelligence, Colonel Masson.

'It is, sir,' he began, 'both a great pleasure and honour to meet you, especially in these wonderful surroundings. I know how difficult it must have been for you to take time off from your duties to come over here this evening, especially right now, and I want to tell you how much I appreciate it. For my part, I have come here to make it known that if we Americans can be of any help to you in maintaining the neutrality and independence of your country, we shall do so with enthusiasm. I have been an admirer of Switzerland for many years, in fact since my first sojourn here during World War I, so I can assure you that these words come from the heart.' It was clear to all present that Dulles was going out of his way to get off on the right foot with the head of the Swiss intelligence service on a personal level.

Masson's response, given in French, ostentatiously in French, made it immediately obvious that he intended to proceed more cautiously. Nancy Reichman, aware of the fact that Allen Dulles was not fluent in French, immediately began a simultaneous translation into English, murmuring it into his ear as the colonel spoke.

'We Swiss appreciate your sentiments, Mr Dulles. Very much. And I am personally honoured that you are here this evening. We also have a great respect for your country, and your person I might add. But as a long-time observer of us you know, Mr Dulles, that we Swiss take our neutrality very seriously and intend to defend that neutrality against any belligerent, by military force if necessary. It is the possibility that just such action might be forced upon us in the near future which prompted me to suggest this meeting.'

'And not any desire to get cosy with you Americans' were the words which were left unsaid, but certainly implied. And everybody in the room knew it.

Peter Burckhardt sprang into the breach of silence which followed. He spoke in English, also ostentatiously. 'All I have to offer at this point is a humble Baselbieter Riesling, but if you all agree I would suggest that we raise our glasses in celebration of the friendship which has always existed between the two oldest democracies on earth, Switzerland and the United States.'

After the five glasses were half emptied, the silence broke. Nancy Reichman began a conversation in impeccable French with Colonel Masson, one initially composed of the usual banalities about how well the Swiss population was coping with such wartime hardships as rationing and blackouts, but then moving on to more serious matters, such as the role of the Swiss Red Cross in monitoring the prisoner-of-war camps in Germany where many downed American fliers were being held, and how appreciative the American government was of such action and the results it was producing in terms of greatly improved conditions. Masson, who had an eye for pretty women being a rather handsome man himself, seemed flattered by the attention, and appeared to gradually relax. This process was hastened by the arrival of the red wine, a superb 1934 Pomerol. The main course consisted of marinated wild boar, accompanied by mashed potatoes and carrots. A second bottle of Pomerol was needed almost immediately. By the time dessert was served, Schwarzwälder-torte, the atmosphere had changed to one of apparent total congeniality.

At nine o'clock Peter Burckhardt consulted his watch, and then addressed his military superiors seated across the table. 'If you agree, I would suggest we retire to the library and move on to the more serious part of the evening.'

Colonel Masson nodded his agreement. And as soon as the only woman present rose from the table assisted by her boss, Allen Dulles, the two American diplomats and the two Swiss officers followed Peter Burckhardt into the library of the Benkener Schloss. As they entered the room they were greeted by the heat emanating from another huge fireplace as well as by a valet holding a silver tray bearing glasses filled with either cognac or Kirschwasser. All of the men went for the Kirschwasser. Nancy Reichman declined, but then immediately accepted the suggestion of a glass of champagne, which turned out to be a 1940 Veuve Clicquot when it arrived minutes later. The room itself was dominated by leather-bound objects: hundreds of books on the ancient oaken shelves, the massive furniture arranged in three different groups on top of huge Persian rugs which partially covered the original stone floor. Peter Burckhardt suggested that they seat themselves at the group which formed a semicircle in front of the fireplace. Dulles and Nancy Reichman took their places on the left side of that semicircle facing the two uniformed Swiss officers, with Peter Burckhardt in the middle. The lines having been drawn, as if on a signal all eyes turned to the Swiss colonel, for all knew that the next move was his.

Masson was a somewhat portly man with a kindly face which resembled that of the English actor who would soon make himself known to movie goers around the world, Alec Guinness. Masson, a native of the French-speaking part of Switzerland, had been a career officer all his life in an army which was composed almost exclusively of part-time militia under a system in which each Swiss male was obligated to military service, either full-time or part-time, during most of his adult life. After an initial four-month period of full-time training as recruits which began when each Swiss boy reached the age of twenty, they were required to return for yearly refreshment training up to the age of thirty-two, and then less frequently, depending on their rank, until they were fifty. Even the majority of the officer corps was made up of militia, complemented by a very small corps of professional officers. Masson was one of these and, in the tradition of the French-speaking part of Switzerland, had received his principal military training at the *Ecole supérieure de guerre* in Paris in the 1920s. In 1936 he had risen to the rank of *Oberstleutnant*, and was appointed head of Section 5, the military intelligence unit. At that time the entire intelligence service of Switzerland was made up of just two people, Masson and his secretary. Two years later, however, in February of 1938, just weeks before the annexation of neighbouring Austria by the Nazis, the intelligence service was radically upgraded in importance, 'radically' at least by Swiss standards, and by early 1943 had a full-time staff of 130 professional intelligence officers. But these numbers also radically understated the capability of Swiss Intelligence, for in the eighteen months between its reorganization and the outbreak of war in September 1939, Colonel Masson's organization had recruited hundreds and hundreds of part-time informants and agents abroad, predominantly Swiss nationals who lived and worked as architects, doctors, teachers, housewives in the countries surrounding Switzerland – in France, Italy, Austria and Germany. This network of agents was for the most part situated in a zone 100 kilometres wide on the other side of the Swiss border, and the greatest concentration was in south Germany, north of that stretch of the Rhine which flowed between Basel and the Lake of Constance. The man in charge of these agents, in fact in charge of all espionage conducted against Germany, was the officer who sat to the left of Colonel Masson, Captain Max Waibel.

It was to this network of agents that Colonel Masson alluded in his initial words directed at Allen Dulles. He spoke in French, and once again Nancy Reichman leaned over and made a running translation for Dulles.

'I am sure you know,' Masson began, 'that we in Swiss Intelligence regard the detection of a potential surprise military attack on our country as our prime mission. We have reason to believe that one is being organized right now. Our problem relates to the fact that we would have no problem in verifying this were conditions today similar to those which prevailed in World War I, when troops moved on foot and artillery was often horse-drawn. Prior to any assault there had to be a massive military buildup relatively close to the territory to be attacked. I repeat: were that true today, we would not be here this evening. Unfortunately the nature of warfare has changed so much during the past thirty years, as has been repeatedly demonstrated since the fall of 1939 by the Wehrmacht in their Blitzkrieg assaults on Poland and France and Russia, that an attacking army can cover a hundred kilometres a day. Which means that if they intend to invade us, the massing of their forces will no doubt take place beyond the geographical range of our primary intelligence capability . . . which generally extends no more than a hundred kilometres beyond our border.

'However, we do have channels of information other than our net of agents and informers in the territory immediately adjacent to Switzerland. Sources in high places. Needless to say, I can go no further than that. Two of these sources, impeccable sources I might add, have informed us that an attack is planned for either March 6th or March 25th.'

For some reason this last sentence caused Captain Waibel's eyebrows to rise ever so slightly, though nobody except Nancy Reichman appeared to notice it.

Masson continued, looking directly at Allen Dulles as he spoke. 'To be truthful, Mr Dulles, and I pride myself on always being so, we have been unable to verify this from any third source. Which leaves us in a quandary. If we, and I refer now to the General Staff of the Swiss army under the command of General Guisan — and the general himself personally authorized me to come here this evening — are to take this threat seriously, we will have no choice but to order a general mobilization on a scale similar to that undertaken at the outbreak of the war in Europe. At that time we put a half million Swiss under arms and at full alert, and this in a country that has a population of less than five million. Needless to say, the cost of this was enormous, not only in terms of the direct costs incurred by the defence department, but even more so as measured by the loss of national output brought about when all able-bodied men of this country had to leave their factories and farms and desks and join their military units in the field. Right now our troop strength stands at 100,000 men. If we have to go back to a full mobilization now, the economic paralysis which would result would have much more serious consequences for our population. As you must realize, we are a much weaker nation today than we were in 1939 and 1940. Our situation is the most critical where supplies of foodstuffs and fuel are concerned. They are already down to dangerously low levels. Our liquid fuel supply would be almost totally depleted if a full mobilization was required now. For it would result in a huge fuel expenditure as we moved troops and armour into place. The effects of mobilization on our future food supply could be equally disastrous if our farm population were to be diverted into the army just when spring planting must begin. Yet not to mobilize would be tantamount to surrender.'

He paused, and, as soon as Nancy Reichman had completed the translation, Allen Dulles tried to interrupt. But to no avail.

'Then there is the other danger to be considered. *If* our information regarding the invasion plans of the Wehrmacht proves in the end to be incorrect, but *if*, nevertheless, we have mobilized before we could make that determination, our actions could be regarded as a serious act of provocation by the leaders of Germany. And perhaps correctly so. After all, they have repeatedly given us their assurances that they have no intention of violating our neutrality as long as it is strictly adhered to where *all* parties to this conflict are concerned. They might regard a mobilization now as a response to a change in our assessment of the possible outcome of this war – following your recent victories in North Africa and their defeat at Stalingrad. This could prod the Führer into making a preemptive attack on us. Then all this could end up as a self-fulfilling prophecy.'

Masson again paused, but only very briefly. 'Now to the point, Mr Dulles. What we now need, immediately, with your help or anybody else's, is accurate, reliable information about German intentions vis-à-vis Switzerland in the coming three weeks. Lest we make a fatal mistake, one that could have serious consequences for you as well as us, Mr Dulles. For if the Germans, due to some miscalculation on our part during the next days and weeks, were to ultimately gain control of the entire Alps it would make any future attempt on your part to get at Germany from the south essentially impossible.' He paused and then added the following words: 'Maybe it is time for all of us to consider what such a military stalemate in central Europe could lead to. And do something to prevent it and the consequences which would inevitably follow.'

With those cryptic final words Colonel Masson fell silent. Now it was Allen Dulles' turn. He spoke in English but nobody translated, since everybody in the room knew full well that Colonel Masson was quite fluent in that language.

'You've made your situation admirably clear, Colonel Masson. As you know, your Lieutenant Burckhardt relayed to me, through Miss Reichman, a request for two specific bits of information. First, whether our aerial surveillance of Germany has detected any increased concentration of troops or armour in the central part of that country — in other words, in the zone immediately to the north of that which your own people are covering, one which would probably be used as the staging area for any attack on Switzerland. Secondly, any information we might have concerning the status of the 20th Alpine Army in Finland.'

He then reached into the inside pocket of his suit jacket and extracted a brown envelope. He rose from his chair, stepped across the semicircle facing the fireplace and handed it to Colonel Masson. Masson opened it, and took out its contents — two single sheets of paper. As Masson began reading, Dulles, who had returned to his chair, resumed talking.

'The top sheet you are now reading gives a summary of our aerial surveillance of Germany as conducted during the past seventy-two hours as it relates to your specific problem. The report was personally transmitted to me from London by Air Vice-Marshal Matthew Kelly, who is in charge of such matters for the RAF.'

Captain Waibel interrupted for the first time since the 'official' part of the evening had begun.

'Those seventy-two hours. When did they end?'

'At nightfall yesterday. But if anything new, startlingly new, had come up since dawn today, I would have been informed before I came over here this afternoon. I left my office in Bern at 15.25.'

Dulles had his eyes constantly on Colonel Masson, and as soon as he began to read the second sheet of paper began talking once again. 'Now to the 20th Army. We went to the Russians on that

97

one. After all, it is they who are engaged with the Germans – and the Finns – on that battle line along the border between Russia and northeastern Finland. We tend to forget that Finland was attacked by the Soviets two months after the Nazis attacked Poland – in November of 1939 – and that, despite the fact that for 105 days the Finns fought the Red Army to a standstill, the Soviets imposed a humiliating peace treaty upon them in March of 1940. Subsequently, after Germany attacked Russia in 1941 the Finns did the same, resulting in the unholy military alliance between the Germans and Finns which exists today. Be that as it may, the best intelligence on the situation in that part of the world comes from the *Glavnoye Razvedyvatelnoye Upravleniye*, Soviet Military Intelligence. They informed us – yesterday – that the 20th Army, the Wehrmacht's crack Alpine unit under the command of General Eduard Dietl, is fully in place in Lapland.'

'Your conclusion?' Waibel then asked of Dulles.

'That your information concerning a pending invasion of Switzerland, spearheaded by an airborne drop of units of the 20th Alpine Army aimed at securing the Gotthard redoubt, and followed up by an attack across the Rhine by troops and armour being massed in central Germany, is most probably incorrect. That this is a false alarm. And that it would be folly for your general to call for a general mobilization at this time.' Then, turning his attention from Captain Waibel to Colonel Masson, Dulles added the words: 'Or to accept any "deal" that the Nazis may suggest as an alternative to action on their part which would lead to, in your words, "a military stalemate" in central Europe. We believe that somebody in Berlin is cooking this whole thing up in order to lead you down a garden path that will get you nowhere, except, perhaps, further into their economic grasp.'

As he listened to the last sentence Colonel Masson's face turned to stone. He folded the two sheets of paper, slowly, deliberately, and then inserted them back into the yellow envelope. He got up, returned the envelope to Allen Dulles, and then spoke once again – this time in English.

'Thank you, Mr Dulles. Your help is greatly appreciated. We shall be evaluating your information immediately within the context of that which we continue to receive from other sources. I would greatly appreciate it if you and your people would attach a top-secret status to the contents of our conversation this evening, and the very fact that this meeting took place at all. Furthermore, I would strongly recommend that when you report back to your superiors in Washington you do so by courier. Your other means of communication, sir, are not secure.'[5]

He then offered his hand to Allen Dulles who, caught by surprise, rose hastily from his chair to grasp it.

All present in the room were now on their feet, and it was to Captain Max Waibel that Colonel Masson now turned. He reverted to French. 'J'aimerais bien que vous et Lieutenant Burckhardt m'accompagniez à ma voiture.'

His last act before leaving the library was to kiss the hand of Nancy Reichman while murmuring how great his pleasure had been at having this opportunity to meet her. Then the three Swiss officers left the room, leaving Allen Dulles and Nancy Reichman standing side by side in front of the fireplace.

'What was that all about?' she finally asked.

'I think I threw a spanner in the colonel's works,' Dulles answered. 'Or more accurately, into the machinations of some people in Berlin . . . people "in high places" there, to use the good colonel's expression. My guess is that Masson's intentions tonight were to somehow draw me into negotiations with them. And when he realized that he had failed, he simply left in an obvious huff.'

Dulles suddenly reached into the side pocket of his jacket and withdrew first a pipe and then a small packet of tobacco. 'If you don't mind, my dear?'

'Of course not,' Nancy Reichman answered.

Dulles took his time lighting the pipe, and, after a few puffs, said: 'That's better. Now, let me explain what I *think* is going on. There are a couple of key Nazis who are in the process of putting a full court press on Switzerland. They are men who have come to the reluctant conclusion, after seeing what happened at Stalin-

---

5 See Allen Dulles, *Germany's Underground* (New York, 1947), p. 130.

grad and what is happening in North Africa, that the war will be lost if they must continue to fight both us and the Russians. So they are seeking a diplomatic alternative, which would involve Switzerland as the intermediary. To gain Switzerland's support, they are essentially using the bad cop, good cop approach. If the Swiss cooperate with the good cops maybe they can convince the bad cops to lay off.'

'What do they want specifically from the Swiss?' she asked.

'That they use their "good offices" to work out a deal between the Anglo-Saxons and Germany — where we would stop fighting each other to a stalemate, and allow the Germans to devote all their resources to the single purpose of defeating Russia and preventing all of Europe from coming under the influence of the Bolsheviks.'

'But that's absurd!'

'Not in the view of the Swiss foreign minister, Marcel Pilet. He actually summoned our ambassador, and your official boss, Nancy — Leland Harrison — to his office yesterday afternoon to discuss just that. Apparently the German ambassador to Switzerland, Otto Karl Köcher, had put him up to it.[6] That was their initiative through the official channel. My feeling is that Masson intended to try to set up a second channel, a back channel, here this evening — involving all three intelligence services: the OSS, the Sicherheitsdienst of the SS, with Section 5 of the Swiss army in the middle. Or to be more specific, before I shot down his theory of an imminent invasion, suggesting that he was being set up by the Nazis, I think he was on the verge of suggesting a meeting between myself and one of the men behind all this, the head of SS Intelligence, General Schellenberg. We know that Masson has already met Schellenberg twice, once last November just across the border in Waldshut, and a second time in Switzerland, near Schaffhausen, in January. Which brings me to those mysterious goings-on you witnessed at the Three Kings

---

6 See Edgar Bonjour, *Geschichte der Schweizerischen Neutralität* (hereafter cited as 'Bonjour'), vol. V (Basel, 1970), p. 188. Professor Bonjour is the official chronicler of Swiss neutrality during World War II. I had the opportunity to study under him at the university of Basel in the second half of the 1950s.

Hotel the other night. We think they were in the process of setting up a third meeting. Probably near here. One which will no doubt take place very soon, with or without my presence.'

'But why would Masson get so deeply involved with the Nazis?'

'Naïveté, my dear. Plus a thorough mistrust of Soviet intentions after the war is over . . . a mistrust which I fully share, I might add.'[7]

'But what if all this gets back to the Russians?'

Dulles just shrugged, for precisely at that moment the door to the library had opened once again. Burckhardt and Waibel were returning.

---

7 For a history of Swiss–Soviet relations, see Bonjour, vol. V, pp. 373ff.

Chapter 11

Waibel immediately approached Dulles. 'My apologies for the behaviour of Colonel Masson. My only explanation is that he is under a great deal of stress.'

'Not to worry. We all are.'

'I agree,' said Peter Burckhardt, 'and I think that the situation definitely calls for remedial action, such as a strong dose of cognac. By the way, you are still staying the night, aren't you?'

'Of course,' Dulles answered. 'We're definitely staying the night and we are definitely interested in the cognac.' He then sat down in front of the fireplace once again and began to relight his pipe.

The cognac arrived shortly, and this time even Nancy Reichman accepted one. It was then that Max Waibel initiated the conversation for the first time that evening.

'If you don't mind, sir, I would like to return to the matters we were discussing. To make it clear that my views are not necessarily always those of Colonel Masson. Before I expand on that, may I ask you a question first?'

'Surely,' Dulles answered.

'What did you mean by "being led down the garden path"?'

'Perhaps I can better answer your question by suggesting who is doing the leading. We believe that the "who" is General Walter Schellenberg, acting on behalf of Heinrich Himmler.'

Waibel nodded rather grimly. 'The second "impeccable" source.'

'I sense that you disapprove,' Dulles said.

'I and my entire staff thoroughly disapprove of Masson consorting with the likes of Schellenberg,' Waibel answered. Then he asked: 'How much do you know about Masson and Schellenberg?'

'Enough. But allow me to ask you a question, Captain Waibel.'

'Max.'

'All right, Max it is. Who is "impeccable" source Number One?'

'That I will take to my grave. But I will tell you this: it is beyond any doubt the best and most reliable source of top-secret information that we have in Germany.'

'Our British colleagues tell me you have given that source a codename: you call it the "Viking Line".'[8]

'British Intelligence is seldom wrong.' Waibel then fell silent for a moment. 'All right, since you have been so forthright with your intelligence findings tonight, I will tell you this. Viking is often privy to the deliberations of the German General Staff. And sometimes privy to the actual military decisions taken in Berlin and, more importantly, at the Führer's command post in the Wolfschanz in East Prussia where he now spends most of his time. Although I thoroughly mistrust *any* information that comes down the line from Himmler and Schellenberg, I have *complete* trust in all information provided to us by the Viking Line. I repeat: it hasn't been wrong yet.'

'I assume that the Viking Line is one of your personal "accounts".'

'It is. And it will stay that way.'

'OK. Following up on what Colonel Masson said, can you be more specific about the information you've gotten from the

---

8 This 'Viking Line' is alluded to in all histories of Switzerland's role in World War II, but in no case is the exact identity of the German or Germans who were providing the Swiss with their most important intelligence during the war ever revealed. It is thought, however, that he or they were attached to Hitler's personal communications centre, and were thus privy to all of his decisions as soon as they were communicated to the German High Command, or directly to the commanding generals on the various fronts.

Viking source? And when you received it?'

'It first came through to me on January 16th. And it has subsequently been reconfirmed twice.'

'Specifics,' Dulles repeated.

'That in the event of an invasion, or serious threat of invasion of southern Italy, and I quote the exact words which came from Viking, "since the Swiss army will act as a shield, protecting the Anglo-Saxon military forces as they move towards us", Switzerland will be attacked in two stages. The battle plans had been worked out by General Dietl, acting under direct orders from Hitler. His 20th Alpine Army will spearhead the attack in night parachute drops and glider landings aimed at securing the Gotthard Redoubt. Other drops will be made in the northern foothills of the Alps. This first wave will involve 100,000 men. Simultaneously, there will be a massive bomber attack on the major Swiss cities north of the Alps – Zurich, Basel, Bern, Lucerne and Schaffhausen. An hour after Dietl confirms that his attack behind the main Swiss line of defence has been successful, a Panzer column stationed 500 kilometres north of the Swiss border will begin to move south at a speed of 70 kilometres an hour. These units will secure the major centres of population. Immediately behind it, motorized units of the Waffen SS will follow. Once on Swiss soil their primary task will be to enter these population centres and "eliminate" any Swiss, military or civilian, who may be inclined toward organizing partisan activities once the invasion is over. The main invasion force which will follow the Waffen SS units across the Rhine will be the new "Southern Army" of the Wehrmacht, now in formation, composed of one million regular troops. All this will begin on March 6th.'

'And you believe it?'

'Yes, sir. Maybe not where the exact date is concerned, but in principle, yes.'

'We don't. In fact, we have been completely aware of this almost from the very beginning, and were highly sceptical even *before* receiving the latest information I gave to Colonel Masson this evening.' Again Dulles reached into the breast pocket of his jacket, and extracted another single-page document. 'Read this.

It is a message relayed to Washington by our military attaché in Bern, Captain Legge, and then relayed back to me by courier. Legge and I don't talk much to each other, since the chief of our legation here tries to keep me out of his embassy.'[9]

Waibel read it. And appeared shaken, although his next words indicated that it was not due to his having any doubts about the Viking Line.

'I don't know how Legge found out about this. But I'll take Viking's word over his any day.'

Dulles shrugged at these last words. 'I guess you have no choice. In any case, we'll keep you informed if anything changes in our intelligence assessment. That is, if you want to remain in contact.'

'Of course I do. And I cannot stress that enough. Although I would suggest that, for the moment, we leave Masson and Lucerne out of this.'

'Agreed. And may I further suggest that our Miss Reichman and your Lieutenant Burckhardt continue to serve as intermediaries?'

'Perfect.'

'Good. And if this arrangement continues to work for you where this "March alarm" is concerned, maybe it could be used for other purposes.'

'Such as?'

'Some joint ventures. In areas where our interests overlap.'

'Why not? Do you have something specific in mind?'

'Yes, and I'll be very blunt with you, Max. We are interested in developing contacts close to the Führer very similar to the one you already have at the other end of the Viking Line. On the surface there might appear to be a major difference in our intentions. Yours has been solely the acquisition of information which will aid you in defending Switzerland's independence and her neutrality. Ours is a more active mission. One that is less benign. We seek conspirators inside Germany who want to end

---

9 See p.106 for a copy of this document (Pierre-Th. Braunschweig, *Geheimer Draht nach Berlin*, Zurich, 1989, p. 269).

WAR DEPARTMENT
CLASSIFIED MESSAGE CENTER

INCOMING MESSAGE

MESSAGE CENTER COPY
CCWD

RC 30
filed 29/1920Z
dm

Jan 29
2108Z

*D-2 report on rumors of German
invasion of Switzerland*

From: Bern
To: Milid

No. 450   January 29, 1943

    Following 600:303 has been aware some for
Special General Staff studying new plan invasion
of Switzerland under direction Diete recently
in Munich latter reports have stated event invasion of Italy by Allies Germany could not have
large part mountainous frontier held by a nation
which was only advance guard of Allies.

    Plans based on surprise air invasion before
Swiss could concentrate in National Redoubt
parachute and air landings troops neutralizes
troops concentration, Deny roads and destroys
critical points. Motorized and mechanized ground
invading forces in order to retain surprise makes
last march considerable distance from frontier.

    1:25000 scale map of Redoubt prepared by
Germans have been obtained by 303 agent.

    Situation German Army precludes this as
present danger but Swiss alert to possibility.

Legge

ACTION: G-2

INFORMATION: OPD
               CG AAF

CM-IN-14129   (30 Jan 43)   1210Z   emsi

Distribution	
	STRONG
RS	KRONER
BRATTON	MA
SIT	FL
TIB	CIG
SW	SSB
AIR	FIN
NA	TRNG
FE	POW
G-A	PERS
AIC	CC
PUBL	
COLL	CNI
PWB	WH
	16

CONFIDENTIAL   M I S JOURNAL NO. 125 JAN 30 1943
COPY No.

THE MAKING OF AN EXACT COPY OF THIS MESSAGE IS FORBIDDEN

this war as soon as possible. I would like to suggest, however, that ultimately we are both seeking the same end: the defeat of Nazi Germany. And intelligence services, like ours and yours, Max, are ideal vehicles for fostering conspiracies which may bring the day of that defeat much closer and save millions of lives by doing so. Agreed?'

'Agreed.'

'Any suggestions as to how we might go about this?'

Now Peter Burckhardt, after receiving an approving nod from his superior, Captain Max Waibel, broke out of his role as the neutral host for the first time that evening.

'Two suggestions. Have you ever heard of the "Mittwochgesellschaft" in Berlin? The "Wednesday Society"? Or of the "Kreisau Circle" in the eastern part of Germany?'

'No to the first. Yes to the second, but only vaguely.' This was not 100 per cent true. Dulles knew all about the Kreisau Circle, but was having extreme difficulties in establishing contact with them.[10]

'Both are "discussion" groups of the kind that can commonly be found only in central Europe. The Wednesday Society was started in the middle of the nineteenth century and has always been confined to sixteen members who dine together weekly in Berlin . . . obviously on Wednesdays. Its purpose is to bring together scientists and intellectuals, although at present it even includes a general of the Wehrmacht, who, I am told, was admitted only because of his knowledge of military history.'[11]

Dulles was suddenly very alert.

'You said *scientists* and intellectuals?'

'Yes.'

'Please go on.'

'The Kreisau Circle takes its name from the estate of Count Helmuth von Moltke in Kreisau in Upper Silesia, where the group meets. It includes influential men from many walks of life — professional men, churchmen, militant socialists, men of the

10 See Allen Dulles, *Germany's Underground*, pp. 81ff.

11 Ibid., p. 27.

Right. What they all share is a belief in the Christian ethic. What both groups have in common is their total opposition to the Nazi regime.'

'Continue,' Dulles urged.

'Perhaps we could help you establish contact with them.'

'That could be done here in Switzerland?'

'Actually here in Basel. Assuming we could get the cooperation of two intermediaries.'

'And who might they be?'

'The theologian, Karl Barth. And my boss, Per Jacobsson. I strongly suspect that some of his banking contacts in Berlin, a city he visits regularly — in fact he intends to do so again within a few days — are not unfamiliar with some of the members of the Wednesday group.'

'Knowing Jacobsson's political leanings, this is not surprising. But why Karl Barth?'

'Because he is a vehement enemy of the Nazis, and fosters close ties with fellow clergy of the Confessional Church in Germany who share his views. Especially a Lutheran pastor in Berlin by the name of Dietrich Bonhoeffer. Bonhoeffer has allies to his cause among the theologians and pastors in Freiburg im Breisgau — which is not that far from here, as you know. We also understand that Bonhoeffer is in contact with some Swedes on these matters, in particular the Wallenberg banking family. I assume Per Jacobsson will be able to enlighten you further when you meet him.'

'And how should I go about contacting Barth if the need arises?'

'May I suggest that you activate the Reichman—Burckhardt Line?'

Dulles laughed. I like that. Now one more thing — and then I intend to go to bed. You alluded to the possibility of opposition to Hitler among the ranks of German scientists. We are especially interested in them.'

'Chemists most probably,' Burckhardt said. 'Although I must tell you that we Swiss regard it as unlikely that the Germans will revert to gas warfare.'

'I tend to agree. Yet any contacts with chemists would be highly welcome. And with physicists. Yes, especially physicists.' Dulles then looked at his watch. 'But now I must go to bed.'

Dulles rose from his armchair and the three younger people immediately did the same.

'I will show you to your room, sir,' Burckhardt said.

Dulles shook hands first with Nancy Reichman and then with Max Waibel, adding the following words after he had done so: 'Be careful of that fellow Schellenberg, Max. He's liable to get you — all of you — into trouble. Which would be too bad if it happened now when things are about to get interesting. We Americans need your help. And I think you can use ours. One final suggestion: keep your eyes open for trouble from the Russians. Switzerland is not exactly their favourite country.'

As soon as Dulles and Burckhardt had left the room, Waibel and Nancy once again sat down in two of the armchairs facing the fireplace.

'I like him,' Waibel said. 'Although sometimes it's hard to figure out what he's talking about. Why the interest in physicists, for example? And what was that last remark about us and the Russians supposed to mean?'

'Got me,' Nancy answered. And she meant it.

Peter Burckhardt returned minutes later. The three of them had a last drink — ice-cold champagne — and then they also decided that it was time to head for bed. After Peter had quietly kissed Nancy Reichman good-night at the door to her bedroom, he whispered: 'I hope you won't be cold. I made sure that you have the thickest featherbed in the house. But still . . .'

'If I'm too cold I'll just call you,' she answered.

'Fat chance,' he responded. 'With both of our bosses sleeping down the hall. But maybe some other time. Soon. After all, we are now officially the Reichman—Burckhardt team.'

'Maybe,' she said, kissing him again, and then closing the door.

109

Chapter 12

The following morning, Friday, 26 February, breakfast was served in everybody's room at seven o'clock, and at eight sharp the exodus from the Benkener Schloss began. First to leave was Captain Waibel, who drove himself back to Swiss Intelligence's Bureau D office on the Petersplatz in Basel in a Swiss army car; then Peter Burckhardt, who drove the two Americans back to Basel in his Mercedes, dropping Allen Dulles at the central train station where he caught the 9 am train back to Bern, taking Nancy Reichman to her apartment at Augustinergasse 11, and finally heading for his office at the Bank for International Settlements. An hour later all the servants left, walking down the lane from the castle to the village of Benken, and then taking the bus – which stopped just across the road from the restaurant 'Zum Ochsen' – back to Basel, changing onto a tram which took them out to suburban Riehen and their quarters on the Burckhardt estate there.

Peter Burckhardt had barely sat down behind his desk that morning when the phone rang. It was Colonel Masson. And contrary to Burckhardt's expectations, he seemed to be in the best of moods. 'I hadn't really expected to find you back in the office already, Peter. You must have gone to bed earlier than I thought you would. How did the evening end up, by the way?'

'Very well. Mr Dulles seemed satisfied at how everything had gone and went to bed no more than ten minutes after you left. I dropped him off at the station about half an hour ago. The only

110

business discussed this morning was his repeating the request that I set up a meeting for him with Per Jacobsson next Tuesday or Wednesday . . . after Jacobsson gets back from Stockholm.'

'You'll be talking to Jacobsson first, I assume. To see if he's heard anything further about the situation in Finland.'

'Yes, sir. He's expected back on Monday afternoon. I'll talk to him as soon as I can.'

'And you'll report to me immediately thereafter, even if it's late.'

'Yes, sir.'

'Good. Now Peter, the arrangements you made for our meeting with Mr Dulles yesterday were absolutely perfect. The venue ensured total privacy and the ambiance could not have been better. I want to do it again. Next Tuesday.'

'Same drill?'

'Yes. You can count on the visitors to arrive in Benken around six o'clock in the evening. We expect two of them and there will undoubtedly be a second car with security personnel. Two of my staff will meet them at the border. I'll be coming alone with my driver in a separate vehicle. All will be staying overnight at the Schloss, if that is convenient.'

'No problem, sir. What about the drivers?'

'They can take care of themselves.'

'Do you want me present, sir?'

'Of course. Although I think our guests will feel more comfortable if you were to retire before any serious discussions began.'

'Yes, sir.'

'Good. Then I'll hear from you after you've spoken to Jacobsson on Monday?'

'Yes, sir.'

'Then have a good weekend.'

'Thank you, sir.'

Burckhardt did not have to ask who it was. The fact that no mention had been made of Waibel being present clinched it. It had to be Schellenberg. And the second man? It could go either way: either Schellenberg's boss or one of his obedient servants. Either Heinrich Himmler or that SS Major Eggen, who had obviously been instrumental in setting this thing up with Masson's man subsequent to their meeting at the bar of the Three Kings last Sunday night. Masson must have known already for days that they were coming. Which explains, Burckhardt thought, Masson's highly sceptical attitude toward Dulles last night. Whatever Dulles said had to come, by definition, from secondary sources. Masson, however, was dealing with primary sources. *Men who sat at the right hand of the Führer*, for God's sake. Men who not only knew Hitler's intentions, maybe even his concrete plans regarding Switzerland, *first* hand, but were also in a position to influence Hitler on the execution of such plans. Or non-execution.

'It's worth the gamble,' Burckhardt thought, despite the words of warning that Dulles had expressed the evening before.

Then he called his father, to let him know that the Benkener Schloss would be needed again, since 'some visitors from the north' would be arriving the following Tuesday.

His father understood immediately.

'I want *everything* to be perfect,' the banker said. 'To show those scum how things are run in a civilized country. I'll be sending our people out in advance on Sunday. To make sure.'

'But they're just coming back to Basel this morning on the bus.'

'Too bad. They'll have to get right back on the bus. In fact, I will go out to Benken myself on Sunday. Just to make sure that everybody gets the message. You've got to realize, Peter, that the Nazis, all of them, are very primitive people. Thugs. Had their boss not grabbed power through intimidation, the likelihood of their ever being invited to the Benkener Schloss, or any other Schloss, would have remained zero. Absolute zero. So this is our chance to intimidate *them*.'

'If you say so, Father.' Peter sounded less than convinced.

'I definitely say so.'

Two days later, on that Sunday, 28 February, Igor Scitovsky, alias Werner Lentz, picked up Liselotte Maurer in front of the restaurant 'Zum Ochsen' in Benken at precisely one o'clock. She was dressed in her Sunday best, bubbling with enthusiasm, and talkative. She had barely taken her place beside Lentz in the front seat of his van when she began.

'Oh, what a morning it's been so far!'

'What happened?' Lentz asked, as he turned the van around in front of the restaurant and started to head back toward Basel.

'First, we were late for church because two of the cows got out and onto the highway and all of us — Mutti, Vati, my sisters and I — and mind you, all dressed like this! — had to round them up and bring them back to the barn. Then at church, the Pfarrer started to sneeze right in the middle of his sermon and my dumb youngest sister started to giggle, and so did I. And everybody looked at us. We could have died! Mutti could have killed us. Then after church, we walked home as usual and as we passed in front of the restaurant the landlord saw me and asked if I could help out, just for a little while. Because the restaurant is always busy on Sundays, but then on top of that, totally unexpectedly, the banker Burckhardt, the old one who owns the Schloss, had turned up for lunch — he and his wife — and they had told him that a "separate party" would be arriving later on the bus, and that they wanted us to prepare a really special lunch for them too. And to send the bill up to the Schloss. So I helped out in the kitchen, peeling potatoes, cutting carrots, that sort of thing.' She paused, somewhat out of breath, and then continued: 'Now guess who was in that "separate party"? In fact, they are all in there right now.'

'Who?'

'The Burckhardts' servants! The maids, the valet, the driver, two gardeners! Can you imagine! But when you think of it, isn't that nice of the old Burckhardts? They always say that he is very stuck up — talks to nobody in Benken. Just comes and goes like an English lord. But I'll bet English lords don't treat *their* help to lunch on Sundays.'

'But why are they all here in Benken?'

'Well, I put exactly that same question to Heidi — she's one of their maids who is a cousin of a girl I went to school with here in Benken and she came out here one summer to stay with her and I

113

got to know her — well, Heidi said that it was unbelievable. That they were all just here at the castle a couple of days ago for that big do on Thursday night — you remember, you were also here — for some big-shot Americans, she said, and had all gone back to Basel on Friday, and now here they are again, this time to prepare for some more visitors who are expected on Tuesday.'

'But why did they come here already today?'

'Because the old man Burckhardt said that he wanted every-thing — the castle, the gardens, everything, to be in absolutely tip-top condition. Because he wanted to show the "chaibe Schwobe" who are coming here on Tuesday how things are done in Switzerland. Well, Heidi then said to me: "You can imagine, Liselotte, knowing how all of us hate the Germans, that we are going to *kill* ourselves making sure that everything is perfect. Especially after this lunch that the Herr and Frau Doktor are putting on for us!"'

Now she had the full attention of Lentz/Scitovsky. 'Chaibe Schwobe, huh. German bastards right here in Benken! That is something.'

Liselotte, having unburdened herself of the news of such monumental events, now settled back in the front seat of the Opel van as it sped toward Basel. But she did not remain quiet for long.

'Du Werner, what kind of movie are we going to?'

'That was supposed to be a surprise. But I'll tell you. We're not going to the Kino after all.'

He glanced at her as he said it, and saw a pout starting to develop.

'But . . .' she began.

'We're going to the opera.'

The beginnings of a pout were instantly replaced by a frown.

'Now don't worry. It's an operetta. *Die lustige Witwe.*'

'Oh Werner!' she exclaimed. 'I love that music.' And to show that she meant it, Liselotte began to sing, in her little girl's soprano, the first lines of that operetta's theme . . . the first two lines, since she ran out of the words after that. Which did not prevent her from humming the rest. And while she hummed she slid across the front seat of the van until her thigh met his. And when his right hand descended upon it, and stayed there, she made no effort to remove it. Quite the contrary. As they passed through Biel and then Oberwil, she snuggled ever closer. And by the time they reached the centre of Basel, her hand was on his thigh — a chubby peasant hand that took a firm grip. Which led Werner Lentz to wish that they could just skip the goddamn operetta and get on with it.

Lentz was able to park his van within a half block of the theatre, and he and Liselotte immediately rushed to join the crowd entering the Stadttheater on this last Sunday in February 1943, a crowd which was a typical Sunday afternoon one: lots of mothers with little children, but also many young people in their teens or early twenties. All were dressed neatly, and the mood was somewhat festive as two o'clock approached. For they knew that they were in for a treat. Basel had one of the best provincial opera companies in central Europe, one which could manage Mozart and Puccini, and manage them well. But it was not above Lehar or Strauss, especially where Sunday matinees were concerned. And since the performers knew that their audience was there for fun, and not heeding the call for cultural improvement, they performed with that extra bit of panache which was so appreciated by the otherwise so stolid Swiss Bürger.

As soon as the theatre darkened and the overture began, Liselotte's hand found his, but now Lentz barely took notice. His mind had already begun to move beyond the moment and was beginning to focus on the import of the revelation which had been contained in the flood of words which had poured from the peasant girl just minutes earlier.

It was completely obvious that the upcoming meeting at the Benkener Schloss she had been babbling on about was the direct product of the conversations which his men had observed taking place — first at the bar of the Three Kings, and then in that room in the Schweizerhof Hotel — between Swiss Intelligence and Colonel Eggen of the Waffen SS. But, according to Liselotte, there were *two* Nazis coming this time around. One would be Eggen. And the other would be . . . Eggen's boss.

It had to be Schellenberg!

There was no man alive more feared and more despised by the Rote Kapelle. It was he, as the general in charge of the counter-intelligence operations of the SS, who had personally supervised the hunting down and subsequent summary execution of dozens of Scitovsky's colleagues in Germany, then Belgium, then Holland, then France, a manhunt which had been so relentless and so successful that almost all that was left of the Soviet Union's espionage apparatus in Western Europe was its operations in Switzerland.

No doubt one of the key reasons for Schellenberg's coming visit to Switzerland was to prod the Swiss police — who were as bad as the Nazi Gestapo in Scitovsky's judgement — into eliminating even that remnant. Scitovsky was no fool. He knew that the Swiss were fully aware of the activities of the Rote Kapelle on Swiss soil. He knew that their radio transmissions from Geneva and Lausanne were being increasingly intercepted. He knew that, in the end, his transmissions from Basel would likewise be intercepted and also traced to their exact source. He suspected that, even now, his house on the Rheingasse might be under surveillance, if for no other reason than the fact that his dossier with the Fremdenpolizei contained full documentation of his origins in the Soviet Union — or at least those of Walter Lentz — which, by itself, was grounds for suspicion. He also knew, however, that even if such suspicions were already beginning to deepen, the Swiss authorities, fully aware of the precariousness of their neutrality, would not move precipitately, especially now when the tide of war seemed to be turning. Unless there was a quid pro quo in the offing from Germany which, despite what was happening on the Eastern front, still had a great deal more leverage than the Soviet Union did where the Swiss were concerned. One that only a man of position in the country, a man like Schellenberg, could offer.

Which meant that he had to move now and move decisively. Such an opportunity would never present itself again.

He would kill Schellenberg on Tuesday and then get out. The situation in Benken was perfect for both. An ambush, and then immediate flight over the border into France where he would undoubtedly be able to find refuge with the underground. And then just wait out the end of the war before returning to Moscow as the hero who had assassinated General Walter Schellenberg and dealt a blow to the Nazi leadership on a scale equal to that which had followed the assassination of that other symbol of the SS elite, SS Obergruppenführer and Reichsprotektor of Czechoslovakia Reinhard Heydrich, less than a year ago in Prague. What made it all the more beautiful, the more symmetrical, was the fact that Schellenberg had been Heydrich's protégé! And what a beast Heydrich had been, even by Nazi standards. They called him the 'Butcher of Prague' and he had been proud of it. Following Heydrich's assassination the SS had embarked upon a frenzy of savage massacres which began on 9 June 1942, the day of Heydrich's funeral in Berlin, where Hitler had compared his death to a lost battle and where Himmler had declared: 'It is our holy duty to avenge him.' The first to go were three thousand Jews. On the morning of that 9 June, a special train had left Prague marked 'AaH' (*Attentat auf Heydrich* or Assassination of Heydrich) carrying 1,000 Czech Jews to their deaths in SS extermination factories. It was followed by two more transports from the ghetto at Terezin. Then on that same 9 June of 1942, in the evening, the Waffen SS had carried out the total destruction – the *levelling* – of the Czech village of Lidice and the mass murder of almost all of its totally innocent inhabitants. Then came the arrest and execution of thousands of non-Jewish residents of Prague, many of them tracked down as suspected spies; others simply picked out at random. Scitovsky, like all members of the Rote Kapelle, knew of these events all too well, for at least a dozen of their colleagues in Czechoslovakia had been executed in the process.[12]

The victims of revenge this time would be the Swiss. There were rumours of German plans to invade Switzerland floating around all over the place. The killing of Schellenberg on Swiss

---

12 For a chronicle of all this see Callum MacDonald, *The Killing of Reinhard Heydrich*.

soil – and who was to know by whom? – would most probably end all further indecision on the part of Hitler. The maniac would attack immediately! And from his safe vantage point in France he, Igor Scitovsky, could then watch as the hypocritical, double-dealing Swiss went down in flames! No doubt the German attack on Switzerland would be spearheaded by the Waffen SS, and what it did to one village in Czechoslovakia in the summer of 1942 following the assassination of SS Obergruppenführer Heydrich would be nothing compared to what would happen to a dozen Swiss villages in the winter of 1943 following the murder of SS Brigadeführer Walter Schellenberg. Goodbye Binningen, Bott-mingen, Biel and Benken! Which would delight *both* Adolf Hitler *and* Joseph Stalin!

For it would be the Soviet Union itself which would be the prime beneficiary of all this. A German attack on Switzerland would divert at least a million troops from the Eastern front – just at a time when the very outcome of the Nazis' war against Russia was hanging in the balance. Without reinforcements, the defeat of the German Sixth Army at the gates of Stalingrad could now be followed by into a general route along the entire German Eastern front. Then the Soviets could achieve victory over the Third Reich *without* the help of the capitalist powers who kept promising the establishment of a second front in Europe, but never fulfilling that promise.

In fact, now that he thought of it, the consequences of the assassination of General Walter Schellenberg might go deeper still. Was it not possible, no *likely,* that the two meetings at the Benkener Schloss, organized by Swiss Intelligence, were linked? That their purpose was to open the way for a *third* meeting – between Schellenberg and Dulles? And to what end was perfectly clear: to set up a deal for a separate peace between the Western Allies and the Germans, allowing the Nazis to direct their entire war machine against Mother Russia, which harboured their common enemy, Communism – the enemy not just of the Germans but also of the Americans and the British, and, last but not least, the ultra-capitalistic Swiss. No wonder that the banker Burckhardt was in essence co-sponsoring the whole conspiracy at his Benkener Schloss!

And all this would now come to naught!

Scitovsky-Lentz was so carried away with the enormity of the havoc which he personally was about to wreak that, involuntarily, his grip on Liselotte's hand tightened to the point where she squirmed with pain and, yes, pleasure. And precisely at this moment the curtain came down on the first act, and the theatre lights came on.

'Isch das nit toll gsi,' she exclaimed.

'Wonderful,' he responded. 'I need a cigarette.'

They got up and went to the lobby, where he immediately lit up a Gitane while heading for the bar to order a Warteck beer for himself and a tea for Liselotte. She, for once, remained silent, basking in the joy of being in the midst of the matinee theatre crowd in the big city. He, ever wary, scanned the same crowd. And his head suddenly stopped moving. There, way across the lobby, also smoking a cigarette: wasn't that one of Lützelschwab's men? Why would a man from the *political* police force be in the Stadttheater for a Sunday matinee instead of at the football stadium where all the cops got in free and where FC Basel were playing their arch-rival, the Grasshoppers of Zurich, that afternoon? He would have gone there himself – had it not been for . . .

Scitovsky did not even want to finish the sentence mentally in the presence of one of Lützelschwab's men. Nervous now, he took a last drag on his first cigarette and immediately lit another. Even Liselotte noticed.

'Something wrong?' she asked.

'No, no. It's just getting a bit stuffy here. Let's sit down.' He drank the rest of the beer, crushed out his second cigarette in an ashtray, waited impatiently while she finished her tea, and then escorted her back to their seats.

As the crowd settled in after the curtain rose for the second act, Scitovsky's thoughts now started jumping all over the place. If, for whatever reason, they were keeping an eye on him, what should he do next? Could there possibly be any connection between the police presence here and his two trips to Benken? No, he concluded. Not a chance. There had been nobody there the first time – just those locals playing cards and one couple who had not even noticed him. And the first as well as the second time, if anybody had been outside monitoring the recent comings and goings in Benken and made any inquiries about him or his van, Liselotte would have been involved and would have blabbered her head off about it. So forget that angle. Then what other angle could there be? One for sure: all the radio traffic that week from the attic of the house on the Untere Rheingasse. But was that likely? There had been other weeks with traffic almost at the same level. The much more likely explanation for Lützelschwab's man's presence was the surveillance of somebody else. After all, they now had 120 men detailed to that operation in the city of Basel alone! They had to be watching hundreds, no thousands, to justify that force strength. Or, and you never knew, maybe he was just a cop who actually hated football and loved operettas. Although that was probably just wishful thinking.

The only way to be sure was to test it. Leave early – not now, but in the middle of the third act. Before anybody could get lost in the crowd. And see if it was he who was under surveillance. Simple. In fact, he could test it twice. First by taking Liselotte to his place, and then, afterwards, by taking her back to Benken. He couldn't fail to spot them if, indeed, he was being watched. After all, he was a professional and they were a bunch of dumb Swiss local cops.

In the middle of the third act, just as the merry widow was about to latch on to the man of her dreams, Scitovsky leaned over to tell Liselotte that he needed some fresh air, and thought it best that they leave. Since they had aisle seats they were able to get out without creating any undue commotion, much to her relief. After the episode in church that morning, the last thing she wanted was to call further attention to herself – especially in Basel.

Within minutes they had collected their coats from the cloakroom and were out on the Theaterstrasse. It was now four in the afternoon, and although the sun still shone, it was already getting very cold. As they hurried toward Scitovsky's van, Liselotte looked at him anxiously. 'Are you feeling better, Werner?'

'A little bit. But I think that the sooner I get something to drink, something strong, the better.'

'A Kirschwasser,' she suggested. 'Mutti always has one when she feels a bit faint. Let's find a restaurant.'

'I've got a better idea,' he said. 'Let's go to my place. It's not far, and it will be a lot more comfortable than a restaurant.'

Liselotte agreed immediately. And when they reached the van, as he opened the right door for her he checked, then re-checked, the Theaterstrasse in both directions. No one, he knew, had followed them out of the theatre. And there were only two pedestrians on the street: a young couple walking arm in arm in their direction. As they passed Scitovsky judged their age at no more than eighteen years. No problem there.

As soon as he entered the van, he checked the rear-view mirror, and as he pulled out into the Theaterstrasse he kept his eyes glued to it. Nothing. He turned right on the Steinenberg, still nothing; a block later, he turned left into the Freie Strasse. Since this was the main street of downtown Basel, Scitovsky immediately found himself in traffic. Three blocks later they passed through the Marktplatz, and he did not like the looks of a black Citroën which had been parked there, and then abruptly pulled out behind him.

'Du, Werner,' Liselotte began at just this moment, pointing out the window on her side, 'look at that display in the window of Globus department store. Isn't it . . .'

'Shut up, I'm trying to drive,' he said, regretting it immediately. The last thing he wanted to do was alienate her.

A minute later they were on the Mittlere Rheinbrücke, the twelfth-century bridge which took them across to Kleinbasel. The black Citroën was still behind them. Then came the critical moment. At the first intersection on the other side of the bridge, Scitovsky turned right onto the Rheingasse, and then immediately pulled over to the kerb, stopped, and turned off the engine.

Nothing. No black Citroën. No traffic whatsoever. A minute passed. Two minutes.

'May I finally say something now?'

Scitovsky was so relieved that he laughed out loud before

121

leaning across the seat to give Liselotte a big hug. 'My dear,' he said, 'you can say anything you want.'

'*Finally!* What I want to say first is that I'm starting to freeze! Why in the world are we just sitting here?'

'Because this is where we get out. My house is just fifty metres up the street.'

'Then why stop here?'

'Because . . . I like to park under the streetlamp here. Now let's go and get that Kirschwasser.'

As they walked up the Rheingasse, now arm in arm, Scitovsky was still on full alert for anything unusual: a parked car that was normally not seen on that street; a curtain that twitched; a vehicle that might enter the street from the other end and stop there. Still nothing. So it had been a false alarm. At least it appeared so thus far.

When they got to the front door of Rheingasse 37, Liselotte watched in amazement as Scitovsky produced a rather large key-chain from his pocket and then proceeded to select three different keys and insert them in three different locks before the door could finally be opened. At home in Benken they had only one lock on the front door, and they never used it. But for a change she kept her silence.

She had another moment of uneasiness when she found herself inside the door: the room they entered was absolutely pitch-black in spite of the fact that outside darkness had only begun to fall. When Scitovsky finally turned on a lamp she could see why: all of the windows in the living-room were hidden behind thick, impenetrable drapes. The third moment of surprise came when a man suddenly appeared on the staircase which led from the living-room to the second floor, a man dressed in black and carrying binoculars. The man appeared as startled as she was.

'I'm sorry,' he blurted out to an obviously annoyed Scitovsky. 'I had no idea that you intended to bring her back here.'

'I must have a word with you. Now!' was Scitovsky's response. Turning to Liselotte, he said: 'My dear, allow me to take your coat.'

She surrendered it. Reluctantly. He then took off his coat and proceeded to hang both in the closet.

'Now just make yourself at home. I'll be back in a few minutes.'

With that, Scitovsky mounted the staircase and then, along with the strange man, disappeared into the darkness of the second floor.

Chapter 13

Minutes after Scitovsky had disappeared up the stairs behind his radio man, there was suddenly action in the back of another van which was parked just 200 metres east of the house on the Rheingasse, in the secluded courtyard of Basel's Waisenhaus — the city orphanage. There, sitting hunched in the middle of an array of radio equipment and wearing earphones, was Dieter Wenger, the sergeant in the Basel political police in charge of its short-wave radio monitoring activities.

'They're at it again,' he whispered to another policeman, a corporal, who was sitting beside him, monitoring another frequency. Wenger then took both hands and pressed his earphones as tightly as possible to his head.

Just as he did so, somebody opened the back door of the van. Without even looking to see who it was, the police sergeant waved his hand violently in the direction of the intruder, indicating that no interference would be tolerated. That done, he took up pen and pad, ready to take notes.

Then, just seconds later, he tossed the pad aside, and took off the earphones while the intruder watched in dismay.

'What's wrong?' he asked.

Now the sergeant saw who was standing behind the van. 'Entschuldigen Sie, Herr Doktor,' he stammered, 'I didn't know it was you.'

Lützelschwab ignored the apology and simply repeated his question: 'What went wrong?'

'Nothing, sir. They're at it again, just like we anticipated. But it's so damned frustrating. They keep transmitting, and we keep intercepting and recording. But we don't know what they're saying.'

'When did this transmission start?'

'Just when you opened the door, sir. One short burst and *finis*.'

'What does that mean?'

'Only one thing. They're alerting Moscow that they will be transmitting at length later tonight.'

'On the same frequency?'

'I hope so, at least initially. As you know, Herr Doktor, during the past month — since our pylon crew traced their transmissions to the source on the Rheingasse — we've narrowed it down to six frequencies from which they switch back and forth at two-minute intervals. We cover them all, six per van. The one they just used is 8,750 Kilohertz and I lucked out because that was the one I was monitoring today. My guess, knowing the past pattern, is that they will switch back and forth between that frequency and 10,365 Kilohertz later tonight.'

'What time tonight?'

'Again, if they follow the same pattern they will start transmitting at exactly 23.20.'

The chief radio man then asked: 'Herr Doktor, are we having any luck deciphering any of their signals?'

'No. But as you know, we are fully aware of who's sending them: the local cell of the Rote Kapelle. And we think that certain actions, planned tentatively for this evening — not here in Basel, I might add — if they come off as planned, may allow us to decipher what's in these signals. Maybe as early as tomorrow night. That is why, Dieter, it is so extremely important that you and your men in the other two vans take exact notes of each transmission.'

The other two vans, with the familiar markings and colours which designated them as being part of the large fleet of PT&T vehicles, were positioned in a pattern designed to triangulate the source: the second being parked on the other side of the Rhine next to the cathedral and thus overlooking the river and its

125

opposite bank; the third on the Claraplatz in Kleinbasel. The house at Rheingasse 37 was in the exact middle of the triangle. So they had both sides of the Rhine 'covered'. If the source moved, so would they, with the objective of re-triangulating the radio transmissions at their new source.

'What's the drill going to be for this evening, Herr Doktor?'

'I want your men to take time out for dinner and some rest. But I want you all back at your posts no later than 23 hours this evening. After that I want you constantly monitoring all six of the frequencies known to be currently in use by the Rote Kapelle until 23.20.'

'And if nothing starts to happen then?'

'Your men are going to have to scramble like mad, sweeping to ten thousand Kilohertz bands as quickly as they can, hoping they can pick them up on whatever new frequencies the people at Rheingasse 37 may have switched to. I want you, however, to stay with 8,750 Kilohertz, just in case for some reason the start of transmission was just delayed beyond the usual time. With our limited resources, we cannot cover all the contingencies, Sergeant, as you full well know. We have to hope that tonight they stick to their usual pattern of behaviour.'

'Maybe this is out of line, Herr Doktor, but some of my men have been wondering why we don't simply go in and shut them down.'

'If we could be sure that we could make a clean sweep we would go in and get them right now. But we don't know exactly how many are involved . . . others perhaps at another location which we are not aware of. After all, we've only been onto them for less than a month. And we believe that they are up to something — something that goes way beyond the simple gathering of military intelligence here and in Germany and passing it on to Moscow. We won't be able to stop them unless we know what action they are planning — through our intercepts of their transmissions. And their radio traffic will tell us all we need to know, since in their organization nobody does anything without first getting clearance from Moscow Centre.'

He paused before continuing. 'But I will tell you this: I already have a very, very good idea of what's going on. But before I can take countermeasures, I need confirmation. And that, Sergeant, is why you and your colleague are going to be spending the next few nights camped out in this van.'

Dr Lützelschwab looked at his watch. 'Now I've got another errand to run, Sergeant. I may be checking back with you before midnight.' With that he climbed out the back of the PT&T van and was soon sitting in the front seat of a black Citroën parked just ten metres away.

'Now we're going to move out of the courtyard,' he said to the driver, another police sergeant in plain clothes, 'and then I want you to park at *this* end of the Rheingasse. I have the definite feeling that it's all starting to come together.'

It had been in late December of 1942 that, as a result of their constant random sweeps of the shortwave bands, Sergeant Wenger's unit had first detected the presence of a powerful illegal shortwave transmitter in the region of Basel. On 24 January 1943, his mobile short-range monitoring devices had pinpointed its exact location. They had subsequently deduced that it was a unit of the Rote Kapelle from the call signals being employed. Since then, Lützelschwab's men had been monitoring every movement to and from the house on Rheingasse 37 from an observation point in the attic of a house across the street. Where the owner of Rheingasse 37, Walter Lentz, was concerned, the surveillance went beyond this, for the police file kept on him had immediately revealed his family history: their emigration to Russia, and his subsequent return, facts which automatically elevated him to the status of prime suspect. But due to lack of manpower, it could hardly be maintained on a twenty-four-hour basis. Needless to say, however, every member of the Basel political police force was now thoroughly familiar with Lentz's particulars: his home, his store, his van, his face. Hence the phone call from the lobby of the Stadttheater less than an hour before by one of Lützelschwab's men — who was there on a totally unrelated matter — to police headquarters in the Spiegelhof, reporting, out of sheer boredom, that he had just seen 'der rote Lentz' in a most improbable place in most improbable company. Lützelschwab, who checked into headquarters around four o'clock every day of the week, including weekends, had been routinely informed about the contents of the phone call and had decided – on pure instinct – to immediately put Lentz under intensive surveillance under his personal supervision. One of the unit's black Citroëns – with Lützelschwab sitting beside the driver – had picked up on Lentz twenty minutes later while he was driving through the Marktplatz, just minutes away from police headquarters, en route from the theatre to the Rheingasse, and after Lentz had turned into the Rheingasse on the other side of the bridge had then circled the block, pulling into the courtyard of the orphanage just minutes before the radio transmission had started.

As soon as the Citroën had started moving again, following his orders, Lützelschwab suddenly changed his mind.

'Stop,' he said to the driver. 'There can be no doubt whatsoever any more that Lentz is a professional. And that he might very well have picked up on us. Go back to the Spiegelhof.' Lützelschwab activated the police car's shortwave radio and arranged for a replacement surveillance unit in a different car – anything but a black Citroën – to be in place in no more than fifteen minutes.

Back at police headquarters, Lützelschwab had barely taken off his overcoat before he was on the phone to his counterpart in the canton of Geneva.

He came right to the point. 'This is Lützelschwab in Basel. Is that raid you told me about last week still on for tonight?'

The answer was affirmative.

'Would you mind if I send one of our men over to Geneva right away tomorrow morning? If you're lucky you're going to get everything we need: radio frequencies, call-signs, and, most important for us, the Rote Kapelle's codebook.'

Again the answer was affirmative.

'His name is Rudolph Sarasin. He's our resident cryptanalyst. I assume he will be working with your Marc Payot. You can expect him to show up at your place before noon. Et merci bien.'

Lützelschwab hung up with a satisfied look on his face. Then he referred to the telephone directory on his desk, and dialled again. Frau Dr Sarasin, Rudolph's mother, answered the phone. She was reluctant to summon her son — after all, it was a Sunday! — since she had still not grown used to the fact that her boy was subject to calls of duty regardless of the time of day. For her son Rudolph was really an academic turned policeman. That strange metamorphosis could be traced directly back to the intervention of Dr Lützelschwab, which had occurred a year and a half earlier. At the time, Rudolph had been in his eighth semester at the university in Basel, studying mathematics and philology, two disciplines which lent themselves to the science of cryptology, which he had taken up as a hobby. Lützelschwab, who knew his father, a prominent lawyer in the city and a member of the 'Teig', had got wind of this and one evening, at a dinner in the Sarasin home arranged by Rudolph's father, had argued that he could better serve his country by applying his hobby full-time for the duration of the war than he could studying and serving part-time as a foot soldier in the Swiss army. Rudolph, who hated his periodic stints in the military with a passion, needed no further convincing when it was indicated that he would be excused from any further duties of that sort. His father had been the one who insisted that, at the very least, he should be given the rank of sergeant in Basel's political police, and this in turn had convinced his mother that, as an exception, she could acquiesce, even though being a policeman represented a station in life to which Sarasins could hardly be expected to lower themselves, even in wartime. Given all that, she now had no choice but to again acquiesce and call Rudolph to the phone, allowing Lützelschwab the opportunity to give her dear boy his marching orders.

That accomplished, Lützelschwab, a pedantic man — as were most of Basel's Lützelschwabs, who inevitably, it seemed, ended up as postmen, firemen, clerks, or, in this case, with the police — decided to memorialize where he was, and where this might all be leading to. He wrote:

1   *SS Major. Eggen meets Masson's man at bar of Three Kings Hotel observed by me, Burckhardt, the American vice-consul, and — the bartender, who is a frequent caller at Rheingasse 37!*

He reread what he had just written, and then nodded approvingly.

2   *Eggen and Masson's man go to Euler Hotel, observed by us, and the room clerk — who is a frequent caller at Rheingasse 37!*

Lützelschwab paused.

3   *Question: Why this meeting?*
    Answer: To set up a further meeting between Swiss and Nazi Intelligence, but at a much higher level. Purpose? To establish framework for future collaboration with SS Intelligence.

Lützelschwab shook his head in disgust.

4   *Who? Where? When?*

Then he wrote his answers:

5   *Schellenberg + Himmler?? Masson + Waibel?? + Burckhardt??*
    In Switzerland/In or near Basel???
    Very soon.

And added:

6   *Who knows about this?*
    Answer: Swiss Intelligence: Masson/Waibel??/Burckhardt??
    SS: Eggen, Schellenberg/Himmler???
    Rote Kapelle: Lentz + at least 2 — But how much?
    Americans??: Vice-consul/Dulles?? — How much?
    Basel Political Police: Lützelschwab.

Finally:

7   *Is Rote Kapelle planning action against Eggen/Schellenberg/Himmler???*
    Answer in radio intercepts. Makes it imperative *we can*

decipher immediately (Geneva). If confirmed, two options: a.
Intervene. b. Not intervene.

8   *But first must know: where? and when?*

Lützelschwab admired his finished work once more. Then he
fished a small box of wooden matches out of his jacket pocket,
withdrew one match, lit the piece of paper containing his notes,
put it in his ashtray, and then watched it burn. It left very little
ash.

He picked up his phone once again, and dialled the internal
number that connected him with the corporal who had the
all-night watch.

'This is Lützelschwab. I put surveillance on Lentz . . . the Rote
Kapelle Lentz. I'm going home now. If they report in with
anything unusual, I want you to call me there. Immediately. No
matter what the hour.'

The object of the now intense interest of Basel's political police
had remained upstairs in his house on Rheingasse 37 for an entire
twenty minutes before finally rejoining Liselotte Maurer in the
dark living-room below. By that time she was mad as hell, but
also increasingly fearful. Had this happened to her in Benken,
she would have simply walked out of the door and gone home.
But this was Basel. And she was with a stranger. Worse still, she
was alone in the house of a stranger. And nobody knew where
she was or whom she was with – not Vati, nor Mutti, nor even
the innkeeper of 'Zum Ochsen'.

By the time Werner Lentz finally appeared and offered her the
long-ago promised cognac, she had worked herself into such a
state that she simply burst out in tears and demanded: 'Ich will
jetzt Heim! Und sofort!'

She punctuated her demand to be taken home – and right
away! – by going to the closet, getting out her coat, and putting it
on, sniffling all the time. Lentz/Scitovsky was not about to argue
with her. The last thing he needed now was a hysterical girl
throwing a spanner into the works – works which had just been
set irrevocably in motion. Moscow Central had been alerted to

the fact that a priority one transmission would be coming their way at 23.20 that evening. In fact, he had already dictated the contents of that message to his radio man upstairs, who was now in the process of coding it. That's what had kept him upstairs so long.

'Liselotte,' he said. 'I must explain. You know I didn't feel well. So I had to spend some time . . . in the bathroom. You know how it is.' He actually managed to look embarrassed.

She stopped sniffling. But the set of her peasant chin made it quite obvious that she was not going to change her mind about leaving. And Lentz/Scitovsky, who now had much more important matters on his mind, was actually relieved at the prospect of getting rid of her. She probably would not have known what to do had he got her into bed anyway. If she was hysterical now, God only knows how she would have reacted once he had gone to work on her upstairs. And now that it was just a matter of days before he left dreary Switzerland for France . . . where there were plenty of girls ready, willing and especially able to perform . . . who needed the doubtful pleasure of a Liselotte?

So Lentz/Scitovsky got his coat out of the closet, took Liselotte Maurer firmly by the arm, escorted her out of the door, and after locking all three locks, walked her down the street to his van . . . watched all the way by Lützelschwab's man in the attic of the house across the street from Rheingasse 37. And while he watched, he picked up the phone that was positioned right in front of the window, and dialled the number that connected him with the headquarters of Basel's political police.

'This is Roth,' he said. 'The Rote Kapelle Lentz is about to move out in his van. He's got a girl with him. Better let the boys up the street know right away.'

Seconds later the shortwave radio in a grey Peugeot which had only just arrived and was parked a block away, where the Rheingasse curved into the Lindenberg, crackled out the message to the two plain-clothes policemen inside. A half-minute after that, the Opel van passed them going in the opposite direction, and already moving fairly fast. The driver of the Peugeot managed to execute a fast U-turn, but by that time the van was out of sight. This part of Basel was a warren of narrow streets of medieval origin, and the police knew that they could lose Lentz there very easily . . . if they had not already done so.

'Let's take a chance on the Wettsteinbrücke,' the second policeman suggested to the driver of the Peugeot. The bridge he referred to was a modern concrete and steel structure.

And sure enough, as soon as they turned right onto the Wettsteinstrasse which led to that bridge, they could see Lentz's van 100 metres to the south, already halfway over the Rhine which lay fifty metres below. From there it was easy. The van kept moving south, through Dufourstrasse to the Äschenplatz, then to the Bahnhof via the Elizabethengraben where it took a right, and then, after three blocks, moved left onto the Binningerstrasse and began to pick up speed. It was now getting dark. Ten minutes later, the police in the Peugeot, which had kept well behind the van to this point, knew that within a few minutes they would have to turn on their headlights; they also knew that as they proceeded into the suburbs of Basel, traffic would soon thin to the point of non-existence. So they radioed in, explaining the situation and their location — in Bottmingen and heading at a fairly high speed toward Oberwil — and asking for instructions. The desk man at police headquarters put them on hold while he telephoned Lützelschwab at home.

'Dr Lützelschwab says you are to break off the surveillance immediately,' came the surprising directive. Then the desk man rapidly looked up seven phone numbers and phoned them in to his boss.

Twenty minutes later, when the Opel van pulled up in front of the restaurant 'Zum Ochsen' in Benken, it was carefully watched by a man on a bicycle. The man was Benken's one and only policeman. Fifteen minutes earlier while he was in the middle of dinner — composed of Bratwurst and Rösti — he had received a totally unprecedented call from the head of Basel's political police, who wanted him out on the street immediately to watch for an Opel van with the licence number BS 49672. If he spotted it, he should call back. Lützelschwab had then given him his private number and abruptly hung up. The call had lasted all of twenty seconds. Biel's policeman had received a similar call, as had his counterparts in the villages of Bättwil, Therwil, Ettingen and Witterswil. All had been home eating, since this was Sunday evening in rural Switzerland. And all bets were now covered: the direction Lentz was taking was leading him into what was essentially a cul de sac, since immediately beyond these villages lay the French frontier . . . and it was completely sealed off. So Lentz had to be headed for one of the seven villages. And as soon as he had made his last phone call, there was a growing conviction in Lützelschwab's mind about which one it would be — which one it *had* to be: Benken, or more specifically, the Schloss in Benken which was owned by Peter Burckhardt's family. Which meant that his earlier suspicions concerning Peter Burckhardt — after he had spotted him that night in the Three Kings Hotel — had been fully justified. He was in this thing with Masson, and right up to his ears!

But how in the world had the Rote Kapelle found out about that location?

Maybe the girl could be of help. If they could identify who she was. And then she might even be able to help them with the answer to the last remaining open question: When?

To be sure, the obvious way to clear all this up was to simply confront Peter Burckhardt and his boss. But then Colonel Masson, alerted to the fact that he could no longer play his little games with the Nazis in secrecy, would probably just call everything off and reschedule the meeting, or meetings, for another time, and, no doubt, another place far removed from Basel and thus from Lützelschwab's jurisdiction . . . into the territory of a police chief who was ready to look the other way while the chief of Swiss Intelligence, and his obedient servant Peter Burckhardt, were consorting with the Fascist enemy!

No, no. That route was now out of the question. More than a few people had to be taught a lesson. And he, Lützelschwab, fully intended to play the role of teacher. And, if necessary, executor.

The devious mind of a secret policeman was now fully engaged.

Then his phone suddenly rang. It was a return call from the village policeman in Benken. The van had stopped in front of the restaurant 'Zum Ochsen'. Then it had turned around and begun heading back towards Basel. A man in his mid-forties was driving. A girl? Ja, ja. A girl had got out of the van and gone directly into the restaurant. Did he know her name? Of course. It was Liselotte. Liselotte Maurer. A local girl who served in the restaurant. A nice girl. Always thought of as being perfectly harmless. Everybody liked her. Hardly the type to get mixed up with something that had drawn the attention of the political police. When he told her father about this, there was going to be hell to pay, that was for sure.

That was when Lützelschwab got adamant. No mention of this to Liselotte's father, or anybody else. Not one word. Understood? Otherwise . . .

Then Lützelschwab changed his tone somewhat, thanking the rural gendarme for his help and telling him that he would be calling on him soon for further assistance. Maybe as early as next day.

After he hung up, Lützelschwab decided to call it an evening . . . at least until he heard from his man who was spending the night in the courtyard of the orphanage with earphones clamped to his head.

At exactly 23.30 his phone rang again. It was Sergeant Wenger. He had just intercepted a lengthy transmission emanating from Rheingasse 37.

'Good, very, very good,' was his boss's response. 'Now you can all call it a night. But on the way back I want you to drop off your notes of the intercept with Sergeant Sarasin. He's going to Geneva first thing tomorrow morning, and I want him to take them along. He lives with his parents on the Bruderholz . . . Bruderholzallee 26. And Dieter, thank your men for a job very well done.'

One half hour later the Geneva political police made two midnight raids: one on a villa — a secluded private villa — located at 192 Route de Florissant, owned and occupied by a Swiss couple by the name of Olga and Edmond Hamel; the other on an apartment located at No. 8 rue Henri Mussard, rented by a woman, also Swiss, Margrit Bolli, who operated under the codename Rosa. In charge of these raids was Inspector Charles Knecht of the canton of Geneva's political police. Earlier that evening Wilhelm Lützelschwab had spoken to his boss.

The reason for the raids: to close down two of the now four known transmitters being operated by the Rote Kapelle in Switzerland – two in Geneva, one in Lausanne and the fourth in Basel, at Rheingasse 37. Two weeks earlier, using the same methodology as that employed by Lützelschwab's unit in Basel, namely triangulation, the whereabouts of the Geneva-based transmitters of the Rote Kapelle had been narrowed down to these two locations. Two days after that, visits purportedly from the Geneva electricity board had allowed the police to get men inside.

Their objective was to establish the floor plans of the two dwellings, and to identify all possible escape routes. For the intention of the raids was not just to seize and thus close down the transmitters, but also to put everybody on the two premises into immediate and secret custody. Subsequently – at least for a few days – both sites would become traps for anybody who showed up. This method of operation had become standard Gestapo practice throughout Europe, and the Swiss police were nothing if not quick students when it came to entrapment.

Due to the secluded location of the villa, the police had been able to apply full force. Two dozen armed men, half of them aided by police dogs, had surrounded the place at 23.45, and precisely at five minutes before midnight Inspector Knecht had personally entered the villa, flanked by four other policemen. After determining that the ground floor was deserted, they had silently made their way up the stairs to the second floor, and, after moving a few metres down the upstairs corridor, had burst through the first door on the right directly into the master bedroom. And there was Olga Hamel in her nightgown, actually seated at the transmitter. The reason: whereas Lentz/Scitovsky in

Basel always began his transmissions to Moscow at precisely 23.20, Olga Hamel always began hers at 24.00 on the second, as Inspector Knecht's monitoring activities during the past fourteen days had established. The Geneva station was, it seemed, the *primus inter pares* among the Red Orchestra's Swiss establishments. Therefore it controlled the midnight hour.

That hour also meant that Olga's husband was, as usual, lying in the adjacent bed sleeping, while his wife was about to toil for the good of her adopted fatherland – she being a member of the 'Partei der Arbeit', the Swiss Communist Party. But that happy arrangement was now to end permanently, for both were soon in handcuffs, while the search for and seizure of evidence of their treasonous activities went on. That search and that seizure proved to be extraordinarily productive, since everything lay exposed in front of Olga, who was rather exposed herself since her choice of nightgowns was not above reproach, at least as judged by Swiss standards. Among the items seized was a large notebook containing the texts of previous transmissions, and most important of all: a list of call-signs, three code tables and two codebooks.

The raid on Margrit Bolli's apartment was less successful. The visit by the men from the electricity board might have alerted her to what was about to happen. She was not there and the transmitter was gone, although they did find various radios and two codebooks – one of which subsequently proved to be the same as that found at the villa on the Route de Florissant. Fortunately, the Geneva police had been keeping her under surveillance during the prior two weeks and determined that she had a boyfriend, a hairdresser of German nationality by the name of Hans Peters. One hour later they raided his Geneva apartment and caught them both in bed. The transmitter was in the bedroom closet. By three o'clock that morning all four were being held incommunicado in Geneva's Saint-Antoine prison.

This left just two Rote Kapelle transmitters still operating in Switzerland: one in Lausanne, and the other in Basel. Though not for long.

Chapter 14

Fourteen hours later the last express train of the day bound for Bâle, as the city is known in the French-speaking world, left Geneva's train station at exactly 5 pm on Monday, 1 March. Two cryptologists were the sole occupants of a compartment in the first-class section of its second car: Marc Payot, a civilian who acted as a consultant to Geneva's police, and Sergeant Rudolph Sarasin. They had met at noon in Geneva's central police station, where Sarasin had gone directly after arriving on the morning train. It had taken four hours of negotiation and at least five phone calls from Basel to convince the Geneva authorities to release, temporarily release, into the official custody of Sarasin's boss, Dr Lützelschwab, some of the material seized during the midnight raids on the Geneva-based cells of the Rote Kapelle. After further discussions, permission had also been given to Marc Payot to accompany that booty, together with Sarasin, on the next train back to Basel. Upon boarding that train, Sarasin had arranged for the conductor to post a 'Reserved' sign on the outside of the sliding door leading from the corridor into their compartment. Then, after getting two cups of coffee from the dining car, he had drawn the shade on the window of that door, sealing himself and his colleague off from the eyes of other passengers.

First Marc Payot opened the suitcase he had brought with him and began extracting the code sheets, two copies of an obscure thriller published in France decades earlier, and a notebook containing the clear texts of transmissions, and placed them on top of the table which he had folded out from its storage space beneath the outside window of the compartment. Sergeant Sarasin, who sat facing him on the other side of the small table, could not keep his eyes off the 'evidence' as it was placed, piece by piece, in front of him. But protocol forced him to keep his hands away. After all, it was still the sole preserve of the police force of another canton . . . until otherwise indicated.

They were almost halfway to Lausanne, the first stop on the Genève–Bâle route, when Payot gave that indication.

'C'est tout à vous,' he said to Sarasin, smiling mischievously in full appreciation of the bureaucratic behavioural nuances so prevalent in the German-speaking cantons of Switzerland, practices which were already being strictly adhered to despite the fact that the train was still in the canton of Vaud.

Only upon hearing Payot's words did the reserved, rather ascetic-looking sergeant from Basel open the briefcase which lay at his side. Now it was he who extracted a series of documents, transcripts of the signals sent during the preceding thirty days by the Rote Kapelle's Basel transmitter — totally useless transcripts, since all they contained were series of numbers, blocks of numbers, separated by minuscule pauses, which, in the absence of a means to decode them, represented nothing more than an unintelligible babble.

But that was now about to change.

Sarasin took two documents from the top of the small stack, and handed one — a copy — across to his colleague from Geneva, keeping the original for himself. Then he started to talk shop.

'That is a transcript of their most recent transmission to Moscow. I think we can probably agree that they have abandoned the traditional Russian method of cryptology in favour of using books of obscure origins on both ends, and transmitting ciphers indicating sequences of letters or numbers on those pages which, when strung together, would form the messsage in clear text.'

'I agree.'

'Good. Then we probably also agree that the identification of

139

key words, or phrases, and/or luck in matching coded messages with passages in these novels, will determine whether or not we are going to be successful.'

Again Payot agreed.

'Now, we both have copies of the same codebook, found in both places in Geneva. One way or the other, we should be able to find a match which will open this whole thing up. Agreed?'

'Yes.'

'Then let's both of us start with one of the messages which we have found in the clear, and work through the codebook trying to find a match. If we find one, it will confirm that we're using the right codebook. Why don't you work from the front of the codebook while I work from the back? That way we won't duplicate our efforts. If one of us succeeds, then we can start working on the coded messages sent from Basel. All right?'

'Bien sûr,' said Payot when Sarasin had finished, 'et maintenant, au travail.'

At which point Sergeant Sarasin finally reached out and grabbed the top code sheet and one of the codebooks which, barely fifteen hours earlier, had been lying open just inches below the ample breasts of Olga Hamel, which had also been on display, perhaps not openly, but at best thinly veiled by her peach-coloured silk nightgown, as she sat poised in front of her transmitter at the very moment when the privacy of her bedroom was violated by the heavy boots, and later the searching hands, of the Geneva gendarmerie. Marc Payot now also reached out for the copy of the same codebook which had been seized in the Geneva apartment of 'Rosa', which he had brought along, and laid it open beside the document which he had just received from Sergeant Sarasin.

The men now worked in total silence, turning pages here, then there, then back – referring occasionally to copies of earlier Geneva transmissions as first drafted and then coded, as contained in the notebook seized from the villa on the Route de Florissant – and taking notes all the while. After stopping briefly in Lausanne, the train began to move at much higher speeds. As it accelerated, the cars began periodically to lurch, and lurch

rather sharply, as they entered and then left the many curves of
the main line between Lausanne and Bern, curves dictated by the
topography of Switzerland. But neither man took notice. They
were like chess players: totally absorbed by the intellectual
exercise. To be sure, each was partially motivated by the desire to
beat the man on the other side of the table. But the ultimate
objective of the game being played on a train racing through that
war-darkened night in Switzerland was to achieve 'Schachmatt'
where the invisible opponent was concerned: to neutralize the
last operating cell of the Rote Kapelle in central Europe.

The train arrived in Bern at 18.45 and left at 18.49.

At 19.23 it was Sergeant Rudolph Sarasin who suddenly
exclaimed: 'I've got one!'

After hearing Rudolph Sarasin's excited words, Marc Payot
immediately got up and took his place beside him.

'Here,' Sarasin now said, as he pointed to the top of page 185
of the 'codebook' found at both addresses in Geneva, the 1910
edition of *Le Miracle du Professeur Teramond* by Guy de
Lacerf,[13] adding:

'Now watch.'

Payot watched as Sarasin, working from the text of a short
coded transcript of a message which had been found in a pile
beside the transmitter in the villa on the outskirts of Geneva,
began to decode it:[14]

RTO to KWT. 23/2. 2400. 29 wds. No. 363.
Source: Emil
Two new German poison gas substances now in production
in IG Farben plant outside of Lyon.
1. Nitrosulfluoride. Formula HC2F. 2. Kakodylisocyanide.
Formula (CH3)2AsNC.
Rado

---

13 Flicke, *Spionagegruppe Rote Kapelle*, p. 61. The use of this particular book
was in keeping with standard Soviet practice of only using codebooks which
were rare, old, and of obscure origins.

14 Ibid. This is the text of an actual message (slightly edited) sent by the Red
Orchestra, as documented in Flicke's history of that organization.

Payot now began comparing it to the notebook which had also been seized at the villa, the one which contained the clear-text messages which had subsequently been coded prior to transmission. It lay open at one numbered 363 and read:

RTO TO KWT 23/2. 2400 29 wds no 363
Source: Emil
Two new German poison gas substances are now in production in IG Farben factory outside of Lyon.
1. Nitrosulfluoride. Formula HC2F. 2. Kakodylisocyanide. Formula: (CH3)2AsNC.

The only difference was that the original draft of the clear-text message did not contain the sender's signature, and Payot caught that immediately.

'You *have* got it!' Payot yelled as he compared the two. 'The clincher is that we know that it is a Hungarian who operates under the codename "Rado" who is running the whole operation in Geneva.' Then he pounded Sarasin on the back and said: 'Congratulations!'

Sarasin remained cautious. 'Hold on,' he said. 'We don't know if Basel has been using the same codebook. Where *this* is concerned,' and he paused to point at the papers in front of both of them, 'it was only by luck that I noticed from the codebook that the pages up to and including 187 had been used . . . you can tell that in any book. But not beyond. So it did not exactly require any genius to work backwards for a match that began to make sense. I found it only two pages back on 185.'[15]

'But still,' Payot insisted, '*if* Basel has been using the same codebook, it will only be a matter of time, days at most, before we begin to find the right matches which will allow us to start deciphering their messages.'

'Agreed. *If*. But even then, remember, that book has 286 pages and we are going to have to search through each and every one of

---

15 For a full explanation of the code system used by the Russians in World War II, including that used by their agents operating within the framework of the Rote Kapelle, see Heinz Höhne, *Kennwort: Direktor* (Frankfurt am Main, 1970), pp. 87–91.

them to find the passage that fits each and every message that we've been able to intercept in Basel. On the plus side, though, is the fact that, at least at this point, we are interested in deciphering only one message, the one which was sent from Basel at 23.20 last night. You've got a copy of it. Let me give you some clues, especially names and places, which we think could well be key elements of the message sent.'

While Sergeant Sarasin did so, Marc Payot took notes.

When Sarasin had completed his dictation he then said: 'All right. It worked last time and maybe it will work this time. You start at the front of the codebook and I'll start at the back.'

An hour later, as soon as the two cryptologists stepped onto the platform inside the Bahnhof in Basel, they were met by no less an authority than Sergeant Sarasin's boss. Without bothering about any formal greetings, Lützelschwab immediately put a question to Sarasin.

'Did you get the codebook?' And he used the familiar 'du' with Sarasin, due to the family friendship.

'Yes, sir. In here.' He lifted his briefcase.

'And . . . ?'

'And we've already managed to match one of the messages sent by "Rado" from Geneva with a passage in the book.'

Lützelschwab was all smiles now. 'Rudolph,' he said, 'I've always told your parents that you are one smart kid!' What he didn't say was that he had always thought Rudolph to be a little strange also.

'But that doesn't mean that the Basel cell has been using the same codebook,' Sarasin now added.

Lützelschwab's face darkened almost as intensely as it had lit up just seconds earlier.

'But it's *likely,* isn't it?'

His question obviously demanded an affirmative answer, so Rudolph Sarasin gave him one. 'Yes.' Then: 'But we won't know for sure until we either find a match for a Basel message . . . or fail to do so. Don't you agree?' he added, turning for the first time to his colleague from Geneva.

Marc Payot just nodded. He'd already sized up Lützelschwab

and had come to the conclusion that the less said to him the better.

Lützelschwab, who was not long on social graces, decided that since he needed this fellow from Geneva, he might as well recognize his existence. So he extended his hand.

'Lützelschwab,' he said.

'Payot,' came the response.

They shook hands. And that was that. Payot now knew for sure that he was in the German-speaking part of Switzerland.

And, as if to remove any doubt whatsoever on that score, Lützelschwab looked at his watch and said: 'Since time is of the essence, we must now proceed quickly and efficiently. And with the utmost discretion.' As he uttered the final sentence, he glared at Payot, indicating that he considered anyone whose mother tongue was French to be highly suspect where the keeping of state secrets was concerned.

It soon became apparent that the head of Basel's political police also intended to keep what the two cryptologists were working on away from the prying eyes and ears of even his own people. He had arranged for them to stay out of sight in a room in the Pension Erika, located in the low-rent district which began just off the square facing the railway station. After seeing to it that they were properly installed, he let both of them know that he expected them to get right back to work. If they needed something to eat, the Bahnhofbuffet was open all night. And they should not bother him any further unless they had something new and significant to report.

Lützelschwab had parked his car close by, though in a much higher-rent district – just the other side of the opulent Schweizerhof Hotel, which was on the square facing the station. And as he walked by it he could not help but reflect on the fate of its night clerk who was probably just coming on duty . . . the one who was a frequent caller at that house on the Rheingasse.

One thing was sure. If that rather odd Sarasin boy came through, and confirmed his suspicions, the Schweizerhof would soon have to find a replacement.

Chapter 15

The very next day, at exactly 3.26 pm on Tuesday, 2 March 1943, in his room in the Pension Erika, that rather odd boy hit the jackpot. In the second paragraph on page 219 of that 1910 edition of *Le Miracle du Professeur Teramond* he found the match to the message sent by the Basel cell of the Rote Kapelle at 23.20 on Sunday, 28 February, to Moscow Centre. It had proved to be the second last message they had sent. The final transmission had occurred the following night.

Since then: complete radio silence.

This radio silence had almost driven Dr Wilhelm Lützelschwab to distraction. For he knew that one conclusion which could be all too logically drawn from it was an extremely ominous one: that the Basel cell had somehow found out about the Geneva raids, knew that it would only be a matter of time before the jig was up for them too, and had simply shut down their transmitter in an orderly process of preparation for physical flight. Furthermore, knowing that their codebooks were now in Swiss hands, it was possible that they had completely cancelled any further actions on Swiss soil which would have been given away as soon as the Swiss police broke their code and began reading their previous messages to Moscow. That was the worst-case deduction. Second worst was that nobody — neither in Basel, Lausanne, nor Moscow — really knew about the raids, the arrests and the seizures that had taken place in Geneva at the beginning of the week. That they just *suspected* that something might have gone

145

wrong due to the fact that neither Geneva transmitter seemed to be operating, and that, merely as a precaution, both the Lausanne and Basel cells of the Rote Kapelle had decided to lie low for a while. Best interpretation of all: that nobody had a clue about the happenings in Geneva, and that the Basel members of the Red Orchestra were now so involved preparing for a project of major proportions that they were temporarily forgoing the usual gathering and transmission of routine intelligence data.

Needless to say, Lützelschwab preferred the latter interpretation. And although the phone call from Rudolph Sarasin at 16.05 on that first Tuesday in March of 1943 began badly, it confirmed, eventually, that he had opted for the right one.

'Guete Tag, Herr Doktor,' were young Rudolph's first words. 'Do isch Rudolph Sarasin.'

'Rudolph! Where are you? And why, for God's sake, haven't I heard a word from you in two days?' Lützelschwab's nerves were getting the better of him.

'I'm still in the Pension Erika. And you haven't heard from me since you told me not to bother you unless I had something to report.'

'Well, report!'

'I've got it.'

Lützelschwab paused before speaking, as if he dared not ask.

'Are you telling me, Rudolph, that you have been able to . . .'

Rudolph Sarasin actually interrupted him at this point. 'Decipher the last two messages sent from Rheingasse 37? Yes, sir.'

Now slowly *and* softly: 'Are you absolutely, I stress *absolutely*, sure you've got it right?'

'Yes, sir.'

'You've got them written out, on paper?'

'Of course.'

'Then stop talking and bring them over!' Lützelschwab thundered into the telephone.

But then, immediately, he reversed course. 'Rudolph,' he yelled, 'are you still there?'

'Yes, sir.'

'As a major exception to all the rules we follow in this business, I want you to do something.'

'Yes, sir.'

'Read me those messages. Now.'

'I'll have to get them. They're lying on the bed across the room.'

'You get them, Rudolph. I'll be here, waiting.' Lützelschwab's voice was now soft, almost tender.

Thirty seconds later. 'This is Rudolph again.'

'Go ahead, Rudolph. Read.'

'The message sent at 23.20 on 28 February 1943 was deciphered as follows:

SCV to KWT 28/2 23.20 57 wds no. 176.
Attention: Director
Source: Igor
Absolutely reliable information that Swiss Intelligence has arranged meeting with SS in Switzerland outside of Basel on the evening of 2 March, repeat 2/3. SS group to most probably include Schellenberg, perhaps also Himmler. Know exact venue. Recommend we take action to eliminate both and then exit Switzerland for France. Please advise.
Scitovsky

'That's it. Shall I re-read it, sir?'

'No need to do that, Rudolph.' Lützelschwab's voice was very controlled. 'Just read me the text of the second message.'

'Yes, sir. It reads as follows:

SCV to KWT 1/3 23.20 42 wds no. 177.
Attention: Director
Source: Igor
Will proceed on 2/3 as directed. Confirm to Lucy that I will seek to contact her in Belfort on 3/3. Will then report to you results of action. This is our last transmission. Closing down as instructed.
Scitovsky

That explained the radio silence, was Lützelschwab's first

147

thought. The signatures on both messages also confirmed his suspicions about Werner Lentz, the obvious leader of the local cell, being a professional. He was Russian and his name was Scitovsky. He would get back to his colleagues in Geneva to see if, after going through all the records they had seized during their Sunday night raids, they had more on the man. In the meantime Rudolph waited patiently and silently on the other end of the phone in the Pension Erika, awaiting further instructions.

He got them immediately. 'Check out of that hotel right away, and then come over here. Needless to say, I do not want one scrap of paper left behind. By the way, is that Payot fellow still with you?'

'Yes, sir.'

'Has he communicated any of this back to Geneva?'

'Not that I know of, sir.'

'Well tell him not to, or it's going to be his hide. And then bring him along. He's going to spend the rest of the day with us whether he likes it or not.'

After hanging up on his resident cryptologist, Lützelschwab immediately dialled the long-distance number of Section 5 of the General Staff of the High Command of the Swiss army. He identified himself and asked for Colonel Masson, indicating that it concerned a matter of great urgency and extreme importance. After more than a full minute, another voice came on the phone to inform him that Colonel Masson was not available.

'But I insist!' Lützelschwab had then roared into the phone, putting all of his full six feet four inches and 225 pounds behind that roar. For it was paramount that he learn as quickly as possible the exact scheduled time and duration of that meeting between Swiss Intelligence and the SS. And while he was at it he could also reconfirm the venue, although there was not even a shadow of doubt in his mind that they planned to meet at the Benkener Schloss.

'I beg your pardon, sir,' came the reply. 'I have my instructions.' And before Lützelschwab could demand the name and rank of the officer with whom he was speaking . . . whoever it was simply hung up on him.

'Sauhund!' Lützelschwab bellowed. But it was too late. The line was already dead.

'All right,' he then said to the room in general, 'if that's the way Masson wants to play it, that's the way I'll play it. Each according to his own mandate. And each according to his own rules.'

During the next fifteen minutes Lützelschwab just sat there in silence behind the plain wooden desk in his office on the fourth floor of the building known as the Spiegelhof, which served as the headquarters for all units of Basel's police department. Ever the deliberate man, he was thinking through his battle plan before issuing any further commands. His thought process was broken when the phone rang and he was tempted to just not answer it. But he finally did, and regretted doing so the moment the caller identified himself. For it was only the head of the Verkehrs-bureau – the traffic division, which was situated on the ground floor of the same building, and housed the unit which issued drivers' licences and imposed traffic and parking fines. It was also the place where the residents of Basel had to go to register their vehicles and get their licence plates.

'Salut, Hans,' said Lützelschwab, adding immediately: 'I'd appreciate it if you'd keep it short. I'm very busy.'

The caller obviously chose to ignore that admonition, and so did Lützelschwab, for during the next two minutes he just sat there, his ear glued to the phone, not seeking to interrupt even once. Because he was listening to an astounding story.

Apparently about ten minutes before, at 16.40, fifteen minutes after Sarasin had called him from the Pension Erika, three huge automobiles, one a Mercedes and the other two BMWs, all three bearing the standards of both the Third Reich and the Waffen SS, had pulled up on the German side of the border crossing in Lörrach, a crossing which before the outbreak of war had been a very busy one, but was now closed to normal traffic. The only exceptions were border crossings officially sanctioned by both governments, these exceptions almost always involving trucks transporting goods specifically agreed to under the bilateral trade agreements periodically entered into between Bern and Berlin. The guards on both sides were always fully informed well ahead

149

of the time they actually took place, so it was understandable that the unexpected and unprecedented appearance of these three automobiles caused a high degree of, first, consternation, then apprehension, especially when a Waffen SS major emerged from the black Mercedes – its back windows were curtained – and demanded that the barriers be raised: they were expected on the other side, and they were going through!

The officer in charge on the German side of the crossing, also a major, though in the Wehrmacht, immediately appeared on the scene. Politely, but firmly, he demanded to see papers and orders. And just as politely, and just as firmly, the request was denied. Then the SS major walked back to the Mercedes, opened the back door and, with the slightest motion of his hand, indicated that the Wehrmacht officer would be well advised to come over and join whoever was sitting in the back seat. He did so, and after two minutes emerged a much paler man. Seconds later, up swung the barrier.

At this moment, precisely 16.25, or five minutes ahead of the pre-agreed time, a Fiat, painted in that sickly grey-green typical of Swiss army vehicles, pulled up behind the barrier on the Swiss side of the border, and two lieutenants emerged. One barked an order to the man in charge – a lowly corporal in the Swiss infantry – and up swung the barrier on the Basel side of the crossing.

Three engines were then started, and three marvels of German automotive engineering soon left the soil of the German Vaterland and rolled onto that of the Swiss Eidgenossenschaft.

But they did not roll very far. The Swiss intelligence officers who had just arrived and who were to serve as escorts to the German visitors were under strict instructions from Colonel Masson: no car bearing German standards or licence plates would be allowed through. The standards had to be removed and the German plates replaced with Swiss.[16] A huge Mercedes bearing German plates travelling through the streets of Basel in broad daylight would have stood out like one of Rommel's Panzers

---

16 See Braunschweig, *Geheimer Draht nach Berlin*, p. 236.

moving through the desert of North Africa, and the rabidly anti-Nazi journalists of Basel − despite the heavy censorship under which they laboured − would have pounced immediately, jeopardizing the entire process of Nazi−Swiss rapprochement that Swiss Intelligence − at least one faction within Swiss Intelligence − was trying to achieve.[17] The problem was that Masson's men, all stationed in Lucerne, had anticipated two, not three, vehicles, and thus had brought only two sets of licence plates with them, both bearing, in addition to the registration numbers preceded by LU, a lion's head, the emblem of the canton of Lucerne, which the local police department had issued them only after a long bureaucratic hassle.

Where to get the third? Lucerne was two hours away, at a minimum, so that was out. It had to happen fast, very, very fast, so it had to be the police department of the canton where they now stood facing a total impasse, one that would undoubtedly develop into a total fiasco unless a quick solution was found. Thus the phone call to the Verkehrsbureau in the Spiegelhof at 4.30 pm on that first Tuesday in March of 1943, and thus, at 4.40, the phone call from the head of the Verkehrsbureau to the head of Basel's political police.

'Give it to them,' was Lützelschwab's immediate response. 'No. Hold on, Hans. Give me the licence plate and *I'll* give it to them. I'll be right down!'

---

17 For a history of the attitude of the vast majority of the Swiss press − vehemently anti-Nazi and pro-Allies − and the heavy censorship which the Federal government imposed upon them, see Bonjour, vol. V, pp. 161−241.

Chapter 16

On that same Tuesday, 2 March 1943, just as Dr Wilhelm Lützelschwab had started driving at breakneck speed toward the border crossing between Basel and Lörrach with a licence plate bearing the number BS 1147 lying beside him on the front seat of his unmarked police car, a black Citroën, the late afternoon train from Bern was arriving in Basel's main station. When Allen Dulles stepped from the smoking section of the first class car, the American vice-consul stationed in Basel was standing on the platform, waiting for him.

'Is everything still on schedule?' Dulles immediately asked, as he shook her hand.

'Yes. I was not able to get through to Mr Jacobsson, since he's been constantly tied up in meetings ever since he got back from his trip to Sweden. But I did speak again to his secretary, in fact just an hour ago. And she reconfirmed both the time and place. In case you don't recall, we will be meeting him at the Schützenhaus restaurant which is Mr Jacobsson's favourite. It's where he always entertains the central bankers of the world when they come to Basel for their regular meetings – or at least *used* to come to Basel until the war broke out.'

'Fine with me, as long as you know where it is.'

'I do. And it will only take us fifteen or twenty minutes to get there.'

'And what would you suggest we do in the meantime?'

'Check you into your hotel, sir. And then, if you would like, we

152

could perhaps go to my apartment for a coffee. I'd like to tell you about some very peculiar rumours which are making the rounds in intelligence circles here in Basel.'

That caught Dulles' attention. And when, a few minutes later, he checked into the Schweizerhof Hotel, it was his name that caught the attention of the desk clerk as Dulles filled out the registration card and handed over his passport for verification, as the law required. This particular desk clerk did not normally work days, but had, as an exception, arranged to swap his night duties with the day man, explaining that something very important had come up that required his presence after five o'clock that afternoon. No sooner had Dulles disappeared into the elevator, accompanied by the bell hop, than the desk clerk picked up the phone behind the desk. After seven rings, somebody finally picked up on the other end.

'Do isch Rolf,' he then said in a very quiet voice. 'Guess who just checked in? Mr Allen Dulles. In person! And our American girl is with him.' While he spoke he watched as she sat in an armchair across the lobby, mechanically paging through the afternoon newspaper, the *Basler Nachrichten*, waiting for her boss to reappear.

'How does she look close up? Great, even though she now has all her clothes on. Great legs, by the way. We never were able to see that far down, right?'

Whatever the response to that was on the other end, it evoked a rather dirty grin on the desk clerk's face, plus the words: 'Maybe we'll both get our chance tonight, Urs.' Then: 'Look, you'd better tell Lentz about Dulles right away. It might change his plans for this evening.'

He hung up, and minutes later Allen Dulles reappeared in the lobby. Then both he and the American girl walked out of the hotel.

'Something wrong, Nancy?' he asked, the moment they were outside.

As they walked in the direction of where she had parked she rather grudgingly replied: 'Nothing really. It was just that desk clerk. He kept watching me the entire time you were upstairs.'

'Maybe he works for the local police. They've got people everywhere, but especially in hotels. That's how they keep tabs on foreign visitors.'

'By leering at them?' The moment she said it she regretted it. 'Sorry, Mr Dulles, I'm obviously over-reacting.'

'Not to worry, Nancy. These are not the easiest of times for any of us. And being alone here, cut off from the rest of the world, hardly helps.'

After they had walked another fifteen metres, Nancy stopped beside her Fiat Topolino and said: 'Well, here's the limousine!'

Dulles looked at the pathetic little car and laughed. Then after he had squeezed himself into the tiny two-seater, he watched as, after three abortive tries, she finally managed to start the engine, and then, after applying full gas and shifting like mad, got the thing all the way up to 30 kilometres an hour.

'I sense that you do not believe this to be one of the world's great cars,' she said, 'but in its defence I must point out that in the summer you can roll back the canvas roof on this buggy, and, voilà, you've got a convertible. And it's as if you're back in California.' She paused. 'Except for the weather. I don't think I've seen the sun for two months. Does it get to you like it gets to me?'

'In Bern it's even worse.' And then he changed the subject. 'Tell me, how is that young man of yours, Peter Burckhardt?'

She blushed deeply, and hoped he hadn't noticed. That was the first time anybody had referred to Peter Burckhardt as 'her' young man.

'He's fine, thank you. In fact, it was he who filled me in on the latest gossip.'

'Which is?'

'Just what you thought was going to happen: Colonel Masson is meeting with Walter Schellenberg. In Switzerland. Today.'

'Is Burckhardt going to be involved?'

'Only peripherally. They're meeting in Benken . . . where they met you. So he's got to play host again.'

Dulles just nodded.

'Another item: the Swiss police closed in on the Rote Kapelle in Geneva. They seized their transmitters, and are holding three or four of their agents incommunicado. Peter thinks that the fine hand of Colonel Masson was behind this. That he put the pressure on the Geneva police to act now, and that it represents a gesture of good will on his part vis-à-vis Schellenberg. The Germans have been trying to force this action on the Swiss for many months . . . to eliminate the last remnants of the Soviet espionage apparatus still operating in central Europe. And now, just prior to Schellenberg's visit, Masson's given them what they want. And one other thing.' She paused.

'Go ahead,' Dulles said.

'Somebody within Swiss Intelligence has put forth the idea that you were consulted in this matter and acquiesced.'

'Nonsense!' Dulles retorted. 'Why should I do such a thing?'

'For the same reason the Swiss acted. To open the door for negotiations with the Germans. In fact, Peter heard somebody suggest that you were probably going to be present at the meeting tonight.'

'And sure enough, here I am in Basel.' He paused, and then continued. 'Which raises the thought: Are we being suckered into something? And if so, by whom? You remember, I warned both Burckhardt and Waibel about getting mixed up with that gangster Schellenberg. In fact, it was the last thing I said at the close of our evening in Benken last week. Now that son of a bitch – excuse me, Nancy – is going to get all of us into trouble. The Russians will go crazy if they hear about this. At the very least, it would confirm their worst paranoid suspicions where I'm concerned.'

Both Dulles and Nancy Reichman now fell silent until, just a few minutes later, she pulled up in front of her apartment building on the Augustinergasse.

As they both climbed out, Dulles finally broke the silence. 'You know, Nancy, I think I'll skip that offer of coffee. Maybe both of us could use a Scotch. Assuming you have some.'

She did, and soon both were in her third-floor apartment sitting in front of her fireplace, enjoying a good belt of Scotland's finest. Although it had made a big dent in her vice-consul's salary, knowing Allen Dulles' proclivities she had invested in a bottle just the day before. Since she hated the stuff, she took it with a lot of water. He drank his straight.

'How long do you think dinner with Jacobsson will last?' he now asked.

'In Basel such affairs seldom go beyond ten-thirty, maximum eleven.'

'You know, I've been pondering everything I just heard from you in the car. And I must assume you got all of it from Peter Burckhardt . . . which tells me that he continues to be eager to cooperate with us. Since both he and we are going to be hearing a lot of new things this evening over our separate dinner tables — relating, in both cases, to matters of *mutual* interest — maybe it would be a good idea if Peter were to join us for a nightcap. We could compare notes, so to say. I know this would require his coming back from the country, but I have the feeling it would be worthwhile. Maybe you could call him and suggest eleven-thirty. Here.'

Despite the way Dulles framed it, Nancy Reichman knew that this was an order, not a suggestion. So she got up and went to her phone. Like most telephones in Switzerland it was ugly, black, and mounted on the wall, but it was possible to use that ugly Swiss phone to direct dial the number of every other telephone in the country . . . which is more than one could say about the telephone system in any other country in the world in 1943, including the United States. One added advantage of the system was that there was normally no danger that conversations would be overheard by nosy long-distance operators. Nancy Reichman of course knew that her situation was hardly normal. But she also knew that if her phone was tapped, it was probably being monitored by a colleague of the very man she was in the act of calling . . . with his full knowledge and complete acquiescence.

Basel was a complicated place in 1943.

While Nancy Reichman was on the phone extending Dulles' invitation to Peter Burckhardt in Benken, where he had gone earlier that day to make sure that all the advance preparations were in order, Lützelschwab's black Citroën was just pulling up on the Swiss side of the border crossing which separated Basel from the German town of Lörrach. The two Swiss intelligence officers from Lucerne approached him the minute he stepped out of the car, licence plate in hand.

'I'm Lieutenant Sannwald and this is my colleague, Lieutenant Holzer. We are both from Section 5 of the General Staff. I assume you know what that means, since I also assume you are from the Basel police.'

'Indeed I am. What exactly is going on here?'

'What's going on here need not concern you. It is a military matter. Military intelligence. I see you've brought the licence plate. Just hand it over, and then you are dismissed to go about your business.'

'Ah, yes. But perhaps you are my business. You see my name is Lützelschwab, Dr Wilhelm Lützelschwab, and I happen to be head of the political police and responsible for *counter*-intelligence here in the canton of Baselstadt. In other words, you are in *my* territory, and when I put a question to you, Lieutenant, I want that question answered. So I will try a second time: What exactly is going on here? And who is in those three cars?'

Lützelschwab could have sworn that there was a flicker of recognition, in fact more than a flicker, when the lieutenant had heard his name. No doubt over the years word from Colonel Masson had filtered down to the rank and file of Section 5 that the political police in Basel, a city known for its liberals, was dead set against any act that even hinted at cooperation with the Germans. The provincial cops in Basel would only see it as collaboration with the Nazis.

'I don't think you understand, Lützelschwab. We are here under the direct orders of General Guisan.'

Evoking the name of the commander-in-chief of the Swiss army in Switzerland in 1943 was normally tantamount to citing the authority of Yahveh in Old Testament Israel: it demanded immediate obedience. Every Swiss knew this and accepted it. Well, almost every Swiss.

'Oh, really? Let's see those orders,' said Lützelschwab.

'Impossible.'

157

'All right. Let me try a new approach. Less than an hour ago I came into possession of some information which directly bears on what may or may not be happening here. If my information is correct, it would mean that whatever your boss Masson is up to with *those* people,' and when he used the word 'those' the contempt in his voice was all too evident, 'may be in serious jeopardy. In fact, those people might themselves be in jeopardy. Physical danger. Understand?'

No response . . . except for the fleeting appearance of what very much looked like a smirk, masking the thought that probably went something like: Who does this Basel policeman think he's kidding with a story like that?

'All right, let me make a suggestion. I think you should *either* arrange for me to talk by phone with your Colonel Masson immediately and I mean right now, *or* you let me talk directly to whoever is inside that Mercedes with the Lucerne licence plate.'

Now the lieutenant came to full attention. 'I don't think you understand, Lützelschwab,' he said, 'or more likely you don't *want* to understand. So I'll make it crystal-clear. Unless you hand over that licence plate right now and then get the hell out of here, I am going to place you under military arrest.'

Lützelschwab's eyes narrowed to slits. Then, practising all the self-control he could muster, he gave the lieutenant the plates, turned on his heel, and climbed back into his black Citroën.

As he drove off with a roar he uttered but one word, 'Schoffseckel!', the expletive widely used among the Swiss working class which describes that part of a sheep's anatomy which is never referred to in mixed company.

But he didn't roar off very far. In fact, he pulled in to the kerb just before the intersection of Riehenstrasse and Bäumlihof-strasse, for he knew that the convoy of cars he had left behind at the border — the Swiss army officers were no doubt still busy mounting the licence plates on the second BMW — had to take one or the other of these main streets into the centre of Basel and places beyond, such as Benken. Lützelschwab intended for them to be closely observed all the way, so he immediately activated the car's short-wave radio.

158

'Do isch Lützelschwab,' he began, before giving the desk sergeant his location. 'I want four cars to move out immediately, with four men in each car. I want everybody fully armed, including automatic rifles and grenades. Two cars should station themselves at the intersection of the Wettsteinallee and the Schwarzwaldstrasse. The other two I want on the corner of Riehenstrasse and Riehenring. The object of the exercise is to pick up three German automobiles, a Mercedes and two BMWs, all black and travelling together, led by an unmarked Swiss army car, grey-green of course. Whoever spots them first should let the rest of us know by radio immediately. All are bearing Swiss licence plates reading as follows: the Mercedes − LU 14321; one BMW − LU 2131; the second BMW − BS 1146; I didn't get the number on the Swiss army vehicle. All right? Get moving!'

It was now approaching a quarter past five in the afternoon, and Rolf Seiler, desk clerk, was just alighting from the No. 9 tram which had taken him from the Heuwaageplatz across the Mittlere Rheinbrücke to Kleinbasel. From the stop at the intersection of the Greifengasse and the Rheingasse he walked the half block to the house at No. 37. When Werner Lentz opened the front door and let him into the semi-darkness of the living-room − the drapes were, as always, tightly drawn − three other men got up to greet him. One was the bartender from the Three Kings Hotel who had likewise taken the evening off and who had answered the phone when Seiler had called from the hotel a half-hour earlier. The other two, when introduced, spoke in a rather pathetic mix of bad German and worse Schwyzerdeutsch, which identified them as coming from the French-speaking part of Switzerland. They were, in fact, members of the Rote Kapelle's cell in Lausanne, which, after what had just happened in Geneva, was the only other such cell still operating in central Europe.

Rolf Seiler was about to quietly take his place on the sofa and allow the four men to resume the conversation which his arrival had obviously interrupted when Lentz decided otherwise.

'No, Rolf. I heard about what you saw at the hotel a half-hour ago and I strongly suspect that they are about to end up at the apartment on the other side of the river. So I want you up in the attic with the binoculars right now. Keep an eye on the place for the next fifteen minutes. If nothing happens, then come down and join the rest of us.'

'Yes, Herr Lentz. But would you mind if I first got something to eat in the kitchen? If there's anything there.'

'There's bread and salami. And beer. Help yourself. But don't take too long. In fact, why don't you just get what you want and take it up to the attic with you.'

'Yes, sir.'

As soon as Seiler had disappeared, Lentz resumed his conversation with the other three men gathered in his living-room.

'You just asked me if I knew what was going on in Geneva,' he said, now directly addressing the visitors from the French-speaking part of Switzerland, 'and I must confess that I don't know. I can only conclude that they must have somehow got word that they were about to be raided, and then, from one hour to the next, they simply closed down and got out.'

'Got out to where?' one of the men from Lausanne asked.

'To France. Where else? Because if they had been arrested in Geneva the press would be onto it by now. You know how they are in that city. And you would then have heard about it in Lausanne immediately thereafter.'

Both men from Lausanne looked sceptical and worried, very worried, and Scitovsky/Lentz could hardly help but notice it.

'All right. Then who's got a better opinion? What does Rado say?' Scitovsky referred here to Alexander Rado, a professional spy of Hungarian origins who had been trained in Moscow by the Soviets and then sent to Switzerland in the 1930s for the purpose of setting up and then running the operations of the Red Orchestra in the French-speaking part of that country. He was, therefore, the man who was in charge of all three of their transmitters in that region, including the one in Lausanne which was still intact — or at least had still been that morning when the two men now sitting in the living-room of the house at Rheingasse 37 had left that city in order to take the train to Basel — as well as the two in Geneva which had now gone silent.

'Rado is extremely worried. In fact, this morning he took the train to Geneva about the same time we took our train to Basel. He'll find out today or tomorrow . . . unless they catch him too.'[18]

Scitovsky/Lentz then said: 'But when I talked to him yesterday and arranged for you to come to Basel, he did not sound worried.'

'How long was your conversation?' one of the men from Lausanne asked.

'Very brief, of course.'

'And very guarded. We were both there, you know.'

Now Lentz's attitude seemed to change. 'Maybe you would be well advised to stay completely clear of that situation until we find out what is really going on.'

Both men from Lausanne eagerly agreed, and one of them then asked: 'Can we stay here?'

'No. Nobody is going to stay here.'

'Then where?'

'I'll take care of that, don't worry.' Whether he would, whether he *could*, depended upon how everything played out that evening, but that was the last thing that Scitovsky was going to admit to at this juncture.

He looked at his watch. 'We've got to get moving. Now I'm going to tell you exactly what we are going to be doing tonight and what role each of you is going to play. I want you to listen very carefully, and to ask questions if you don't understand. Your life and mine depends upon each of us executing our jobs perfectly. Understood?'

'All right,' Scitovsky continued as he rose from the sofa, 'now let's all go into the dining-room. I've got my maps and some photographs laid out on the table there.'

---

18 According to Professor Bonjour, Rado escaped arrest in March of 1943 by immediately going underground in Geneva, protected by the community of local Communists. In 1944 he escaped to France on a milk train. See Bonjour, vol. V, pp. 99ff. Also M.R.D. Foot, *Resistance* (London, 1978), p. 216.

It was just after he had spoken these words that a loud shout came from upstairs: 'Herr Lentz! You've got to come up here. Now!'

It was Rolf Seiler's voice. When Lentz burst through the open trapdoor after climbing the ladder which led from the second floor hall into the attic, he was immediately handed the binoculars.

'Take a look. Just like you said, Herr Lentz. They are both there.'

Lentz looked through the binoculars, and then at his watch. It was almost 17.30. 'The goddamn Americans must be in on it too. They *must* be, otherwise why would Dulles show up in Basel now?' The words were not directed at the young man standing at his side, watching him: they were directed at himself, as if he were trying to convince himself that his worst suspicions were now actually being confirmed before his very eyes. He again raised the binoculars to his eyes.

'They don't exactly look like they're about to move, do they?' And this time he *was* talking to the Swiss desk clerk with the Communist bent.

'No, Herr Lentz.'

Again Lentz/Scitovsky referred to his watch. And then he made a decision.

'Rolf, I've changed my mind. Instead of coming with the rest of us, I want you to stay here and keep an eye on that apartment the entire evening. It's now obvious that Dulles is going to meet Schellenberg, but not in Benken. I can hardly imagine him compromising himself in front of the Swiss.'

'Nor vice versa, in my opinion.' Rolf Seiler's opinion, despite his current desk clerk status, was usually worth hearing. Though he had not gone on to university, he had been a brilliant student at the local Humanistische Gymnasium, where he had come under the influence of a teacher of philology, a closet Marxist who had soon made a convert out of young Rolf. When, in his final year of secondary education, Rolf had started ranting on about dialectical materialism over the dinner table at home, it so put off his father – who was a teller in the Kantonalbank and thus ultra-conservative and a rabid anti-Communist – that there was

162

no question of his further supporting such a wayward son in any further pursuit of higher education. An embittered Rolf became a waiter and then a desk clerk at the Schweizerhof Hotel, with the help of his Marxist tutor who knew the manager. It was the same professor who, in a much more subtle way, made sure that Rolf also crossed paths with a local jeweller by the name of Werner Lentz. All three, for quite different reasons, of course, hated what they saw around them in bourgeois Switzerland, and were dedicated to bringing about its destruction . . . again, each in his own way. Initially Rolf had agreed with the non-violent approach to change advocated by his academic mentor, but then gradually, over the years, Lentz/Scitovsky had managed to wean Rolf away from such illusions, convincing him that, in the end, it would be kill or be killed.

'That does not mean, however, that you're going to miss all the fun this evening, Rolf. Because I now think it is going to take place in two quite different locations.'

'Perhaps one rural and one urban?' Rolf now ventured.

Scitovsky liked that. 'You're a smart young man, Rolf,' he said, patting him on the back and grinning. 'Maybe the division of labour may more aptly be described as taking care of, first, the Germans, and then the Americans. After all, we now seem to be their common enemy.'

Then: 'These are your instructions, Rolf. I want you to keep that apartment under constant observation. Don't worry if they leave for a while. That is to be expected. After all, they've got to eat. But I'm convinced they'll be back, because I'm convinced that they are expecting company, either late tonight, or perhaps some time early tomorrow morning. By company I mean the SS, most probably a general in the SS by the name of Walter Schellenberg. Is that clear?'

'How would I recognize him?'

'Like I just said, Rolf, you're a smart young man. I should have thought of that. He's a lot younger than you would expect. In his very early thirties. About six feet tall. Slim. Very elegant for a German. And a very stylish dresser. Remember, *if* he shows up, he will be in civilian clothes.'

'Yes, sir. But assuming he does show up, what are we going to do about it?'

163

'Kill him. And if the Americans get hit in the process, so be it. They're asking for it. But if all goes well out there in Benken, any further action along those lines will be made unnecessary.'

'How will I know that?'

'I'll either telephone, or deliver the news personally. By no later than 23 hours. In any case, you must realize, Rolf, that this is the last night any of us will spend here. More important, this is probably the last night that we can finally make a *real* difference where the outcome of this war against us is concerned.'

'I realize that.'

'And as I told you earlier, no matter what happens, I'll take care of you.'

'I know that too. But just in case, in case I don't hear from you, the professor has let me know that I can stay at his place, at least for a while.'

'Good. But you'll hear from me by eleven. By the way, I'm leaving three different weapons with ample ammunition for all three in the cellar. You know where. All right?'

With that, Lentz disappeared down the trapdoor. It was now 5.35 pm and there was absolutely no further time to waste.

The three other members of the Rote Kapelle, perhaps the last surviving active members of the Soviet espionage apparatus in central Europe, were waiting for the NKGB colonel when he returned downstairs and entered the dining-room.

'Now I want all of you to look at this map. It's a blowup of the western end of the Birsigthal. It's a valley formed by the Birsig River which starts in France and then works its way through Switzerland on its way to the Rhine. Here.' Lentz/Scitovsky's finger traced the river's path for the benefit of the two men from Lausanne, who were totally unfamiliar with the topography of this part of Switzerland.

'Now the last Swiss village before the French frontier is Benken. Here.' Again the finger pointed.

'Above Benken, at the top of the ridge overlooking the valley below, is the Benkener Schloss.' He had marked the spot with a red X. 'This is where our target will be spending the night. As you can see, there is only one road leading up to it. Actually it's more

164

a lane than a road. It's about a half-kilometre long, and goes through forest most of the way.

'Now come over to this end of the table.' They did. 'That's the front view of the Schloss.' It was again a blowup, but this time of a photograph not a map. 'As you can see, it's surrounded by a moat, and you approach the front entrance across that narrow bridge. The rather formidable oaken entrance door and the massive stone structure of the castle itself, with its very small windows, rule out any attempt at frontal assault. Even grenades would be useless. So we won't even try that approach. And after all, there are only four of us.'

But Scitovsky knew that although they were 'only' four, the two imports from Lausanne were superbly qualified for assaults of a paramilitary nature, frontal or not. Although in civilian life one was a butcher and the other a physical education teacher, both were members of the elite mountain division of Switzerland's militia, where they spent four months of each year in active service, one as a sergeant, the other a corporal. The Swiss navy might be a joke, but this division of the Swiss army was definitely not. The mountain troops were accustomed to undertaking all-day climbs from the valley floors of central Switzerland to the upper reaches of the Alps which formed the Gotthard massif, lugging 50 kilos of weapons and ammunition on their backs, and this on skis fitted for the ascent with non-skid chamois skins. There they set up their tents in the snow in sub-zero temperatures with winds blowing at 40 kilometres an hour in preparation for spending weeks up there participating in manoeuvres aimed at improving their abilities to respond to an aerial attack on central Switzerland by Nazi paratroopers. The exercises left little to the imagination, since the use of live ammunition was often the order of the day. Scitovsky himself, though out of shape, had been thoroughly trained in the art of guerrilla warfare back in Russia as part of his NKGB training. However, the fourth man in that dining-room, the bartender from the Three Kings Hotel, had none of these qualifications. He was, therefore, the designated driver.

'So,' Scitovsky continued, 'we are left with two options. Either we ambush the target's automobile on the way up to or down from the Benkener Schloss, using the forest as our cover. Or we try to somehow get inside the Schloss surreptitiously and kill him there. I'm leaving those options open until I see how things develop.

'Now,' and he addressed the following words to the young Swiss who tended bar, 'in either case, I want you to stay with the van. But no matter what happens, I want you to call in to this house, to Rolf who will be remaining here, at 23.00 hours, and bring him up to date. No matter what. There are two public telephone booths you can use – one in Biel and one in Benken, both on the main road. I'll point them out to you on the drive out. Got that?

'All right.' Now Scitovsky turned to the two men from Lausanne. 'I know that you can handle weapons of all types, but I want to be absolutely sure that you are familiar with the ones we will be using this evening. They're down in the cellar. Let's check them out right now.'

Twenty-five minutes later, at 18.10, Werner Lentz's van pulled away from the kerb in front of Rheingasse 37. It was loaded with four men, as well as three submachine guns of Russian origin, four pistols manufactured in Germany, 5 kilos of ammunition, plus a dozen hand grenades which had been made in Switzerland. The observer from Basel's political police, stationed in the attic of the house directly opposite Rheingasse 37, immediately alerted headquarters in the Spiegelhof. There it was duly noted, but no further action was taken. All of the department's available cars and manpower had already been commandeered by Dr Lützel-schwab to monitor the movements of SS General Walter Schellenberg and his entourage as they moved further and further onto Swiss soil.

Chapter 17

Although the hours during which the Deutsche Generalkonsulat in Basel was open to the public, 9 to 12 am, Monday through Friday, were long past, the activities within the German consulate were at a pitch not seen there since the outbreak of war in 1939. At 5 pm that afternoon the German ambassador to Switzerland, Otto Carl Köcher, had arrived from Bern. Then forty-five minutes later, the reason for the ambassador's presence in Basel had appeared in the person of no less than General Walter Schellenberg, an Obergruppenführer in the SS (which had its own ranking system), accompanied by his 'man in Switzerland', Major Hans Eggen, a Sturmbannführer in the SS.

When the two principals met in the library where the ambassador had been waiting, it was apparent to the consul-general, who was allowed to remain there only during the introductions, that the ambassador and the general had an instant mistrust of each other. This was hardly surprising, since they came from completely different worlds. The ambassador was a diplomat of the old school, a product of the nineteenth century rather than the twentieth, a man who believed that the rules of the diplomatic game, as defined at the Council of Vienna in 1815, still applied in 1943. They were firmly anchored in the assumption that intercourse between governments should take place through established diplomatic channels. In other words, when the men who ran Germany from Berlin wanted to communicate with their counterparts in Switzerland they should do so through his embassy. In this regard, the attitude of Otto Karl Köcher was no different than that of his American counterpart in Bern, Minister Leland Harrison. What neither man wanted to recognize was that the world in which they operated in 1943 was radically different from that which had endured, essentially unchanged, for well over a century. A new element had interjected itself into the affairs of state, the intelligence services, a rogue element which paid no attention whatsoever to the old rules of the game. In the case of the American envoy, the new cross that he now had to bear had been thrust upon him in the person of an intelligence officer by the name of Allen Dulles . . . a *spy* who had arrived four months earlier, and who had immediately let the world know that he and he alone had a direct line to President Roosevelt. It soon became apparent to America's friends and foes alike that if they wanted immediate action it was Dulles who should be contacted. Thereafter, it had only been a matter of time before the back channels established by Dulles, channels which ran through the OSS (America's newly established professional intelligence service) directly to the White House, displaced the diplomatic channels which ran through Harrison back to the State Department, which, more often than not, turned out to be a cul de sac. The spy had displaced the diplomat.

SS General Walter Schellenberg, the German ambassador knew, was trying to do exactly the same thing: to circumvent diplomatic channels and establish direct contacts with foreign leaders, and to this end he had enlisted the help of his intelligence counterpart in Switzerland, Colonel Masson (who was now *also* operating outside of the accepted parameters which forbade the interference of the Swiss military in political affairs), leaving Köcher out in the cold. The trouble was: there was nothing he could do about it. Because just as Dulles had the ear of Roosevelt, so Schellenberg had Hitler's. Once a week, every week, he, as the man in charge of Germany's foreign intelligence service, personally delivered their intelligence estimates to the Führer. On top of that Schellenberg was SS, not a cookie pusher.

Not that Schellenberg was a product of Munich beer halls, like so many of the slobs who had risen to positions of power within the SS. Rather he was a product of Germany's middle class, a man with academic credentials, a lawyer. Köcher had arranged to have Schellenberg's 'card' pulled from the Berlin document centre to get a better feel for the man. It was a classic example of Teutonic concision.

The *Personal-Bericht* contained nothing out of the ordinary — Schellenberg was unmarried, had no criminal record, and believed in God — except, perhaps, the fact that he was born in Saarbrücken in 1910, which made him just thirty-three, very young for a general in the SS. But in the second half of the report, under *Beurteilung*, which recorded the judgement of his superiors (as well as those who kept him under observation due to the highly sensitive post which he held within the SS), what emerged was the portrait of a man who was not only to be reckoned with, but also one to be very careful of. It read:

Rassisches Gesamtbild: Pure northern European.
Charakter: Candid and sincere, a man of impeccably pure character. He is a security service man.
Wille: Firm, tough, endowed with energy.
Gesunder Menschenverstand: Very sharp thinker.
Wissen und Bildung: Good grades in law exams; has an above average general education.
Auffassungsvermögen: Gets to the heart of problems with amazing speed.
Nationalsozialistische Weltanschauung [Belief in Nazi ideology]: Totally firm.
Auftreten: Carries himself like a soldier both in and out of uniform.[19]

And indeed, although in civilian clothes, there could be no doubt that the tall, trim, extremely good-looking Aryan who stood at the centre of attention in the library of the German consulate in Basel in early March of 1943 was a man of high military rank. But despite that bearing, Walter Schellenberg

---

19 See p. 171 for a copy of the original *Personal-Bericht* on Schellenberg (Braunschweig, *Geheimer Draht nach Berlin*, p. 227).

knew how to turn on the charm, which he immediately did.[20]

'Herr Botschafter,' he began, after the consul had left the room, leaving the Nazis of high authority among themselves, 'you have honoured me by coming over from Bern for what, out of necessity, must be a very brief meeting.'

The ambassador acknowledged these words with a nod.

'Let's sit down together on the sofa over there, Herr Botschafter. I'm sure we can arrange for some coffee to be brought in. In fact,' and he addressed these words to Rittmeister Eggen, 'why don't you see to that?' It was obvious that Schellenberg wanted to hold his conversation with the ambassador in strict privacy.

And only after his man had left the room did Schellenberg continue. 'First, I want to extend to you personal greetings from the Führer. I was with him yesterday morning, and he specifically requested that I do so.'

That broke the ice. The ambassador actually flushed with surprise. 'I am greatly honoured, Herr General. I hope that the next time you meet the Führer you will relay to him how much I appreciate his continuing trust in me. My only remaining mission in life is to be able to serve him and the Reich to the best of my abilities.'

---

20 Compare David Kahn's description of Schellenberg in his book, *Hitler's Spies. German Military Intelligence in World War II* (New York, 1985), p. 260: 'He had a quiet way about him, quite different from the bullying pretentious hardness of most SS types. He spoke softly, almost shyly, in a clear tenor with exceptionally precise enunciation and with a boyish charm that was one of his greatest assets . . . Not everyone liked him. Some of the older, street-brawler types of the SS despised him; some officials regarded him as too pushy . . . He was bright and perceptive: people meeting him often had the impression he could form a clear picture of people and events on the basis of a few key facts . . . he could lunch smoothly with foreigners and befriended young officials in the Foreign Office and the Propaganda ministry. He was credited with understanding foreign affairs.'

The British historian, Hugh Trevor-Roper, had a quite different view: 'The excellent reputation which Schellenberg, their youngest general, commanded within the ranks of the most narrow-minded fanatics of the SS was completely without substance . . . To be sure, he did not believe in the use of force but rather in cunning, since he believed himself to be a cunning man. That was his biggest mistake.' *The Last Days of Hitler* (London, 1947), p. 59.

Personal-Bericht

des **Walter Schellenberg** .... (Dienststellung und Einheit) .... **SS-Oberscharführer.**
(Vor- und Zuname) .... (Dienststellung und Einheit) .... (Dienstgrad)

Mitglied-Nr. der Partei: **3.504.508** .... SS.Ausweis Nr. **124.817**

Seit wann in der Dienststellung: .... Beförderungsdatum zum letzten Dienstgrad: **13.9.36**

Geburtstag, Geburtsort (Kreis): **16.1.1910 zu Saarbrücken**

Beruf: 1. erlernter: **Jurist** .... 2. jetziger: **Angestellter**

Wohnort: **Berlin SW 68** .... Straße: **Wilhelmstr. 102**

Verheiratet? **nein** Mädchenname der Frau: ———— Kinder? ——— Konfession: **gottgl.**

Wirtschaftliche Verhältnisse: **geordnet**

Vorstrafen: **keine**

Verletzungen, Verfolgungen und Strafen im Kampfe für die Bewegung: ....

....

....

Beurteilung:

I. Rassisches Gesamtbild: **Rein nordisch.**

....

II.   1. Charakter: **Offener, einwandfreier, lauterer Charakter; er ist SD-Mann.**

2. Wille: **Fest, zäh, besitzt Energie.**

....

3. Gesunder Menschenverstand: **Sehr scharf denkend.**

Wissen und Bildung: **Assessorexamen: gut; überdurchschnittliche Allgemein-**
bildung.

Auffassungsvermögen: **Erfasst überraschend schnell das Kernproblem.**

Nationalsozialistische Weltanschauung: **Durchaus gefestigt.**

III. Auftreten und Benehmen in und außer Dienst: **Soldatisches Auftreten in und ausser Dienst.**
(Besondere Neigungen, Schwächen und Fehler)

....

....

171

'I am sure he will be very pleased when I repeat your words to him,' Schellenberg replied. Then: 'I feel obligated to mention that the Führer is in a rather agitated state. As you know, things are not going well on the Eastern front, at least for the time being. And he is becoming increasingly worried about our exposure on the southern flank, especially now that one must reckon with an Allied landing in Sicily or southern Italy. And that has raised the issue of Switzerland, of what to do with Switzerland. As you know, the Führer is not overly fond of this country. I recall being present at the meeting he had with Mussolini in June of 1941 when the subject of Switzerland came up. And all of us were shocked at how hostile, *emotionally* hostile, he was. He described the Swiss as "das Niederträchtigste und erbärmlichste Volk", "the most devious and detestable of people" and as the "Todfeinde des neuen Deutschland", "the deadly enemies of the new Germany".[21] Mussolini was the most shocked of all, since he had spent a year or so right here in Basel in the early 1920s and had apparently been treated very well. Be that as it may, Herr Hitler is currently in such a frame of mind that just a little more provocation on the part of the Swiss might tip the scales dangerously in the direction of military intervention aimed at securing our southern flank by integrating Switzerland into the Reich, and then using the Alpine redoubt as a bulwark against any invasion that the Anglo-Saxons may contemplate mounting against the fatherland from the Italian peninsula. In the Führer's headquarters, already there is talk about this as "Aktion Schweiz", "Campaign Switzerland".'

At this point Rittmeister Eggen reappeared, followed by a young woman bearing a tray with coffee and some local Konfiserie.

Ambassador Otto Karl Köcher waited until they had left before responding: 'I am fully aware of this danger. And in fact, just a month ago I had a long conversation with the Swiss foreign minister and suggested that it would be in everybody's interest if

---

21 Bonjour, vol. V, p. 66. His source, in turn, was *Staatsmänner und Diplomaten bei Hitler*, compiled by Andreas Hillgruber (Frankfurt, 1967).

all of us began to work towards a German/American détente
before it is too late. The alternative could be the Bolshevization
of all of Europe. Minister Pilet was very sympathetic, and, I am
told, communicated this desire to the American ambassador
here, Leland Harrison, a fine diplomat of the old school, I should
add.'[22]

'You did this acting on whose authority?'
'State Secretary Ernst von Weizsäcker.'[23]
'And what was the American response?'
'Negative.'[24]
'Maybe you used the wrong channel of communication.'
'What does that mean?'
'Maybe you should have gone through Allen Dulles.'

'He is not accredited in this country,' was the immediate,
haughty response, one that carried with it the definite suggestion
that neither was Schellenberg, an impression reinforced by his
next words: 'And what, might I ask, is your mission here, Herr
General?'

'It is very similar to yours. To warn the Swiss. To suggest that it
is in their best interests to cooperate with us, especially in the
economic and financial realm. That by doing so, they can
demonstrate in a concrete fashion that they are indeed neutral. In
Berlin there are those in the circle around Hitler who now talk
about their "Anglo-Saxon" neutrality. Heinrich Himmler, for

---

22 Bonjour, vol. VI (Basel, 1970), p. 116. This meeting between Köcher and the
Swiss foreign minister took place on 5 February 1943.

23 Ernst von Weizsäcker was the father of the current President of Germany,
Richard von Weizsäcker.

24 Pilet told Harrison that since the Germans' military reserves were almost
exhausted, the danger of a 'Bolshevization' of Europe was becoming acute,
something that was hardly in the interests of the Anglo-Saxons. He then
suggested that the Americans and British pull out of the war and let the Russians
fight it out with the Germans. The American ambassador relayed these thoughts
immediately to the State Department. Their laconic response: Roosevelt had
already given his answer in previous statements to the effect that the Americans
intended to fight on without compromise until the Axis powers agreed to an
unconditional surrender. Bonjour, vol. VI, pp. 117–18.

one. If they have their way, the Führer may be talked into going for the "Aktion Schweiz" right away.'

These last words appeared to shock the ambassador. 'But that would be a great mistake. We have good friends in very high places in this country. Foreign Minister Pilet, for one.'

'And Colonel Masson of the Swiss army's General Staff for another,' added Schellenberg.

'So you will be meeting with him.'

'This evening.'

'Be careful. There are also people in both high and low places, such as the police in this city, who harbour such a deep hatred for us that they may act irrationally, totally ignoring the dire consequences which would follow. They very badly need to be reminded about what happened to the Czechs after they killed your good friend Reinhard Heydrich.'

'I appreciate your concern. But I think it is misplaced. Nobody except for a very few officers in the High Command of the Swiss military knows that I am here,' Schellenberg answered. 'In fact, and you must keep this entirely to yourself, Herr Köcher, my visit has been sanctioned by no less than their commander-in-chief, General Guisan. If all goes well, I will meet him tomorrow.'

The ambassador was stunned. All he could say as a response to this news was: 'Congratulations, Herr General.'

Schellenberg looked at his watch. 'Regrettably I must leave in a few minutes. But before I do, I want to ask you how our negotiations are working out with the Swiss in regard to their future deliveries to our defence industries, and especially those of electricity, turbines for our U-Boats, and aluminium for our aircraft. We are running desperately short of all of these and the Führer himself is concerned. And there is also a question of gold and dollars. To fund my operations around the world I am constantly in need of both. And, as you know, Herr Ambassador, our only remaining reliable source for such financing is the Swiss National Bank. That source cannot be allowed to dry up.'

'I am doing my best, you can reassure the Führer of that, but the negotiations are not going at all well in any of these categories. The major reason is that the Americans are beginning to put pressure on the Swiss. There are those in the circle around Roosevelt, such as the Jew Henry Morgenthau, who are likewise promising dire consequences where the Swiss are concerned if they continue to cooperate with us. The Swiss greatly resent this pressure, especially Foreign Minister Pilet. We need to encourage men like Pilet, to reassure them. But also to impress upon them that they really have no option other than not only continuing, but even expanding our bilateral economic cooperation. I hope you will mention this to your colleague, Colonel Masson, and to General Guisan when you meet them.'

'Now that you have mentioned the Americans, allow me to return to the person of Mr Dulles. How, in your judgement, does he fit into all this?'

'I wish I knew. He is an enigma even to the Swiss. Why do you ask?'

'I have the feeling that he might be a reasonable man. One who understands the enormity of the Soviet threat. A man one can talk to.'

'Do you intend to do that?'

'Perhaps. Maybe you could be of some help there, Herr Ambassador, by dropping a word here, one there, in Bern.'

'Perhaps.'

General Schellenberg chose this moment to rise from the sofa. The audience was over. Five minutes later he and his adjutant, Rittmeister Eggen, climbed into the back seat of the huge black Mercedes which had been waiting outside the consulate, along with the two BMWs and one rather pathetic-looking grey-green Fiat. As they pulled away from the kerb and began to move off they were observed by a total of twelve Swiss policemen in three different cars.

Schellenberg's clandestine visit was a lot less secret than he thought.

Chapter 18

And it was not only the Swiss police who were in on that secret.

It was now a quarter past six on this evening of 2 March 1943, and NKGB Colonel Igor Scitovsky, alias Werner Lentz, though unaware of the arrival of the SS general on Swiss soil three hours earlier, was proceeding on the assumption that sooner or later that evening he would show up at the medieval castle located atop a hill overlooking the village of Benken. And Scitovsky intended to be fully prepared beforehand. That, in turn, required some further work in his field of expertise: intelligence. It was a delicate operation, since the source of the information he now required in order to ensure the success of his mission was Liselotte Maurer, the young lady who had not been overly enamoured of him the last time they had parted company after their Sunday afternoon at the operetta.

Dusk had begun to fall when the Opel van, driven by the bartender at the Three Kings Hotel and carrying Scitovsky and his two colleagues from the Rote Kapelle cell in Lausanne, entered the outskirts of the village of Benken, and then pulled to the side of the road just short of the lane which led off to the right and then up the hill through the forest to the Benkener Schloss above. Immediately on the other side of that lane was the restaurant 'Zum Ochsen'. The van's lights went out. Its four occupants now waited in total silence. There was no movement whatsoever in the village. Then Lentz gave a curt order and the driver started the engine, pulled away, and immediately turned right into the lane. Although the headlights remained out, since there was a full moon, despite the tall fir trees which lined both sides of the lane the driver had no difficulty staying on it. After 300 metres he was once again ordered to stop. Lentz and the other two men now jumped out, opened the back door of the Opel van, and removed, piece by piece, the weaponry stashed there — the three Russian-made submachine guns, three of the four pistols, all of the ammunition, plus ten of the twelve hand grenades. With these they disappeared off into the forest to the left. Ten minutes later they returned, now empty-handed and climbed back into the van. Very carefully the driver now backed down the narrow lane until he had once again reached the main road. Once on that road, and after he had confirmed that the streets of Benken were still deserted, he switched on the headlights and pulled forward about twenty metres before stopping again, this time in front of the restaurant 'Zum Ochsen'. The three passengers had barely got out again when the van moved quickly off. The driver took it a kilometre further down the road, and then pulled into another lane which he knew — from the map which had lain on the kitchen table at Rheingasse 37 — led to the village cemetery. There the driver shut off the motor, consulted his watch, and decided to take a nap. He had many hours to waste.

Scitovsky had entered the restaurant warily. Was Liselotte working this evening, and if she was, would she revert to her usual talkative form? She was not only there, but the moment she spotted him she came directly towards him.

'So, so,' she began, 'I thought I had seen the last of *you!*'

'I've missed you,' he said, 'and I apologize for acting so badly last Sunday. To prove it, I've brought you a little something.'

He handed over a small package, elegantly wrapped in silver paper and bearing a red ribbon. A small envelope was discreetly attached to the ribbon. She immediately removed the envelope, opened it, read the enclosed card, and blushed.

'That is very sweet of you, Werner,' she said, 'but we can't just stand here. Are these other two gentlemen with you?'

'Yes.' Scitovsky did not bother to introduce them.

'Are you going to be eating, or just . . .'

'We've come for a full dinner.'

'I can't give you the best table, because it's already reserved. But the one next to it is really just as good.' She led them to an alcove area of the restaurant which lay off to the left.

After they had taken their places she then asked: 'Now what can I get you to drink?'

Scitovsky ordered a large carafe of the local Riesling, and Liselotte promptly went to fetch it, all the while carrying the small package in both hands. After the door leading into the kitchen had closed behind her, she walked over to one of the wooden tables there and immediately untied the red ribbon. Then she began to work on the packaging, though very carefully. After all, the ribbon and the paper could be used again. Once they were removed, she neatly folded both, hardly daring to look at the exquisite little leather jewellery box that had now been revealed and which she had placed in front of her on the table. Finally she took it back into her hands, opened the lid, and gazed down upon the ring that now lay displayed.

'Du lieber Gott im Himmel! Das isch en echte Perlring!' It was indeed a real pearl in the ring, and a rather large one at that. And just as Liselotte had spontaneously called out to her Father in Heaven upon seeing it, it had been inevitable that religious thoughts would also enter Scitovsky's mind when he had had the ring packed earlier that day in his jewellery store in Kleinbasel, namely those expressed in the Gospel according to St Matthew, chapter 7, verse 6. But what the hell, he had concluded: the store would inevitably be raided and all of its contents confiscated once the Swiss authorities got to the bottom of the things which were about to transpire later that evening. So one pearl cast to a Swiss could hardly be regarded as wasted.

Very slowly, in fact very shyly, she put it on her ring finger — which had remained a virgin so far — and it fitted perfectly! Her joy at discovering this might have been somewhat diminished had she known that Lentz had sought out the second largest ring size in stock, recalling how pudgy that hand had been which had lain so briefly, yet with such great promise, on his right thigh as they had driven together to the theatre just a few days earlier. Her immediate impulse was to show it off to the cook and his helper, who were both busy, one chopping vegetables at another table, the other stirring a sauce at the wood-burning stove. But she immediately decided against it. The cook knew her father. Instead she took the beautiful little box, the wrapping paper and the ribbon and carefully stuffed them into the pocket of her winter coat, which hung on the wall opposite the stove; but the ring remained on her finger. If somebody noticed it and asked her about it she would say it was from . . . an aunt. A rich aunt who had lived all alone in Basel for many years and who had just died.

Then Liselotte fetched a carafe of Baselbieter Riesling and, after putting it and three glasses — the type known as Römer — on a tray, she returned to the table in the restaurant occupied by her admirer, Werner Lentz, and his two friends.

Once the wine had been poured, she caressed Lentz's back very briefly, leaned down and whispered in his ear: 'Du bisch ein Schatz, Werner.' Then she added: 'I'll take a break in an hour or so. Maybe we could meet for a few minutes outside.'

He nodded his agreement. And as soon as she moved away, he looked at his watch. An hour was just about right. If he found out what he wanted to know, it would leave ample time to plan the details, especially the schedule, of the operation accordingly.

Twenty minutes later there was a pause in the conversations going on in the restaurant 'Zum Ochsen', which was almost full by then, as everybody became aware of unusual noise, unusual at night in wartime Switzerland: that of traffic on the road outside, of cars, heavy cars, being shifted down, and then, after a pause, of engines, big engines, at least three or four of them, being revved up as they started to move off again. Liselotte Maurer, nosy as always, could not help but go to the front door and peek out onto the road. And there in the glare of headlights she could see, turning off the main road into the lane which led up to the

Benkener Schloss, the biggest Mercedes she had ever seen in her life, followed by two other huge cars — they were BMWs, of course, but she did not recognize the make since they were rare in Switzerland.

After closing the door, she immediately headed for Werner Lentz's table, where she leaned down and again began to whisper in his ear. 'Remember what I told you on Sunday? About the Germans coming? Well, they must have arrived this very minute. I just saw their cars. I've never seen such big cars!' Then she stood straight up and, in a normal voice, asked: 'Would the gentlemen now like to see the menu?' They did. And five minutes later they ordered dinner — all three went for the Rehschnitzel with Spätzli — and another carafe of wine, this time a Dôle, the heavy red wine from the Valais which would go well with the venison.

About a half-hour later the phone rang behind the bar, and since Liselotte happened to be there drawing beer from the keg for a large group which had just arrived for their regular evening of Jass at the Stammtisch in the back of the restaurant, she answered it. After she hung up, she delivered the eight steins of Warteck lager and then went directly to the table adjacent to that occupied by the three men from the Rote Kapelle — the one that had remained reserved — and arranged two additional settings. On the way back to the bar she paused ever so briefly behind Werner Lentz and whispered another message: 'Four of them from up there will be here in five minutes. That means I can't take a break until much later, maybe another hour. Are you going to stay that long?' When Lentz nodded his head affirmatively, her hand again moved to caress the back of his neck very quickly. Then Liselotte was off again.

Almost exactly five minutes later, two men and two women entered the restaurant 'Zum Ochsen'. Immediately every eye in the place was drawn to them. For they were not ordinary men: both stood well over six feet tall, and neither weighed under ninety kilos. But it was not just their size that was so striking, but also their bearing. Each wore a long black leather coat, and although beneath they were in civilian clothes, it took very little imagination to see them in what must be the dress of their choice: a military uniform. When one beckoned impatiently to the waitress, Liselotte, and then addressed her in a loud voice in impeccable high German, everyone in the room could not help but conclude that the uniform of their choice was that of the Wehrmacht: green and bearing an eagle with folded wings mounted above a swastika over the breast pocket, or maybe even worse: black, which along with the icon on their caps, a skull and crossbones, identified the wearer as a member of the Nazi elite. Such guesses were close – but no cigar. In fact, the two men who had just walked into that small Swiss inn were indeed members of the military elite in their German homeland, but hardly SS: they were both Fallschirmjäger, paratroopers, and as such wore blue-grey uniforms, and in contrast to the officers in the regular army, the eagle wings worn on their right breast pocket were spread and curved. One of Hitler's own 'ten commandments' to his Fallschirmjäger had been: 'Against an open foe, fight with chivalry, but extend no quarter to a guerrilla.'[25] As Schellenberg's bodyguards in a neutral but hostile country, they were definitely in guerrilla territory.

But it was their two companions who caused an even greater stir among the locals who had gathered to dine out, as Liselotte Maurer showed all four new patrons to their reserved table.

They had all arrived forty minutes earlier, at precisely 1900 hours, as prearranged, in one of the BMWs which had been part of the four-car convoy. The lead car had been occupied by two officers attached to Section 5 of the General Staff of the Swiss army. As soon as the convoy had stopped, they had sprung out to greet the man who stood in front of the drawbridge which led across the moat to the main entrance of the castle which was bathed in the bright light shed by lamp posts standing at the edge of the forest surrounding the Schloss, there to provide both show and security. In the centre of that light stood the son of the

25 Bruce Quarie, *German Airborne Troops 1939–45* (London, 1983), p. 6.

181

chatelain, Peter Burckhardt, and the greeting he received came in the form of a salute, recognizing the fact that he was a fellow officer in the Swiss army, although the fact that he too was attached to Section 5, Intelligence, was known by only a few.

Simultaneously the driver of the huge black Mercedes opened the back doors of his vehicle and out stepped General Walter Schellenberg and his adjutant, Sturmbannführer Rittmeister Hans Eggen. As Burckhardt approached them, four heels clicked, and two closely shorn heads nodded in unison. For a split second it looked as if they were also going to salute, Nazi-style, but instead Schellenberg took one step forward and merely extended his right hand. For another split second it appeared as if Burckhardt was hesitating. But then he grasped that hand firmly, very firmly, and said: 'Willkommen in der Schweiz, Herr General.' He also shook hands with Eggen, and, addressing both, continued: 'My name is Peter Burckhardt and I will be your host. Colonel Masson has already arrived and has asked me to tell you that he is eagerly looking forward to meeting you. If you agree, we will all meet for dinner at seven-thirty. In the meantime, one of the servants will escort you to your accommodation for the evening. If there is anything you need, please let me know immediately.'

Then, as if to a signal, the door at the main entrance to the Schloss opened and two valets followed by six maids approached them.

Schellenberg appeared to be not in the slightest fazed by the display put on by the Basel aristocracy. 'Your Swiss hospitality is indeed overwhelming, Lieutenant Burckhardt. We Germans, as your neighbours and friends, hope that our ties with you, which have always been close and include the language which we share, will become even closer in the days ahead.'

His heels clicked and his head nodded yet again. And at this moment the back doors of one of the other two cars which had been part of the convoy opened. Two strapping examples of classic Aryan breeding emerged from the BMW, and immediately approached Peter Burckhardt.

'These men,' Schellenberg explained, 'always accompany me.

This is Major Gerhardt von Göhler.' Göhler stiffly stepped
forward and shook Burckhardt's hand. 'And this is Lieutenant
Reichardt.' He did the same. And then came what could have
been the more embarrassing part of the arrival ceremony. For
when the back doors of the second BMW opened for the first
time since it had rolled onto Swiss soil, what emerged were two
further prime specimens of the Nordic race, equally tall and well
built — but in a somewhat different way. As they neared the four
men who now awaited them in front of the entrance to the
Benkener Schloss, their appearance caused more than a slight stir
among the six Swiss maids as they stiffly stood waiting, clad in
their black dresses and white aprons, since they had never seen
two women quite like this, except perhaps on the screen in the
kino. Neither had a coat on and both wore silk dresses — one red,
the other bright green — that began well below the neck and
stopped well above the knee. The bosoms that were displayed
were equally ample; the legs equally trim, and the effect the latter
had on their audience was further enhanced by the fact that they
were encased in black silk stockings. One of the ladies was
blonde; the other had red hair. And both were absolutely
gorgeous.

General Schellenberg again proved himself equal to the situation. 'Darf Ich vorstellen?' he asked. 'These are my two secretaries, although in many ways they are much more than that,' and he
grinned slightly as he said it. 'I think they would like to room
together this evening, if that can be arranged.' Their names were
Hannelore and Marlene and both looked quite boldly at Peter
Burckhardt as they were introduced.

'Since neither will be joining us for dinner,' Schellenberg
continued, 'I thought that perhaps they would enjoy eating in the
village below. I noticed what appeared to be a very quaint inn
there. I am sure that Major von Göhler and his colleague would
be gallant enough to accompany them.'

'In fact,' Peter Burckhardt said, 'I anticipated that this might
arise, and took the liberty of reserving a table at the inn — it's
name is "Zum Ochsen" — for seven-thirty.' The reservation had
been for only two, but that could be corrected to four by

telephone. 'Is that convenient?' He addressed the question to Hannelore, the one with the red hair.

She leaned forward to touch his arm, while saying in the husky voice which seemed so typical of women from Berlin: 'It is very kind of you, Herr Burckhardt. Do you think we could go like this?' The question evoked an inadvertent but understandable response in the young Swiss: his eyes went directly to the red dress and the body it so tightly enclosed. 'Of course,' he said, and then added: 'But it being such a lovely moonlit night, I suggest you walk down through the forest. And since it gets quite chilly here at night, you might consider wearing a coat, or a very warm wrap, over your . . . costume.'

And so it came to pass that a half-hour later the four Berliners were ushered to their table by Liselotte Maurer, a table which was situated immediately adjacent to the one occupied by the last three active members of the Soviet Union's espionage network in central Europe. In this year of 1943 a situation such as this could only have arisen in very few places on earth, probably no more than four: Lisbon, Istanbul, Geneva and Basel. These were the cities, with the areas immediately surrounding them, where the agents of all of the warring parties were free to go about playing their games not only without undue interference on the part of the local authorities, but often under their protection. For it was in the interest of all of the neutrals in 1943 to ward off any incidents arising on their soil which could endanger their avoidance of direct involvement in the bloodiest war that mankind had ever waged.

And thus also on this March 2nd of 1943 the comings and goings at the Benkener Schloss and at the restaurant 'Zum Ochsen' in the village itself were under official surveillance, supervised by the head of Basel's political police. Lützelschwab and his men had arrived in Benken in three unmarked police cars just minutes after the convoy had turned up the lane leading to the Benkener Schloss. Two of the police had been assigned to watching the restaurant; the rest had fanned out around the

Schloss, taking advantage of the cover provided by the surrounding forest.

There could be little doubt that Schellenberg and *his* men were aware that the local authorities were keeping a close eye on them, for subtlety was never one of the strong suits of the Swiss, nor finesse a distinguishing characteristic of that country's police force, as evidenced by the three black Citroëns they had been using to trail the Germans since four o'clock that afternoon. This may have explained the uncharacteristically leisurely attitude which the two Fallschirmjäger were demonstrating inside the 'Zum Ochsen' when Wilhelm Lützelschwab entered it around 8.30 on that evening of 2 March 1943: they felt sure that a protective screen had been erected around the SS general whose safety was their personal responsibility – all the more so because Hitler himself had expressed misgivings about General Schellenberg going to Switzerland at this time, fearing that Schellenberg could be kidnapped by the British, or for that matter by Swiss agents in the employ of the Americans. The Führer did not want to lose a second close confidant to the enemy, as had happened less than two years earlier in the case of his deputy and successor designate, Rudolf Hess,[26] who had flown solo to Scotland and then parachuted to earth near Glasgow on a mission that was eerily similar to that now being undertaken by Schellenberg, namely to establish contacts with influential people in the West who he imagined were in favour of a negotiated peace.[27] Be all that as it may, where the here and now was concerned it had been General Schellenberg himself who had personally and emphatically suggested that they undertake this little outing with the

---

26 See Bonjour, vol. V, p. 74. Professor Bonjour points out that an additional reason for Hitler's initial opposition to Schellenberg going to Switzerland was his fear that the Italians might get wind of it, and conclude that Germany and Switzerland were discussing the formation of a common Alpine defence line designed to frustrate any Allied invasion from the south – a move which would allow Germany to tell its Axis partner, Italy, that it would now have to fend for itself.

27 Chambers, F.P., Harris, C.P., Bayley, C.C., *This Age of Conflict, 1914 to the Present* (New York, 1950), p. 673.

ladies — 'to keep them busy', as he had put it, since he had serious work to do that evening.

Lützelschwab's purpose for entering the restaurant was two-fold. The first was to verify that the Basel members of the Rote Kapelle, most particularly their leader, Werner Lentz, were indeed inside. Their arrival in Benken had been observed by the local gendarme and duly passed on to Lützelschwab's headquarters an hour earlier. Since Lützelschwab had put the restaurant under surveillance immediately after arriving in Benken, there was little doubt in his mind that they must be still inside. Nevertheless, he wanted to be absolutely sure. He spotted Lentz immediately, and hurried to the back of the room before Lentz had an opportunity to see and most probably recognize him. He was shocked that he did not recognize either of the other two men sitting with Lentz. Lützelschwab had assumed upon hearing from the local constable that three men had entered the restaurant around 6.45 that he was referring to Lentz and his two local compatriots — the one who doubled as a bartender at the Three Kings Hotel, and the desk clerk at the Schweizerhof. If these other two were not here, then where were they? And, come to think of it, where was Lentz's van? And who were these two strangers? 'Dammit.' Lützelschwab swore under his breath. He had thought that he had this thing totally under control, and now . . .

The second reason for his appearance inside 'Zum Ochsen' was to check out what had just been reported to him by the sergeant in charge of maintaining a watch on the restaurant: that two men who appeared to be Schellenberg's Leibwächter had entered the inn a half-hour earlier. That was not surprising. What was unexpected was the further information that they had been in the company of two women . . . women of questionable origin. 'Zwai gueti Stück' were the words in the Alemannic dialect the sergeant had first used to describe them — 'two nice pieces' — which, switching to French, he had then upgraded to 'deux poules de luxe' . . . 'two high-class tarts'.

It had hardly required the eye of an eagle to spot the ladies in question. Clad as they were in their low-cut red and green frocks they could scarcely be mistaken for two of the local Swiss Hausfraus in their dowdy dresses buttoned up to the neck. Furthermore, it took no more than a cursory glance to conclude that their presence in Switzerland was in no way related to the secret mission the SS general was embarking upon in his country — Schellenberg was probably working on Colonel Masson up in the Schloss at that very moment. No, Lützelschwab concluded, these women were here for one purpose and one purpose only. And the Basel police chief who sat in the front pew of his Protestant church every Sunday, who was proud of the fact that he had never even thought of sleeping with any woman other than his wife, Bertha, was suddenly brimming with righteous indignation when faced with the unmistakable truth that an SS general had imported two undocumented aliens (for he was sure that not only did they not possess diplomatic passports, but they had no passports at all) onto Swiss soil for lewd purposes. For the briefest of moments he was tempted to walk out of the restaurant, withdraw his men, and simply let matters run their course. But the thought soon passed as he was approached by the Serviertochter — who, he concluded, was probably none other than the peasant girl his man had spotted in the Stadttheater the previous Sunday in the company of that Soviet spy who, he now realized, was sitting not more than a few metres away from the Nazis.

'Do you want to have dinner, sir?' she asked, and despite his lifelong loyalty to Bertha the policeman from Basel could not help but notice that she was a very attractive young lady. A bit plump, to be sure, but compared to Bertha . . .

'No,' he replied. 'In fact, I just came by for a quick beer. That's why I sat at a table back here.'

He was trying to remain as unobtrusive as possible, which was not easy for Lützelschwab, since he was very big for a Swiss — well over six feet tall and weighing in at 225 pounds. But any further curiosity about him on the part of the waitress disappeared when he ordered his Warteck beer 'temperiert', meaning that he wanted it to be warmed up before he drank it, a vulgar custom practised only by the uninteresting Swiss men.

'Unobtrusive' was hardly the word to describe the behaviour of the four Germans seated at their table in the restaurant's alcove, however: boisterous, raucous, in fact downright loud-mouthed would have been the more accurate adjectives. As a result, 'Typische Schwobe' – 'typical Germans' – was the phrase that now began making the rounds among the Swiss patrons in the restaurant. But this criticism had perhaps less to do with the decorum of the strangers in their midst than with their envy of the Germans' ability to have a good time. Because having a good time they certainly were!

In the half-hour following their arrival, and before they had even ordered any food, they had already gone through three carafes of white wine. And the more they drank, the louder were the voices in which the two Fallschirmjäger told their jokes. The responses of the two Fräuleins, which came in the form of giggles and shrieks, became even shriller. To make matters even worse, every now and then the two hussies brazenly surveyed the other patrons in the restaurant in a manner which indicated that they could not care less what the local peasantry was thinking.

It was the beginning of a night that would be long remembered in the village of Benken.

The atmosphere in the dining-room of the Schloss which lay atop the hill overlooking that village could not have stood in greater contrast. There were six people at the table, all men, and all officers in their respective armies: four Swiss and two Germans. But the usual hearty comradeship which typifies get-togethers of military men, regardless of their nationality, was singularly absent: the mood could best be described as subdued, reserved, even restrained. It was as if acquaintances from those student days at the Gymnasium or the Universität had suddenly dropped dropped in after many years, creating a situation where both host and guest were struggling very hard to bridge the gap that had grown between them due to so much time apart. For despite the fact that Germany and Switzerland shared a common border stretching from France to Austria, meaning that for centuries many Swiss had lived, literally, within shouting distance of their

German neighbours (and had they shouted they would have understood each other perfectly, since the same Alemannic dialect, more or less, was spoken on both sides of that border), since the late summer of 1939 the two nations had lived totally apart. A steel curtain had been dropped between them. Normal intercourse had been reduced to zero, absolute zero. And while during these years the German people had become, perhaps, the most powerful on earth, conquering Europe from the Atlantic almost to the Urals without any outside help (that provided by the Italians being more of a hindrance than a help, as current events in North Africa were now proving), the Swiss had simply disappeared from history. They were a people who for over three and a half years now had been held captive in their own country, totally isolated from the mainstream of world events. The fact that two of their imprisoners now sat in their midst certainly added to the strain.

By the time the party of four in the restaurant below had finished their third carafe of white wine without even as yet ordering any food, the six men in the Schloss were already finishing the first course, Forellen blau, the blue trout coming from a stream that flowed through the grounds surrounding the Benkener Schloss into the Birsig River in the valley below. And the conversation had also moved on . . . to the Eastern front, deliberately moved there by Lieutenant Peter Burckhardt, in an effort to somewhat level the field they were playing on tonight by introducing the thought that their 'captors' were hardly invincible. For it was just over a month now since the Nazis had suffered their first major defeat when, on 31 January, Field Marshal Friedrich Paulus had surrendered his Sixth Army to the Russians at Stalingrad. When Colonel Masson, Burckhardt's boss, a professional soldier who was a graduate of France's military academy, tried to press General Schellenberg on details of the current military situation in Russia, it soon became apparent that the SS general was not really informed, that his vague answers were not a result of his being coy, but rather due to his inability to intelligently discuss military tactics and strategies with a professional in that field. The conclusion which he drew from the military fiasco at Stalingrad, and now shared with the five other officers sitting at the dinner table, showed beyond any doubt what kind of a general Walter Schellenberg was: a political general.

'Stalingrad,' he now stated, 'is precisely one of the main reasons why I am here this evening, meine Herren. The military catastrophe that occurred there, and no one is denying that it was just that, a catastrophe, has served to further emphasize a truth that is now inescapable: the enemy of *all* of us who are seeking to preserve our common European culture are the Bolsheviks. Should the Russian barbarians be allowed to overrun Europe, it would be the end of the Abendland as we know and love it.

'We Germans stand ready to defend Europe to the death.' Then he added: 'All that we ask is that as we do so, others who share our European heritage are not yet again preparing to stab us in the back.'

The 'back' he was referring to was Germany's southern flank, and the 'stabbing', a dagger-thrust that would come from or, more accurately, through Switzerland.

This all grew clear when Schellenberg became even blunter: 'As you know, Colonel Masson, we are in possession of certain documents which our army managed to seize at La Charité-sur-Loire in 1940 that are very damaging where your nation's claim of strict neutrality in this conflict is concerned. As you know, the person who was most compromised was your commander-in-chief, General Guisan.'

What Schellenberg was referring to here were protocols of a totally secret military pact which had been worked out between General Guisan and the General Staff of the French army which were discovered in a railroad car full of highly sensitive French government files. They were obviously being transported to some hiding place when, inexplicably, that railroad car was left abandoned in a siding in the village of La Charité-sur-Loire, 150 kilometres west of Dijon, where it was discovered by the advancing German troops on 16 June 1940 during their Blitzkrieg attack on France. These protocols fully documented the astonishing fact that Franco-Swiss joint military planning had begun as early as

October 1939, immediately after the outbreak of World War II, and that by late November precise details of a joint military response to a German attack had already been worked out.

Phase One would have involved a massive artillery barrage directed against the invading Germans in the region of Basel by the Swiss army. Phase Two would begin three to four hours after the Swiss artillery (which would fire from their fixed positions in concrete bunkers in the hills around Basel overlooking the German–Swiss border) had begun their barrage and would be triggered by the Swiss High Command granting permission to the French military to cross the border. It was foreseen that a full French division would then move through Switzerland and begin its counterattack on the Germans from a totally unexpected direction – from the *south*. This tactic would allow the French to make an end run around the fixed East–West lines of defence which had been built up along both sides of the Maginot Line. In Phase 3 the entire Eighth French army would engage the enemy, as would the Swiss army, under joint French–Swiss command. The total evacuation of the city of Basel was foreseen, since it would be right in the middle of the war zone. In the early months of 1940, the units of the French army which were to be thus deployed had been moved into the southernmost region of the province of Alsace. Ironically, the route they would have taken over 'neutral' Swiss soil in their march to join battle with the German Wehrmacht would have been through Biel/Benken and then down the Birsig Valley to and then beyond Basel, following the same path – but in the opposite direction – that Schellenberg and his entourage had just taken from the German–Swiss frontier.[28]

But it never happened that way.

For on 17 May 1940, three days after the Dutch had surrendered and Sedan had fallen to the advancing German army, the

---

28 For a full history of this episode, see Bonjour, vol. V, pp. 12ff. Bonjour had to rely completely on German sources, since all Swiss documentation of these negotiations was destroyed in 1940 on orders of General Guisan. Bonjour's repeated attempts to gain access to any of the original French documentation were rebuffed by the French government.

army, the Eighth French army that had stood poised near the French–Swiss frontier ready to intervene was withdrawn under orders to do so 'as secretly as possible'.[29] A few battalions were left in place so that the Swiss would not immediately notice what was going on. The Swiss army, particularly General Guisan, was never informed.

Thus the heroic French military had lived up to its reputation once again, this time leaving the Swiss in the lurch. Which, of itself, would have been bad enough where the Swiss military leaders were concerned. But now, to be confronted with these highly secret and extremely dangerous revelations based upon fully documented facts *on Swiss soil* by a general in the SS, and in front of Swiss officers of lesser rank, who, of course, had no knowledge of any of this – that was too much for Colonel Masson . . . especially when Walter Schellenberg now said: 'Unless I can convince the Führer that similar plans are not now being made between your General Guisan and the Americans and British, allowing the Allies entry onto and free passage through Swiss territory for the purpose of attacking Germany from the south, I am afraid that he will proceed with a preemptive attack – and soon.'[30]

There it was right out in the open: the spectre of 'Aktion Schweiz'!

When Schellenberg had completed his ultimatum, Masson signalled to Lieutenant Peter Burckhardt – and that signal must

---

29 See Bonjour, vol. V, p. 16.

30 According to the then secretary of state of the Third Reich, Ernst von Weizsäcker, when Hitler received a full report on the documents found at La Charité-sur-Loire in the fall of 1940 it only served to further increase his highly developed animosity where Switzerland was concerned. This prompted Weizsäcker as well as Admiral Canaris, who was in charge of German military intelligence (both men being friends of Switzerland and anti-Hitler), to inform Swiss Intelligence that these documents had fallen into Nazi hands, and to warn them about the military consequences which might follow any further provocation of the Führer were the Swiss to be again caught compromising their neutrality through any future cooperation with the Allies. See *Ernst von Weizsäcker: Erinnerungen* (Munich, 1950), edited by his son Richard, pp. 301ff.

have been prearranged, since it prompted Burckhardt to abruptly rise to his feet and suggest that his fellow staff officers and Rittmeister Eggen retire for dessert and coffee in the library. As one man they immediately rose, and after appropriate murmurs and gestures to their respective commanding officers, left the dining-room.

Once they were alone, Colonel Masson turned to General Schellenberg and said: 'Now let us talk soldier to soldier, Herr General,' implying that these matters had become much too serious to be left to the political leaders.[31] The first thing I want to now tell you is that General Guisan is prepared to meet with you tomorrow in order to personally give you his assurances that, despite any conclusions your government may have drawn from those documents found at La Charité-sur-Loire, this nation and this nation's army intend to maintain absolutely strict neutrality in its relations with *all* warring parties. *All!*'

'I am grateful that this meeting could be arranged, Colonel Masson,' Schellenberg responded, 'because I am sure that you must be aware of my deepest admiration for your country, and my sympathy for the plight in which you currently find yourselves. You can rest assured that I will do all in my power to convince the Führer that he has been misinformed concerning the *current* attitude and intentions of the Swiss military, and that it would be extremely imprudent to proceed with "Aktion Schweiz".'

When he used that term he could not help but notice the reaction on Colonel Masson's face. 'I see you are acquainted with that codename, my dear colleague . . . despite the fact that it has been categorized as top-secret in Berlin. My congratulations.'

Having just demonstrated how easy it was to trap his Swiss counterpart into revealing that his intelligence organization had a direct line to the innermost circle of the Nazi High Command in Berlin, Schellenberg then began to apply additional pressure.

'But if I am to help you and your nation, Colonel Masson, I am

---

31 This is the exact phrase, 'er wolle als Soldat zum Soldat reden', which Masson used vis-à-vis Schellenberg. See Bonjour, vol. V, p. 72.

going to have to return to Berlin with certain items in hand. I must have a written statement, written and personally signed by your commander-in-chief, stating unequivocally that this nation and its army intends to remain neutral, in the strictest sense of that word, for the duration of this war.'

To Schellenberg's surprise, Masson immediately nodded his agreement. Thus encouraged, the German general continued. 'Now, and this hardly need concern your General Guisan, there are certain concessions in the realms of industry and finance that must also be agreed to if I am to convince our Führer of your nation's good intentions. First, there is a matter of our gold shipments to your National Bank, a matter in which I have a personal interest, since, as you know dear colleague, in order to finance some of my operations abroad I have a continuing need for hard currencies.'

What Schellenberg failed to mention was that he maintained a large espionage network in Switzerland, using Swiss nationals sympathetic to the Nazi cause but, being Swiss, not so sympathetic that they were willing to risk their necks for nothing, nor willing to accept payment in any other currency than the world's hardest, the Swiss franc. Ironically, the source of those Swiss francs was the Swiss National Bank!

'Then there is the vital issue of our rights of transit through the Gotthard tunnel. We cannot tolerate any backsliding on our agreements in this respect, especially now when an Allied landing in Italy appears imminent. The tonnage must, in fact, be increased and . . .'

While Schellenberg droned on in the dining-room of the Bonkener Schloss, Peter Burckhardt now found himself alone with Schellenberg's adjutant, Rittmeister Eggen, in his study on the second floor . . . alone because the SS major had insisted on it, suggesting that the junior officers who had left the dining-room with them take their dessert and coffee elsewhere. The reason for this insistence became immediately obvious.

'I understand,' Eggen began, 'that your father is chairman of the Swiss Bank Corporation.'

'Indeed he is,' Peter Burckhardt responded.

'I have never had the pleasure of meeting him, although we have done business with his bank. As you may know, I have been involved with some major business transactions between our two countries, the most recent involving the importation of pre-fabricated wooden army barracks made here in Switzerland. Our Swiss partner in this business is a firm by the name of Extroc S.A., domiciled in Lausanne. Since the name "Guisan" came up more than a few times this evening, it might interest you to know that General Guisan's son is one of the directors of Extroc.'

Major Eggen paused here, no doubt to provide a moment for that last little bit of information to sink in. For Eggen was certain that having Colonel Guisan, the general's son, as a reference automatically elevated him to a privileged status in this country, especially where the Swiss elite were concerned, and there was no doubt in his mind that the Burckhardts of Basel were as blue-blooded as they came in this land that was mostly populated by descendants of cowherds. But if he had expected that this name-dropping would produce some immediate magic effect, Eggen was disappointed. For the young Burckhardt just sat there, not saying a word, waiting for him to come to the point . . . sure that it would come very soon. And it did.

'The reason I wanted to see you in private, Herr Doktor,' Eggen now continued, showing that he was aware of Burck-hardt's academic credentials and appreciated them, 'is to discuss some new business that I have been asked to offer to your country. Not business in the sense of army barracks, however; this time it involves pure finance. Banking. Banking in the classic Swiss sense. One that requires the type of discretion that can only be found in your country, since bank secrecy here is backed up by law . . . and by severe sanctions if these bank secrecy laws are broken. I am talking about deposits. Large deposits. In hard currencies. If necessary in non-interest-bearing accounts.'

Again he paused to let all this sink in . . . as if it were necessary!

Then Eggen went on: 'From the very outset I want to point out that those persons who have asked me to act as intermediary on their behalf in this matter are fully aware of the fact that in these troubled times it goes without saying that access to such protection is a privilege which is hardly automatically extended to all. Especially where foreigners are concerned. However, I can also say that it goes without saying, Herr Doktor, that should I succeed in bringing this very limited number of new private clients to, say, your father's bank, they would be more than willing to discuss, no, to *offer* reciprocity. That such reciprocity may take on unusual forms is also fully understood since, as I just mentioned, these are indeed troubled times for us *all*. And if we do not help each other out, each in our own way, who will?'[32]

The offer could hardly have been presented more bluntly. And it was an offer that could hardly be rejected out of hand. In fact, the more Peter Burckhardt thought about it, the more it became apparent that it was an offer that could not be refused.

'I cannot speak on behalf of my father or his bank, as you must realize, Herr Major,' he began, speaking slowly and carefully choosing his words. 'Nevertheless I can assure you, as one professional to another,' and this time it was Burckhardt who paused to allow the import of these last words to sink in, 'that this matter interests me. So much so that I am willing to take the matter up with my father immediately. Tomorrow, in fact. But knowing him as well as I do, I can assure you that he will require further information before he would agree even in principle. As

---

32 Bonjour confirms that Eggen was deeply involved in secret financial transactions in Switzerland on behalf of Nazis. 'Unter Schellenbergs Schutze konnte sein Adjutant versteckterweise Nazigelder in die Schweiz verschieben und persönlich lukrative Geschäfte machen.' Vol. V. p. 89. That there was a connection between these financial deals and intelligence activities benefiting Switzerland was revealed in a letter from Swiss Federal Councillor and Minister of Justice, Eduard von Steiger, to the Generalstabschef of the Swiss army, Jacob Huber, dated 20 December 1944: 'Man weiss nie was nun bei Eggen die Hauptsache ist, sein Nachrichtendienst gegen die Schweiz, seine privaten Geldgeschäfte oder seine Tätigkeit im Nachrichtendienst zugunsten der Schweiz.' Translation: 'One never knows with Eggen whether his principal interest lies in spying on Switzerland, his private financial transactions, or his intelligence activities on behalf of Switzerland.' Ibid., p. 90.

you yourself just said, the protection of Swiss bank secrecy is hardly automatically granted to all comers. And contrary to the mythology which has developed in regard to the use of numbered accounts in Swiss banks, and it *is* true that they represent the key safeguard where privacy is concerned, Swiss banks — *responsible* Swiss banks, and you can certainly count my father's bank as such, which is one of the reasons it is today Switzerland's largest — *must* know the true identity of its clients. That identity is made known to two executives of the bank, and two executives only, from the time the account is opened until it is closed. Where everybody else within the bank is concerned — from tellers to secretaries to auditors — that account and all transactions made through it are identified only by a number. And I can assure you, Herr Major, that since 1934, when criminal penalties were attached to any violation of our bank secrecy laws, no serious penetration of the system has ever occurred. I trust that your clients are familiar with all this?'

Whether they were or not, Waffen SS Major Rittmeister Eggen nevertheless nodded his head affirmatively.

'Then might I suggest that this entire matter could be expedited were it possible for you to more closely identify one or two of the potential bank clients on whose behalf you are acting. Now I hasten to add that you have my solemn word as a fellow officer that such information will remain totally confidential, and that I will pass it on to one person and one person only, my father.' Peter Burckhardt meant it and Eggen knew that he meant it.

Eggen then reached into the inside breast pocket of his jacket and removed a small notebook and a pen. He wrote three names on one of the pages, ripped it out, and handed it to Burckhardt. After Burckhardt had read the three names — Schellenberg, Bormann and the initial H — Eggen again reached out his hand to retrieve the paper. 'Where the third party is concerned, I think it would be wise if he had the protection of *both* the number and a pseudonym. And I think it should also be said that he would hardly have anything to do with any "reciprocity" that might be forthcoming as a result of these financial arrangements.'

Then he asked: 'Do you perhaps have an ashtray?' Burckhardt

went over to his desk and returned with a large crystal one. After he had handed it to Eggen, the German officer withdrew a small box of wooden matches from the side pocket of his jacket, withdrew one, lighted it, and then watched the small piece of paper as it burned in the ashtray. Then he took the ashes and, very nonchalantly, put them and the box of matches back into the pocket of his jacket.

While Eggen was going through all this Burckhardt was trying to think fast, for he knew full well that his father and his bank would not even consider taking the men on Eggen's short list as clients — well, on reflection maybe Schellenberg, but not the other two, especially 'H'![33] But there was a bank right across the

---

33 The 'H' which Eggen had so mysteriously listed was *not* Hitler, although there can be no doubt that he was not averse to leaving that impression. Rather, as it later turned out, it was Heinrich Himmler, the head of the SS. According to no less an authority than General Guisan's son (see Braunschweig, *Geheimer Draht nach Berlin*, p. 179), Eggen had a close relationship with Himmler and, no doubt, as the man responsible for SS procurements in Switzerland, shared with him some of the profits resulting from the SS major's dubious business deals there — that share being deposited in Swiss francs in Swiss banks.

Whether Hitler had accounts in Switzerland has never been proven, in spite of reports such as that which appeared in the *Weltwoche* of 15 March 1990 (the *Weltwoche* being Switzerland's equivalent of *Time* magazine) to the effect that Hitler had deposits of over 1 million Swiss francs in three different accounts in Switzerland, using a false name. This was reported as early as 12 July 1945 by London's *Evening Standard* and then, somehow, forgotten or buried. The reason for this could well be due to the fact that the bank where these deposits were made was in the highest probability the Basler Handelsbank, one that specialized in German business. As a result it failed shortly after the war and was liquidated under Swiss government supervision. No doubt all records which could be potentially damaging to Swiss national interests were destroyed in the process, just as all documents relating to the Swiss—French military pact of 1939/40 were destroyed under direct orders of General Guisan. In both instances the Swiss again proved that they are past masters at revising history in their favour by simply destroying any damaging historical evidence.

In recent times, they have been less successful in doing so, however. In the second half of the 1980s alone, it became known that at least five of the worst of the post-World War II dictators had, collectively, deposited *billions* in Swiss banks: Marcos of the Philippines, Duvalier of Haiti, Noriega of Panama, the Ceausescus of Romania, and Honecker of East Germany.

street from the headquarters of the Swiss Bank Corporation — the Basler Handelsbank — which specialized in German business, loans and deposits. In fact, the bank's exposure in Germany was so great that there were whispers among the innermost circle of bankers in Basel that if the tide of war continued to turn against Germany, that country, those loans, and thus the Basler Handelsbank could end up in deep trouble. Which would be all the more reason for them to accept new deposits now, no matter from where or from whom.

'Well?' the SS major now asked.

'I think something can be arranged,' Burckhardt replied.

And with that he rose and went to fetch a decanter of port, two glasses and two cigars. He would obviously have to pass a good deal more time with this scum from the SS, and he might as well try to make it as painless as possible.

Chapter 19

At ten o'clock on that evening of 2 March 1943, the discussions in both the dining-room and study of the Benkener Schloss ended simultaneously.

In the interim, Colonel Masson and General Walter Schellenberg had agreed on the agenda which would be followed the next day during Schellenberg's meeting with the Swiss commander-in-chief, General Guisan. In keeping with the desire of both parties to avoid any publicity, that meeting would also take place in an obscure Swiss village, Biglen, situated in the canton of Bern. The venue there would be a restaurant – the back room of the restaurant 'Bären'. They were expected to arrive at twelve noon, and since it was about a two-hour drive from Benken, Masson suggested that perhaps they should adjourn for the evening.

The Swiss colonel and the German general then went to the study on the second floor to inform their host, Peter Burckhardt, that they were both retiring for the night. To Burckhardt's enormous relief, SS Major Rittmeister Eggen announced his intention to do the same. So after another series of bows and heel clicks, the two Nazi visitors disappeared out into the second-floor corridor of the Benkener Schloss and proceeded to their respective bedrooms. Masson soon did the same, leaving Peter Burckhardt alone in his study, where he decided to sit in the dark for a while and watch the fire burn down while enjoying a last glass of port and one more of Havana's best.

*

Down in the village below, events that evening had been considerably more boisterous and the amount of alcohol consumed considerably higher. Where noise and alcohol were concerned, the table occupied by the four visitors from Berlin was out in front of all others in the restaurant by margins which were quite substantial: at least 40 decibels where the average noise level was concerned, and a full litre and a half in terms of wine consumed. By ten o'clock, therefore, the two Fallschirmjäger and their two Fräuleins were pleasantly drunk.

At the table adjacent to theirs, Igor Scitovsky and his two colleagues from Lausanne had been much more judicious in their drinking as they sat there, nursing a few beers and then a series of coffees, biding their time, waiting, as the rest of the restaurant gradually emptied. For the final element in his plan of attack had fallen into place in Scitovsky's mind as he observed the behaviour of the Germans next door: all that its implementation now required was an opening.

That opening arrived very suddenly. It began with a totally unrelated event – unrelated, however, only in the immediate sense. Herr Doktor Wilhelm Lützelschwab, like the local delegation from the Rote Kapelle, had also been forced to play the waiting game. And, like them, he too had moved on from beer to coffee as the evening progressed. By ten o'clock this had led to a desperate need to seek relief, and so he left for the toilet, situated down a corridor in the rear of the restaurant. At precisely this moment, one of the German paratroopers called for his bill, and Liselotte Maurer went behind the bar to fetch it. Scitovsky immediately rose from his table, and his two colleagues automatically did likewise, and then followed him as, like Lützelschwab just moments earlier, he headed toward the rear of the restaurant. But instead of entering the corridor which led to the rest rooms, he stopped at the end of the bar and addressed no more than half a dozen words to Liselotte, who was bent over behind it, adding up the Germans' tab for the night. She stopped what she was doing, walked quickly to the door leading to the kitchen, and pushed it open for Scitovsky and his colleagues. As if nothing out of the ordinary was going on, she then went back behind the bar, finished her calculations and rushed to present the bill to the taller of the German men, who was by now waiting impatiently just inside the front entrance: the other three Germans had already walked out. He glanced at it in the most cursory fashion, took out his wallet, extracted a 100-franc note and handed it to Liselotte with a bow.

'Vielen Dank, gnädiges Fräulein,' he said, and disappeared out of the front door in the wake of the other three, leaving Liselotte with the change and thus the largest tip she had ever received in her life.

Dr Lützelschwab emerged from the men's room just in time to witness this scene, and, without even sitting down at his table it was he who now called out to Liselotte for the check. His was already prepared and in Liselotte's apron pocket, so she went right over to him. He studied it, handed Liselotte a ten-franc note, and then likewise headed for the front door of the restaurant, also leaving Liselotte with the change, which in this case amounted to 25 centimes and represented one of the smallest tips she had received in recent memory.

Lützelschwab was halfway through the front door when he stopped short and looked back. *Both* tables in the alcove of the restaurant were now completely vacant, as was the rest of the dining-room, meaning that Scitovsky and his two men must have left the restaurant immediately in front of the Germans. The Swiss policeman then plunged out into the night and hurried past the four Germans, who were standing in front of the restaurant involved in a loud discussion. None of them took any notice of him whatsoever. And the three men who had been sitting at the table next to the Germans all evening? Once onto the road in front of the restaurant Lützelschwab frantically looked in all directions for them. Not a trace.

They had simply disappeared.

In fact, they were sitting at a table in the kitchen of that restaurant, waiting for Liselotte Maurer to join them. And she did so almost immediately. A few minutes after that, the back door to the kitchen opened and in came two young women about Liselotte's age. After they had taken off their coats Scitovsky/

Lentz, with growing certitude that things were going his way, noticed that both were dressed in the black and white uniforms worn by maids. Liselotte immediately brought them over to the communal kitchen table and introduced them to her now-back-in-favour boyfriend from Basel, Werner Lentz. One, it seemed, was Liselotte's best friend, Hilde, who had gone to school in Benken with Liselotte and who sometimes helped out at the Schloss when there was a big do there. The other girl was her cousin Heidi, who was a full-time maid with the older Burckhardt's family in Riehen. She had come out to Benken by train with the other maids that afternoon, but now that dinner was over and her help no longer required, instead of spending the night with the rest of the maids up in the Schloss, Heidi was going to spend it with her cousin in the village. This all took a long time for Liselotte to explain, but Werner Lentz managed to keep himself under control, feigning eager interest in every word until, finally, he was able to break in.

'I understand,' he began, addressing his words to Heidi, 'that you are entertaining a very important person up there tonight.' He used the German expression 'ein grosses Tier'.

'Ja,' Heidi answered, 'a general. And I was responsible for his rooms. He even spoke to me. In high German. He seemed to be a real gentleman, in spite of being a German.'

'What kind of rooms would they be? I mean, for a person like that they must be something special.'

'He's in what Frau Doktor Burckhardt calls the "blue suite", because the wallpaper and all are blue.' And then she turned to Liselotte. 'You know it, Liselotte. Remember last summer when Hilde and I managed to sneak you into the Schloss through the back door and then up the back stairs? It's right at the top of those stairs on the left – the one with the huge Himmelbett.'

Liselotte now nodded her head. She definitely remembered the Himmelbett.

And then Heidi continued in a very low voice. 'That's why the general spoke to me. While I was turning down the bed for him this evening, just fifteen minutes ago, he came into the bedroom and asked me to bring two additional pillows.' Now she turned to address her fellow maid, Hilde. 'I think that one of those Fräuleins who are supposed to be staying together in the pink room might be paying him a little visit later on tonight. Maybe both! In the Himmelbett!' And then all three girls broke out into loud giggles.

Werner Lentz now knew everything he needed to know.

A minute later, after a short whispered conversation with Liselotte at the back door of the restaurant, Lentz and his two comrades slipped out of that door and into the darkness. The moon had disappeared, and a cold drizzle had begun to set in.

The drizzle was the reason why the two German Fräuleins, Hannelore and Marlene, after stepping outside the restaurant, had resolutely refused to take the path through the forest as they had done earlier in the evening at the suggestion of Peter Burckhardt. Maybe Swiss Mädchen liked that sort of thing, but for them once − downhill − had been enough. After all, they were girls from Berlin! Since their two male companions had by now broken into song − 'Trink, trink, Brüderlein trink' − it took a bit of shouting before they got the message across, but in the end they succeeded. A few minutes later, leaving the two girls from Berlin huddled in the doorway of the restaurant, Major Göhler and his fellow officer began trotting up the hill to get one of the BMWs, and it was a fairly fast trot since, as paratroopers, they were in top condition.

All this noise and coming and going had left Lützelschwab's surveillance team in a state of disarray. And so it was relatively easy for Scitovsky and his two foot soldiers to slip into the forest after leaving the restaurant through the back door of the kitchen.

Lützelschwab now had no choice but to rethink his entire strategy. As he stood in silence in the darkness across the road from the restaurant, joined now by the sergeant he had charged with keeping an eye on any and all activities in the village of

Benken, he had to admit to himself that he was in trouble . . .
that he might have made a strategic error in dealing with this
entire situation. For days he had had the option of simply moving
in on the house in Rheingasse 37, taking Lentz into custody, and
effectively and very quietly closing down the Rote Kapelle's
operations in Basel at the source. But, and perhaps this was just
rationalization in view of what was now happening, that would
have left an unknown number of Lentz's co-conspirators still free,
and more or less in the clear. He had wanted to catch them all
red-handed, and in the process teach Colonel Masson and the
faction he represented within the Swiss military that they had
been playing with fire by bringing a high-ranking Nazi onto Swiss
territory. In one respect at least he had been proved right, namely
in suspecting that there were more active members of the local
Communist cell than those who had been identified during the
weeks of constant surveillance of the house at Rheingasse 37 by
his political police, as evidenced this evening by two complete
unknowns showing up at Lentz's table.

But now all of them, knowns and unknowns alike, had
somehow eluded him. He had been sure that Lentz and his two
cohorts had left the restaurant immediately before the Germans.
But when he had checked with the sergeant in charge of surveillance, he had been assured that it simply had not happened that
way. What about the back? Well, the man he had stationed there
had momentarily left his post to see what all the noise was about
in front of the restaurant. He had felt that his help might be
needed.

Then it struck Lützelschwab: that stupid peasant girl! She'd let
them out the back way in the middle of all the turmoil in front of
the restaurant. And by now they were probably halfway through
the forest on their way up to the Schloss – and Schellenberg. To
be sure, he had six men up there on the periphery of the clearing
in the forest which surrounded the Schloss. But the Schloss
was big and the night now dark. And after a phone call to
his counterpart in Geneva earlier that evening, he now knew
that Lentz was in reality an NKGB man, known by the Geneva
cell of the Rote Kapelle as Colonel Scitovsky. The Russian was

205

obviously on his way home to a hero's welcome – provided he succeeded in this one last job on Swiss soil.

Lützelschwab now decided to radically change tactics. Speaking in a very low voice he addressed the sergeant at his side: 'I'm going into the restaurant through the back door.' He did not explain why. 'I can only assume that the two Germans have gone to fetch a car to take the ladies back up to the Schloss. If and when that happens, we are all going up after them.'

'On foot, sir?'

'No, by car.'

'But . . .'

'The plans have changed. I believe that at least three members of that Communist cell are in the forest right now, working their way up towards the Schloss. And there are probably others that were planted in the forest earlier this evening who will join them. I'm going to make one last attempt to surprise them in the act. If it doesn't work, or doesn't work completely, then we are going to break our cover and openly go after them . . . or what's left of them. Get your men who are down here ready. There's no time left now to alert our men up at the Schloss without alerting the enemy. And after all this, Sergeant, I'll be damned if I'm going to let them get away.'

Then both the sergeant and Lützelschwab moved off into the darkness . . . though in opposite directions. Lützelschwab ran 100 metres down the road on the side opposite the 'Zum Ochsen', then very carefully crossed it and circled back through the pasture behind the three houses immediately adjacent to the restaurant, an open space which separated all the buildings there from the forest beyond. When he opened the back door of the restaurant and burst into the kitchen, the sudden appearance of this huge man in a dark trenchcoat with a fierce scowl on his face prompted two of the three girls sitting at the communal table there to let out shrill shrieks of terror. But not Liselotte. Instead she went right for the butcher table and was about to pick up the largest knife there when Lützelschwab grabbed her arm and simultaneously hissed: 'Quiet! All of you!' And then, directly addressing Liselotte who was now firmly in his grasp, 'Is your name Liselotte Maurer?'

She just nodded, as the tears started to pour down her chubby cheeks.

'You stupid little goose! You had those three men back here, didn't you? Lentz and his two friends.'

Again she nodded.

'When did they leave?'

She just sobbed. So Lützelschwab really applied the pressure on her right arm while saying: 'Enough of that, young lady. Now listen to me. I am with the Basel police and here on official duty. Any more of your hysteria and I'll take you outside, put you in one of our cars, and have you taken to the Lohnhof in Basel where you will spend the rest of the night.'

That did it. Everybody who lived in the region surrounding Basel knew about the jail there known as the Lohnhof, a prison which resembled a dank medieval monastery . . . but with none of its comforts. So the sobbing stopped immediately, and Liselotte Maurer suddenly managed to find her voice.

'No more than ten minutes ago, sir,' she said.

'And where were they headed?'

'I don't know, sir. But Werner — Herr Lentz — said that he would be back in less than an hour. That I should wait for him here.'

His fall-back position, Lützelschwab thought. 'Now one more thing — these two girls here,' and now he let go of Liselotte's arm, 'they're maids from up there, aren't they?'

'Yes, sir.'

'Did Lentz talk to them?'

'Yes, sir. About the general who's up there.'

That did it.

'Where's the telephone?'

'Inside the restaurant. Behind the bar.'

'Show me.'

After she had done so, he said: 'Now I want you back in the kitchen, where you and the other two girls are going to stay until I tell you differently. Understood?'

She nodded, let out one last stifled sob, and then disappeared back into the kitchen.

207

Lützelschwab now picked up the receiver from the wall phone and dialled 11 for information.

'Benkener Schloss,' he said when the operator answered.

A pause. 'We do not have such a listing.'

'Verdammt nochmal,' he swore. Then: 'Try Burckhardt . . . with a "ck" and a "dt" . . . in Benken.'

Five seconds later: '42-13-81.'

He hung up without another word and dialled the number. It rang only twice, and then a man answered in a low voice: 'Burckhardt.'

'Is that *Peter* Burckhardt?' Lützelschwab demanded.

'Who is this? Don't you realize what time it is?'

'This is Wilhelm Lützelschwab and I want you to listen to me very carefully. I'm calling you from the restaurant "Zum Ochsen". I know that you've got Schellenberg up there in the Schloss. There are at least three men, no doubt very heavily armed by now, on their way up to kill him. All are connected with the local cell of the Rote Kapelle.'

Suddenly there was the sound of an automobile braking outside the restaurant.

'Hold on!' Lützelschwab exclaimed, adding: 'And don't even think of hanging up!'

Leaving the receiver dangling from the wall-mounted phone, he ran to the front window of the restaurant, arriving there just in time to see the two German Fräuleins getting into the Germans' BMW. Seconds later he was back on the phone. 'They are led by a major in the NKGB. I strongly suspect that within no more than five minutes – *five minutes*, Burckhardt – they are going to try to get in through the back door, and then head up the back stairs to the blue suite to kill Schellenberg. I've got men up there, but I can't get to them in time. And I fear that their attention is about to be diverted. So Peter, it's up to you. My advice: shoot to kill.'

'I understand,' Burckhardt replied. Then the line went dead.

After he had hung up the phone, Peter Burckhardt hurried out of his study to his bedroom, directly across the hall. Once inside, he went straight to the closet and reached down into the left corner, where he kept a 'Bergman' Maschinenpistol, a 7.36 calibre Mauser made in Switzerland by Schweizerische Industriegesellschaft in Neuhausen, one of Europe's leading arms manufacturers. It was an experimental weapon, and the limited number which had been made thus far for the Swiss army had been issued only to a select number of officers attached to special forces such as Burckhardt's unit. He then retrieved three clips of ammunition from the closet (due to the experimental nature of this Maschinenpistol, the ammunition was not yet manufactured in Switzerland, but imported from Germany, where it was made by the Deutsche Waffen- und Munitionsfabrik in the Ruhr), snapped one in place, and stuck the other two under his belt beneath his jacket.

Then he ran out of the door of his bedroom and down the hall to the head of the stairs at the rear of the Schloss, the 'back stairs' which led up from the kitchen and servants' quarters which were located adjacent to the kitchen on the ground floor. There he stopped. And listened. It was dead silent. He could see light coming from the door on his immediate right — the one which led into the rooms which his mother insisted upon calling the 'blue suite'. Schellenberg must still be awake.

Then, at first very faintly, the noise began, and it came from outside, through the open window at the end of the hall. Seconds later, as it grew in intensity, the source became obvious: the engine of a high-powered car which was coming up the lane from the village below. The squealing of tyres was soon heard above the roar of the engine. Somebody was pushing the automobile to the limit.

'It's them!' was the immediate thought that entered Burckhardt's mind. Somehow the men from the Rote Kapelle had got by Lützelschwab's men below and were mounting a frontal attack on the Schloss! His next thought was to simply burst into Schellenberg's rooms in order to warn him to take cover. But that impulse was instantaneously suppressed when Burckhardt recalled what Lützelschwab had just told him on the phone . . . that the men he had stationed up near the Schloss were 'about to be diverted'. And Burckhardt had no doubt that by now this had already occurred; that Lützelschwab's men had abandoned their earlier lookout positions around the Schloss and were moving to counter the frontal assault that was now so obviously under way.

Meaning that it was already too late to involve Schellenberg. He might just decide to put himself in the line of fire. He was better off in his bedroom, even if they knew where that was.

Burckhardt then swiftly descended the back stairs of the Schloss to the kitchen below. It lay in total darkness. He knelt behind the massive wooden table which stood in the centre of the room, one which for centuries had been used for cutting and chopping and kneading by the cooks and their helpers.

And waited.

Ninety seconds later, the driver of the automobile which had been roaring up from the village slammed on the brakes and came to a screeching halt in front of the Benkener Schloss. Doors were slammed and voices, loud voices, soon joined by loud *angry* voices — no doubt those of Lützelschwab's men — were heard.

Ten seconds later the back door of the Benkener Schloss leading into the kitchen opened. And as a man entered, followed immediately by two others, Burckhardt yelled out: 'Halt! Oder ich schiesse!'

They did not stop as he had commanded. So he opened fire, using up the entire ammunition clip in one long burst. Although Burckhardt was not yet aware of it, Igor Scitovsky was killed instantly. One of the men behind him was hit in the chest and also dropped to the kitchen floor, barely alive and bleeding profusely. The third man was unscathed, and fled back through the door.

Burckhardt put a new clip into his Mauser, but maintained his cover behind the table until he was sure that no second wave of attackers had been held in reserve.

A minute later he heard more gunfire, and shortly after that a voice from right outside the kitchen door.

'This is Major von Göhler. I want everybody inside the room to identify themselves. Then I want somebody to turn on the light in there. Otherwise I'm going to come in firing.' The words were spoken in impeccable high German.

'Herr Major,' Burckhardt immediately answered, 'hier ist Peter Burckhardt. And I'm alone. Hold your fire. I'm going to turn on the light.'

When the light went on it revealed the German paratrooper standing poised in the doorway, a submachine gun at the ready. The first thing he did was check the status of the two men lying prone on the kitchen floor immediately in front of him. Neither showed any signs of life. But taking no chances, the German soldier stripped both of all weapons — tossing their guns one by one into the rear corner of the kitchen, and then taking the grenades from their belts and carefully carrying them to the table in the middle of the room and depositing them directly in front of Burckhardt, who remained standing on the other side.

'Where's Schellenberg?' von Göhler now asked.

Burckhardt, without turning his head, pointed his thumb in the direction of the back stairs. The German major now charged across the room and up those stairs.

The next thing Peter Burckhardt did after this brief interchange with the German bodyguard was to ensure that the door leading from the kitchen to the servants' quarters remained closed. To be absolutely sure, he bolted it. He wanted no maids wailing over the dead and wounded as a prelude to their spreading war stories through the village of Benken and later the entire city of Basel.

The next man to arrive through the back door of the Schloss was one of Lützelschwab's men, and he entered the kitchen, very, very carefully, with gun — this time a pistol — drawn. He first inspected the room, taking special note of the two bodies, and then addressed Burckhardt. 'You're Burckhardt. Right? And you're alone, except for these? Right?'

When Burckhardt nodded affirmatively, the policeman said: 'We just got the third one. And we're combing the forest for more.' Then he knelt down to assess the condition of the two men who were lying there.

'This one's dead,' he said after a brief examination of Scitovsky. And after taking the pulse and raising the eyelids of the second man, he added: 'And this one's dying.' Satisfied, he put away his pistol. 'One of our men is a medic. I'll get him in here right away.'

When he returned a few minutes later with the medic, they were accompanied by their boss. Lützelschwab, after a glance at the two bodies on the kitchen floor, went directly to Peter Burckhardt and shook his hand vigorously. 'Damn well done, Burckhardt.' Then: 'Where's Schellenberg?'

'I assume he's still in his rooms. Probably Eggen's with him. One of their bodyguards came through here, and then went up the stairs — to join them, I would think.'

'And Colonel Masson?'

As if on cue, the head of Section 5 appeared coming down the back stairs. When he saw Lützelschwab he was visibly startled, but ignoring him, addressed Peter Burckhardt. 'Is the situation under control, Lieutenant?'

'Yes, sir. Completely.'

'They were obviously after Schellenberg. Do you have any idea who they are?'

'Yes, sir. They're all members of the local cell of the Rote Kapelle. Dr Lützelschwab can explain it better than I can.'

'In a minute,' Masson answered, still avoiding even looking at Lützelschwab. 'Who are these men?' He pointed at the two policemen who were bent over the dying man who lay in front of the kitchen door.

'They're mine,' said Lützelschwab.

'Well tell them to get those two wounded men out of here. Immediately.'

'One's dead, sir,' Burckhardt interjected.

'All the more reason. I don't want Schellenberg to see this.'

Lützelschwab chose not to argue with Masson, and went over to his men to relay the order.

As he did so, Colonel Masson kept up his interrogation of Burckhardt. 'Who did the shooting?'

'I did, sir,' Burckhardt answered.

'How did you happen upon them?'

'I didn't. Dr Lützelschwab alerted me just in time. By phone, from the village.'

'Were just these two involved?'

'No, sir. There was a third one. Lützelschwab's men have got him.'

'Lützelschwab is going to have a lot of explaining to do,' Colonel Masson then said.

Peter Burckhardt mulled that one over for a few seconds. Then he said: 'May I suggest something, sir?'

'By all means. After all, you have been the host to all this.'

Ignoring the implied insult, Burckhardt plunged on. 'I think, sir, that we probably agree that it would be in everybody's interest if knowledge of this incident is very strictly contained.' He paused, and, taking Masson's silence as an indication of his agreement, went on: 'That will require Lützelschwab's full coop-eration.' Masson still said nothing. 'If you agree, sir, I'll have a word with him to that end. It may be necessary to invoke the name of General Guisan, and the meeting he will be having with Schellenberg tomorrow. In order to drive home the point that whether Lützelschwab likes it or not, our national security interests are at stake. With your permission, sir.'

'Hold on, Burckhardt. Lützelschwab obviously knew some-thing like this was being planned. Why, for God's sake, did he let it go so far?'

'Let's face it, sir. To embarrass you. But now we are in a position to more than embarrass him. If they had succeeded in killing Schellenberg, God knows how Hitler would have reacted. By the way, have you spoken with Schellenberg?'

'Very briefly.'

'How much does he know?'

'Hard to say. But I don't think he will be a problem. From the very beginning we have been in complete agreement on the necessity of keeping his presence here in Switzerland as secret as possible.'

'If you agree, I would like to have a word with that paratrooper major. Do I have your permission to approach him too? As with Lützelschwab?'

Masson chose not to answer that question. 'Where were those two German paratroopers all the time?'

'With the two Fräuleins. So my guess is that they would like to

213

forget this evening, in totality, as soon as possible.'

'All right. I'll have a brief word with Schellenberg and tell him that the incident is over and that you'll brief his Major von Göhler on the details. And then I'll suggest that we go back to bed. Where Lützelschwab is concerned, do what you feel is necessary. Just don't involve me.' Then the chief of the Swiss Intelligence Service disappeared up the back stairs.

In the meantime more of Lützelschwab's men had gathered in the kitchen. Minutes later they left, taking the two bodies with them. The second man, it seemed, had just died. After asking Burckhardt's permission, they also took the dead men's weapons and grenades.

When they were gone, Lützelschwab came back across the room to talk once more to Peter Burckhardt, who was now sitting behind the kitchen table, his submachine gun lying in front of him.

'If you agree, I'm going to leave five men here for the rest of the night. They'll be outside. Three in front and two in back. Just in case.'

This startled Burckhardt. 'Why?'

'We're still missing two members of the cell. One's driving a van. Probably been parked somewhere outside the village, waiting for his compatriots. When they don't show up, he'll move out. And we'll get him. We've set up road-blocks.'

'And the other one?'

Lützelschwab shrugged. 'No idea. Probably in Basel. We know who he is, so it will only be a matter of time. After all, he can hardly leave the country, can he?'

Lützelschwab then turned as if to leave, which prompted Burckhardt to say: 'Before you go, Herr Doktor, I would like to ask that we meet as soon as possible, preferably tomorrow morning, to discuss how we handle this incident.'

'What's to discuss? It's been handled.'

'You know what I mean.'

'All right. Nine o'clock. My office.'

'Ten.'

'All right.'

214

'By the way, what are you going to do with those two bodies?'

'What bodies?'

He'd already got the message, Burckhardt concluded.

Lüzelschwab, being Lützelschwab, then added: 'Which means that since nothing happened up here this evening, I'm no longer indebted to you for saving my skin. Right?' He grinned . . . and immediately left the Benkener Schloss through the back door.

Peter Burckhardt then suddenly remembered: Nancy Reichman! Dulles! And looked at his watch: 11 pm exactly.

When he reached the top of the back stairs on his way to the phone in his study, he was immediately challenged by Major von Göhler, as well as by one of the Swiss army lieutenants who had been charged with escorting the Germans during their secret mission to Switzerland. That the lieutenant knew that he had failed in the discharge of his duties was apparent from his ashen complexion, so when Burckhardt suggested that he spend the rest of the night in the kitchen below, armed and ready, he was off like a shot.

Burckhardt turned to the German paratrooper. 'Alles in Ordnung?' he asked. Then he heard the loud giggling of a girl – no, girls – from behind the door which led into the rooms of General Walter Schellenberg.

'In bester Ordnung,' the German replied, 'as you can no doubt hear. I assume that everything else is now under control?'

'It is.'

'Then could you, perhaps, spare a minute or two with me. *Alone*?'

'Certainly. In my study, just down the hall.'

'First I have to get my colleague to replace me on guard duty.'

'I'll wait.'

As soon as Göhler had returned with his fellow paratrooper, who now took over the watch in the corridor outside Schellenberg's door, he followed Peter Burckhardt into his study. Burckhardt immediately went to fetch two glasses and a bottle of cognac. He poured a more than generous portion into one of the glasses and offered it to the German officer. Then he did the same for himself. Both remained standing in front of the fireplace, where the dying embers were still radiating enough heat to keep the study comfortable despite the hour.

'I'll be blunt,' von Göhler began. 'I have given the general very few details of what happened tonight. Yet he seems to be under the impression that I played a key role in preventing his assassination.' He paused and took a good slug of cognac. 'Needless to say, my dear colleague, nothing could be further from the truth. In fact, if the truth comes out, I'm afraid it will provide me with excellent grounds for immediately seeking political asylum in Switzerland.' And he laughed.

Burckhardt took an immediate liking to the man. 'So what do you suggest we do in order to remedy the situation, and save both of us unnecessary embarrassment? After all, Herr Major, we have too many refugees here already.'

'Needless to say, I have the germ of an idea. But first I must ask you something. Those two dead men downstairs − were they not dining in the village inn earlier this evening?'

Burckhardt thought that one over, and, recalling that Lützelschwab's warning call had originated from the restaurant below, answered: 'Most probably, yes.'

'In fact, I am sure that they spent almost the entire evening at the table right next to ours. As you know, my colleague and I, along with the two ladies, also dined at the "Zum Ochsen" this evening, as you suggested we do.'

'I'm aware of that, yes.'

'Yes, indeed. Good food, by the way. And good wine. Needless to say, we perhaps enjoyed just a wee bit too much of the latter.'

'I understand.'

'Well, what I'm leading up to is this: would it be at all within the realms of possibility for you to not contradict me if I were to suggest to the general − perhaps *imply* would be the more apt verb − that it was I who became suspicious of the men at the table next to mine and, when they suddenly left, alerted you by telephone? Put you on guard, so to say. Allowing you − and you

216

alone, that will be stressed, dear colleague — to save my general from an early death at the hands of . . .' And then his voice fell off. When he continued it was with a question: 'Who *were* they, by the way?'

'Members of the local Soviet spy ring, led, I've been told, by an NKGB colonel.'

'Du lieber Gott! It was *that* serious?'

'I'm afraid so.'

'Could you perhaps spare a drop or two more of that cognac, dear colleague?'

Burckhardt poured him another glass, and said: 'Upon further reflection, I can now appreciate that when all this comes out it might, at a very minimum, mean that any promotion to colonel will become a very remote possibility where you are concerned, Herr Major.'

'Remote is hardly the word, my dear fellow.'

Burckhardt continued: 'May I ask you something which may seem a bit obtuse, but your name — von Göhler — am I correct in assuming that your family belongs to what we in the provinces of central Europe might regard as the Prussian landed aristocracy?'

'One could say that, yes.'

'Are you by any chance acquainted with the Kreisau Circle?'

'One might also say that, yes. But not out loud.'

'Well, back to our problem. I think I have what might prove to be a useful suggestion. How about this: I came down the stairs in the same moment that you burst in through the back door. We opened fire simultaneously and caught the intruders in our crossfire. You killed one, I killed the other.'

'How very chivalrous of you!'

'In fact,' Burckhardt continued, 'as far as I'm concerned, you can have them both.'

'No, no. *That* I could not agree to. It is *exceedingly* thoughtful of you, my dear colleague, but no. I think *one* will be more than sufficient.' Then: 'Which one did you have in mind?'

'The Russian.'

'You are generous to a fault, my dear Lieutenant. But I will accept the offer. Vielen, vielen Dank.'

Then Burckhardt looked at his watch. 'I must go,' he said, 'but before I do, I want to ask one more question. And if you do not choose to answer, it will not change my decision to back you up completely in regard to what transpired this evening.'

Major von Göhler nodded his head in appreciation.

'And I will reciprocate your bluntness,' Burckhardt continued. 'We have heard that your General Dietl, acting under direct orders from Hitler, is now at one of your army's staff headquarters in Freising, just outside Munich,[34] and that the reason he is there is to supervise the transfer of his 20th Alpine Army to southern Germany, and that, within a matter of weeks, they will parachute into the Swiss Alps, spearheading an invasion of our country.'

The expression these words produced on the German major's face could not possibly have been anything but spontaneous: he appeared totally flabbergasted.

And when he finally spoke, it was to utter but one word: 'Unsinn!'

Nonsense.

Then, raising himself to his full height, which was well over six feet, he added: 'I, sir, served as General Dietl's adjutant before being temporarily detached to my current duties in Berlin. We still telephone each other at least once a week. The last time we spoke was two days ago, I from Berlin, he from his command post in Lapland. To be sure, he *did* mention the possibility of the 20th Alpine Army being moved. But to the Eastern front, not southern Germany!'

'Are you totally convinced this is true?'

'Dietl would never lie to me. And you have my word, sir, as a German officer, that what I have just told you is the truth.'

Burckhardt then reached out to shake the hand of the German officer. 'Thank you,' he said.

'It is I who must thank *you*, Herr Burckhardt. And something else before you go. I would like to stay in contact with you. Because who knows? There might be other occasions, other

---

34 See Bonjour, vol. V, p. 57.

reasons . . .' He left the rest unsaid. 'I assume you will be travelling with us tomorrow.'

'No I won't,' Burckhardt answered.

'Then I will leave the details of where and how I can be reached with one of your lieutenants who will be escorting us to the meeting with General Guisan.'

Burckhardt immediately reacted. 'It might be better if you merely left a note on the bureau in your bedroom. I will have it picked up in the morning.'

'Then I will do it that way.'

Burckhardt again looked at his watch. It was now 23.05.

'I must be on my way,' he then said. In the corridor outside his study on the second floor of the Benkener Schloss the Swiss captain and the German major again shook hands. Minutes later Peter Burckhardt was in his Mercedes, headed for Basel. The lateness of the hour meant nothing to him, for after all, what was involved was the most important mission the Swiss Intelligence Service had been involved in since the outbreak of the war: to determine, beyond any reasonable doubt, whether or not a Nazi invasion of Germany was imminent. If Allen Dulles was able to reconfirm what he had just heard from the German paratrooper, it would undoubtedly allow for a much firmer negotiating stance for the Swiss government vis-à-vis the Nazis, and pull the rug from under those factions within both the Swiss military and Swiss Intelligence who favoured collaboration with the Germans.

Rolf Seiler, the member of the Rote Kapelle who had been left behind in Basel for the purpose of maintaining a continuing surveillance on the American vice-consul from his post in the attic of the house on the Rheingasse, had started to get nervous at 10.30 that evening. For before he had left for Benken with the rest of the remaining active members of the Swiss cells of the Rote Kapelle, Igor Scitovsky had made a promise to call him at that time. Seiler knew that, where timeliness was concerned, the NKGB colonel was a fanatic.

Chapter 20

Allen Dulles and the American vice-consul in Basel had spent the entire evening over dinner with the Swedish banker, Per Jacobsson. The restaurant they had gone to was the city's finest, the Schützenhaus, located on the site of a medieval hunting lodge which had, for centuries, lain outside the walled city of Basel. By 1943 the wall had been long gone, though three of the massive gates through which one could enter the city in medieval times still survived: the 'Spalentor', the 'St Johanntor' and the 'St Albantor'. Copper-plate engravings of each graced one of the walls in Nancy Reichman's apartment, and, as the hour approached 11.15 on this 2 March of 1943, Allen Dulles stood in front of them, cognac glass in hand.

'That man Jacobsson may be a Swede, but he could just as well be Swiss. He seems to be completely in love with this city.[35] And when you look at these lovely engravings, and recall Basel's history, its architecture, its university and the humanistic tradi-

---

35 As Jacobsson's daughter, Erin E. Jacobsson, points out in her biography of him, *A Life for Sound Money*, he loved Basel so much that he planned to retire there. Unfortunately, the six years he spent between 1956 and 1962 as head of the International Monetary Fund in Washington took such a toll that he died in 1963 before he could fulfil that wish. Poignantly, among those she lists as sending condolences and tributes at the time of his death, alongside President Charles de Gaulle, President John Kennedy and Chancellor Ludwig Erhard, was Per Jacobsson's Basel shoemaker.

tion it has always stood for, Jacobsson's love affair is certainly
understandable. Even though at times it seems to me that he goes
a bit too far in defending some of their actions.'

'You mean when you brought up the subject of the Swiss
selling arms to the Nazis in return for gold,' Nancy Reichman
said. She sat on the sofa, sipping a cup of coffee.

'Precisely.'

'But you did offer to pass on his explanation to Washington
that the Swiss have no choice. That they are literally under the
gun.'

Now Dulles turned away from the prints, and walked to the
windows which faced north and looked out on the River Rhine. It
reminded him how close he was to the enemy: that those German
guns were just three kilometres further north. 'I will do that
immediately, but I fear that it will meet with very little understanding in Washington. And much, much less in Moscow. Stalin,
I hear, is really starting to get worked up over the Swiss. And
when he hears about Schellenberg's visit here, he's going to get
even more agitated, you can be sure.'

Dulles then looked at his watch. 'Speaking of Schellenberg, I
assume we can rely on your friend showing up.'

Nancy Reichman now also looked at her watch. 'He has always
been completely reliable and absolutely punctual, like all the
Swiss. I hope nothing has happened.'

Just one hundred and twenty metres away, on the other side of
the Rhine, the last surviving member of the Rote Kapelle in
Switzerland who was not in police custody now also looked at his
watch, and thought exactly the same thought as Nancy Reichman. It was as if Rolf Seiler were reading her lips, which he
almost could, since he had kept his binoculars directly focused on
both her and Allen Dulles from the minute they had stepped into
her apartment and turned on the lights. The American woman
had obviously forgotten to draw the curtains, as was required
after ten o'clock in all of Switzerland by the blackout edict which
had been in effect since November of 1940. It was probably

because on most nights she was already in bed before that ten o'clock deadline.[36]

He had already begun to worry a quarter of an hour before that. The exact words of Colonel Scitovsky were perfectly fresh in his mind: 'I'll either telephone or deliver the news personally,' had been his promise about the outcome of their mission in Benken. 'By no later than 23 hours.'

After almost three years of experience of working with the NKGB intelligence officer, Seiler knew that Scitovsky always kept his promises and was, if that was possible, even more punctual than the Swiss. As he continued to watch the two Americans in the living-room on the other side of the river, he could tell from their body language, especially the pacing up and down of Allen Dulles, that they too were becoming increasingly disturbed. They had obviously been expecting the arrival of someone . . . who had not shown up at the appointed hour. Which was good. For if that someone was Walter Schellenberg, the most likely reason for his failure to appear was the fact that he was dead. They would probably give him until midnight, and then Dulles would return to his hotel, Nancy Reichman would go to bed — he would keep his glasses trained on her until she was out of her clothes and into her pink nightgown just to make sure — and then he would do what he had told Scitovsky he planned to do in the absence of any new instructions to the contrary: he would quietly slip out of the house on Rheingasse 37, and seek asylum for the duration of the war in the house of his ex-professor and mentor. For him, the war would be over.

At exactly 11.38 all that changed. He watched as Nancy Reichman suddenly rose from the sofa, where she had been sitting during most of the last half hour nursing one cup of coffee after the other, and rushed towards the front door of the

---

36 The blackout edict was revoked on 12 September 1944 after repeated bombings of Swiss cities, including Basel and Zurich, by British and American planes, piloted, the Swiss government claimed, by young inexperienced men who erroneously assumed they were still over German territory. As in many cases where this government was concerned, this was a half-truth: some raids were no doubt accidental, others deliberate.

apartment. The entrance itself was out of his view, but there was no doubt in Rolf Seiler's mind that the visitor had arrived and that she was pushing the buzzer that would unlatch the door leading into her apartment building from the Augustinergasse. That meant that the newcomer should appear within minutes.

And sure enough, just two minutes later a man still clad in his overcoat appeared in his binoculars as he crossed the living-room to shake hands with Allen Dulles. After he had taken off his coat and handed it to Nancy Reichman, he remained chatting with Dulles, both now standing immediately in front of the huge panoramic window facing the Rhine below, and the house on Rheingasse 37 on the opposite bank of that river. The visitor fitted Colonel Scitovsky's description of Walter Schellenberg to a 'T': Six feet tall, slim, in his early thirties and immaculately dressed in a suit that could have been tailored on Savile Row.

It was now 11.41, and still no word from Colonel Scitovsky.

Decision time for young Rolf Seiler. In trying to make that decision, he attempted to put himself in the place of the Soviet colonel. Scitovsky's intention had been made crystal-clear: Kill him!

But how?

Then he remembered Scitovsky's last words to him before he had left: 'I'm leaving three different weapons with ample ammunition for all three in the cellar.' That should narrow down the options. So now, for the first time since Scitovsky had ordered him to maintain a constant surveillance of the apartment across the Rhine, Rolf Seiler abandoned his position in front of the rear attic window of the house on Rheingasse 37, clambered down the ladder which led to the upstairs corridor of that house, and then ran down two sets of stairs to the cellar below. The weapons lay, neatly arrayed, on a table in the middle of the cellar: a pistol, a fully automatic assault rifle and a carbine.

The sight of them reduced the options to two, and Rolf Seiler immediately dismissed the one that was implied by the presence of the Sturmgewehr, the standard German assault rifle, and the pistol: a direct raid on the apartment on the other side of the Rhine. That would require an assault team of three men: at the very least two, if one of them had been Colonel Igor Scitovsky.

The third weapon was the ideal weapon of choice for a single assailant such as he was now destined to be: a high-powered special issue Mauser Kar 98K rifle with scope, one with a muzzle velocity that would more than suffice for the purpose he now had in mind. He picked it up off the table to get the feel of it. It was lighter than he had expected. He also picked up six rounds of ammunition and put them in his jacket pocket.

Then, suddenly, Seiler did not feel at all well. The knot in the pit of his stomach which had been growing during the past forty-three minutes had brought him to the edge of nausea. For Rolf Seiler, now barely twenty-two years old, whose motives for joining the Rote Kapelle had been purely ideological, no, idealistic, the prospect of killing − of cold-bloodedly sniping at − another human being was nothing short of sickening. But then, deliberately, he sought to conjure up images of those atrocities being committed each and every day by the Nazis: the shooting of as many as fifty French Communists at a time as revenge for a single terrorist act against the military occupiers of the country which lay just a few kilometres to the northwest of where he stood; the massacre of entire villages in Czechoslovakia and Russia; the increasingly puzzling disappearance of Jews from every single country in Europe occupied by the Germans − and that included most of them. And his resolve gradually returned.

Two minutes later he was back in the attic of the house at Rheingasse 37 and in front of the open window which faced the Rhine and the southern bank of that river which lay a football-field length across the water. Carefully he steadied the barrel of the rifle on the lower sill of the window, and, after putting his eye to the scope, began focusing in on the top floor of the apartment building situated on that opposite bank, immediately facing where he stood crouched behind the Mauser 98K. The three occupants of the apartment were now standing together talking, just a few metres inside the huge window which faced directly north. The problem was that the girl was closest to him, standing with her back to the window, meaning she was positioned in such a way as to block shots on both Schellenberg and Dulles.

Seiler now took the six rounds of ammunition from his jacket pocket, loaded one into the carbine and, after laying the other five bullets to his right on the window sill, repositioned the rifle.

About ten seconds later he heard something. In the building. A few seconds later he heard it again, though very faintly. Someone was in the building. Colonel Scitovsky! He must have returned. But . . . but if it were he, why was it so quiet again? Scitovsky was an impulsive man, a Russian. He would be shouting up to him by now, ready to celebrate.

His eye remained at the scope as all this raced through his mind. Then the American woman finally began to move. Once she was out of sight, Schellenberg and Dulles were both fully exposed. Rolf Seiler shifted the carbine ever so slightly.

And fired.

Schellenberg was down immediately. Dulles dived to the floor. Both were still in view. Seiler reloaded and was about to fire again when two things happened: the lights went out in the apartment across the Rhine, and someone burst into the attic through the trapdoor which led from the second-floor corridor below. As young Rolf Seiler turned in the darkness to confront the intruder, he was tackled by a huge man whose momentum sent Seiler flying violently back, smashing his head against the window sill from which he slid, unconscious, onto the bare wooden floor.

Seconds later, the man who had felled him was joined by two, then three, then four other members of Basel's political police. After recovering his balance, their chief had immediately reached to his belt for his flashlight and directed its light onto the young man lying at his feet and bleeding rather profusely from a scalp wound. Now he was projecting its beam around the rest of the attic, probing until he was satisfied that he had been dealing with a lone gunman.

But who had been the target?

It took Lützelschwab only a few seconds to come up with an answer. He knew Basel like the back of his hand. Most of the buildings on the opposite bank were institutional – owned by the Church, the city, the university – and were occupied only during the day. The exceptions were half a dozen apartment buildings on the Augustinergasse. The American vice-consul lived on the top floor of the one that lay directly across the Rhine from the attic window of Rheingasse 37. He had worried about her being a possible target of the Germans, who had already attempted to kill the British ambassador. He had even warned Peter Burckhardt about it after he had seen them together dancing at the Three Kings while that Nazi Eggen was watching them. And all the while it was the Communists he should have been worried about!

'Somebody turn on the light in here,' he said. Somebody did so immediately. Then, pointing: 'You and you. Take him to the emergency room of the Bürgerspital, get him bandaged, and then lock him up in solitary in the Lohnhof.'

Once they were all down in the front living-room of the house at Rheingasse 37, he ordered one of the other two policemen to plan on spending the night there. The reason they had come directly to the Rheingasse from Benken was simple standard police follow-up procedure: now that those members of the Basel cell of the Rote Kapelle who had been involved in the attack on the Benkener Schloss were either dead or in custody, it was logical that the base from which they had operated should now be occupied – as quickly and quietly as possible – before the news got out. The objective: entrapment of any remaining cell members who might seek to check in with their now very dead leader in the hours and days that lay ahead.

The last thing he had expected to encounter was a lone assassin at work in the attic of that house . . . although Dr Lützelschwab had already decided that it would be unnecessary to admit that when this entire operation was put under scrutiny during the inevitable review which would now take place. Everybody would seek to get into the act – the army, the intelligence service, the Federal police – and all with the same thought in mind: to cover their backs. For they had all failed where he had succeeded. Singlehanded!

But it had not been a total success. Somebody had been shot just minutes earlier in the centre of the city of Basel, i.e. on the territory for which he was primarily responsible. He only hoped to God, if it was the American girl – and who else could it be? –

that she was not dead. And he might as well find out right away.

'Come on,' he said to the remaining police sergeant. 'We're going across the river to take a look.'

Across the river, after Nancy Reichman had finally had enough sense to draw the curtains, she again switched on the lights in her living-room. Then she knelt by Allen Dulles, who was at the side of the man who lay shot.

'How bad is it?' she asked in a voice that was trembling with fright.

The answer came not from Dulles but from the wounded man, who was now struggling to sit up. 'It got me in the right shoulder. Barely.'

She could see the blood that started to flow out of the right sleeve of his jacket onto his hand. Now it was dripping onto her carpet. As if sensing what she was thinking, he added: 'Don't worry, we'll get you a new carpet right away.'

With the help of both Dulles and Nancy, he managed to rise fully to his feet.

'Let me . . .' she then said, starting to remove his jacket to get at the wound.

'No,' he said. 'We are all getting out of here. Now! You are first driving me to the Bürgerspital. Then, Nancy, you are taking Mr Dulles back to his hotel, where you will also be spending the night.' He then added: 'If you agree, sir.'

Allen Dulles responded immediately. 'I agree. Nancy, go down and start your car. We'll follow you.'

Peter Burckhardt countermanded that order. 'No. Your car's too small. Get the keys to the Mercedes out of my left jacket pocket.'

She did as she was told, and within three minutes the Swiss intelligence officer who looked somewhat like Walter Schellenberg and the chief of America's espionage operations in Switzerland were in the back seat of Burckhardt's Mercedes as it pulled away into the Augustinergasse. The hospital, the Bürgerspital, was less than ten minutes away. Burckhardt insisted, and insisted absolutely, that they simply drop him off and proceed immediately to the Schweizerhof Hotel. 'To avoid unnecessary complications.'

When Allen Dulles agreed, Nancy Reichman had no choice but to, once again, do as she was told.

After both the ringing of her bell and the subsequent pounding on her door had produced no response, Dr Lützelschwab and his two men broke into Nancy Reichman's apartment and turned on the lights which Allen Dulles had so carefully turned off just five minutes before, after helping Peter Burckhardt out of the door. At first glance everything appeared normal. On second glance, however, it definitely did not. For that red wine stain in the middle of the living-room carpet turned out to be of a quite different origin, a substance that was a lot thicker and still warm. Blood. And when the curtains were drawn open, they revealed a huge window that, again, at first sight appeared intact, but, under further examination, contained a bullet hole situated almost exactly in its middle. Upon measurement, it was 165 centimetres above the apartment floor.

Shoulder high. Although the amount and colour of the blood on the rug indicated that the wound had not been serious.

But if it was Nancy Reichman who had been hit by that bullet which had come across the Rhine from the attic of the house at Rheingasse 37, where was she?

'Goddamn it,' Lützelschwab now swore, and then asked himself a question: 'And why, come to think of it, did they shoot her?' It didn't make sense.

For the next half-hour the political policemen of Basel went through Nancy Reichman's apartment, examining every object in it, looking for an explanation. Needless to say, not one thought was wasted on the propriety of it all. Political police in Switzerland were above any laws that might theoretically have guarded against invasion of the privacy of its citizens or residents and called for search warrants issued by a court. In Reichman's case, diplomatic immunity from search or seizure no doubt also applied. On the other hand, she was only a vice-consul. And a woman. Neither gained her much respect in Swiss official circles in 1943.[37]

It was well past midnight when Lützelschwab and his men finally gave up and returned to police headquarters. He immediately put out a bulletin to all local police forces to be on the lookout for the missing American woman. Then, just as the police chief was finally preparing to leave for home, the two sergeants whom he had put in charge of the assassin also arrived at headquarters, after having delivered their prisoner to the local jail. One of them went directly to Lützelschwab's office.

'Guess who checked into the emergency ward of the Bürgerspital while we were having that young Communist punk bandaged up there? That Burckhardt fellow who's attached to Section 5. He was apparently shot in the shoulder.'

Lützelschwab was so excited by this news that, bone-tired though he was, he jumped up from the chair behind his desk. 'Did you talk to him?'

'Tried to. But the doctor that was treating him interfered.'

'Was anybody else being treated?'

'No. Just that Seiler boy and the guy from Intelligence.'

'Nobody with him?'

---

37 Such acts of Switzerland's political police, it turned out, did not cease when the war ended. Quite the contrary. In 1989 it came to light that they maintained secret card files — 'Fichen' — on no fewer than 900,000 citizens suspected of being somewhat less than loyal to the Swiss Vaterland. The political police were empowered to spy on their citizens (through wire taps, mail intercepts, etc.) by a secret edict of the Federal Council put into effect in 1951 in order to 'protect the security of the nation'. It remained valid until 1990. This edict further allowed the political police, in times of national crisis (such as an attempted coup d'état, the definition of which remained extremely hazy), to take 'preventive action' in the form of committing Swiss citizens of questionable loyalty to internment camps without any due process of law whatsoever. Denunciations by 'loyal' citizens were sufficient cause for the taking of such action, and were in fact to be encouraged. Revelation of all this led to the greatest political scandal in Swiss postwar history. Needless to say, no member of the Swiss conservative ruling establishment suffered any serious consequences. One of the aftermaths was a proposal in parliament to abolish Switzerland's secret police. The proposal was defeated. See the Tages Anzeiger of Zurich for a complete history of this affair.

'No.'

'Then how the hell did he get there?'

The sergeant shrugged, but said nothing. How the hell would he know?

Lützelschwab looked at his watch. It was almost a quarter to one in the morning. But it could not be put off. Vice-consul or not, that young woman was still a full-fledged member of the diplomatic corps. And she was missing. He knew that she and Burckhardt were more than just acquaintances from university days. After all, he had personally watched them dancing cheek to cheek in the Three Kings Hotel not so long ago.

He pulled the Basel phone directory from a desk drawer, and after finding the number, dialled the Bürgerspital. After he had identified himself and asked about Burckhardt it was immediately confirmed that he was spending the night there. He then had the call transferred to the resident in charge of the night shift. He again explained who he was, and said that he would be showing up in about ten minutes and expected to see the patient Burckhardt immediately. When the doctor began to protest, Lützelschwab simply hung up the phone. It was too late to put up with any crap from some smartass young doctor.

Peter Burckhardt felt a bit woozy from the local anaesthetic and sedatives, but was still lucid enough to handle the questions which Lützelschwab was firing at him. Yes, it was he who had been hit by that bullet while in Nancy Reichman's apartment. What was he doing there at that hour, especially after all that had just transpired in Benken? Meeting with Allen Dulles.

That stopped even Lützelschwab for a few seconds.

'On matters that concern Section 5 of the General Staff, and them only,' Burckhardt added.

'Any ideas about who shot you?' Lützelschwab then asked.

'Maybe.'

'Well, you don't have to puzzle over it any longer. We not only know who did it, but we've got him in custody.'

Lützelschwab then explained. After he was done, he asked a

further question: 'Now that you know *who* did it, maybe you can explain *why*?'

'One explanation more or less leaps out,' Burckhardt replied. 'They were out to get Schellenberg and were covering all the bases. They knew that he would be meeting us — meeting Colonel Masson — in Benken. But they must have also somehow learned about Dulles being in town, and concluded that a clandestine Schellenberg—Dulles meeting was also being planned — and what better place to hold such a meeting than the American vice-consul's apartment? So when I showed up, the shooter assumed, quite logically when you think of it, that I was Schellenberg.'

Makes sense, Lützelschwab thought. And we'll find out tomorrow for sure, even if I have to personally beat the hell out of that young Communist son-of-a-bitch.

Lützelschwab decided to press no further on that matter. Burckhardt now appeared totally fatigued. But he had to add a final word. For it was now apparent that at least one officer in Section 5 had enough brains to consort with the Americans, instead of with criminals like Schellenberg. He was beginning to change his mind about Peter Burckhardt. The young man was no doubt running a great personal risk by meeting the Americans at the same time as his boss, that fool Colonel Masson, was so focused on cutting a deal with the goddamn Nazis. Well, more power to him.

'We need more of your type, Burckhardt,' he said. 'And you can rest assured that in so far as I am able to do so, I'll leave Dulles out of this.'

'I'd appreciate that very much.'

'Where's the girl?'

'Staying the night at the Schweizerhof. Dulles is there too.'

'I'll send a man over there right away just in case there's still a loose cannon rolling around. By the way, the driver of their van tried to run through our road-block outside Benken, and got shot up pretty badly in the process. So we don't have to worry about him.' Then: 'Speaking of shots, how's the shoulder?'

'Could be worse. They say I can check out in the morning.'

231

'Take care of yourself, Peter. And thanks again for what you did for us in Benken. I owe you one.'

With that, Lützelschwab left. And Peter Burckhardt fell immediately into a deep sleep.

The 2nd of March 1943 was finally over, but the events of that day were destined to cement a relationship between the intelligence services of Switzerland and the United States which would have far-reaching consequences for both nations before the war was over. In the process, however, the two junior members of this clandestine alliance, Nancy Reichman and Peter Burckhardt, would face a much closer brush with death.

PART THREE

Chapter 21

The incident which was so dramatically to affect their lives – and the very conduct of the war in its final stages – had its origins in the early hours of 3 March 1943. A man jumped ship – a German ship – in the Rhine at a village just a few kilometres upstream from the spot where Nancy Reichman's apartment was situated and swam ashore, where he was immediately spotted and taken into custody by one of the Swiss border guards. The sergeant in charge of the guard-house where the man was subsequently held waited until 7.30 that morning before carrying out the standing instructions for such a situation: he placed a telephone call to Basel, using the number that had been given him, and explained the situation.

At 8.30 a black Citroën arrived. In it were two of Dr Wilhelm Lützelschwab's men. They presented their credentials and written orders and waited as various phone calls were made seeking verification of both the orders and the credentials.

An hour later they pushed the handcuffed man into the back seat and headed back to Basel, to the Spiegelhof where the headquarters of the regional counter-intelligence unit were located. There he was put in a holding room. Lützelschwab arrived in his office at ten o'clock. The desk sergeant had left a note on his desk to the effect that they were holding a man – a Frenchman, or at least he spoke French – and awaited further instructions as to what to do with him. So far he had refused to talk to anybody, insisting that he would only speak to someone in high authority.

Normally Lützelschwab would not have wasted his time on such a petty matter — the arrival of refugees or escapees from both Germany and France was an almost daily event — but following that instinct which had been so important all through his career, he decided to take a look at the man.

What he saw when he entered the holding room was a man in his early thirties, unshaven, haggard, and shivering in mud-stained clothes.

'Il paraît que vous voulez parler avec celui qui commande ici,' Lützelschwab began.

'Exactement!' the prisoner replied eagerly.

Lützelschwab then explained who he was, and suggested that if his guest had something important to tell him, now was the time to do it. Now or never.

The man — he was short, only five feet six inches — then said that he was a Frenchman, from Strasbourg. He was by profession a sailor and had, from his youth, worked on the Rhine barges, travelling the stretch between Rotterdam, the Ruhr, Strasbourg and Basel literally hundreds of times. In late 1942 he had been pressed into service by the Nazi occupiers of his home town and taken to north Germany. There he had been given a peculiar job, very peculiar indeed. Perhaps the Swiss authorities would like to hear more about it.

Aha, Lützelschwab thought: we've already arrived at the *quid pro quo* stage. And again his instinct led him to show a readiness to cooperate.

'I assume that what you want to tell us must be very important. Otherwise you would hardly have taken so much trouble, so much risk, to come here, would you? And if it really does turn out to be of value to us, I can assure you, monsieur, that the Swiss government will be most willing to express its gratitude in a concrete fashion. Especially,' he then added, 'where a neighbour from Strasbourg is concerned.'

The man seemed to carefully weigh these words before speaking again. Then he made up his mind.

'All right,' he said, 'I will explain. I worked out of two ports immediately adjacent to each other on the Baltic Sea. Their names are Wolgast and Peenemünde. I lived in a barracks on Peenemünde. It's an island.'

Lützelschwab had never heard of either of them.

'I was assigned to a small coastal steamer. This steamer had only one destination: the port of a small city on the southeast coast of Norway by the name of Skien. It was like a shuttle. Peenemünde and Wolgast to Skien, and then straight back. But what was so bizarre was that we always left the German port completely empty; we carried no cargo whatsoever. And on the way back we carried just one piece of cargo, a *single* piece.'[1]

Now the French sailor had Lützelschwab's full attention. And, despite himself, he could not help but break in and ask: 'Et qu'est-ce que c'était?'

'What was it? I tell you what it was. A cask. That's all: one single cask. And do you know what was in the cask? Eh?'

Lützelschwab waited.

'Water! Can you believe it: one cask of water! One cask per trip!'

Lützelschwab just stared at the man. A crazy. He must be a crazy.

Then someone knocked on the door.

'Herein!' Lützelschwab bellowed.

The door was opened, barely, just enough to reveal the desk sergeant's head. 'A Herr Doktor Peter Burckhardt is here to see you, sir.'

Lützelschwab looked at his watch. Of course. They had agreed last night to meet here at ten o'clock. But after what had happened to Burckhardt, he had hardly expected him to show up. At least it meant that he could immediately end any further conversation with this poor demented man. So without even glancing back at the Frenchman he left the holding room.

Peter Burckhardt, pale and with his right arm in a sling, was waiting in his office. Lützelschwab was still shaking his head as he came in.

---

1 For the OSS version of this 'improbable story', see Richard Dunlap, *Donovan: America's Master Spy*, pp. 401ff.

'What's bothering you?' Burckhardt asked, grinning at the look of dismay which was still on Lützelschwab's face.

'Do you want to hear something *really* crazy?'

'Sure. Why not?'

Lützelschwab told him. And to his surprise, when he was done Burckhardt was not laughing. In fact, he had a frown on his face. Which prompted Lützelschwab to say: 'I thought you got shot in the arm, Burckhardt, not the head!'

'Hold on,' Burckhardt replied. 'There's something stuck in the back of my mind. About water. But for the life of me, I can't remember where or when or from whom I heard it, whatever "it" is. Let me think for a moment.'

Burckhardt thought while Lützelschwab stared at him.

Then: 'My sister!'

'Your sister!'

'She studies physics at the university.'

'What's physics got to do with this, for God's sake?'

Ignoring the question, Burckhardt asked: 'May I use your phone?'

'Be my guest.'

He caught Felicitas while she was still at home at their parents' place in Riehen before leaving for her lectures at the university. Peter repeated the story he had just heard from Lützelschwab and then asked what the significance, the scientific significance, might be. He listened for at least three minutes without saying anything, then thanked her and hung up.

'I think we're on to something,' he said to Lützelschwab.

'Onto what? What was the phone call with your sister all about?'

'For the moment, matters which concern only Section 5. And if I could put a few questions to that Frenchman, it should bring us even closer.'

Lützelschwab glared at him and then led him out of his office and into the holding room down the corridor. When Burckhardt saw the wretched man, he immediately said to Lützelschwab: 'Why don't you get him some clean clothes? And, in the meantime, a cup of coffee.'

238

At first Lützelschwab appeared to resent the suggestion, but then disappeared through the door, leaving Burckhardt alone with the prisoner.

'Dr Lützelschwab told me your story,' he began. 'Tell me, how in the world did you manage to get all the way here from north Germany without being caught?'

'I got to Rotterdam on another coastal steamer with the help of some of its crew, also Frenchmen. Their ship made regular calls at Peenemünde and that's how I came to know them.'

One of Lützelschwab's men arrived with not only coffee but also two 'Weggli', the Basel version of a breakfast roll. Burckhardt watched in silence as the man devoured them. After he had washed them down with the coffee, the Frenchman breathed a deep sigh of relief and continued.

'In the port of Rotterdam it was easy to find some of my old buddies from the days I worked the Rhine barges. With their help I was able to make my way up the Rhine to Basel. Almost got caught once – in Rüdesheim, when the crew took me with them to a Weinstube. We got stopped for inspection by the police on the way back to the barge. Fortunately, nobody had any documents on them and we were so drunk that, rather than get stuck with us for one night, they just let us go.'

'Just a minute,' Burckhardt said. 'You said that this coastal steamer made regular calls at Peenemünde.' In contrast to Lützelschwab, Burckhardt knew where that little town was. As a boy, his parents had once taken him to the little port of Travemünde, not far northeast of Lübeck, from which they had gone on a Baltic sailing trip with the family of a German banker friend of his father, and had spent a night anchored off the tiny island of Peenemünde. 'What kind of cargo did it carry?'

The Swiss intelligence officer was in his element, taking advantage of the unexpected appearance of an odd source of very puzzling new information.

The Frenchman answered immediately: 'Cement.'

Burckhardt thought that one over before asking his final questions. 'And that Norwegian port. What was its name again?'

'Skien.'

This time Burckhardt drew a blank.

'But the origin of the flask of water was another town to the north of Skien by the name of Rjukan.'

'How do you know that?'

'From the guards – heavily armed guards – who always brought the flask to our ship.'

A new piece added to the puzzle: heavily armed guards!

'Let's move back to Peenemünde. You said you lived in a barracks?'

'Yes.'

'Did a lot of sailors live there, or was it just for foreign sailors who'd been forced to come to work in Germany?'

'Yes.'

'Yes to which question?'

'The barracks were for foreigners. But not only sailors. There were many barracks. And all kinds of workers from all over Europe, but especially Eastern Europe. Poland.'

Another piece had fallen into place.

But now the man Burckhardt was questioning suddenly appeared to be on the point of collapse. And it was just then that the door opened again and another of Lützelschwab's men appeared, carrying clothes. Lützelschwab walked in behind him. 'How are you doing?' he asked Burckhardt. If he was expecting an explanation of what this was all about, again he did not get it.

'We're done. At least for the time being.' Burckhardt then rose and walked around the table to extend his hand to the French sailor, saying: 'Thank you, monsieur. You have told me some very interesting things. I may have to talk to you again.'

'That means that I can stay in Switzerland?'

Burckhardt glanced over to Lützelschwab, who nodded ever so slightly.

'For the time being, yes.' These words brought, for the first time, a smile to the face of the French sailor. He gripped Burckhardt's hand fiercely, pumping it repeatedly and saying: 'Merci, bien, monsieur. Merci. Merci.' Then Lützelschwab's man took charge of him.

Back in Lützelschwab's office, Burckhardt asked: 'How do you plan on handling his case?'

The policeman answered: 'Normally, we would have no choice but to take him to the frontier this afternoon and hand him back to the German authorities. That's been the official policy under a decree issued by Bern on September 26th of last year. Since then exceptions can only be made for military deserters, escaped prisoners of war, and for genuine political refugees.[2] The French sailor does not qualify under any of these, since there are literally millions of foreign workers just like him who have been forcibly brought into Germany since the beginning of the war. And a lot have tried to escape their fate by escaping to Switzerland. We could hardly allow that to continue since, as you know full well, Burckhardt, our boat is full. We've already got 73,000 refugees here. So it was stopped. We are now forced by law to send them right back to Germany.'

'So they just try again later.'

'Not any more.'

'What's that supposed to mean?'

'You don't want to know,' was Lützelschwab's first response. Then: 'All right I'll tell you. Under a new German law any foreign worker who remains absent from his place of work for more than forty-eight hours is deemed to be a saboteur. As such, when caught he automatically receives the death penalty.'[3]

'Sorry. I should have known about that new law. I've been busy with other things. And the German courts go along with this?'

'Of course.'

'It gets worse and worse over there.'

'That's what I keep telling Bern. That's why I am so vehemently opposed to even the thought of consorting with any of them in any way whatsoever. And I would put Schellenberg right on top of the list of Germans who should be avoided like the plague. Why your boss Masson invited him onto Swiss soil will escape me for as long as I live.'

---

2 Bonjour, vol. VI, pp. 25ff.
3 Ibid., p. 19.

'Sometimes you have to deal with the devil in order to survive.'

'You can include me out of such exercises in sophistry, Burckhardt.'

'I'll try to remember that. But back to the French sailor. We might still need him. And if you want it officially, I am now speaking on behalf of Section 5 of the General Staff.'

'Then I'll keep him. For a while.'

'Thanks.' And now Burckhardt made ready to leave.

Lützelschwab decided to get in a last question. 'Before you go, allow me to get back to Schellenberg. What happens next, now that we've managed to save his life?'

'To use your expression, you don't want to know.'

Burckhardt knew that just about then a small convoy of automobiles was leaving Benken, one which included Schellenberg's Mercedes, guarded now by two additional Swiss army vehicles full of heavily armed military personnel which had been brought in hurriedly during the night, and headed for a secret rendezvous with Switzerland's General Guisan. He had spoken to Colonel Masson earlier that morning, from the hospital, to tell him that he had had confirmation from two sources that no German attack on Switzerland appeared imminent: first, from the German paratrooper, and then, very briefly, from Allen Dulles. He did not bother to explain why his conversation with Dulles had been so abbreviated, nor how it was so abruptly ended. There would be time for that later.

Masson's response could not have been more cordial. He promised to pass on this information to General Guisan *before* he began his talks with Schellenberg. And then he apologized that he had to hang up. They were scheduled to leave within a few minutes on a trip which would take them first to Bern, where Masson would install the general and his entourage in the Hotel Bellevue. Later that afternoon, he would proceed alone with Schellenberg and their army escort to the rendezvous with Guisan.

*

The meeting of the two generals, one a member of the High Command of the Nazi SS, the other the commander-in-chief of the Swiss army, was one of the strangest affairs to take place on the periphery of World War II. For it was inconceivable to the Swiss citizenry that their general, their commander-in-chief, would even *consider* such a meeting. General Guisan was to them the very antithesis of all that the Nazis stood for, and he had convinced them that if necessary, rather than bend to their will, he would be the first to die for his beloved fatherland.

The unique status of Guisan can be partially attributed to the fact that Switzerland does not have a general in peacetime. So the very elevation of a military officer to this rank guarantees him a singular place in Swiss history. In Guisan's case, that occurred at 5 pm on 30 August 1939, when the combined legislature of Switzerland elected him general with nine-tenths of their 460 votes. Simultaneously, a partial mobilization of the Swiss armed forces was ordered and put under his command. These actions were deemed necessary to protect the neutrality and independence of Switzerland in the event of the outbreak of a general war in Europe. That war started four days later when Britain and France declared war on Germany in response to its invasion of Poland.[4]

Guisan subsequently made two moves which established him as the hero of World War II in the minds of all right-thinking Swiss. The first occurred on 25 July 1940, a month after the surrender of France, and thus at a time when it appeared inevitable that the Nazi darkness was destined to descend on all of Europe. The commander-in-chief, fearing that the Swiss could now well succumb to defeatism, decided to stage what was in essence a theatrical event designed to re-establish the will of both the army and the people to resist the forces of totalitarianism which now totally encircled Switzerland. He organized a 'secret' convocation of the 400 most senior officers of the Swiss armed forces, where

---

4 For the definitive biography of General Guisan and the role he and the Swiss army played in World War II, see Willi Gautschi, *General Henri Guisan. Die Schweizerische Armeeführung im Zweiten Weltkrieg.*

he asked that they solemnly renew their oaths of allegiance to their country, and to the democratic way of life for which it stood. The time: 25 July 1940. The place: the 'geheiligte Boden' — the holy ground — of the Rütli meadow in central Switzerland near Lucerne, where in 1291 the peasant population of the original Swiss cantons of Uri, Schwyz and Unterwalden had first declared their independence from foreign tyranny.[5]

Word of the 'Rütlirapport' soon spread like wildfire throughout Switzerland, and on 1 August 1940 General Guisan took to national radio to repeat the message he had given to his officers. The overwhelmingly favourable response to his appeal allowed him to subsequently usurp the role of national leadership from the seven-man Federal Council which formed the executive branch of the Swiss government, some members of which — especially Foreign Minister Marcel Pilet-Golaz — were (correctly) suspected of being not only defeatist but downright pro-German.

It was, of course, all well and good to reinforce the will of the Swiss army and people to resist any attack by totalitarian forces — from the Germans to the north, the Italians to the south, or both together — but how could a small country like Switzerland possibly survive in the face of such overwhelming odds?

General Guisan had already provided the answer to that question when addressing his senior officers on the Rütli meadow. It came in the form of his commitment to quickly build, at whatever cost, an Alpine 'Redoubt': a mountain fortress in central Switzerland to which the main military forces would retreat in the event of an attack and from which they would wage relentless and uncompromising guerrilla warfare after having destroyed all North–South transportation and communication links running through their territory.[6]

By spring of 1943, the Redoubt was already in place. In the mountainous region of central Switzerland with a sparse popula-

---

5 Ibid., p. 268.
6 For a history of the Redoubt concept and its construction, see ibid., pp. 294–328.

tion of 300,000 inhabitants, housing facilities for an additional 300,000 soldiers had been erected. Food, clothing, and fuel for 600,000 men had been stored in the fortress, and 40,000 horses stabled there. The supplies and ammunition were deemed sufficient to allow the Swiss army to withstand a siege of from six to eight months.[7]

To be sure, this strategy had left the Swiss civilian population out in the cold, at the mercy of invaders who would, within days, be able to overrun all the heavily populated areas of Switzerland. Rather than putting a damper on Swiss enthusiasm for the general, however, this prospect of martyrdom for the greater good had raised the national spirit to new heights and elevated the stature of General Guisan one notch higher – to that of national Saviour.

And now the Saviour was going to have dinner with an SS general on holy Swiss soil!

Knowing the uproar that this would cause were it to leak out among the general populace, but also seeking to avoid giving the meeting any 'official' status by holding it at General Guisan's headquarters in Interlaken, it had been decided that the meeting would be held in a small restaurant – the Gasthaus 'Bären' – in the village of Biglen in the canton of Bern. The Gasthaus had a reputation for maintaining high culinary standards even under wartime conditions, and General Guisan was a regular guest there. Masson had arranged for a small private dining-room in the rear of the restaurant to be put at their disposal, starting at six o'clock on Wednesday, 3 March 1943. The table would be set for six.

There can be little doubt that the meal was a success. Much of the talk consisted of 'frohe Unterhaltung' – happy conversation – mainly about horses, about buying horses, about the cavalry. Although only six people dined – General Guisan, General Schellenberg, Rittmeister Eggen, Colonel Masson and two of his adjutants – along with their food they managed to down one bottle of white wine, a 1940 Johannesburg, three bottles of red

---

7 Ibid., pp. 318ff.

wine, a 1937 Pommard, and eleven liqueurs. After dinner, they switched to champagne, Moët et Chandon Brut, and managed to go through another three bottles. Around ten o'clock that evening, the two generals withdrew and spent two hours alone in another private room. At midnight the meeting finally broke up, one hour after the official closing hour known in Switzerland as 'Polizeistunde'. The landlord, Herr Berchtold-Schneider, added an additional Fr. 5.50 to the bill for the inconvenience it caused him.[8] Carried away by the occasion, all participants signed the guestbook of the Gasthaus. Masson, as he paid the bill before leaving, had second thoughts about that, and arranged for the page to be torn out and destroyed. It was torn out, but never destroyed. Since Masson had made sure that no other records of Schellenberg's stay in Switzerland existed – for instance, they were never registered at the hotel – the only paper trail the Nazis left behind were that page and that bill for 259.20 francs, which Masson also neglected to destroy.[9]

After midnight, the Swiss general's car took him to his head-quarters in Interlaken, while Colonel Masson drove Schellenberg back to the Hotel Bellevue in Bern. Early the next day, the two girls from Berlin – who were getting very bored in safe, neutral Switzerland by this time – conspired to convince 'Schelli' that they could use a bit of fun before returning to the war-torn German capital. So they sneaked into his bedroom from their adjoining suite and woke the young general with a series of perverse sexual acts that could only have been thought up by two girls who had been born and raised in the world's most decadent city, Berlin. Exhausted by fifty-five uninterrupted minutes of being used in so depraved a fashion by the two Fräuleins clad only in black silk stockings – prized possessions which they had, unselfishly, put at high risk during some phases of their acrobatics in this third-floor bedroom of the Hotel Bellevue – Schellenberg

---

8 Ibid., p. 540.

9 See pp. 247 and 248 for copies of the bill and of that page (Willi Gautschi, *General Henri Guisan*, Zurich, 1989, pp. 541, 539).

Kellereien und Hotel „Bären"

H. Berchtold-Schneider, Biglen (Bern)

Postscheck-Konto III 5822   Telefon 6 56 84

Spezialität: Feine Waadtländer-, Wallloer- und Neuenburgerweine - Franz. Rot- und Weissweine - Fremdweine - fl. Liqueurs

Biglen, den .1. .2. ....1943.   6071 *

Rechnung für *Herrn Schroth, Mannan*

Ihrem freundlichen Aufträge zufolge sende ich Ihnen auf Ihre werte Rechnung und Gefahr per Bahn nachstehend verzeichnete Waren und wünsche guten Empfang.

Zahlungen:

H. B.					
		Familie Thом' l Bären	12. -	72.	-
	6	*Opera*	- 80	4.	80
	1	*fl. Marmsburg* 1940	4. -	4.	-
	2	*fl. Pommard* 1937	8. -	16.	-
	8	*Pork Kaffee ca*	70	5.	60
	11	*Lagerwein*	60	6.	60
		Cigarren u Cigaretten 2.15		2.	15
		4 Telefone - 50		2.	-
		Tee 4	1.50	3.	-
		fl. Vermougen 1		7.	-
	3	*fl. Weik et Claudan* Bordeaux 25.	75.		
				194.	55
	4	*Claussens 1 Bären*	6. -	24.	-
	1/6	*G. Burgenau 1 Opera, 1 Verres*		7.	40
	3	*Cigarren* 1/25, 1/50, 1/25		1.	25
	1	*Kaffee u Tee*		2.	40
	4	*Likör*		8.	40
		10% *Service*		237.	-
				23.	-
		Freiquartierverrechnung		253.	70
				6.	-

Fässer, Kisten u. Korbflaschen bleiben mein Eigentum u. sind, sofern fest, franko Biglen zurückzusenden. Nach 6 Monaten noch ausstehendes Leergut wird zum Tagespreis fakturiert, dabei späterhin Alters zurückgenommen.   *Total Fr. 259.70*

Gasthaus Bären, Biglen.

immediately caved in to their request to go skiing. Where? Arosa. When? Now. Right away.

He nodded his agreement and then crawled out of bed and staggered across the room to his bathroom before they could dream up something new to express their appreciation.

By four that afternoon they were back at it in the Hotel Excelsior in Arosa where, upon arrival, they had immediately been given the best rooms in the house thanks to the invisible hand of Swiss Intelligence − one which also made sure that they were not bothered with such formalities as registration or such details as payment. They took a break for dinner, which they had served in Schellenberg's suite, and then resumed their activities for much of that night, having now regained their strength from the Wienerschnitzel and Rösti which were the specialties of the kitchen of the Hotel Excelsior, and no doubt also refreshed by the pure Alpine air that poured in through the windows which the young SS general insisted on keeping open, a practice he had learned as a teenager in the Hitlerjugend. As it turned out, Schellenberg stayed in bed for almost all of his forty-eight-hour stay in Arosa.[10]

At dawn on Sunday morning, 7 March 1943, enough was finally enough. Schellenberg and his entourage hurriedly packed and headed directly for the Swiss—German frontier. Prior arrangement allowed them to roll right through. From there they drove directly back to Berlin, stopping only for a brief overnight layover in Nuremberg. On 9 March, Walter Schellenberg gave his personal report to Hitler. They were later joined by the German foreign minister and the Nazi minister of economic affairs.

To this day, exactly what transpired during this strange episode is unknown, since no protocol was kept of the Guisan—Schellenberg conversation, and because the general subsequently acted as if it had been a non-event.[11] But its substance was summarized in a secret communiqué sent to the German ambassador to Switzerland, Otto Karl Köcher, by his boss, Foreign Minister Joachim von Ribbentrop. In that communiqué Ribbentrop quoted from a formal letter from General Guisan which had been hand-delivered to Schellenberg in Arosa and in which Guisan reaffirmed that he, the Swiss army and the Swiss populace intended to defend Switzerland's integrity against attack from *any* foreign army at whatever cost necessary, and would take advantage of the country's unique topography to achieve that end. He had initially given this same commitment

---

10 To explain his rather odd behaviour, Schellenberg told the hotel management that he had an upset stomach and even went so far as to have a local doctor visit him in his room and prescribe 'Opiumtröpfe'! Gautschi, p. 544.

11 When, five days after the meeting, he was questioned by Switzerland's civilian minister of defence about rumours of a meeting with a high-ranking German general in Biglen, Guisan said that he had indeed met with a German 'personality' but that he did not know his name. Asked whether it had been a political, industrial or military 'personality', Guisan replied that he apparently was in the military, in fact a general, but what kind of a general he did not know. Gautschi, p. 548.

orally to Schellenberg during their talks in Biglen, and, when pressed to further define it, Guisan had empowered Schellenberg go 'give the Führer his solemn word as an officer that if the Allies attacked Switzerland on its southern flank, the Swiss would defend themselves to the last drop of blood' — 'zum letzten Blutstropfen'. Furthermore, according to Ribbentrop, during their meeting with Hitler, Schellenberg quoted Guisan as saying that: 'Since Switzerland wanted to avoid any possibility of Germany mounting a preventive military action against Switzerland, he would seriously entertain the thought of demobilizing a major proportion of the Swiss army and redeploying the manpower in the civilian sector, allowing Switzerland — under conditions of continuing strict neutrality, of course — to contribute indirectly to the buildup of Germany's war potential.'[12]

In addition to von Ribbentrop, Hitler had also brought in Walther Funk, his minister of economic affairs, to give his views on this matter. According to Ribbentrop, it was Funk who finally convinced Hitler that it would be extremely unwise to attack Switzerland due to the invaluable services which Switzerland provided the Third Reich by acting as its international turntable — 'Drehscheibe' — in financial matters, and further due to Switzerland's willingness to serve as Germany's only major outside supplier of large quantities of both industrial and military equipment of the highest quality, with no questions asked as to their ultimate deployment.[13] Their cooperation went so far, Funk pointed out, that General Guisan's son was a director of a firm which was supplying wooden barracks to house the Jews in the concentration camps in Poland! So from the economic point of view, there could be no doubt that Switzerland was Nazi Germany's most valuable ally. Funk concluded that as long as the Swiss continued to cooperate — and thanks to the Schellenberg

---

12 For the original text of this communiqué from Ribbentrop to Ambassador Köcher, see the Swiss National archives, BAr EDI 1005/2. See also Gautschi, p. 546.

13 See Walter Schellenberg's memoirs, *Aufzeichnungen* (Wiesbaden/Munich, 1979), pp. 313ff. Also Gautschi, p. 534.

mission General Guisan had given his guarantee that they would, provided the Germans did not initiate a preventive attack against them – it would be folly to seek to change the status quo. Hitler finally agreed. That ended any further consideration of an 'Aktion Schweiz'.

Only a handful of Swiss ever learned about all this during the war, and it left them bitterly divided from that time on. This was especially true where the 'insiders' within Swiss Intelligence were concerned. Those in the Masson camp defended the general's action as a classic example of 'Realpolitik', one born of the necessity to avoid any unnecessary provocation of the Nazis, and which had been key in convincing Hitler to drop, once and for all, any further consideration of waging a preventive war against Switzerland. The evidence of this, they claimed, was provided just three weeks after Schellenberg's return to Berlin, and came in the form of a non-event on 22 March 1943. According to the information provided by the 'Viking Line' – that line of communication which allowed Swiss Intelligence to go directly to a source in the inner circle of Hitler's High Command – that was the date when the 'Aktion Schweiz' was to begin. Despite the Berlin source sticking to his story to the bitter end, General Guisan did not order an all-out mobilization. On 25 March, after nothing even remotely unusual had occurred north of the border, Masson and Guisan declared the 'emergency' over and subsequently claimed that it was Schellenberg who had played the key role in 'saving' Switzerland.[14]

As a result of the assurances to the contrary which Lieutenant Peter Burckhardt of Section 5 had received both from the German paratrooper Major von Göhler and from the man who ran America's intelligence operations in Switzerland, Allen Dulles, those in the Waibel camp knew that it had been a false alarm all along and that Schellenberg had duped Masson into believing otherwise. They regarded the entire Guisan–Schellenberg

14 In fact, on the evening of 22 March Rittmeister Eggen met Masson in Zurich and they stayed up until midnight drinking champagne to celebrate the fact that due to their intervention the Swiss people had been spared 'the bitter cup' of being directly involved in World War II. Gautschi, p. 556.

episode as appeasement, and were appalled by the content of the Ribbentrop communiqué, a copy of which was provided to Waibel by a clerk in the German embassy in Bern just two days after it arrived. It strengthened their resolve to do everything within their power to undermine the Nazi influence upon Switzerland. This resolve was not just a matter of ideology, but also grew out of the conviction that such Swiss–German cooperation was bound to lead to extremely serious difficulties with the Allied powers.[15]

And it soon did. The root cause was gold. For gold was the key to understanding how the invaluable 'Turntable Switzerland' worked, and represented the reason why Walther Funk had told Hitler that it was essential for Germany's future war efforts that it remain intact and undisturbed.

The subject was unexpectedly raised by Dulles' 'man in Basel', the American vice-consul there, during dinner with Peter Burckhardt on Tuesday, 30 March 1943. It had been she who set the rendezvous in a telephone call earlier that day, suggesting that, since she had to work late, they could meet at a restaurant – perhaps his favourite little place, the one in the old city of Basel which was owned by the Widow Hunziger. Burckhardt said that he would make the reservation.

When she walked in, he was already at a table waiting. It was the first time she had seen him since that night in her apartment

---

15 The ideological split within the Swiss army's High Command, and especially within Section 5 of the General Staff (Intelligence), dated back to an earlier event which occurred on 21 July 1940, when 37 young officers in the Swiss army got together to found a secret organization designed to counter the appeasement tendencies which were then becoming rampant both in the army High Command and in Switzerland's political leadership. They swore to fight on even if the Swiss government ordered the Swiss army to surrender to the Nazis. When they were found out, eight of the members of this 'Officers' Conspiracy' were given 14 days of 'sharp arrest'. Max Waibel and Peter Burckhardt were among them, since they were among the ringleaders. Subsequently the entire affair was played down as a 'children's crusade' and both officers were not only rehabilitated but were later given leading positions within Swiss Intelligence, directing all of its operations aimed at Nazi Germany. See Gautschi, pp. 235ff.

when their meeting with Allen Dulles had been so rudely interrupted by a bullet from across the Rhine.

'Are you all right?' were her first words as he stood up to greet her.

'Yes, completely healed, and I'll prove it.' He then put his 'bad' arm around her shoulder and, after drawing her closer, planted a firm kiss directly on her lips.

'Peter!' she scolded, looking around the restaurant to see if anybody was watching. Good Swiss girls did not allow this to happen to them in public, nor did good American-Jewish girls. Ignoring the rebuke, Burckhardt helped her out of her coat, and while handing it to a waiter ordered a carafe of Dôle.

When it arrived, and their two glasses had been half-filled, he took his and raised it, saying: 'To the first major success of the Reichman—Burckhardt Line! We were certainly right about the March emergency being a false alarm, thanks in part to your intervention with Mr Dulles, Nancy. We thank you.'

She appeared flustered by his words, but nevertheless raised her glass and drank with him.

He noticed. 'Something new is apparently on your mind, Nancy. Official or private?'

'Official. That's why I called. Or at least it was one of the reasons why I called.'

'Let's get to it. Or would you rather order first?'

'Let's order. I'm absolutely famished.'

He watched her as she looked at the menu. She was wearing a skirt and sweater, a pink sweater which could not help but draw attention to the fact that she was a mature woman. She seemed to notice his attention, and, as if to ward it off, said: 'You order, Peter. After all, it's your restaurant.'

'Steak, pommes frites and salad,' he immediately said. 'And since you're famished, I'll ask for the entrecôte to come with a Café de Paris sauce.' He called the waiter over and placed the order.

Once the waiter had withdrawn, she began. 'Mr Dulles asked me to preface what I'm about to say with the comment that *he* is on your side, fully cognizant of your dilemma, but that an

253

increasing number of people in high places are not.'

'Before we get to the "dilemma", I assume that the high places Mr Dulles is referring to are in Washington?'

'Unfortunately not just in Washington. Also in Moscow. And London.'

Now Nancy Reichman had his full attention.

'All right. What's the problem?'

'Gold.'

'What gold?'

'Gold looted by the Nazis and transferred to Switzerland.'

Burckhardt's face darkened as he heard these last words.

'Where did this information come from?'

'The Soviets. It was communicated to our Treasury Department, and went directly to the man who runs it, Mr Morgenthau.'

'How do you know the information is authentic?'

'We can't know that. However, according to the Soviets, it comes from a source "in Basel, Switzerland". They offered no further clarification.'

Whoever the source in Basel was had no doubt arranged to have the information transmitted to Moscow by Colonel Igor Scitovsky before Lützelschwab closed down his operation, was the thought that flashed through Burckhardt's mind. Lützelschwab had briefed Section 5 on this affair.

'All right. Why are you telling me this?' he then asked.

'Because unless this sort of "monkey business" – as Mr Dulles termed it – stops, it could prove to be extremely damaging for Switzerland. It openly invites severe reprisals, he said, and due to the magnitude of the gold transfers, if they continue there would be very little he could do to ameliorate the consequences.' She then added: 'Mr Dulles is as good a friend of Switzerland as you will find anywhere these days, Peter, so, believe me, all this is meant well.'

'I accept that. But I don't know how much I can do about it. We're dealing with something that is so delicate that there are no more than half a dozen people in this country who know the details of what you are talking about. And all of them are, to use your phrase, in *extremely* high places.'

'I understand,' Nancy Reichman commented. 'The last thing we want – and now I am quoting Mr Dulles directly – is that you do anything that could put you personally in jeopardy. Because, as he pointed out, the cat is already out of the bag.'

'I understand, and appreciate your concern. But that doesn't mean that I am going to let the matter rest there. Before I say anything else, Nancy, I will want to look into the matter further. If the situation is as bad as I suspect it might be – both in regard to the facts and the leak of these facts to the Soviets – you can rest assured I'll be back to you in very short order. And my reason for doing so is to try to contain the amount of damage done.'

The entrecôte Café de Paris arrived minutes later, and an hour after that it was a very subdued Peter Burckhardt who drove Nancy Reichman back to her apartment overlooking the Rhine. He even turned down her invitation to stay for coffee.

At 7.30 next morning, 31 March, Burckhardt was on the phone to the head of Basel's counter-intelligence unit.

'You're calling about that Frenchman we fished out of the Rhine,' was the policeman's initial response.

'No, but I assume you've still got him.'

'I have. But there are limits to how much longer.'

'What I'm calling about is much more serious. I know you briefed us on the Rote Kapelle affair, but I'd like a few more details. First question: I assume you were monitoring all their transmissions for quite a while before you closed them down?'

'Not for that long. Maybe two months. Of course, it was all gibberish then. But yes, we made complete transcripts.'

'I trust you've still got them.'

'Of course.'

'Did you decipher them?'

'Just those transmissions which took place immediately before the incident in Benken. We've had other matters that were much more pressing.'

'If I could convince you that there is a strong possibility that some of those transmissions might have contained information that would be extremely, I repeat extremely, compromising to Switzerland, would you put some of your people on it immediately?'

'Maybe. You're talking about a tedious, time-consuming task. Remember, Burckhardt, I have a very limited budget, and the resources I do have must be devoted exclusively to the task I am responsible for, namely supervising our counter-espionage in this region. If what you are talking about falls within that category, then we'll help you.'

'What if I tell you that it involves one of the most important single acts of espionage conducted against Switzerland since 1939? And it all happened here in Basel.'

'I'd say come over here right now.'

'I'll be there in half an hour.'

Once behind closed doors in Lützelschwab's office, Burckhardt got right down to business.

'What I'm about to tell you is highly secret. I wouldn't even think of discussing it with you if I didn't have to convince you that deciphering every single intercept of the transmissions to Moscow by the local unit of the Rote Kapelle is of the utmost importance. All right?'

'Convince me.'

'We're going to be talking mainly about gold. To date, since the outbreak of the war, the Nazis have shipped to us, to Switzerland, a grand total of over a thousand million Swiss francs' worth of gold. To put this in perspective, the physical amount of gold involved equals more than a third of the entire world production of gold during this same period. It is gold that has been looted by the Nazis, and subsequently either sold to our Swiss National Bank, or is being stored in that bank for the account of the German government, and then, in accordance with instructions regularly relayed to Bern from the Reichsbank in Berlin, transferred to similar gold accounts which other governments maintain with the Swiss National Bank. The recipients are chiefly the central banks of Spain, Portugal, Turkey, Romania, Sweden, and Argentina. These gold disbursements are all directly related to the Nazi war effort. As regards the sale of this gold to us, it is being used to buy weapons − chiefly anti-aircraft guns from Oerlikon, artillery fuses and timing mechanisms for the Wehrmacht from our watch industry − plus machine-tools, generators, pharmaceuticals, aniline dyes from Basel's chemistry industry. Romania gets Nazi gold, via Switzerland, for oil. Where Spain and Portugal are concerned, these countries buy strategic metals from all around the world − manganese, chrome, wolfram − for German account, and then re-export them to Germany. According to our information at the BIS, the Nazis get 100 per cent of their manganese this way, 99 per cent of their chrome, and 75 per cent of their wolfram. Without these exports, and our providing the financing for them, German production of the specialty steels − extremely hard steel − required for such things as shell casings, artillery barrels and ball bearings would have to be shut down within two months.'

Burckhardt paused to see what effect all this was having on Lützelschwab. From the now grey complexion of the man who sat facing him behind the desk, it was apparent that even this tough, cynical policeman, who thought he had seen and heard it all, was shaken. 'Who else knows about all this, Burckhardt?'

'I'll get to that in a minute.' Then Burckhardt continued with his dry, factual narrative. 'Turkey is a special situation. From what we have been able to ascertain at the Bank for International Settlements, gold held in the "German account" at the Swiss National Bank is transferred to the Turkish central bank's account there. The Turks then provide the Germans with counterpart funds in Ankara in the form of hard currencies − dollars, Swiss francs, sterling − which are subsequently used to finance the extra-European intelligence efforts of the SS, to pay their agents all around the world via bank transfers from Turkey.

'The proceeds from their gold sales to Argentina − and again, these sales took place here − are used to purchase fuel and supplies for the German submarine fleet in the South Atlantic when they re-supply there. As regards Sweden, our fellow neutral,' and Burckhardt's sarcasm was heavy, 'that country supplies Germany's steel industry with 40 per cent of the iron ore it requires. The Swedes are also beginning to demand "Swiss" gold in return, although thus far the quantities transferred to their account in Bern appear to be small.'

Again he paused. 'I think you get the message.'

'I'm getting it all too well,' Lützelschwab replied. 'Continue.'

'All right. But let me back up a bit. This whole extremely unsavoury episode for our country started with, of all people, King Leopold III of Belgium.'

Lützelschwab interrupted. 'Before you do, and excuse my ignorance since I am but a lowly policeman with a degree in law, but would you mind explaining exactly how all these transfers take place? Where is all that gold kept?'

'The gold that belongs to Switzerland is now dispersed through-out the country. It used to all be kept in Bern, but now most of it is kept in highly secret vaults maintained in Zurich and Lucerne, as well as in the Alpine Redoubt. But the gold which other central banks keep here is still all stored in a large underground vault beneath the Swiss National Bank's building in Bern. As you must know, the building proper has been totally sealed off since the war began, and is guarded by a special heavily armed unit of our army. The vault itself is currently divided into fourteen separate compartments – steel cages. The gold, in the form of twelve-kilo bars, is stacked up inside these cages. Each gold bar is stamped with the mark of the central bank that had the bars poured, a mark which guarantees its exact weight and purity. On the door leading into each cage, there is a listing of the number of bars, the central bank of origin. Once a week, three officials of the National Bank make the rounds to confirm each inventory count.'

'Have you been there?'

'Yes. You see one of those fourteen cages contains gold belonging to the Bank for International Settlements. One of my duties at the BIS is to oversee that gold, and to give the instructions to the National Bank whenever there are to be movements into and out of our depot there.'

'How is that done?'

'How is what done?'

'Moving the gold.'

'On a trolley. For instance, say that we at the BIS want to buy $50 million equivalent in Swedish kroner, in exchange for gold. We tell the Swiss National Bank to roll out the trolley. They load up $50 million worth of gold bars in our cage, wheel it over to the Swedish cage, and stack them up there. Then they adjust the inventory posted outside both cages. Upon confirmation from Bern of the gold transfer, the Swedish central bank credits our account in Stockholm with the kroner. Transaction complete. It's exactly the same setup as they have in the vaults of the Federal Reserve Bank in New York where there is also a lot of gold being held for the account of other countries. Our country has an immense amount there. When our government buys US government bonds or bills, it pays in gold, and the New York Federal Reserve Bank rolls out the trolley deep under the streets in New York and gold moves from our vault to that of the US Treasury. The one place where it can't move, however, is out of the United States. Since 14 June 1941 the assets of all continental European nations in the United States, including those of Switzerland, have been blocked, and the reason given was "to prevent the liquidation in the United States of assets looted by duress and conquest".[16] In other words, to prevent a recurrence of what had already happened in Europe. Which brings me back to King Leopold, assuming you want to hear me out.'

'If you feel it's necessary.'

'It is, if you want to know what to look for in those intercepts,' Burckhardt replied, adding: 'And if you want to get an idea of the trouble all this can lead to for us Swiss.'

'Go ahead.'

'All right. On 26 June 1940, four weeks after the surrender of the Belgian armed forces, the Belgian king, now a prisoner of the German Wehrmacht, sent a personal message to Hitler. In it he

---

16 This was done by President Roosevelt under Executive Order 8785. See Paul Erdman, *Swiss–American Economic Relations* (Basel, Tübingen, 1959), p. 94.

informed Hitler that prior to the outbreak of war a substantial amount of gold belonging to the kingdom of Belgium had been shipped to the Banque de France in Paris for safekeeping. According to his information that gold had been moved to a hiding place in the vicinity of Bordeaux. The letter went on to let Hitler know that he, Leopold III, would appreciate it if Hitler would arrange for that gold to be returned to its rightful owner.

'OK. First, how much Belgian gold are we talking about? And who controlled it? Under the 22 June 1940 armistice agreement between France and Germany, which confirmed the German military victory over France, it had been agreed that it would be the Pétain government in Vichy which would exercise the civilian administrative power over all of France, including its overseas territories, and also including the Banque de France. So, under Hitler's instructions, an urgent communiqué was sent from Berlin to Vichy demanding full details on the Belgian gold. It came back immediately, and the Germans got more than they had bargained for. According to Vichy, the amount of Belgian gold that had been sent to France for "safekeeping" in face of the threat of German invasion amounted to,' and now Burckhardt stopped talking and removed a folder from his briefcase, opened it, and read, '4,944 cases containing 221,730 kilograms. But in addition, France was also holding 57,000 kilos of gold belonging to the Polish National Bank, as well as an additional 10,000 kilos belonging to the national banks of Luxembourg, Lithuania, Latvia, Norway and Czechoslovakia.'

Burckhardt closed the folder.

'The problem was: none of that gold was any longer in France. Four days before France's surrender, all of it − plus all the gold that France itself owned − had been loaded onto two French cruisers in the port of Brest, and they had subsequently disappeared into the Atlantic. Under the original plan, laid out in an agreement which the French had entered into with the British, the gold should have gone out on British warships and been taken to New York. But when the British failed to show up, the plan had to be changed. And so was the ultimate destination: Africa, not the United States. Consequently, ten days after the French cruisers had set sail, they reappeared, entering the port of Dakar. Dakar is the city from which France governs all of its territories in West Africa. And you have to keep in mind, Wilhelm, that France controls one-sixth of the entire African continent, ranging from Algeria and Tunisia in the north to the Gulf of Guinea in the south; from Senegal on the Atlantic way over to Lake Chad.'

Burckhardt paused. 'And I warn you: before this odyssey ends, and it does end, finally, here in Switzerland, that gold passed over almost every damn bit of that territory.

'After being offloaded in Dakar on 28 June of 1940, the cargo was now put under the guard of the French colonial army. And there it sat for the rest of the year. Until the Nazis started to get tough with both the Belgian and French central bankers . . . and we know about all this in detail at the BIS since, despite the war, they still come regularly to Basel for board meetings. And to get something decent to eat, I might add. Anyway, in November of 1940 the Germans sent an ultimatum to the governor of the Banque de France, Bréart de Boisanger: No more stalling. We conquered Belgium. All rights of the Belgian National Bank are now our rights. Their gold is now our gold. We want it brought back now to a safe place. Berlin.'

Burckhardt glanced at his watch. 'Don't worry,' he said. 'I'm almost done. The Vichy government ultimately caved in to the German demands. But it was considered too dangerous to bring the gold back by ship, since the Atlantic was now a full-fledged war zone, and British warships essentially controlled the waters off the west coast of Africa. So it was decided to bring the gold by land, through central Africa, and then across the Sahara desert to the Mediterranean port of Algiers, from where it could be flown to Marseilles and then on to Berlin. So off the gold went, first by train, to the end of the line at Bamako on the left bank of the Niger. Then, after months of delay caused by the winter rains, the gold continued to move across Africa, first by truck and then by river boat, to Timbuktu. There a shortage of fuel caused it to be stranded for a long time. Next stop: Gao in the Sudan. And a long, long delay. Then, a few tons at a time, either on trucks or on the backs of camels, it was moved 1,700 miles north, through

261

the Sahara to Colomb-Béchar, where it was again loaded back onto railroad cars which took it another 1,600 kilometres to Algiers. Then, finally, by German military air transport to Berlin, and the vaults of the Reichsbank. The last ton arrived in Berlin on May 26th of 1942, about eight months ago.[17]

'Since then, most of it has been transferred to Switzerland, first to the depot of the Reichsbank in the vault of the Swiss National Bank in Bern. And then it was sold, ton by ton, transferred to the Swiss gold depot in exchange for Swiss francs which were then used to buy turbines or aluminium from Swiss manufacturers, or to the depot of the central bank of Sweden in exchange for kroner which were then used to buy Swedish steel. And so forth. Which takes us full circle. Right?'

'Right.'

'Now so far we have just been talking about the gold the Nazis looted from Belgium. They looted a similar amount from Holland. Most of that gold, in fact probably all of it, also came to Switzerland, in 1941 and last year. Then there is Czech gold,

---

17 For an exhaustive factual account of the movements of looted gold from Germany into Switzerland during World War II, see Werner Rings, *Raubgold aus Deutschland*. This episode was one of the best-kept secrets of World War II, both during and after. The Swiss government had put under seal all references to these matters, and it was only by chance that in the winter of 1978/79 a Swiss student at the university of Bern by the name of Peter Utz stumbled upon a mass of material which documented these events and which had somehow, by mistake, found its way into the Swiss Federal Archives (Schweizerische Bundesarchiv). His findings were subsequently presented before the Historical Seminar at the university of Bern, under the leadership of the Swiss historian, Dr Walter Hofer.

Much earlier than this, in 1958, I found out how touchy these matters were in the view of the Swiss government. I had chanced upon references to the German–Swiss gold deals during World War II from American sources, and included some of that material in my doctoral dissertation at the university of Basel. When the Swiss Federal Council, the collective presidency of Switzerland, found out about this, it tried to block publication of the dissertation. The head of the economics department, Professor Edgar Salin, who was at the time also chancellor of the university, termed this unacceptable interference in the freedom of the university and threatened to go public with the issue. The Swiss government backed down, and the dissertation was published in 1959 in unabridged form.

some of which was brought to the BIS by the Nazis. Schacht himself engineered that one. That is going to prove damned embarrassing for the BIS when it comes out.'

'Who knew all this?' Lützelschwab now asked.

'The three general directors of the Swiss National Bank for sure. They engineered the whole thing. My guess is that at least two members of the Federal Council must have also been in on it from the very beginning, and one of them is our minister of foreign affairs, Marcel Pilet. You have to also include my boss at the Bank for International Settlements, Per Jacobsson. But there were a few men in not-so-high-places who were fully in the know: me, for reasons which I've now explained to you, and it seems a Soviet plant who also works inside the Bank for International Settlements.'

'On what do you base the last part of that statement?'

'At this point, only surmise. But it is not pure conjecture. I think it extremely unlikely that it is somebody in the National Bank since . . .'

'Hold on. How do you know this information has leaked to the Soviets?'

'Because they passed it on to the Americans.'

'How much did the Russians find out?'

'I don't know. That's why I'm here. To find that out, with your help. Assuming, of course, that the information was transmitted to Moscow from that house on the Rheingasse.'

'And how do you know that the Americans know?'

'I think you ought to be able to figure that out yourself.'

'How many Swiss have heard about this leak?'

'Where I'm concerned, only my boss in Section 5, Captain Waibel. I can hardly know if other people in Bern have also been told. Although somehow I doubt it.'

Lützelschwab liked that answer. 'Look, Peter, you've done me an immense service by coming here this morning. I'll put young Sarasin on it right away. And I'll see if I can borrow another excellent cryptologist by the name of Marc Payot from the police in Geneva. It was these two who cracked their code in the first place. We can only hope that we started our intercepts of their radio traffic with Moscow early enough to have caught this.'

'I think the odds are in our favour. I just heard about it last night, and knowing the Russians' attitude toward Switzerland, I doubt that they would have kept this sort of thing to themselves for very long.'

Two weeks later, the deciphering of the earlier radio traffic between the Rote Kapelle in Basel and their Moscow Centre confirmed Burckhardt's worst fears. It was all there, and more. The clue to where it originated came from detailed statistics on *direct* gold transactions between Germany and Salazar's Portugal, deals which had been brokered by the Bank for International Settlements, deals in which the Swiss had played no role whatsoever. That information could *only* have come from inside the Bank for International Settlements.

When Lützelschwab summoned Burckhardt to his office in mid-April of 1943 to show him what the team of Sarasin & Payot had come up with, he immediately summed up what now had to be done. His own job was to find the leak inside the BIS and plug it. Assuming that could be accomplished, then Burckhardt's job was to *either* get to the men who ran the National Bank and convince them of the folly of their ways – a prospect which he considered very unlikely – *or* seek to convince the Allies, especially the Americans, that all gold traffic between Germany and Switzerland had now been halted, permanently. 'Whether it is true or not,' the policeman had added.

How to find the leak?

'Why not take the obvious course of action?' was the question put to Burckhardt by Lützelschwab.

'Which is?'

'Go to your boss and ask him if we can interrogate those persons who have access to the type of information that was passed on to Moscow. In fact, that will be the only way, since the Bank for International Settlements enjoys the same status as that of an embassy, and is thus otherwise strictly off-limits where we are concerned. To get in we have to be invited in.'

'Bad idea,' Burckhardt immediately countered.

'Why?'

'Because even if you do find out who it was, what are you going to be able to do about it?'

'Arrest him and charge him with espionage.'

'Espionage against whom?'

'What do you mean?'

'All he did was gain access to some confidential information inside the BIS, and make it available to a foreign government. Such action certainly violates the rules of the BIS, but hardly the laws of Switzerland. If you wanted to accuse anybody of espionage it would be the BIS itself. After all, it was its internal staff that gathered all the information in the first place.'

'All right. I can't really argue with that. But we certainly can't tolerate any more such information being passed on to the Russians.'

'So we have to find another way. You forget, Wilhelm, you've already got somebody inside the bank. Me.'

Lützelschwab liked it. 'And do you have any suspects in mind?'

'Yes. A few, but there is one in particular.'

Then Lützelschwab suddenly slapped his right hand across his forehead. 'We've got that kid!'

'What kid?'

'The one that shot you, Burckhardt.'

'So?'

'He was in and out of the house on the Rheingasse almost every day. If their man inside the BIS came there to deliver documents to Colonel Scitovsky on a recurring basis, it is highly likely that he saw him. Probably even talked to him.'

'You're right.'

'I assume that the personnel department at the BIS must have photographs on file of all the staff and employees.'

'It must. I know that when I was hired one had to be attached to one of the many forms I had to fill out as part of the hiring process.'

'Who runs the personnel department?'

'A Swiss, since for the most part the job requires that he deal with secretaries, clerks, and the like. Locals. So he must handle Schwyzerdeutsch and know the local scene so he can check out the credentials of new hires. Not that it's such a big job. The whole bank only employs 115 people.'

'How old is he?'

'Around forty, I would guess.'

'Healthy?'

'As far as I know.'

'Terrific. Then he must be a reservist in the army. Pull rank on him, Burckhardt, get copies of the photographs of your suspects, and I'll run them by that kid, Rolf Seiler. In fact, get their entire personnel files while you're at it.'

'And if Seiler refuses to cooperate?'

'He won't.'

It required four hours of interrogation, five broken ribs, and two sessions of 'shock therapy' before they got the answer three days later. The breakthrough came when Dr Lützelschwab told Seiler that so far during the war sixteen men had been secretly executed in Switzerland for espionage and that he was going be number 17 within thirty days unless . . .

Rolf Seiler then fingered a Pole by the name of Stanislaus Kryzinski before passing out for the third time that day.

When Lützelschwab telephoned with the news, Burckhardt immediately knew that they had the right man. Poland had become a shareholder in the Bank for International Settlements in June of 1930, but it had to wait a long time before it got staff representation – until 1939, when a young man from the Polish central bank was assigned to the Central Banking Department of the Bank for International Settlements, the department that monitored and sometimes participated in official gold movements throughout the world. The reason that Stanislaus Kryzinski had immediately come to mind as a prime suspect when Burckhardt had become convinced that someone inside the BIS had to be the source of the leak, was a discussion that had arisen inside the bank just a couple of months earlier. News of the German surrender at Stalingrad had come through on the BBC on the evening of 31 January 1943, a Sunday. So it had been quite natural that first thing Monday morning this would be topic 'A' during the coffee break. There had been six or seven senior men gathered there, and opinion was sharply divided. For a change the German who headed the Banking Department, Dr Huelse, and the Frenchman who ran the Central Banking Department, Monsieur Quesnay, were in agreement: if the Germans were unable to stop the Bolsheviks, then who could? And what would that mean for the future of capitalism, and for institutions like the BIS which were right at the centre of the capitalist system? That had, to the surprise of all, provoked an emotional outburst by one of M. Quesnay's deputies, the Pole, who, in his defence of the Soviets and all that they stood for, had even quoted a rather long passage, word for word, from memory, from *Das Kapital* to make his final point. From then on he had become known inside the bank as 'Der rote Pole'.

So they had him. Just to make absolutely sure, after first checking with Burckhardt to make sure that the Pole had showed up for work at the bank, Lützelschwab delegated three of his political policemen to break into Kryzinski's apartment. They found a whole stack of documents dealing with international gold movements, the last dated just two days earlier. All had been stamped 'Highly Confidential', and all were on paper which bore the logo of the Bank for International Settlements.

The following morning Peter Burckhardt was back in Lützelschwab's office. The first thing Lützelschwab did was hand over samples of the material his men had found in the Pole's apartment and photographed with their Minox cameras. Then he produced three additional blow-up photographs of typescript which summed up the dates and amounts of recent gold transactions involving the German Reichsbank, the BIS, and the Swiss National Bank. They were very sizeable.

'That comes from a portable Olivetti we also found in his apartment,' Lützelschwab explained as Burckhardt read. 'Looks like he's getting ready to send off another dispatch to his friends in Moscow, wouldn't you agree?'

267

'How? Did you find a transmitter there too?'

'Unfortunately not. If we had, that would have been the end of the story. Without the need for any other evidence or explanations we could have put him behind bars immediately.'

'So how's he planning on getting it there?'

'I suspect the same way he always did. Except that this time when he goes to the house on the Rheingasse he's going to get a little surprise.'

'Don't you think he's heard about what happened there?'

'How? We made sure that nothing was reported in the press about either the shooting out in Benken or our raid on their house here in Basel. And everybody connected with the Rote Kapelle in Switzerland, be it here, in Geneva, or Lausanne, is either dead or locked up incommunicado.'

'The system works,' Burckhardt commented, drily.

'And it is my duty to ensure that it continues to work.'

'What does that mean?'

'It means that I am informing you that the Pole now falls under the exclusive control of the Political Police Department of the Canton of Baselstadt and that from here on, Peter, matters relating to his person need no longer concern you.'

'What about the damage he's already done?'

'*That* falls under your jurisdiction.'

'I'm not so sure. They might disagree.'

'Who are they?'

'The men who run this country, Lützelschwab.'

At dawn two days later a body was fished from the Rhine about a half-kilometre downstream from the Mittlerebrücke. An autopsy revealed a very high level of alcohol in the deceased. Also a few unusual bruises. The conclusion was reached that the unidentified man had most probably got drunk the previous evening in one of the dives in Kleinbasel, and, on the way home, fallen off the embankment below the Rheingasse and drowned. The local police made the usual cursory checks of the many bars in that area in the hope that somebody would remember him and possibly provide information which could lead to his identification. They came up empty-handed.

Then, two days later, they received a report from the personnel department of the Bank for International Settlements that one of their staff was missing. He had not reported for work the entire week, and repeated attempts to contact him at home had proved futile. When the personnel director came first to the police, and then the morgue later that day, he immediately identified the dead man. Although going through such an ordeal almost always shook people up, the BIS man seemed unusually nervous. And when the two policemen who had accompanied him suggested that they go back to the bank, where they could take a look through the Pole's file and collect a photograph of the deceased, he became even more agitated. The reason, of course, was that he had given that file out just a week earlier to Lieutenant Peter Burckhardt, under strict orders to tell nobody. So as a loyal Swiss soldier he kept his silence. Which gave the police the idea that maybe the dead man had been pushed. So instead of going to the bank, they took him back to the police station and started interrogating him about his relationship with the dead Pole, beginning with the question as to whether or not either of them was married. They finally let him make a phone call to one of the officers at his bank, a Dr Peter Burckhardt, who, he said, could explain everything. After listening for no more than thirty seconds Burckhardt asked the man in charge of personnel at the BIS to tell him the number of the phone he was calling from. When he got the answer he then told him to hang up. No more than a minute later that same phone rang. It was Dr Wilhelm Lützelschwab.

The police file on the dead Pole was closed permanently one hour later with the notation 'Death by accidental drowning. No further action required.'

The system worked. The leak had been plugged.

The system also worked when Burckhardt attempted to further pursue this matter within Switzerland's financial power structure.

First he had to gain permission from his superiors in Section 5, Colonel Masson and Captain Waibel. He finally won them over — Masson, reluctantly, and only after he had been convinced that the Americans, who had alerted Burckhardt personally about the leaking of this highly sensitive information to the Soviets, not only expected but deserved an answer as to what, if anything, the Swiss proposed to do about gold and the Nazis. In order to come up with an appropriate response, it was imperative that he talk to somebody who was on the receiving end of that gold in Switzerland.

That somebody was Ernst Weber, president of the Board of Directors of the Swiss National Bank. Getting to him was not easy. In fact for a mere lieutenant attached to Section 5 of the General Staff of the Swiss army it would have been impossible — no matter what the reason — had it not been for the fact that Peter Burckhardt's father was president of Switzerland's largest commercial bank. Nobody in Switzerland *ever* said no to him. Burckhardt Sr made a personal phone call to Weber. An appointment was set for his son for 2 pm the next day. No doubt the fact that Peter Burckhardt also worked at the Bank for International Settlements, and was in fact their liaison man with the Swiss, also played a role.

For mere mortals the atmosphere inside the Swiss National Bank would have been intimidating, at the very least: marble floors and pillars; dark wooden panelling; clerks, all male, dressed in sombre black suits and talking only in hushed tones. But even before one encountered this *inside* the bank a visitor had to convince the commandant of a heavily armed crack unit of the Swiss army which stood guard around the building — and had since the day after World War II broke out — that he had come on legitimate business. Burckhardt, as a result of his frequent visits there, had no trouble doing that, nor was he in the slightest intimidated when one of the ushers opened the door to the inner sanctum of the office of the president, who did not even bother to rise from behind his massive desk — one which did not have even a single piece of paper on top of it — when Burckhardt entered the room. He motioned him to a straight-backed chair immediately in front of that desk and then uttered the words: 'Um was geht es?' And before Burckhardt could even begin to explain what his visit was about, he added: 'You have a total of ten minutes.' After which he looked pointedly at his watch.

It took at least eight of these ten minutes for Burckhardt even to describe the bare bones of what was involved, beginning with his being alerted by the Americans that the Soviets had found out all about Nazi gold shipments to Switzerland, giving Weber some examples of the information that had already been passed on, and ending with his assuring the central banker that the leak had been plugged.

When Burckhardt finally fell silent, Weber simply repeated his original question: 'Why are you here?'

Burckhardt was so taken aback that for a moment he simply did not know how to respond.

'If you are worried about what the Americans or the Russians think, I am not. *We* run this country, not they. And we run it *our* way.'

'But, sir, a large part of the gold we have been receiving from Germany was looted.'

'Who says that? We do not have even the slightest idea — Wir haben nicht die leiseste Ahnung[18] — regarding the ultimate source of the gold you are referring to. You especially ought to know, Burckhardt, that it is impossible for us to determine the origin of *any* gold bars which are delivered here from abroad. It is the simplest thing in the world for a foreign government, or central bank, to falsify the stamp of the mint of origin on the bars, to change the numbers stamped there, to provide counterfeit certificates of ownership, or to falsify the dates of changes in ownership on certificates that are not counterfeit. Do you think we here at the National Bank have either the time or the ability, or I might add, the inclination, to check out every bar of gold that comes in here? We are not the policemen of the world, Burck-

---

18 These are the exact words used by Ernst Weber, the president of the Swiss National Bank, in 1943 when confronted with this issue. See Werner Rings, *Raubgold aus Deutschland*, p. 48.

hardt. Nor, if you need reminding, are *you*. We Swiss are in a situation which requires – no, Burckhardt, *demands* – solidarity. Solidarity! Understood?'

The president of the Swiss National Bank then rose, while simultaneously pushing a button mounted at the edge of his desk. An usher opened the door moments later, and Peter Burckhardt had no choice but to also rise from his chair, and leave. The audience was over. But before Burckhardt disappeared out the door, Ernst Weber had one last message for him: 'E Gruss an Ihren Vater.' 'Greetings to your father.'

This was the signal that the ranks, which obviously also included his father, had just closed. The system worked. Which meant that the case had been closed in *both* Basel and Bern.

But not in Washington, Burckhardt knew. And, like it or not, he also knew that it was up to him to exercise damage control. To at least put a lid on this matter for the time being. Not by lying, at least lying outright, to the Americans, but perhaps by somehow diverting their attention, at least temporarily, to something of much more importance for them. But what did he and Section 5 have to offer the Americans?

Burckhardt immediately knew the answer: that French sailor they had fished from the Rhine! Provided they still had him.

272

Chapter 22

To Peter Burckhardt's great relief, when he called Dr Lützel-schwab first thing the next morning, the policeman confirmed that he still had the French sailor locked up in the Lohnhof, but gently reminded him that he could not do so much longer. This prompted Burckhardt to show up for dinner that evening at his parents' place in suburban Riehen, where he not so gently reminded his sister that she had promised to follow through on the matter. He did so just as they were finishing their coffee.

That incited the immediate intervention of Peter's father, Dr Maximilian Burckhardt, who was presiding over dinner from his position at the head of the table.

'What Frenchman are you talking about?'

Peter explained, briefly, about the Alsatian who had been indentured as a sailor in the German coastal merchant marine and who had had the peculiar task of repeatedly escorting a single flask of water from Norway to Peenemünde.

'What kind of nonsense is that?'

'Don't ask me,' his son Peter answered. 'Ask her. I did a month ago and still haven't got an answer.'

'Why in the world would you ask Felicitas?'

That got her dander up. 'Because, dear father, we are in the middle of the twentieth century. At least the rest of the world is.'

'What's that supposed to mean?'

'That women have brains too. In fact, in some countries they are even deemed intelligent enough to vote.'

'Now, now, Felicitas, *that* is not up for discussion this evening,' her mother said.[19]

'All right,' Felicitas continued. 'Peter asked me because he suspected, recalling a totally unrelated conversation we'd had earlier this year about what I was currently involved in at the university, that what the man told him had some connection with nuclear physics, the study of the atom.' Then turning to her mother: 'As *you* may or may not remember, mother, that is one of the subjects I am studying.'

Her mother's face indicated that she did not appreciate the sarcasm, but she said nothing further.

'About eleven years ago British scientists found a way to shatter the nucleus of an atom by bombarding it with an atomic particle called the neutron, thus opening it up for the first time to examination. In our physics laboratory at the Bernoullianum we have a machine called the cyclotron, a rather small one, that does that. But compared to what they are doing in England, Germany and America, our research in Basel definitely represents very small potatoes. Even in Zurich at the Federal Institute of Technology they are way ahead of us. Which is quite natural, since it was there that Einstein got his start.'

'What has all this got to do with Peter's story?' her father asked, impatiently.

'I can only guess, but it probably relates to the fact that the Germans are working on developing a new weapon. Everybody in the field of physics knows that, at least theoretically, ways can be found to force the nuclei of atoms to give up some of their enormous energy.'[20]

'And?'

'Well, again theoretically, that could result in an enormous explosion. Perhaps even an uncontrollable one.'

That silenced the rest of the family.

---

19 Twenty years later, the male population of most, but not all, Swiss cantons finally voted to enfranchise Swiss women. The half-canton of Appenzel-Inner Rhoden held out until 1990, when it was forced to do so by court order.

20 See Richard Rhodes, *The Making of the Atomic Bomb* (New York, 1986), pp. 23ff.

'Explain that,' her brother suggested.

'It relates to what they call a chain reaction. In chemistry such a process is self-limiting. But in physics this is not necessarily true. The bombardment I've been talking about could create a chain reaction that could run away in geometric progression − 1, 2, 4, 8, 16, 32, 64 . . . 67108864, 134217728 and far, far beyond, indefinitely.'[21]

'And the Germans know how to do this?' her mother asked.

'Nobody knows exactly how to do this, mother. At least yet,' her daughter answered. 'But the Germans are no doubt trying. That's probably where Peter's Alsatian sailor and his flask of Norwegian water fit in.'

Felicitas Burckhardt then continued: 'I'll try to explain how. It is generally known among physicists today that the key to making an atomic explosive is uranium . . . that if a neutron hits the nucleus of a uranium atom something is bound to happen, like the beginnings of a chain reaction. If you use a pound of uranium as the target, you might be able to set off a chain reaction of millions of other atoms and get an extremely large explosion. But "normal" uranium won't work. The chain reaction would fizzle. You need to "enrich" it. And to do that you need to separate a special type of uranium isotope known as U-235 from the much more common U238.[22] One way of doing that is to use a "uranium burner", a separation system which, however, requires the use of a moderator to slow down the movement of the neutrons inside the "burner" to the speed required for achieving that separation. It was first thought that plain water would serve this purpose. But it doesn't. What does work is "heavy water" − a chemically different kind of water consisting of deuterium, instead of hydrogen, molecules.'

'You have totally lost all of us, dear,' her mother said.

'It doesn't matter. The point is that "heavy water" is probably key to developing the substance that will serve as the material at the core of a device that could set off an atomic explosion. And it

---

21 Ibid., p. 28.

22 Ibid., pp. 294−7.

was no doubt "heavy water" that was in those flasks.'

'How do you know all this?' her mother asked in absolute awe.

'After Peter called me I waited for the visit of a professor who comes over from the physics department at the Federal Institute of Technology once a month to give a lecture on nuclear physics here in Basel. His name is Wolfgang Pauli. He's Austrian. Before he came to Zurich he was at the university in Göttingen where many of the big names in this field either taught or studied: Max Born, Enrico Fermi, Edward Teller, John von Neumann, Walter Elsasser, even an American, Robert Oppenheimer. They all left, because almost all of them were Jews. Pauli and Elsasser came to Switzerland: the rest went to America. One of the giant figures in nuclear physics stayed, however, Walter Heisenberg.[23] And according to Professor Pauli, he is no doubt in charge of the project which is using that heavy water coming from Norway.'

'But why from Norway?' Peter now asked.

'You have to distil an immense volume of ordinary H_2O in order to get even very small quantities of "heavy water". That takes enormous amounts of energy. Professor Pauli explained to me that to get just one ton of heavy water a year would require an installation that would burn 100,000 tons of coal a year. This is impossible in Germany today. So when I told him about your story, Peter, he said that it made complete sense. There was only one source of heavy water in quantity in the whole world before the war broke out. Norway. It was not deliberately being produced there but was simply a chance by-product of a process employing hydrogen electrolysis in order to produce synthetic ammonia. That was, and no doubt still is, taking place in a huge electrochemical facility, known as a High Concentration Plant, powered by a waterfall at Vemork, a little place near Rjukan, 130 kilometres west of Oslo in southern Norway.'[24]

Now Peter Burckhardt was flushed with excitement. 'I spoke to that sailor again after I telephoned you, Felicitas, and what you just told me tallies *completely* with what he told me. They would

---

23 Ibid., pp. 168–97, where Richard Rhodes tells the story of this exodus of nuclear physicists from Germany in the 1930s.

pick up those flasks at a small port in southern Norway by the name of Skien, but when I pressed him further he told me that they were transported there under heavy guard from another town nearby, Rjukan.'

'The Norway connection makes obvious sense, Peter,' his sister said, 'but I should add that Professor Pauli seemed puzzled when I mentioned Peenemünde as the destination.'

'Why?'

'Because just last week he had spoken by telephone to the man in charge of Germany's nuclear research, Professor Heisenberg. He and Professor Pauli were colleagues at Göttingen. Anyway, Heisenberg was where he has always been since the war broke out: at the Kaiser Wilhelm Institute in Berlin.'

Then Peter's father broke in. 'That's just a detail, Felicitas. Let's stick to the substance of the matter, one which appears to me to have extremely serious implications.' Then he turned to his son. 'What do you intend to do about it, Peter?'

'Talk to my immediate superior in Section 5, Captain Waibel. And if he agrees, I will then repeat the story to somebody who is in a much better position to do something about it than anybody else in Switzerland.'

'And who might that be?'

'Allen Dulles.'

As usual the meeting with Allen Dulles was arranged through Nancy Reichman, but this time Dulles was very specific as to the

---

24 The danger inherent in German control of this heavy water installation had already led to two British attempts to sabotage it. The first occurred during the night of 19 November 1942, and involved the landing of two gliders carrying British commandos in the vicinity of the Vemork High Concentration Plant. Both crashed into the side of a mountain, however. The fourteen men who survived the crashes were captured by German occupation forces and executed the same day. On 16 February 1943 the RAF tried again, this time parachuting in six Norwegians who were native to the region. They managed to disable the plant using explosives. However, the plant had resumed operations by April, and by the summer of 1943 was back up to full production. See Rhodes, pp. 455–7, 468.

details. He wanted to talk directly to the Alsatian sailor. He insisted, furthermore, that the meeting be so arranged as to escape any possible notice by hostile outside observers. Dulles knew that German agents were everywhere in Basel, gathering signs and portents however veiled, which meant that any unusual happening that would provoke their interest — as a visit to Basel's jail by Allen Dulles would definitely do — was out. So was a meeting at police headquarters. And for the same reason, he certainly did not want the sailor brought to either the American consulate or Nancy's apartment.

After first checking with Peter Burckhardt, she came back to Dulles with two suggestions. Burckhardt, who would have the sailor with him in his Mercedes, could simply pick up Dulles at some prearranged spot and they could drive around while Dulles interrogated the man. No. Dulles did not like it. It was too intense a situation. The sailor might just clam up under those circumstances. All right, Nancy countered, then how about a chance meeting and then a stroll around the zoo in Basel? Dulles liked its sense of the absurd: it was the sort of rendezvous that seemed to be standard practice in spy fiction, especially when the spies were operating in the heart of central Europe.

This was no doubt one reason why Dulles was in an exuberant mood when he arrived in Basel's railway station at ten o'clock the next morning. The other was the fact that it was a sunny, warm spring day. Nancy had put on a yellow summer frock for the occasion, and, to Dulles' delight, was accompanied by an extremely beautiful young lady similarly outfitted. When Nancy had suggested she come along after explaining why, Dulles had reluctantly agreed. That reluctance not only disappeared, but was immediately replaced by almost boyish enthusiasm when he saw that the 'woman scientist', as Nancy had described her, looked and acted like anything but.

Felicitas Burckhardt was providing the transportation from the station, and it came in the form of a red Alfa-Romeo convertible. Since it only had a front seat, Dulles soon found himself wedged between the two shapely young ladies in their rather daring — at least by Swiss standards — summer attire. Dulles had come in a dark suit, jacket and all, and was wearing a hat of the homburg variety, so the scene they presented was incongruous at the very least – and hardly in keeping with the ground rules Dulles had laid down, as was immediately evidenced by the stares the threesome attracted from the bourgeois Swiss as Felicitas pulled away from the kerb in front of the Bahnhof. Dulles was apparently not taking this matter *that* seriously. It took them just five minutes to drive to Basel's Zoologischer Garten, and when they arrived the parking lot in front of it was still almost empty, since the zoo had opened at ten o'clock. One of the few cars there was a black Citroën.

After Felicitas Burckhardt had paid the entrance fees – she had insisted, since, after all, Basel was her home and the Americans therefore her guests – they proceeded down a walk adjacent to a pond which seemed to be half filled with flamingos. Then came the zebras on the right, the giraffes on the left. All the animals were on display in perfectly natural settings of rocks and ponds and trees – trees everywhere. The zoo in Basel, though small by London or Berlin standards, was known throughout Europe as a jewel, an unexpected treat that could be found right in the middle of one of Europe's older urban centres. The okapis came next, and Felicitas Burckhardt made sure her two American guests found out that Basel was so far the only place outside Africa where these rare animals had been bred.

The total peace in this urban park was suddenly broken by a cacophony of loud honks. It was feeding time for the seals and sea-lions, and as they approached the railing around their large pond they could see one of the keepers standing high on the rocks behind, tossing them fish. Many of the creatures of the sea were clapping their flippers, trying to attract attention, and thus the next fish. The only other spectators enjoying the sun were three men, also standing behind the rail on the other side of the pond: Peter Burckhardt, Dr Wilhelm Lützelschwab, and the French sailor who had been fished from the Rhine a month earlier.

'There they are,' Nancy Reichman now said.

Dulles looked in their direction and was not totally pleased at what he saw.

'Who is the tall man in the dark suit?' he demanded of the American woman at his side.

'I don't know,' she answered, obviously flustered.

'I do,' Felicitas Burckhardt interjected. 'He is with the Staatsanwaltschaft – I don't know the English for that – but everybody in Basel is afraid of him, because they know that he is head of the political police.'

'Then he must be Wilhelm Lützelschwab,' Dulles replied. He was fully aware that in wartime Switzerland the political police were in charge of counterespionage. Was he being set up?

Peter Burckhardt had been carefully watching them since their arrival, and now, sensing that something was wrong, he hurried over. His first words, addressed to Allen Dulles, indicated that he knew what the problem must be. 'The third man, Mr Dulles, is in charge of the prisoner, and it was only with his cooperation that this meeting could be arranged. He is totally, I stress totally, opposed to the Nazis, and completely sympathetic to the cause of the Allies. He has given me his word that as far as he is concerned this meeting is and will remain strictly off the record.'

'He knows who I am?' Dulles asked.

'Of course.'

'And he understands what this is all about?'

'I don't think so.'

'Will he insist on knowing?'

'Not necessarily. It depends . . .'

'On me,' Dulles interrupted. 'His name's Lützelschwab, right?'

'Right. He likes to be called Doktor Lützelschwab.'

'Fine with me. Let's go.'

They all walked over to the two men who had remained at the railing on the other side of the pond, with Dulles and Burckhardt leading the way. After being introduced, Allen Dulles immediately drew Dr Lützelschwab aside, and began to conduct an intense conversation with him that lasted a full five minutes. Whatever it was that he said, it sufficed to win over the man whose specific duty was to stop the kind of activity which Dulles was about to engage in, namely espionage by a foreign agent on Swiss soil. To be sure, as Peter Burckhardt had already pointed out, due to Lützelschwab's violent anti-Nazi stance he had already been prepared to close an eye to what was going on here in any case. But the power of Dulles' personality had set a chemistry in motion that ensured that Lützelschwab was now not only no opponent, but had become a silent ally of the OSS's man in Switzerland. The fact that Dulles had promised to provide him with some extremely damaging evidence on the activities of one of the Nazis' most important agents in Basel – a Swiss lawyer who was in the service of I.G. Farben – certainly helped seal the relationship.

After Dulles and Lützelschwab had returned to the group, Dulles immediately got down to work. He suggested that they break up. If Herr Doktor Lützelschwab did not mind, he would take a stroll with the sailor and the Burckhardts – who would serve as interpreters. He did not bother to explain the role of Felicitas Burckhardt was not to interpret language but rather to explain the possible scientific import of what they were now going to explore. Lützelschwab chose not to mind at all, and immediately suggested to Nancy Reichman that they go to the zoo's restaurant and have a coffee and some pâtisserie on the terrace which overlooked the park. He suggested to Dulles that he join them when he was done.

It was almost an hour later when the foursome finally appeared at the top of the stairs which led from the zoo to the restaurant's terrace. Lützelschwab, sensing that the less they were all seen together in public the better, immediately went over to them and offered to once again take charge of the prisoner and return him to the Lohnhof jail. Without any further ado he put a hand on the sailor's arm, and began guiding him back down the stairs. Peter Burckhardt, hurriedly excusing himself, rushed after them.

'Wilhelm,' he said, when he had caught up with the policeman and his charge, 'what's going to happen to this man now?'

'I've got no choice in the matter. The law dictated that I toss him back over the border within twenty-four hours of his illegal entry into Switzerland, and I've already bent that law rather severely by keeping him here this long. So I'm afraid . . .'

'I understand. You've got to get rid of him.'

281

'Yes.'

'Well, there are ways and there are ways, Wilhelm.'

'What the hell is that supposed to mean, Burckhardt?'

'First a question: over which border are you going to toss him?'

'The German one, naturally.'

'But he's French. From the Alsace.'

'Technically yes. Although you know perfectly well that the Germans have once again reclaimed Alsace-Lorraine as their territory. But so what?'

'This. As you probably know, our estate out in Benken borders on the Alsace.'

'So?'

'Why don't you have him delivered to my custody out there, with the understanding that I will shove him over into France?'

He didn't fool Lützelschwab for one minute. 'I know what you're up to, Burckhardt, but as long as you sign on the dotted line when you take custody of him, it's your funeral after that.'

'I'll sign whatever you require.'

'Then I'll personally deliver him in Benken at six this evening.'

'I'll be there.' Then Burckhardt added: 'For such a mean bastard, Wilhelm, you sometimes surprise me.'

So later that day, Wilhelm Lützelschwab got rid of a prisoner while the Burckhardt estate gained a handyman for the duration of the war. But now, Peter rushed back up the stairs to rejoin the group that was waiting on the terrace. It was going on noon, and Dulles suggested to the two young Burckhardts that they stay on for a light lunch, and declared — while looking directly at Felicitas Burckhardt, for whom he had obviously developed a great liking — that this time *he* was paying. As soon as they had joined Nancy Reichman at the table where she had remained waiting, Dulles called a waitress over and ordered a well-chilled bottle of Fendant. During the next forty-five minutes, upon request, Felicitas Burckhardt delivered to Dulles the same lecture on nuclear physics, uranium and heavy water that she had given over the dinner table at her parents' home in Riehen. While she spoke, Dulles occasionally took notes on the back of a restaurant menu. Lunch came in the form of tiny open-face sandwiches —

asparagus, smoked salmon, salami, ham – followed by equally small tarts for desert – tarts filled with lemon cream, strawberries, mocha cream. It was a perfect Swiss lunch marred only by the coffee, wartime coffee consisting mostly of chicory.

It was nearing one o'clock when lunch finally broke up. Dulles consulted the abbreviated Swiss train schedule, which along with his wallet and passport he always kept in one of the inside breast pockets of his suit jacket, and declared his intention to catch the 1.47 train back to Bern. An eye signal from her brother prompted Felicitas Burckhardt to say that she was due soon for a seminar at the university and, since it was only a few blocks from the building which housed the American consulate, would take Nancy Reichman with her. This left Dulles in the custody of Peter Burckhardt, who volunteered to take him to the Bahnhof. When they got there he suggested that, since they were early, they get a second coffee. Dulles agreed, so Burckhardt parked his Mercedes and the two men headed for the first-class section of the Bahnhof Buffet. Once they had ordered, Burckhardt immediately raised the subject of the inflows of Nazi gold into Switzerland. He began by thanking Dulles for letting Swiss Intelligence know, through Nancy Reichman, that the Soviets had obtained a great deal of information on this subject. He had subsequently checked the matter out and unfortunately had to confirm that it was probably accurate.

'Is it continuing?' Dulles inquired.

Burckhardt chose not to answer. 'These matters are in the hands of a very few men in high places in this country whose perspective and attitude most of my countrymen do not share.'

'I fully understand that, Peter,' Dulles said. 'But most probably the majority of *my* countrymen would not. The same goes for some, maybe most, men in high places in Washington. Their perspective and attitude is quite simple and can be summed up as follows: Those who trade with our enemy can hardly be treated as our friends.'

Dulles paused and then added: 'My attitude is tempered by my knowledge and great love for your country, Peter. And by practical matters, as supremely exemplified by the events of this day. I will do my very best to soft-pedal your country's commercial and financial involvement with the Nazis, but you and your colleagues must realize that my influence in Washington in these matters is definitely limited. I can buy your country some time, but that's about all.' Then he looked at his watch. 'Speaking of time, I think I should be on my way.'

Burckhardt walked him to the train, and as Dulles opened the door to one of the first-class compartments and began boarding, an apparent afterthought struck him and he asked: 'Say, do you by any chance know anybody at the Bally Shoe Company?'

'Yes. One of the sons of the founder. We went to school together.'

'Do you have any feel for his "perspective and attitude" as you so nicely put it?'

'Yes I do. He shares mine.'

'Would you mind letting him know that I will be getting in touch with him?'

'Certainly.'

'I would appreciate that.'

Dulles climbed in, a conductor came by slamming all the doors closed, and at precisely 1.47 the 1.47 to Bern began to move out.

It arrived in Bern at precisely 2.58. Dulles was picked up by an embassy driver, and ten minutes later he was in the American embassy. Within the hour a brief coded message was transmitted to OSS headquarters in Washington:

From: 110
To: 109
Status: Top secret

Text: Just spoke to a French worker who swam the Rhine from Germany to Switzerland. Told following improbable story. Said he was forced labor guard for cask of water from Rjukan in Norway to island of Peenemünde in Baltic Sea. End.[25]

The OSS had assigned the code number 110 to Allen Dulles. The recipient of this message with code number 109 was no less than the head of all of America's wartime espionage efforts, the OSS chief, General William J. Donovan. Reflecting the rather lighthearted attitude he had shown in Basel, and perhaps also due to his lack of any scientific background – his academic strength lay in languages[26] – although Dulles gave the message a top-secret status, he did not assign it any special priority. As a result, it sat on Donovan's desk for weeks since, during this period, he was in North Africa, directing the intelligence penetration of Sicily in advance of the planned invasion of that island in July.

It was therefore not until early August that Donovan passed the message along to the man in charge of Research and Development in the OSS, a chemist and inventor by the name of Stanley Lovell, known within that organization as 'Dr Moriarty'. Matters dealing with science were automatically referred to him.

The chronicler of the role of Donovan and the OSS in World War II described what happened next as follows:[27]

Stanley Lovell pondered the report in his South Building cubby-hole. He knew there was a huge hydroelectric plant at Rjukan. The only water worth guarding would be heavy water needed for an atomic explosive. Lovell suspected that the Nazis might be working on an atomic bomb at Peenemünde. He rushed to Donovan's office and threw down a brace of maps on his desk.

'Bill,' he said, 'this may be vitally important.'

One map showed Peenemünde in the Baltic; the other showed the northern coast of France. On the latter Lovell had drawn in the locations of curious ski-like runways, with odd curved twists at the ends, that Allied planes had

25 Richard Dunlop, *Donovan: America's Master Spy*, p. 401.

26 See Leonard Mosley, *Dulles: A Biography of Eleanor, Allen, and John Foster Dulles and Their Family Network* (New York, 1978). After Princeton, and before embarking on his diplomatic career, Allen Dulles taught English in such diverse places as Allahabad, Shanghai, Canton and Peking.

27 Dunlop, p. 401.

photographed. From west of Boulogne to south of Cherbourg, these strange runways seemed to be aimed at the British cities of London, Bristol, Birmingham, and Liverpool.

'What do you mean?' asked Donovan.

'This little French workman has told us where the German heavy water comes from,' explained Lovell, 'but vastly more important, where the German physicists are working to make a bomb employing nuclear fission. It all adds up perfectly.'

'Adds up to what?'

'To a catastrophic Nazi victory. This explains the ski sites. The Germans are going to attack Britain from those odd-looking launching sites with a secret weapon.'

Donovan ordered Lovell to fly to London and brief the OSS European chief, David Bruce, about his suspicions. According to Lovell, Bruce immediately met with Lord Portal of the Royal Air Force and General Carl Spaatz of the U.S. Air Force. The RAF took to the air en masse on August 17, 1943, and attacked Peenemünde in one of the war's most devastating raids. A thousand Germans, many of them scientists and technicians, died in the attack, and the mysterious facilities on the island were obliterated. The attack knocked out the experimental plants developing the V-1's and V-2's delaying the appearance of these rockets over Britain until June of 1944.

But the German facilities devoted to developing an atomic bomb escaped totally unscathed . . . due to a fact that would later return to haunt Allen Dulles: there had never been any such facility located on Peenemünde. The heavy water was never unloaded at Peenemünde but rather at the neighbouring port of Wolgast, from where it was shipped by rail to Berlin, to the Kaiser Wilhelm Institute, where the German nuclear research was centred all along.[28] Lovell might have caught on to this at the

---

28   Ibid., pp. 402.

very outset had Dulles relayed to him the apparent scepticism of Professor Pauli that the young Swiss scientist, Felicitas Burck-hardt, had detected in her conversations with him, and duly passed on to Dulles during lunch at Basel's zoo. But he didn't. And Heisenberg's efforts aimed at making his country the first to develop an atomic bomb continued unabated and unobserved while American intelligence efforts were being diverted to other matters.[29]

One such diversion involved a plot to kill Heisenberg's patron, Adolf Hitler, and again it was the Burckhardt–Reichman connection which played a key role.

---

29 As Richard Rhodes points out in his definitive history of the development of the atomic bomb: 'One of the mysteries of the Second World War was the lack of an early and dedicated American intelligence effort to discover the extent of German progress toward atomic bomb development.' *The Making of the Atomic Bomb*, p. 605.

Chapter 23

A small factor – infinitesimal, in fact – which played a role in the genesis of this doomed project, the assassination of Adolf Hitler,[30] can be traced back to the same resident mad scientist of the OSS who had instigated the Peenemünde bombing, Stanley Lovell. It was totally unrelated to Lovell's efforts to prevent the Germans from developing the ultimate superweapon, and seemingly laughable by comparison.

It grew out of the fact that Lovell's R&D department was not only responsible for providing scientific analysis of raw intelligence data – such as that contained in Dulles' cable about the mysterious casks of water which were being transported over Nordic waters – but was also charged with creating exotic products for the use of agents in the field ranging from invisible inks for secret messages, to cameras camouflaged in matchboxes, to a candle that was half wax and half explosives.[31] Another invention – and here is where Dulles came in – was a shoe designed to carry messages in hidden spaces. Lovell's people had worked out a technique whereby a shoe sole could be laid over the message, stitched in place, and bevelled, its edge stained and

---

30 This whole episode reached its initial climax in January of 1944 in Bern, where Dulles met with the group conspiring to kill Hitler. See Dunlop, p. 450.

31 See Dunlop, pp. 377ff. Here Donovan is quoted as referring to Lovell as 'my evil genius'. One can hardly avoid concluding that Lovell might have been the model for that scientist who supplied James Bond with his toys in Ian Fleming's novels.

set. He managed to get the design to Dulles in Bern with the help of the French underground in the spring of 1943. Lovell suggested that Dulles find a way to have it manufactured in Switzerland and then use it to communicate with the small but growing number of OSS contacts in Germany and occupied Europe.

This had led to Dulles' cryptic inquiry of Peter Burckhardt before departing the Basel railway station after his day at the zoo in the early spring of 1943 as to whether he might happen to know any of the Bally family, the Swiss founders and owners of one of the world's most prestigious shoe manufacturers. Shortly thereafter, Dulles visited Bally's headquarters in Schönewerd, a small town some twenty-five miles from Zurich. Not only did Bally agree to manufacture Lovell's shoe, but with the help of Bally's management, Bally salesmen were persuaded to help the OSS. Already in this autumn of 1943, as they travelled through Germany and occupied Europe, they were carrying messages written on paper or cloth and inserted in place of a shoe's bottom filler, both to and from Switzerland.

One of the first to take advantage of this Swiss courier service was a member of the Kreisau Circle in East Prussia, the only major surviving force inside Germany seeking the removal of the Führer. This episode grew out of a Swiss–American joint venture in intelligence which, at its outset, received an invaluable assist from a man of the cloth, in fact from one of the twentieth century's greatest theologians, Karl Barth. Although Barth was a Swiss through and through[32] – or better yet, a Basler – from the very beginning his academic career was intertwined with Germany, German universities and German theologians.[33] Although

---

32   In 1926 Barth had also been given German citizenship, due to his status in the Prussian civil service as a professor at Münster University. Eberhard Busch, *Karl Barths Lebenslauf: Nach seiner Briefen und autobiographischen Texten* (Munich, 1976), p. 189.

33   These included Paul Tillich, Rudolph Bultmann and Martin Buber, three of the other towering figures in twentieth-century theology, as well as the philosophers Martin Heidegger and Karl Jaspers (who also eventually moved from Heidelberg to the university of Basel due to the fact that his wife had Jewish ancestors). But Barth's close contacts also extended to leading figures as

most of his theological education was received at the university of Bern, he also spent various semesters at German universities — Berlin, Tübingen and Marburg. It was also in Germany in the early 1920s, at the university of Göttingen, which was then developing into the world centre for the embryonic science of modern nuclear physics, where Barth was first recognized as a major figure in twentieth-century theology. In 1921, despite the fact that he held no academic degrees,[34] he was invited to become a professor there and given the chair of Reformed Theology. In 1926 he moved to the university of Münster, and in 1930 to the university of Bonn, where he stayed until he was expelled from both the university and the country by the Nazis in 1935. Within three days of the announcement of his dismissal from Bonn, the cantonal council of Basel invited Barth to a special chair to be immediately created for him at the university in his home town.

---

well as 'simple pastors' in the Lutheran and Reformed Church throughout Germany. See Busch, *Karl Barths Lebenslauf*. Also the English translation of this work by John Bowden, *Karl Barth: His life from letters and autobiographical texts* (Philadelphia, 1977).

34 A few years later the Protestant faculty at Münster granted him a doctorate in theology, 'because of his many and varied contributions to the revision of religious and theological questioning'. In 1937 the Nazis forced the university to rescind this degree. Busch, p. 128.

35 It would be silly to even try to summarize the main thrust of the theological teachings of Karl Barth in a footnote in a novel! After all, his work consisted of more than nine thousand pages, twice as much as the *Summa* of Thomas Aquinas, with whom a Pope compared Barth. Suffice it to say that after being involved in 'dialectical theology' in the 1920s, he returned more and more to traditional Christian orthodoxy. His principal book is *Kirchliche Dogmatik* (*Church Dogmatics*), and the first sentence sets the tone for the whole work: 'The problem of dogmatics is scholarly reflection on the Word of God spoken by God in revelation and handed down in holy scripture by prophets and apostles.' His reflections led Barth to bring Jesus Christ 'into the centre' of his theology to the degree that he equates the 'Word of God' to 'Jesus Christ'. (Hans Urs von Balthazar, the Catholic theologian who also lived in Basel, termed this 'Christological concentration', the basic formulation of which can be found in Barth's *Anselm: Fides Quaerens Intellectum*.) In Barth's words, 'The relationship between God and man, of which Christian discourse speaks in its pure form as the Church's preaching, is *itself Word*. It does not become Word by being spoken by man; it is Word from the beginning.' See Busch, pp. x, 153–5, 173. Also Georges Casalis, *Karl Barth* (Garden City, New York, 1963).

Thus Switzerland had gained — or better said, regained — one of the towering intellects of this century, while Germany had managed to create an enemy who never rested in his vehement opposition to the Nazi regime until its total destruction.[35] Well before the outbreak of war, Barth's outspokenness on this subject, which even brought him in conflict with the Swiss government on certain occasions, made him a rallying point for all anti-Nazi forces in Switzerland, as well as those in Germany itself, the adherents to the so-called Confessing Church.[36] It was in a new Swiss theological journal, *Theologische Existenz heute*, which Barth had co-founded in the mid-1930s, that many of them were still able to voice their opinions. There was a constant flow of visitors from German Protestant Church circles to Basel, while Barth was constantly arranging study grants from Basel University for German students who had been refused admission to German universities because of their political views, arranging new jobs for German émigrés, and putting up 'non-Aryans' at his home,[37] and this in a country where few foreigners were ever invited into a Swiss home even for dinner!

After 1 September 1939, all this came to an end. The borders

---

36 The 'Confessing Church' was founded by the Lutheran pastor, Martin Niemöller, in 1933, taking its name from the fact that it based its opposition to Hitler and the 'German Christians' on the confession of faith in Jesus Christ as the one Lord and source of belief. Niemöller subsequently spent the war in a Nazi concentration camp. One of the major differences Barth had with the leaders of the Confessing Church centred on their attitude toward the Jews. He accused the Church of having fought for itself 'for the freedom and purity of its proclamation while, on the other hand, it has kept silent over the treatment of the Jews . . . and so much else against which the Old Testament prophets would certainly have spoken out.' *Karl Barth zum Kirchenkampf. Beteiligung-Mahnung-Zuspruch* (Basel, 1956), p. 34. Barth, for his part, was constantly writing letters to Church leaders in other countries, for example Bishop Bell of Chichester, Bishop Eidem of Uppsala, and Marc Boegner of Paris, asking them to aid the reception of Jews into their countries. See Busch, pp. 226 and 271ff; Casalis, pp. 57ff.

37 Beginning in 1936, Barth also made contacts with non-theologians who were now unpopular in Germany, including Thomas Mann and the pianist Rudolph Serkin. It was as if Barth were now involved in a one-man vendetta against the Hitler regime.

between Switzerland and Germany were closed to all but those few travellers whose trips abroad were officially sanctioned by the Nazi regime. Karl Barth was now isolated from his Protestant brethren in Germany, with one major exception: Dietrich Bonhoeffer, the Lutheran pastor in Berlin who was not only a leading figure in the Confessional Church, but also associated with the East Prussian Kreisau Circle — the last remaining force inside Germany which stood in violent political opposition to Hitler. To Barth's amazement he showed up in Basel on three occasions in 1941 alone, on 4 March, 31 August, and 19 September. This was possibly due to the fact that the German Abwehr (officially the Military Intelligence Division of the German High Command which, although specifically charged with counter-intelligence, was also very active in 'offensive' foreign intelligence) provided Bonhoeffer with travel papers. This was done under direct orders of the officer who since 1935 had been in charge of the Abwehr, Admiral Canaris.

Canaris was a very strange man. On the one hand he was regarded outside Germany as a very dangerous man, since his secret service functioned well and he provided Hitler with invaluable information. Yet, at the same time, he tolerated, protected and at times abetted anti-Nazi conspirators in the Abwehr, as well as outside of the military.[38] Where the Church resistance movement inside Germany was concerned, as Allen Dulles was to tell Nancy Reichman in this fall of 1943: 'Canaris's Abwehr furnished the technical facilities for the conspiracy, its lines of communications, contacts with foreign countries, and the cover under which the individual conspirators could operate. It was the Kreisau Circle which provided the spiritual and political ideology.'[39] Chief among these individual conspirators were such Prussian aristocrats as Count Helmuth von Moltke, such military leaders as Colonel Claus Schenk von Stauffenberg, such political leaders as the former mayor of Leipzig, and such Church leaders as the Lutheran Pastor, Dietrich Bonhoeffer.

---

38   Allen Dulles, *Germany's Underground*, pp. 70–2.

39   Ibid., p. 81.

According to Barth, when Bonhoeffer showed up in Basel, 'he spoke to me of the plan to form a military government which would first of all halt the German troops . . . on the fronts they then held and in the occupied territories, and would deal with the Allies on this basis. I remember very clearly Bonhoeffer's great amazement when I told him that I thought it impossible that the Allies would agree to this.'[40] Barth had already anticipated the unconditional terms the Allies would attach to any German surrender. But apparently he had not convinced either Bonhoeffer or his co-conspirators.

This became clear in the fall of 1943 when Barth received an urgent message on microfilm which was smuggled to him via Holland by the Swiss wife of a pastor in the Dutch Reformed Church whose husband was in contact with the Bonhoeffer group. She had been allowed to come to Switzerland for her mother's funeral. The message made it clear that any further trips to Switzerland by Bonhoeffer were out. The reason: Heinrich Himmler and his Gestapo had gained evidence of Canaris's support of anti-Nazi activities. As a result, under direct orders from the Führer the Abwehr had just been totally disbanded.[41] This still left the Kreisau Circle intact, but now without any means to stay in contact with the foreign support it needed if it was to succeed in its main objective: the elimination of Adolf Hitler and the establishment of a new regime in Germany. This message was to introduce a friend of Bonhoeffer's who was likewise a member of the Kreisau Circle. Since he was attached to the Foreign Office in Berlin he was able to gain independent access to travel papers. He planned to come to Switzerland in early November and would contact Barth to seek his help in establishing contact with the highest possible authorities among the Allied powers, preferably the Americans. Due to the now very delicate situation inside Germany, such contacts had to be

---

40 This quotation is taken from a letter by Barth to a J. Glenthoj, dated 7 September 1956. See Busch, p. 315.

41 The four top men of the German intelligence service, including Admiral Canaris, were subsequently executed for treason. Ibid., p. 80.

established with extreme care. The envoy's name was Adam von Trott zu Solz.[42]

On Monday, 16 November 1943, Peter Burckhardt picked up the phone in his office at the Bank for International Settlements and was told by his secretary, in a voice which indicated both awe and amazement, that Professor Karl Barth wished to speak to him.

'This is Peter Burckhardt, Herr Professor,' Burckhardt said as soon as the connection was established.

'You are probably wondering why I am calling you,' Barth began. 'Well, to begin with, my family and yours have ties which go far back. My grandmother on my mother's side was a Burckhardt. She was, in fact, my favourite grandmother. And her older brother, Hans Burckhardt, was my godfather. Alas, they have both been dead for a long time, but I still have fond memories of them.'[43]

Peter Burckhardt responded: 'I know about our family relationship from my father, Herr Professor. He has often mentioned that he is a distant cousin of yours.'

'I just finished talking to your father, Peter, and it was he who suggested I call you. I will come directly to the point and not waste much of your valuable time. I am expecting a visitor from Germany next week who wants to establish contacts with the Americans, specifically with Americans who have influence in high places in Washington. The reason I called your father was because I assumed that, as a result of his position at the head of the Swiss Bank Corporation, he must have such contacts. He did not seem too eager to help. Instead he referred me to you.'

Peter Burckhardt knew the reason behind his father's reticence. When he referred to Karl Barth as a distant cousin, it was

---

42 Ibid., p. 88.

43 See Busch, pp. 4−6. The most famous member of the Burckhardt family was Jacob Burckhardt, the Renaissance historian. He and Friedrich Nietzsche had been rather unlikely colleagues on the faculty of the university of Basel when Karl Barth's father had studied there.

not always in the most complimentary fashion. For in certain circles, especially those of Swiss bankers, Barth was perceived as having leftist leanings, due to his sympathy for the Swiss Social Democrats. They ignored the fact that these 'sympathies' had their origins in its having been the Social Democrats who had been in the forefront of Swiss criticism of and resistance to the Nazis from the very beginning, while it was the bankers who had brought up the rear . . . and still did.

Before Burckhardt could respond, Barth added: 'Assuming you are able to help me out, I must add that it must be done with great care. The Gestapo and their agents are everywhere in Basel. They regard me as their Public Enemy Number One in Switzerland. Unfortunately, it is not just the Gestapo I must worry about. As you know, our own Swiss government is very ambivalent in its attitude towards the Nazis and continues to do everything it can to prevent me from further "provoking" them. They want to ban me from any further public speaking on the subject. They already censor my writing. I now even have it on the best authority that the cantonal police are listening in on all my telephone calls at home. That is why I am calling you from the university. If either the Gestapo or our government gets wind of this, everyone concerned could end up in deep trouble, especially our visitor from Germany, since his very life will be at risk were he to be seen in my company. So we must be extremely cautious.'

'I fully understand, Herr Professor,' Burckhardt said, adding: 'So that you know where I stand, let me assure . . .'

Barth interrupted him. 'I already know where you stand.' Barth did not explain further, but between phone calls to Burckhardt father and son, he had made a third call to one of the leaders of the Swiss Social Democrats who had told him that 'despite his name' Peter Burckhardt was 'on our side'. Then Barth added: 'But the point is, can you help this man meet the right American?'

'Most probably.'

'Can you tell me who that would be?'

'Yes. Allen Dulles.'

295

'You're referring to the man whom President Roosevelt sent here late last year as his personal envoy?'

'Yes.' That was the story that had made the rounds in Switzerland, and Peter Burckhardt was hardly going to contradict it. 'But I'm sure that he will want to know a lot more about this German before he agrees to meet him.' As a fellow intelligence officer, Burckhardt knew that Dulles had to make sure that the visitor from Germany was what he purported to be and not a Gestapo plant.

'I fully understand that. How can we get by that impasse without wasting a great deal of time?'

'The simplest way would be for one of Dulles' men to check him out as soon as possible, which should be no problem, since there is a person here in Basel right now who could do that. They would have to meet, of course. Which just leaves the questions of "where" and "when".'

Barth had an immediate answer to both. 'The German is arriving in Basel this Thursday. Which is perfect. It would be too dangerous to meet either at my home or at the university. My home is under sporadic police surveillance, and there are too many people around at the university. But every Thursday I hold a small informal seminar with some of my students in a place which is completely out of the way. We meet in the back room of the Bruderholz restaurant, which is just a short walk from my house. Only people from the neighbourhood frequent the place. It would, I think, be perfect for what we have in mind. You could bring along the American intermediary, and . . .'

'No. I think it best if I stay out of this. My presence at such a seminar could hardly be explained, and might, through some unforeseen circumstance, draw attention from the wrong quarter.'

'I understand.'

'But there is another way, one that would still keep all this in the Burckhardt family, Herr Professor.'

'Ja?' And Peter Burckhardt could note the hint of a chuckle.

'I have a sister who is matriculated at the university. In the Philosophical Faculty. Phil II. She studies physics. But every semester she tries to expand her horizon, as she puts it, by taking lectures in non-related disciplines. I know that last semester she chose psychology, and attended the lectures of Carl Gustav Jung.'

'Uh,' was Barth's only comment on this. Jung, who came over from Zurich twice a month to lecture at the university of Basel, was suspected in academic circles of harbouring sympathies for the racial theories of the Nazis and, as such, was anathema where Karl Barth was concerned.

But Peter Burckhardt was blissfully ignorant of this at the time, and continued: 'It would be quite appropriate for her to turn up at one of your lectures or seminars this semester. Her name is Felicitas. And as luck would have it, she is a friend of the American intermediary here in Basel whom I have in mind.'

'I will expect to see them at seven this Thursday at the Bruderholz restaurant unless I hear otherwise from you in the meantime. Thank you very much. I only wish all the Swiss in our government were more like you, Peter. God bless you.'

Chapter 24

Felicitas Burckhardt and Nancy Reichman were fast friends during the summer of 1943, a friendship which had begun at dinner at the Burckhardts' house, but come to full blossom in Basel's zoological garden on the day that Allen Dulles had travelled from Bern to meet the French sailor. Following lunch, Peter Burckhardt had taken Dulles to the railway station while his sister drove Nancy Reichman back to the American consulate in her Fiat convertible. On the way they had decided to have lunch again — just the two of them — at Schiesser's, the confiserie overlooking Basel's market square. They chose Schiesser's because it was just a few blocks down from the new university lecture halls on the Petersgraben and a few blocks up from the offices of the American consulate. This soon became a ritual — every other Wednesday at noon. For some reason, although both young women were fluent in both German and French as well as the Swiss dialect, they always spoke English when they were together. And they always got dolled up for their lunches, high heels and all. Although they never admitted it, there could be little doubt that they enjoyed the attention they drew from men and women alike.

At 7 pm on 11 November 1943, when these two very pretty young women entered the Bruderholz restaurant, located on the hill of the same name overlooking Basel, they immediately received the same type of appreciative glances. They just stood there for a minute, wondering what to do next. Then a large bear of a man in his mid-fifties who had been sitting at a table in the rear, smoking his pipe and occasionally taking a sip of beer while listening intently to a much younger man who was sitting at his right, rose and came directly over to greet them.[44]

'You have to be the young Burckhardt woman,' he immediately said to Felicitas.

'I am,' Felicitas replied.

'Well I am your distant cousin, Karl Barth. I knew it had to be you from your patrician nose. And because you are so pretty. All the Burckhardt women are.'

This actually caused Felicitas Burckhardt to blush, and in order to divert attention from herself she introduced Nancy Reichman as the American vice-consul in Basel.

As Barth shook her hand he said: 'I am most pleased to meet you, and most pleasantly surprised, since for some reason . . .'

'You were expecting a man,' Nancy said.

Barth chuckled, and then, taking the arm of each of the young ladies, escorted them to the table where he had been sitting. In addition to the young man, there was also a striking-looking woman in her mid-forties sitting there. Both now rose, to be introduced as Fräulein Charlotte von Kirschbaum and Adam von Trott zu Solz. Then Barth drew up two additional chairs and, once all were seated, said to the woman on his left: 'Lollo, I suggest that we sit here and chat for a while. Maybe when the students start to arrive you can escort them to the back room so that we won't be disturbed.'

The aristocratic woman, her dark hair parted down the middle, her dress in severe black, nodded her agreement while giving Barth a loving glance so obvious that it caused Felicitas Burckhardt to surreptitiously nudge Nancy Reichman's foot with hers. Then Barth continued. 'We have just been finding out once again how small our world is. Young Adam here' — and now both

---

44 Author's note: I attended Karl Barth's seminars in the Bruderholz restaurant during the years 1955–8, and even then the food was good. Now it ranks as Basel's premier restaurant and has even been given two stars in the Michelin Guides Rouges, an honour which is only very grudgingly bestowed on restaurants not located on French soil.

Nancy and Felicitas turned their attention to the German, who was a classic case of tall, blond, and handsome, in his mid-thirties and not wearing a wedding ring — 'not only studied at Göttingen, where I taught in the 1920s, but also went to Oxford on a Rhodes scholarship, a university where I have lectured on various occasions and which saw fit to give me an honorary doctorate of theology in 1938. I very much appreciated it at the time, since it was also in 1938 that the Nazis forced the university of Münster to rescind the honorary degree they had bestowed on me. Win some, lose some as the British say. In the short time we have been sitting here together, Adam and I have identified many mutual friends in both places. As well as in Berlin, where Adam is now with the Foreign Office.' He addressed these words to Nancy Reichman.

And with that, she concluded, Barth has just confirmed Trott's credentials. So for all intents and purposes the objective of this meeting has already been achieved. She could pass Trott along to Dulles with Barth's nihil obstat.

Then Barth proceeded to do the same with her. 'I understand from Felicitas' introduction that you are America's vice-consul here in Basel. I do not wish to pry, but is it not unusual for a young lady to have such a diplomatic posting here on what could become a front line in this war?'

'It is. And my parents were as surprised as you seem to be when I accepted the posting. You see, our family is Jewish.' When she had finished speaking these words she wondered why in the world she had simply blurted them out. But her embarrassment immediately evaporated when Karl Barth reached over to put his hand on hers.

'My dear, I must constantly remind many of my colleagues in the Christian Church that our Lord Jesus Christ was a Jew, and that we are all children of the same God. I constantly pray for your people who are now being subjected to horrors which are almost beyond human comprehension. I admire your courage, young lady. And do not totally give up hope for those of your people who remain under the Nazi yoke. As long as there are still a few Germans left like Adam, perhaps this tragedy can be stopped before it is taken to its final conclusion. Is it not so, Herr Trott?'

The German responded with an emphatic: 'Yes. In fact that is precisely why I am here. To get help in stopping a calamity which is about to engulf not only the Jews but everybody who lives in my country.' What he did not express out loud was his subsequent thought: only in Basel would a Prussian aristocrat determined to kill Hitler be seeking the help of an American–Jewish woman under the protective auspices of a Swiss theologian.

Now the students began to straggle into the restaurant and, under the direction of Fräulein Kirschbaum, who now left the table, were being ushered into the back room where Karl Barth was soon to begin his regular Thursday evening seminar. The two men also excused themselves for a few minutes, leaving Nancy Reichman and Felicitas Burckhardt alone at the table.

'Who is that woman?' was the immediate question that Nancy whispered to her friend.

'His partner, his confidante, and also his girlfriend,' Felicitas answered. 'They say she is the daughter of a Bavarian general who was killed in World War I.'

'Why hasn't he married her?'

'Because he's already married.'

For a few seconds this left Nancy Reichman literally speechless.

'Not only that, but Fräulein von Kirschbaum lives in the same house with the rest of the Barth family.'[45]

---

45 For more on this odd relationship, see Busch, pp. 185ff. Here Barth is quoted as saying that 'Without her collaboration I could only have done a fragment . . . of my work.' Nonetheless, as his biographer put it, 'Many people, even good friends, and not least his mother, took offense at the presence of "Lollo" in Barth's life, and later even in his home. There is no question that the intimacy of her relationship with him made particularly heavy demands on the patience of his wife Nelly.' He adds: 'Barth himself did not hesitate to take the responsibility and the blame for the situation which had come about. But he thought that it could not be changed. It had to be accepted and tolerated by all three.'

'My goodness!' was all that Nancy could manage.

'Most of the hypocrites from the so-called good families in Basel snicker about this. None of them dares admit that the heads of *their* families have always kept a girlfriend in Geneva or a mistress in Paris. Including my father, I might add.'

For a Jewish girl from Palo Alto, this was a strange new world. 'But what do the wives say?'

'Nothing. This is Switzerland, my dear. At least Karl Barth does it out in the open.' Then Felicitas Burckhardt added: 'I really like him, don't you?'

'Oh, yes,' Nancy replied. 'He's like a teddy bear. You almost feel like cuddling him.'

Then the subject of their conversation returned, with the young German at his side. Barth spoke directly to Nancy Reichman: 'I know that you have things to discuss with Adam, Fräulein Reichman, but perhaps before you do you might spend a few minutes with us in the other room.'

When they entered the back room, the dozen students — all male — who had been seated around a large table in the back room of the restaurant, immediately rose out of respect. Barth motioned to them to be seated, and then took his place at the head of the table, with Fräulein Kirschbaum at his side. The three visitors stayed in the back of the room, and took chairs which stood against the wall just to the right of the door, since they only planned on staying for a brief time.

Now Barth took charge. 'As you all know, the winter semester has just begun and I notice that a few of you are here for the first time. For them I will repeat that during this semester and the next we will be discussing principally four works and I expect all of you to be thoroughly familiar with all of them. They are Calvin's *Institutes*, Book III, Anselm's *Cur Deus Homo?*, Luther's *Sermon on Good Works*, and Zwingli's *De vera et falsa religione*. We shall also be addressing some general themes, such as Kant's philosophy of religion and Luther's understanding of "authority".

'But before we begin, I want to remind you that today is November 11th, the day on which the last world war ended.

Unfortunately, the end of this war is not yet in sight. Tens of millions more will no doubt die before it is over. Yet in this war as in the last, we here in Switzerland remain untouched. For we are neutral. What I want to say to you tonight, because you are all Swiss[46] and all of you serve in the Swiss army as do I[47] – with great pride and with the resolve to die for my country if it proves necessary, I might add – is that there must be limits to such neutrality. I have always rejected the interpretation of Swiss neutrality which the supreme authority in the Confederation claims to be orthodox and compulsory. By that I mean the false and forced reinterpretation of our military neutrality in terms of an "integral" neutrality, which our Federal Council used in 1939 as a pretext for preventing not only itself, but all Swiss citizens from demonstrating any Swiss interest in the European conflict. They wanted to tell us to keep a blank face while the others were fighting and shedding blood for the light of freedom – where, I ask, would we who are gathered here this evening be if they hadn't done this? – and to act as though we saw no difference between Peter and Paul, Hitler and Churchill. The Federal President of our country, Wetter, has just reaffirmed this, telling us that this is "the only possible Swiss attitude" and that any further public discussion of it is prohibited, a prohibition which if necessary will be enforced by the police.[48]

---

46 By 1943 the foreign students, the largest contingent of whom had always come from Germany, had totally disappeared from Basel. Even had some remained, there would probably have been no German students in Barth's seminar, since the Nazi regime had issued a decree which prohibited German universities from giving them credit for any semesters spent under Barth at Basel's university.

47 Barth had reported for military duty in April of 1940. He described it thus: 'I had been declared unfit when I was nineteen, but in my fifty-fourth year I was fit (so I had made some progress) and my bedroom now contained a helmet, a complete uniform, a rifle and bayonet, etc. so that I would be able to go out at any hour of the day or night to decide the issue.' He served sporadically on active duty – mostly patrolling the Rhine – for a total of 104 days. Busch, *Karl Barths Lebenslauf*, pp. 305–6.

48 These are direct quotations taken from Barth's *Eine Schweizer Stimme 1938–1945* (A Swiss Voice, 1938–1945) (Basel, 1945).

'Well, I refuse to be silenced. Our national policy is a mixture of cunning short-sightedness and short-sighted cunning. It is a scandal and a blot on the reputation of Switzerland. We Swiss must do everything in our power to help bring this war to an end. That can only be achieved by bringing down the barbarian, Hitler, and all those who surround him. It is our Christian duty to help those who are actively working toward that end, by both word and deed, if we are given the opportunity. At the very least we must pray, and pray often, for their success.'

Barth paused to relight his pipe before he continued: 'Now, let us turn our attention to Calvin and . . .'

As Barth continued to speak, the three visitors who had been sitting at the rear of the room rose and very quietly slipped out of the door which led back into the main room of the Bruderholz restaurant.

'Let's sit over there,' said Nancy Reichman, pointing to a table that was both unoccupied and isolated from the rest of the restaurant's patrons, which were very few anyway.

'May I suggest that we share a bottle of wine?' Adam von Trott zu Solz said, once they were seated. Both young women immediately agreed, and minutes later a chilled bottle of Fendant arrived and was poured.

'I think Professor Barth's words were addressed as much to you, Herr Trott, as to his students,' Felicitas Burckhardt then said.

'I know. They are deeply embedded in my mind and I fully intend to repeat them, word for word if I can, when I am back among my friends in the Kreisau Circle.'

Now Nancy Reichman spoke. 'I think it would be helpful if you explained more about that Circle. Who are they? What are their intentions? And how can the United States help? Before you do, however, let me explain more precisely why I am here this evening. Although I am the American vice-consul in Basel, I also work with a man who has contacts at the highest level within American Intelligence, and who even has direct access to President Roosevelt. His name is Allen Dulles and he is attached to our embassy in Bern. He is aware of the fact that we are meeting this evening.'

'I understand and will treat all that you have just told me with the greatest possible discretion,' von Trott said, speaking in a clipped Oxford accent. 'Since I am attached to the Foreign Office in Berlin, I am well informed as to both the person of Allen Dulles and his mission here in Switzerland. I hope that if all goes well here this evening, I can meet him as soon as possible.'

Adam von Trott zu Solz then went on to explain the basic mission of the Kreisau Circle: to rid their Vaterland of Hitler and the Nazis and replace them with a government based on the principles of Christian Socialism. Once in power they would see to it that the German army was immediately abolished. And as for the punishment of Germans for the war and crimes against humanity, the Circle favoured trials for war criminals before the Court of International Justice at The Hague. Von Trott summed it up by saying that the Kreisau Circle hoped, after Hitler, to guide the German people on the road to individual freedom, to peace, and to decency.

'But first we must rid ourselves of Hitler, and, very frankly, we are sharply divided as to how to achieve that end. Many among us are opposed to using violence. Others are convinced that Hitler must be killed, and that the Kreisau Circle must play a direct part in such an assassination. I am one of them. Since we no longer have the help of Admiral Canaris and the German Abwehr, if we are to succeed in this we must obtain help from outside Germany. I hope I will be able to convince Allen Dulles to give us such assistance . . . assuming that I can get the opportunity to speak to him.'

Nancy Reichman responded: 'I will arrange for that immediately. What is your schedule?'

'I plan to take the last train to Bern tonight. I have meetings scheduled with officials from the Swiss Foreign office at ten. They will probably last all day.'

'Which hotel will you be staying at?'

'The Schweizerhof.'

'Do you know the famous clock tower in the old city of Bern?'

'Of course.'

'Let me suggest this. Take a walk from your hotel after dinner tomorrow night right after the blackout goes into effect and plan to be at the clock tower at ten-fifteen. Either Mr Dulles or one of his men will meet you there. If for some reason this arrangement cannot be worked out I will leave a telephone message at the hotel. It will simply say "Your Aunt Felicitas called".'

This evoked a grin on the face of the Prussian aristocrat and a giggle from Felicitas Burckhardt.

'Nancy! You are quite the Mata Hari! I had no idea.'

But Nancy Reichman remained serious. 'You know, I've never done anything quite like this before. Is what I just suggested silly?'

Now von Trott intervened. 'Quite the contrary. It would be too dangerous for any of us to speak together by telephone. The phones we would be using are all tapped, that is for sure. And I like your suggestion of a walk after the blackout starts.' Then he looked at his watch. 'Which reminds me that I must take a tram back to the Bahnhof before it is too late, since I have to reclaim my baggage before catching that train.'

Felicitas Burckhardt offered to give him a lift in her car, but the German refused. He was certain that no one had had him under observation so far that evening, and he wanted to continue to avoid attracting any attention — which, he suggested, would be inevitable if he arrived back at the railway station in the company of two such attractive young women.

They soon finished the wine and, after von Trott had settled the bill, they walked out into the chilly November night. The tram stop was directly across the street from the restaurant, and, after kissing the hand of both young women, Adam von Trott zu Solz hurried to it, since one of Basel's blue and white trams was just rounding the corner. Minutes later the two women passed the tram in Felicitas' red Fiat. They got a last glimpse of his face through one of the tram windows. It was the face of a man deep in thought.

'Oh, how I hope your people can help him!' Felicitas Burckhardt said to the young American woman sitting at her side.

'Don't worry,' Nancy Reichman answered.

'Do you think we will ever see him again?'

'Probably not.'

'Do you think they will succeed?'

'It seems to me that might depend upon how much help he gets from us.'

Soon they were in front of Nancy Reichman's apartment on the Augustinergasse.

'Before you go, Nancy,' Felicitas Burckhardt said, 'although it's none of my business, has the subject of Heisenberg ever come up again with Mr Dulles?'

'No. Why?'

'Well, as you heard Professor Barth say, the winter semester has just begun, and this week Professor Pauli came over from Zurich to resume his lecture series. The first one was yesterday, and that's why I had to cancel our lunch. I had coffee with him afterwards. At his invitation. He wanted to bring me up to date, he said, on what was happening in his field, and recalled that Peenemünde had played a central role in our previous chat. Then he rather slyly asked me whether I had noticed in the news this summer that that little island had been the object of a devastating bombing attack by the RAF. I said that I had, not telling him, of course, that I heard it from you over lunch at Schiesser's the day after it occurred. Nevertheless, I think that Pauli smells a rat but suspects it is a Swiss rat. Because he went on to ask me if I was the sister of Peter Burckhardt, and when I said I was he said that he understood that Peter was attached to Section 5 of the General Staff. So I told him that he understood correctly. By the way, Nancy, how are things proceeding with my dear brother?'

'I think "proceeding" is not the appropriate term, my dear Felicitas. But to answer your question, we saw a Marlene Dietrich movie last night.'

'And afterwards?'

'There was no "afterwards". He just drove me home.'

'You mean you don't — what do you call it again?'

'Call what?'

'What Americans do in their cars. Neck! Isn't that what you call it?'

'What's gotten into you tonight, Felicitas?'

'Well?'

'The answer is yes, we do neck, but it is none of your business.'

'Good. It's about time.'

'All right, now that we've gotten that out of the way, let's get back to your Professor Pauli.'

'Somehow it is difficult for me to imagine my brother necking. You, yes, but . . .'

'Felicitas!'

'All right, Professor Pauli told me that he regularly corresponds with some of his former colleagues at Göttingen University, including an American by the name of Robert Oppenheimer. He says that there is growing apprehension among atomic scientists in America that now that it is obvious that Germany is beginning to lose the war, the Nazis may turn to very desperate measures. He gave me a copy of one of these letters, as well as his response to it, with the suggestion that they might be of interest to my brother.' She reached into her purse and withdrew an envelope. 'I asked him, by the way, how he managed to get letters to and from America. He said he has friends in our Swiss embassy in Washington who arrange this. Which means that some other people in our Swiss government must also be very interested in these matters.

'Here,' she said as she handed the envelope to Nancy Reichman, 'and maybe it would be best when you're done with the letters if you pass them along to Peter. Then we will all have our stories straight. By the way, when I read it I found the letter from America to be quite disturbing. I hope that if that nice German is going to kill Hitler then he does it soon.' Then the two women said goodbye, and Felicitas Burckhardt drove off.

After taking off her coat, Nancy went into the kitchen to prepare a cup of tea. Once it was ready, she sat down on her sofa and read the letter which had been sent from America to Wolfgang Pauli. It was dated 21 September 1943 and was thus almost two months old:

Recent reports both through the newspapers and through

the secret service have given indications that the Germans may be in possession of a powerful new weapon which is expected to be ready between November and January. There seems to be a considerable probability that this new weapon is uranium. It is not necessary to describe the probable consequences which would result if this proves to be the case.

It is possible that the Germans will have, by the end of the year, enough material accumulated to make a large number of gadgets which they will release at the same time on England, Russia and this country. In this case there would be little hope for any counter-action. However, it is also possible that they will have a production, let us say, of two gadgets a month. This would place particularly Britain in an extremely serious position, but there would be hope for counter-action from our side before the war is lost.[49]

It would be extremely helpful, dear Wolfgang, if you could give us your assessment of the status of nuclear research and development in Germany from your vantage point in Zurich. You have the advantage of being both much closer to Berlin and, as we understand it, in contact with Heisenberg, the man who undoubtedly is in charge of their program.

Wolfgang Pauli's response, dated 28 October 1943 (which seemed to indicate that the courier service between Washington and Switzerland was quite irregular) read thus:

Thank you for your letter of August 21st, which just arrived. I think your worries are somewhat exaggerated. There is no doubt that the Germans are deeply engaged in trying to develop a uranium 'gadget', as you term it. Their reactor is designed to use heavy water which they get from Norway and uranium, which they extract from a huge amount of Union Minière uranium ore from the Congo

---

49 Compare this with a letter written by Edward Teller and sent to Robert Oppenheimer, cited in Rhodes, *The Making of the Atomic Bomb*, pp. 511–12.

which the German army captured in Belgium in 1940 – one speaks of 1,200 tons.[50] However, I have seen one of Heisenberg's drawings of such a heavy water reactor and I doubt if a reactor of that design would be efficient enough to produce enough material to allow them to build the number of 'gadgets' mentioned in your letter in the immediate future.[51] But I may be wrong. And it may well be that the Germans are not using a Heisenberg-designed reactor. Though I also doubt that.

Therefore, dear Robert, although I am as worried as you about what is going on at the Kaiser Wilhelm Institute in Berlin, I do not think that it poses an immediate threat. A year from now things could be quite different, of course.

The next morning Nancy Reichman took the first train to Bern, and from the station went directly to Allen Dulles' apartment on the Herrengasse. He was expecting her, and already had a full pot of real American coffee ready to pour. As soon as she had taken off her coat, she accepted a cup gratefully.

'Let's start with the German,' Dulles said, once both had settled on the sofa in his living-room.

'I spent a full hour with him last night,' Nancy Reichman began, 'in the company of Karl Barth.'

Dulles liked that. For him, style was always as important as substance.

After she had recapped the conversation of the prior evening, without any hesitation or further questions Dulles immediately agreed to meet von Trott zu Solz . . . or at least, to have one of his men meet him. 'It is very interesting to hear about Canaris and the Abwehr. It totally confirms what I have been hearing from other sources. Too bad. We had put high hope in them.'

'That reminds me of one point I forgot to mention. Apparently

---

50 Ibid., p. 607.

51 The Danish nuclear physicist, Niels Bohr, who escaped to Sweden in October 1943, from where he proceeded to Britain and then the United States, had seen similar drawings by Heisenberg and had reached the same conclusion as Wolfgang Pauli. Ibid., pp. 484, 523–4.

the Abwehr provided the Kreisau Circle not only with protection but also with a communications network. Now that it has been dismantled . . .'

Dulles interrupted her. 'I know what you are leading up to, and I think − provided von Trott proves out − that we can be of immediate help.' Then he told her about the Bally shoe network, and concluded by saying: 'That entire arrangement came to pass as a result of an introduction to the Bally family provided by your friend, Peter Burckhardt. Not only that, and I don't know if you recall this, but last spring when I had my first meeting with Swiss Intelligence at the Schloss in Benken, Peter Burckhardt brought up the subject of the Kreisau Circle and how we might work together. In fact, now that I think of it, he even mentioned Karl Barth as a possible intermediary. So that young man really comes through. Next time you see him, Nancy, be sure to thank him on my behalf.' Then: 'What else is on your mind?'

She reached into her purse and extracted the envelope Felicitas Burckhardt had given to her the night before. After she had told him how they had come into her possession, she handed the letters to Dulles. When he had read them, he just sat there in silence as if carefully pondering what to say next.

'This is very serious stuff, Nancy, as you know. I think that Professor Pauli could prove to be an exceedingly valuable asset for us. But we, and by that I mean the OSS, must tread very, very carefully where this matter is concerned. Because to some degree, some unknown degree, the intelligence effort to discover the extent of German progress in developing those "uranium gadgets" has been taken out of our hands. What I'm telling you is, of course, top-secret, Nancy, and must not be repeated to anyone. The reason, I am told, that this is being done is because it is felt in Washington that we have been too cautious. I can tell you that the reason we have been so cautious is that we were told from the very outset that in no case must we risk briefing one of our agents on nuclear fission and then have him captured, or worse yet, turned into a double agent by the Germans. Then *they* might be able to deduce what *we* are doing, and as a result greatly accelerate their efforts. In any case, General Marshall has just put one of his men in charge of intelligence gathering in this field – General Groves. We will, of course, cooperate fully with him if and when we are asked.'[52]

Then he handed the letters back to Nancy Reichman. 'I suggest that you return these letters and that we forget that this conversation has taken place.

'Now I've got something. And again it relates to the reciprocity which has developed between Section 5 and ourselves, one which so far has proven to be highly beneficial for both parties, as you have just demonstrated again with our now establishing direct contacts with the Kreisau Circle. And the Bally Shoe arrangement. Now as another *quid pro quo* from our side, I want you to pass on a warning to Peter Burckhardt, with the suggestion that he see to it that it gets to the highest echelons of Swiss government, industry and banking. In Washington they are getting very perturbed about the continuing economic and financial cooperation between Switzerland and Germany. Very perturbed. They are aware of the fact that, for instance, during this year alone Switzerland has received a record half a billion francs' worth of gold from Germany – all of it stolen.[53] They got this from British Intelligence, I might add, which suggests to me that they must also have a plant inside the BIS. You might mention this in passing to Burckhardt.'

'I suspected that the atmosphere was changing,' Nancy told him. 'I was called into the ambassador's office last week and given a specific laundry list of items the embassy wants me to monitor as part of my consular duties – which barely exist

---

52 For a more extended treatment of this incident see Rhodes, pp. 605ff. There the chronicler of the making of the atomic bomb says: 'Vannevar Bush (who was in charge of the administration of the atomic bomb project) had raised the question of espionage with Franklin Roosevelt . . . on October 9, 1941 . . . but got no satisfactory answer, probably because the United States was not yet a belligerent. Groves in his memoirs passes the buck to the existing intelligence agencies – Army G-2, the Office of Naval Intelligence, and the Office of Strategic Services, the forerunner of the CIA – and attributes the inadequacy of their information to "the unfortunate relationships that had grown up among them".'

53 Werner Rings, *Raubgold aus Deutschland*, p. 145.

anyway, since there are obviously no visas to be issued to Swiss wanting to go to the United States, and no Americans left in Basel who need the usual type of consular assistance. I thought maybe this was just a way to keep me busy, but obviously not.'

'I don't want to tread on the ambassador's turf, but what kind of things are they interested in?'

'Freight train traffic coming from Germany passing through Basel and headed south is right at the top of the list. Washington suspects that since the Italians surrendered in September it has increased dramatically. For now that it is totally up to the Wehrmacht to hold the line against us in Italy, the Basel—Gotthard—Milan supply line has become absolutely critical for the Germans. As are many Swiss industrial exports to Germany. So they want me to get as much information as possible on both the makeup and volume of those exports. I suspect this request is directly related to their hearing about the huge amount of gold still coming into Switzerland from Germany, and wanting to know what's going back out in return. And one last item: anything I might be able to pick up on a company by the name of Interhandel, which is domiciled in Basel. Do you by any chance know anything about it?'

'No.' Then Dulles added: 'It sounds like pretty dull stuff to me. Before you leave to attend to such pressing matters, tell me more about Karl Barth. I have never had the chance to meet the man but I've heard that he is as towering a figure in person as he is in his theological writings.'

Nancy Reichman confirmed this, of course, and ended her brief portrait of Barth by quoting what he had said about his fellow Swiss: 'They are cunningly short-sighted and short-sightedly cunning.'

'Exactly, but exactly right,' Dulles said. 'And in the coming year they are going to begin to live to regret it.'

PART FOUR

Chapter 25

In the weeks and months that followed, Nancy Reichman devoted most of her days and many of her nights to the tedious task of following her new instructions. And it did not take her long to reach the same conclusion that Karl Barth had stated that evening in the Bruderholz restaurant: the Swiss were playing both sides to their advantage, an exercise in amorality which was unique in World War II. It fully explained why Switzerland had remained an untouched island in the middle of a Europe which was totally dominated by the Nazis.

Just ten nights spent intermittently during the first months of 1944 observing the rail traffic through Basel allowed the American vice-consul to confirm Washington's suspicions: that the volume was swelling to immense proportions. From an observation point she had sought out in the outskirts of Basel alongside the main railroad line which led from the Swiss–German frontier through Basel to the Gotthard tunnel and then the Italian frontier (in fact, the lookout spot in suburban Muttenz which she had chosen was at almost exactly the same location as the one used by the Soviet Red Orchestra to develop the same information – until it was put out of business a year earlier by Swiss counter-intelligence), she saw train after train moving south, often only minutes apart. The railroad cars, many tanker cars, were all either German or Italian. All were sealed. All were under heavy guard. They were at the core of the 'understanding' between the Nazis and the Swiss, one that had been struck at the very outset of the war, and which was the real reason for the abandonment of Hitler's plans to incorporate Switzerland into his Thousand Year Reich. For those trains, as she gradually found — and as every informed Swiss knew — were absolutely essential to the German army which was now fighting it out alone against the Allied forces in southern Italy, and which had managed to halt the drive north by the Allied army at Monte Cassino. They were loaded predominantly with fuel, which was now in extremely short supply in Italy. In return for providing the Nazis with transit through neutral (and thus safe) Switzerland, on a ton-for-ton basis the Swiss were able to buy from Germany carefully calculated amounts of coal and oil for their own use. Equally important, the Swiss were allowed to freely transport foodstuffs, especially grain bought in North and South America, to be brought by ships sailing the Atlantic under the Swiss flag into neutral Portugal and Spain and from there, through Nazi-controlled territory to Geneva. Transit for transit.

Her report was duly noted in the Swiss section of the State Department back in Washington, and added to a growing body of evidence that Switzerland had developed into Nazi Germany's most important economic ally.

Although getting a fix on the volume of the Italy-bound German shipments through Switzerland was relatively easy, due to her strategic location in Basel, one of the main railroad hubs in Western Europe, when Nancy Reichman tried to pursue the matter of what the Nazis were getting in return for the immense amount of gold they were selling Switzerland she met stone wall after stone wall. But, as with most intelligence work in the economic sector, as one spliced together a newspaper item here, a bit of a conversation over dinner there, with information which was deliberately provided to her by Swiss who were in violent disagreement with the Swiss policy of providing Germany with everything from precision machine-tools to turbines, ball-bearings to anti-aircraft guns and artillery shells, it gradually became clear that Swiss industry continued to provide absolutely key support to the German war effort in 1944, at a time when, as the months progressed, it should have become clear to any sensible Swiss that they were supporting a losing effort, and running the risk of serious retaliation if such practices continued unchecked. Her conclusions — again duly noted and filed in Washington — were that 40 per cent of Swiss exports were still going to Germany and that more than half of such exports could be classified as 'war materials'. Furthermore, that although this volume of 'war materials' represented no more than 1 per cent of the output of Germany's defence industry, they were often high-precision products which, due to their unique state-of-the-art quality, had become key and irreplaceable components in German tanks, aircraft and U-boats. In this critical war year of 1944, the Swiss origins of such high-tech military hardware became increasingly important, in fact critical, as the Allied bombings of Germany gradually destroyed the ball-bearing factories in Schweinfurt, the Krupp weapons-producing facilities in the Ruhr, the Siemens electrical equipment plants in Berlin. The production gaps were often now filled by imports from such companies as Georg Fischer in Schaffhausen, which supplied diesel engines for U-boats, Brown-Boveri in Baden, where heavy electrical equipment such as generators and turbines was being manufactured to German specifications, or the Bührle concern outside Zurich (owned by Emil Bührle, who was known as 'the Krupp of Switzerland'), which was now one of the principal suppliers of anti-aircraft weapons to the Nazis, as well as cannons for the Wehrmacht's Panzers. In all cases, these firms could be relied on to meet their delivery deadlines, since their factories were, of course, immune from Allied bombardment due to their location on the other side of the border in neutral Switzerland.

And then there was that request from Washington instructing her to look into a holding company registered in Basel under the name Société Internationale pour Participations Industrielles et Commerciales S.A., but popularly known as Interhandel. The request was accompanied by a background memorandum which explained that Interhandel's holdings were predominantly in the field of chemicals, but that its principal holding was a huge chemical concern in the United States, General Aniline and Film, which, as owner of both the Agfa and Ansco film companies, as well as Ozalid, a large blueprint manufacturer, was Kodak's principal competitor in the film industry in the United States. Ironically, GAF also supplied the khaki and blue dyes for the American army, air force and navy uniforms. In 1942 the United States government had seized GAF under the Trading with the Enemy Act. It had justified its actions by claiming that in spite of the purported Swiss character of this holding company, it was in fact merely a front for the notorious German chemical cartel, I. G. Farben. The Swiss had vehemently protested this action, the memorandum went on to say, and would undoubtedly try to reclaim the property. As the United States government's only official representative in Basel, Vice-Consul Nancy Reichman was to develop as much information and especially documentation as possible which could be used to back up the American seizure and to block a potential Swiss counter-action which would undoubtedly be filed in the American courts once the war was over and the dust had settled.[1]

Where to turn? A phone call to Professor Salin produced a suggestion: a lawyer whom she had met at one of Salin's dinners in late 1943. His name was Karl Meyer. Meyer had many corporate clients in Germany, lucrative connections, but he also took advantage of them for other purposes such as keeping the Swiss government, which was constantly involved with trade negotiations with Germany, supplied with information of the type that would allow them to drive hard bargains. Salin was fully aware of this, otherwise he would hardly have been there that evening. But he was also a major in the Swiss army, Salin had pointed out, leaving it up to her to factor in the import of that information.

Very shortly after she had joined Dr Meyer in his offices on the

---

1 For a full history of this episode, see chapter 11, 'The Strange Case of General Aniline and Film', in Joseph Borkin's *The Crime and Punishment of I.G. Farben: The startling account of the unholy alliance of Adolf Hitler and Germany's great chemical combine* (New York, 1978), pp. 200–22. Also chapter 8, 'The Film Conspiracy', of Charles Higham's *Trading with the Enemy: An Exposé of the Nazi–American Money Plot 1933–1949* (New York, 1983), pp. 130–53. Also Paul Erdman, *Swiss–American Economic Relations*, pp. 158–66.

Freie Strasse, that import became very apparent. To be sure, at the outset Meyer responded to her questions with curt, precise answers. Who owned Interhandel was quite clear: the Sturzenegger Bank of Basel, a bank whose ownership was 100 per cent Swiss. And who ran its affairs was equally clear: a Verwaltungsrat, a Board of Directors, which was also 100 per cent Swiss and composed chiefly of partners of the leading law firms in Basel. That alone guaranteed that Interhandel was above reproach. Then came the warning shot across her bow designed to signal that it was one thing to use Basel as a place from which to spy on Germany, but quite another to misuse the city's hospitality to spy on Switzerland. What it revealed was that the vested interests of the legal and banking establishments of Basel in Interhandel were so great that no meddling in its affairs by any outsider would be tolerated. The message was delivered without a trace of subtlety.

'My dear young lady,' Dr Meyer began, 'I must remind you of the basic rules which are embedded in the legal framework of this country and which are meant to govern the behaviour of all those who live here, including guests of our country. They are all contained in this thin volume.'

Without rising from behind his desk, he then picked up a book, indeed a rather thin one, bound in red, and offered it to her. She had no choice but to get up from the chair in front of his desk and take it in hand. She read the title on the cover. *Handkommentar zum Schweizerischen Strafgesetzbuch.*

The Swiss lawyer then continued his lecture. 'What you have is the short commentary to the Swiss criminal code. Some of the laws it describes are peculiar to Switzerland, and perhaps even offensive to Anglo-Saxons, but that in no way affects the will of Swiss courts to impose penalties on anyone who violates them. Anyone. Now I suggest that you turn to page 163 of the commentary.'

She did as she was told.

'You see Article 273 of the Swiss Criminal Code there. Why don't you read it — out loud.'

In spite of herself — her inner voice screamed that she should just throw the little red book at him and leave — she began to

read. 'Wer ein Fabrikations- oder Geschäftsgeheimnis aus-
kundschaft, um es einer fremden amtlichen Stelle zugänglich zu
machen,' it went on and on, ending with the words, 'wird mit
Gefängnis, in schweren Fällen Zuchthaus bestraft.'[2]

'Good. For an American you read German very well.' Unsaid,
but obviously implied, was that it was also known that she was not
a 'real' American, but rather an émigré to the United States from
Germany who had managed to be recycled back to Europe . . .
which made her doubly second-class.

Without waiting for her to thank him for the compliment, he
continued: 'But just to make absolutely sure that you understand
what is at stake here — for *you*, Fräulein — let me bluntly
summarize in English what Article 273 says in no uncertain terms:
Anyone who tries to spy on a Swiss business — any business — in
order to make its confidential affairs available to foreign governments is subject to the penalty of prison, in severe cases to a
minimum of five years at hard labour. All that is required to set in
motion a criminal investigation by the local authorities which
could lead to this unfortunate end for anyone who attempts to
engage in such activities is a complaint by a Swiss citizen,
especially by one such as myself.'

He paused for a moment to let this sink in.

'From the smirk on your face, Fräulein, I cannot help but
conclude that you think I am bluffing.'

She finally spoke up. 'I don't think. I know.' What she knew
for sure was that her diplomatic immunity protected her from any
such thing. What she did not know, however, was whether or not
a complaint by Herr Doktor Meyer might lead to the withdrawal
of her credentials by the Swiss Foreign Office, and ultimately her
expulsion from Switzerland. But she was too mad to give a damn
about that clearly remote possibility. The way the war was going,
even the Swiss would now have to think twice before antagoniz-
ing the United States in such a way.

So Nancy Reichman got up from her chair and slapped the little

---

2 Oscar Härdt, *Handkommentar zum Schweizerischen Strafgesetzbuch* (3
Auflage, Bern, 1943).

red book back on to the top of the Swiss lawyer's desk. She knew she was breaking the rules, but she could not help but get in one more lick before leaving. 'I don't know if you are aware of it or not, Herr Doktor, but we are in the process of putting together a black list of individuals and companies in this country who have been trading and consorting with the enemy. They will be barred from conducting any commerce with the United States and its allies after this war is concluded. I am going to make the recommendation that this list be extended to certain law firms. Needless to say, a complaint by any member of the American Foreign Service should suffice to add someone to the list, especially if it comes from a Foreign Service officer like myself.'

The Swiss lawyer now sprang to his feet, and if the desk had not separated them Nancy Reichman was sure that he would have hit her.

'Raus!' he shrieked at her.

So she left.

Just before noon the next day she got a call from Peter Burckhardt at the consulate.

'I hear you had a run-in yesterday with one of the pillars of our local legal establishment.'

'You heard right,' Nancy replied. 'Don't tell me he's some big friend of yours.' Before waiting for an answer she went on: 'That pompous son-of-a-bitch not only threatened me, but I swear, Peter, if he had been able to get at me, he would have slugged me.' Then: 'By the way, how did you hear about this so soon?'

'My father.'

'Figures.'

'Now take it easy, Nancy. You've disturbed a wasps' nest. Every bank in this little city has a big financial interest in Interhandel.'

'But it's controlled by I.G. Farben.'

'No. It's owned by the Sturzenegger Bank.'

'Come on, Peter. That little bank! It probably doesn't even have twenty employees. All it does is act as a front, a cloak, for the true beneficial owner, which I know, you know, your father knows, and certainly the Sturzenegger Bank knows, is I.G. Farben.'

'Maybe. But you'll never be able to prove it. Not one document that might point in that direction will ever be allowed to leave this country. They are protected under both the bank secrecy laws and those designed to prevent economic espionage.'

'I know about those laws from your pal, Herr Doktor Meyer.'

'He's not a pal, Nancy. He is in fact an arrogant pompous ass. But then, most lawyers in this city are. On top of that they can all be bought. And in the case of Interhandel, they have been totally and irrevocably bought. As have the banks. We're talking hundreds of millions of dollars here.'

'So what do you advise me to do?'

'Lay off. Otherwise you will find yourself totally ostracized in this community. That, in my judgement, would be much too high a price to pay for continuing the pursuit of Interhandel, especially since such a pursuit is bound to prove futile in the end.'

For a few seconds Nancy Reichman said nothing. 'I'll think it over,' she finally said.

'Would you like to go to the opera tomorrow night? *Die Fledermaus* . . .'

'No thank you. I'm not in the mood,' she replied, and hung up.

Later that afternoon she telephoned Allen Dulles and asked if she could come over to Bern the next morning and talk to him very briefly. He immediately agreed. She slept badly that night, and was up before dawn to make sure she would make the first train to Bern on time.

After listening to her story, Dulles had but one comment: 'Peter Burckhardt is right. Lay off. There are potentially many more important issues at stake where we may need your help – life-and-death issues, not just money.'

When she got back, although it was already late in the afternoon, she telephoned Peter Burckhardt at his bank.

'It's me,' she began. 'Is that offer for the opera still on?'

'Of course.'

'Will you pick me up at seven?'

'With pleasure.'

'By the way. I'm taking your advice. So you won't have to be ashamed to be seen with me in public.'[3]

During the intermission between the second and third acts of that opera, just as he was ordering two glasses of champagne, a man who had obviously just come into the theatre, since he was still wearing his topcoat, after rather frantically scanning the crowd in the lobby spotted Peter Burckhardt and immediately rushed over to him. Peter excused himself, and left Nancy standing in front of the bar while he retreated into a corner with the man and entered into an intense whispered conversation.

He returned a few minutes later alone. 'Something urgent. I've got to leave. Do you want to stay, or should I . . .'

Nancy Reichman interrupted. 'I'll stay, and don't worry, I can very easily walk home from here. You'd better get going.' They had been out together many, many times during the past year and a half, but this was the first time that such a thing had happened.

---

3 The advice of Peter Burckhardt and Allen Dulles proved absolutely right. The Swiss bankers and lawyers fought to reverse the seizure of General Aniline and Film for the next twenty years in the American courts. During this period, the Union Bank of Switzerland managed to acquire control of the Swiss holding company, Interhandel, by paying an unknown amount of money to the Sturzenegger Bank and the German interests behind the façade of that bank. In 1959 the chairman of UBS, Dr Alfred Schaefer, got himself appointed general manager and vice-chairman of Interhandel and single-handedly took up the crusade. Well, not quite single-handedly: in August of 1961 he recruited the help of a certain Prince Radziwill, the brother-in-law of President Kennedy. Radziwill, as a member of the Kennedy clan, of course also had direct access to the President's brother, Robert Kennedy, who by chance was the Attorney-General of the United States. In October 1961 Robert Kennedy met with Alfred Schaefer. A deal was worked out which eventually led to the United States government selling the (seized) stock of GAF in the largest competitive auction in Wall Street history. The sale netted $341 million. Interhandel got $124 million of this. A few years later Dr Alfred Schaefer was elected to the board of BASF, the giant German chemical company which was one of the postwar successors of − guess who? − I.G. Farben. See Erdman, pp. 161−2, and especially Borkin, pp. 210−22.

Being in the same business as Burckhardt — at least part-time — rather than paying attention to the music of Strauss, she spent most of the next hour thinking about what it could be that demanded the immediate attention of a Swiss intelligence officer at this late hour.

Chapter 26

The same thought had been going through Peter Burckhardt's mind as he drove to the headquarters of Section D (for Deutschland) of Swiss Intelligence, which stood on the Petersplatz across the wooded park from the university. Immediately upon entering the building he was approached by the sergeant who had the night shift in the communications centre located there.

'Here,' he said, handing Burckhardt a slip of paper. 'The message came in to Masson's people in Lucerne an hour ago and they relayed it here by telex.'

The message had come from the office of General Walter Schellenberg. It was an urgent request that Lieutenant Peter Burckhardt telephone Rittmeister Eggen, and included various telephone numbers in Berlin where he could be reached, day and night. Attached to this were instructions from the head of Swiss Intelligence, Colonel Masson, as to how Burckhardt was to respond: he should telephone Eggen immediately, hear him out, remain noncommittal, and immediately get back to Masson for further instructions.

So Burckhardt got on the phone and reached Eggen on the first try. He was still in the offices of SS headquarters which were situated in Berlin not far from the burnt-out Reichstag building.

'It is so extremely kind of you to return my call at this very late hour. I do hope that it has not too greatly inconvenienced you, Herr Doktor,' were Eggen's first words.

'In fact it has,' Burckhardt replied. Upon hearing Eggen's

voice he immediately visualized the man as he had last seen him in his upstairs study at the Benkener Schloss almost a year earlier, a meeting during which he had developed an instant dislike for this unscrupulous Sturmbannführer in the SS who seemed to have an unmatched talent for cultivating men in high places on both sides of the German–Swiss border . . . a list which now seemed to include Peter Burckhardt, at least in the German's scheme of things.

'My most profound apologies,' Eggen responded, 'but I think it will be immediately apparent why I did so if you will allow me to explain.'

'Bitte,' Burckhardt responded.

'A prototype of an advanced version of one of our fighter aircraft, a Messerschmitt 110 Cg + EN, which had been engaged in an air battle over southern Germany, landed by mistake at Dübendorf airport outside Zurich two hours ago. It is powered by radically new engines and is equipped with highly secret and extremely advanced instrumentation which gives the plane a unique capability where night operations are concerned. The pilot tried to take off again when he realized where he was, but was prevented from doing so. We must have that plane back, Herr Leutnant.'

'But surely you realize that my competence within the Swiss military does not extend to a matter of such importance, from the very fact that this is the first I have even heard of this incident,' Burckhardt responded.

'We understand that. But we, and by "we" I refer to General Schellenberg and myself — the general, by the way, has asked me to extend his personal regards to you and to once again thank you for the exquisite hospitality he enjoyed during his stay at your Schloss last year — anyway, we have decided to approach this matter via two channels. One channel was already established an hour ago between General Schellenberg and General Guisan, with the assistance of your Colonel Masson in Lucerne. We hope to establish a second line of communications between the two of us.' Eggen then added as an apparent afterthought: 'But only if you agree, Herr Leutnant.'

Peter Burckhardt's basic inclination was to tell this piece of Nazi slime to find somebody else with whom he could play his games, but he knew that in a matter of such importance his personal feelings were totally irrelevant. At least his instructions from Lucerne had been quite clear: to remain noncommittal, which was some solace. He would remain *very* noncommittal.

'That is not for me to decide,' Burckhardt said, hoping his voice sounded as cool as his feelings.

If it did, it certainly did not faze Eggen in the slightest. 'We also understand that, Herr Leutnant. However, it is imperative that no time be wasted in this matter. We are acting under direct instructions from the Führer. He has told us that he expects us to resolve this matter within forty-eight hours.'

'I see. Well, obviously I must consult with my superiors.'

'Of course. I assume you will do so immediately.'

'I will.'

'Then I will hear from you again very soon?'

'Most probably.'

'One more thing. I plan to leave Berlin for Basel first thing tomorrow morning, which should mean that I will arrive in your Badische Bahnhof in the late evening. You might want to make your plans accordingly.'

'I shall certainly take that into account.'

As soon as Eggen hung up, Burckhardt rang Section 5 headquarters in Lucerne. He was immediately connected with Colonel Masson. After he had repeated his conversation with Eggen, Masson's response was curt and explicit. 'Tell Eggen that you will meet him when he arrives. General Guisan and I are going to fly over to Dübendorf at dawn tomorrow in his Fieseler Storch to take a look at the machine, and will then return to Bern to consult with the Federal Council as to how to handle this. By late afternoon – well before Eggen gets here – we will get back to you with further instructions.'[4]

*

---

4 For a complete history of this incident, see Gautschi, *General Henri Guisan*, pp. 563–7. Here Gautschi gives the complete text of the message which Schellenberg sent to General Guisan. In it Schellenberg indicated that he

Eggen had booked a room at the Three Kings Hotel, situated no more than 300 metres downstream from where Nancy Reichman's apartment overlooked the River Rhine. Burckhardt, who had driven him there in his Mercedes, rather than join him in his room as Eggen had insisted, suggested that the German take his time to unpack and get refreshed. He would be waiting for him in the bar . . . the same bar, of course, where he had first seen the man twelve months ago, prior to the Schellenberg meeting at the Benkener Schloss. The bar had not changed, but the bartender had: the one who had been there before had gone down in a hail of bullets a year earlier when he had tried to evade a police road-block on the outskirts of Benken. Something else was different: this time the head of Basel's political police was nowhere to be seen. Which was just as well. Lützelschwab tended to get very upset when he saw SS on his turf.

Burckhardt sat there alone at a corner table for ten minutes. When Eggen returned, the German major and the Swiss lieutenant fenced for a while until Burckhardt passed on his government's offer − the destruction of the Me 110 in return for the delivery of twelve Me 109s to the Swiss air force. A relieved Major Eggen ordered champagne, and minutes later he was raising his glass. 'To your twelve Me 109s, Herr Leutnant, and our six million Swiss francs.'

The man is utterly shameless, Burckhardt thought, as he also raised his glass − since he had no choice in the matter. And, as if to second his thoughts, Eggen's next question was: 'Now when

---

wanted to personally come to Switzerland and meet with Guisan in order to work out the details of the return of the Messerschmitt 110. Guisan knew that the political fallout of his meeting yet again with the SS general would be devastating should it become known to the Swiss public. So this suggestion was immediately rejected, leaving Schellenberg no choice but to put the entire matter into the hands of his deputy, Sturmbannführer Eggen.

One further note: Gautschi mentions the role played in this episode by the Swiss military attaché in Berlin, whose name was also Peter Burckhardt, and who held the rank of major in the Swiss army. Lest there be any confusion, there was no relationship whatsoever between the two men. Their having the same names and somewhat similar functions is pure coincidence.

you said cash, did you mean banknotes, or a cash balance in a Swiss bank account?'

'Either. That depends on you.'

Eggen mulled that one over. 'Banknotes might tend to draw a lot of attention, wouldn't you say? I mean, it would require a steamer trunk!'

'Not a trunk, but maybe two large suitcases. We could pay you in thousand-franc notes.'

'Still.' Then: 'The more I think about it, the more I tend toward using a bank. But not just any bank. Where such a large sum is concerned, we would want you to make the funds available at a very large bank, ideally the largest. Is your father still . . .'

Burckhardt interrupted him. 'Yes. He is still chairman of the Swiss Bank Corporation.'

'Well, that would make it all the easier, wouldn't it? I mean, you could, so to say, keep all this in the family.'

Peter Burckhardt remembered that the last time Eggen had tried to get his foot inside the door of the Swiss Bank Corporation on behalf of his 'clients' back in Berlin, his father had adamantly refused to have anything to do with him. Instead he had been referred to the bank across the street in downtown Basel, one which specialized in German financing. But this time, Burckhardt knew, if Eggen insisted, his father would have no choice but to cooperate.

As if reading his mind, Eggen continued to pursue the subject. 'Which reminds me of a related subject. You were kind enough to facilitate my establishing certain financial arrangements at the Basler Handelsbank after our conversation in your study at the Schloss a year or so ago.'

'I assume they are taking good care of you. And your clients.'

'Yes. And no, frankly,' the German said.

'I'm surprised to hear that.'

'Don't misunderstand me, Herr Doktor. They are always most courteous and professional at the Handelsbank. But what has begun to worry a few of my clients who have accounts there is the fact that the bank's loan portfolio is very heavily concentrated in one country.'

Yours, Burckhardt was about to say, but kept his silence.

'They feel that, given the uncertainties of the future, they might be better advised to keep their money in a bank that is more diversified geographically.'

So that their Swiss bank does not go down with the sinking German ship, leaving you and your 'clients' without a financial nest-egg abroad, Burckhardt thought, one which will allow you to fight again another day. And to think that he and his father had no choice but to deal with this scum!

His words were quite different from these thoughts, however. 'I'm sure that something can be worked out, Herr Eggen. Provided there are no new complications in the basic deal we have just finished discussing.'

'That is now up to me.'

Two days later, on 20 May, Germany lost one aircraft and Switzerland gained twelve. That evening, the son of General Guisan, Colonel Henry 'Gigi' Guisan, put on a banquet to honour Rittmeister Eggen for his role in bringing this incident to such a successful conclusion, and in his toast offered the opinion that Eggen 'a rendu d'immenses services à notre pays'.[5]

On 21 May, at precisely 11 am, SS Major Eggen entered the headquarters of the Swiss Bank Corporation in Basel alone and carrying a briefcase. His objective: to now render an enormous service to himself. He was immediately escorted to the office of that bank's chairman, Dr Maximilian Burckhardt-Von der Mühll. The banker did not offer his hand, but just indicated that the German should take his place in the chair in front of his desk.

'I would suggest that we get right to the business at hand, Herr Eggen,' he said, while pressing a buzzer next to his telephone.

The door to his office was opened almost immediately, and a man in a dark suit entered carrying a dossier. He looked at Dr Burckhardt, who responded with the slightest of nods, whereupon the bank executive opened the dossier and handed it over to Eggen. It contained two pieces of paper.

---

5 Gautschi, p. 565.

'You have there, Herr Eggen,' Burckhardt now said, 'our notification that six million Swiss francs are available for payment in full for the twelve Me 109 aircraft which were delivered yesterday to the Swiss military authorities in Dübendorf. The second document, which requires your signature, confirms that you have the authority to accept these six million francs as payment in full for the twelve aircraft, that you also have the authority to dispose of these funds as you see fit, and that you release the Swiss government and this bank from any further claims in this matter. Our only other requirement before we release these funds to you is that you produce documentation from your government authorizing you to act in this matter on its behalf. I assume you have brought that.'

Rittmeister Eggen, who was visibly extremely nervous, reached down into his briefcase and extracted a document bearing the seal of the German Reich and the signatures of Marshal Hermann Göring and General Walter Schellenberg. Again the bank executive who was standing at Eggen's side looked to his chairman for instructions, and after receiving a second nod took the German document in hand. So far Dr Maximilian Burckhardt-Von der Mühll had not touched a single piece of paper related to this transaction, nor would he. He merely watched as his man stood and read what Eggen had handed him.

'In Ordnung?' Burckhardt asked impatiently.

'In Ordnung, Herr Doktor,' came the reply.

Burckhardt now turned his attention back to Eggen. 'Then all we need are your instructions in regard to the disposal of these funds, Herr Eggen.'

'I want to keep the funds here at the Swiss Bank Corporation,' was Eggen's reply.

'I see. I assume they will then be used at a later date for settlements within the framework of our two countries' bilateral trade compensation agreement,' the banker said.

'Not exactly. I would like to open three new accounts – numbered accounts – at your bank and have the six million francs disbursed equally among them.'

The eyebrows of Dr Burckhardt rose ever so slightly. 'And these three new accounts, are they . . .'

Before he could finish his question Eggen interrupted. 'They are to be personal accounts. One for Marshal Göring, the second for General Schellenberg, and the third for myself.'

Burckhardt again turned to his executive. 'Any problem with that?'

Without even re-examining the document describing Eggen's authority in this matter, the man immediately said: 'No, sir. Herr Eggen has clearly been granted a full power of attorney by the German authorities.'

Left unsaid was that the same authorities who had given Eggen these powers — Göring and Schellenberg — were now also to be beneficiaries of that grant of authority. They were in essence stealing from themselves. Since in the Third Reich, 'they' and the state were synonymous, from the viewpoint of an outside institution which was merely facilitating the movement of funds from a client's right hand to his left, there was no problem.

So on behalf of the Swiss Bank Corporation, Dr Maximilian Burckhardt said just that. 'Then there is no problem. You understand that the proper signature cards must be filled out, and that we will also require mailing instructions. You can either have us notify you as to the status of your accounts at your addresses in Berlin, or, if you prefer, we will hold back all such correspondence here at the bank where it will, of course, be available for your review when you are again back on these premises.' Not that there was any question in the banker's mind as to which option *these* three new clients would go for! Again he turned to his assistant. 'Get three sets of account opening documents.'

As the man hurried out of the office to get them, Burckhardt continued. 'You can execute these documents for your personal account immediately. As to the other accounts, as an exception we will also open them up right away on an interim basis since, in this instance, we already have valid samples of the signatures of the two beneficiaries of these accounts, don't we?'

'Vielen Dank, Herr Doktor,' Eggen said. Then: 'There is one other matter, Herr Doktor.'

'Yes. Those accounts at the bank across the street.'

Burckhardt's assistant returned at this juncture with the three sets of account papers and Burckhardt addressed his next words to him: 'That can be taken care of in your office. And I have already spoken to you about some accounts that are to be transferred from the Basler Handelsbank to ourselves. You will go over there with Herr Eggen as soon as you are done here and arrange it.'

Dr Burckhardt then stood up, leaving Rittmeister Eggen no choice but to do the same. Again the Swiss banker did not offer his hand but merely said: 'I think that does it. I wish you a good day, Herr Eggen, and a pleasant trip back to Berlin.'[6]

Eggen was thereupon escorted out of his office. Maximilian Burckhardt's thoughts immediately turned to the next visitor who was due within five minutes: an industrialist from Vienna who wanted to transfer a huge amount of his company's funds – the company exported textiles to Switzerland, and retained the Swiss franc proceeds in an account at his bank – to his personal account at a bank in Buenos Aires. It seemed that all the rats were suddenly preparing to jump ship.

The motivation was reinforced just two weeks later, on 6 June 1944, D-Day, when the Allies finally landed in Normandy and established a second front in Europe. It was the beginning of the end of the Axis domination of Europe. That change, paradoxically, would soon have a very negative effect on everybody who lived in Switzerland. For when word of this cynical deal between the Swiss government and the Nazis got back to the Americans and British (and it did so with no help from Swiss

---

6 This was a classic example of how intelligence service personnel use Swiss banks for their own enrichment. The East German Stasi followed the same practices during the Cold War. And, of course, it was at the Geneva branch of the Crédit Suisse that the principals involved in the Iran/Contra affair kept their accounts, not necessarily for their own enrichment but to further their own causes, which were hardly synonymous with those of the United States government.

335

Intelligence), it merely added fuel to the flames of Allied discontent with Switzerland, one which had heretofore been merely smouldering. It was just another illustration of that country's contemptuous disregard of the legitimate interests of the democratic powers, a further example of the Swiss flagrantly pursuing self-interest when it should have become obvious to the people who ran Switzerland that it was time to drastically cut back on their financial, economic and, in the case of the Messerschmitt 110, military cooperation with the Nazis.

Heretofore there had been very little that the Allies could do to stop the Swiss. To be sure, they had fired a few shots across the bow of the Swiss ship of state. On 17 May 1943, for instance, British planes had bombed the small town of Oerlikon, where the factories of the Maschinenfabrik Bührle were located, factories which were engaged almost exclusively in producing weapons for the Nazi war machine. Eleven days later, British bombs also fell on the Rhine harbour in Basel, the Swiss hub for the huge barge traffic between Germany and Switzerland. Then on 1 April 1944, twenty-four American bombers attacked the Swiss industrial city of Schaffhausen with fire bombs, killing forty civilians, injuring hundreds of others, and destroying sixty-six buildings, principally factories, this city being the home base of one of Nazi Germany's other principal Swiss supplier of war materials, the firm of Georg Fischer. If these attacks had been regarded as deliberate, they would have had to be considered as an Allied declaration of war on Switzerland, with all the ensuing disastrous consequences for the country. So the Swiss government chose to view the bombings as 'accidents'. That way nothing had to be changed.[7]

Now that the Allies had a military presence on the continent, however, one that was growing by the day, Switzerland began to feel the consequences almost immediately. On 7 July, the Swiss government received a 'strong telegram'[8] from the American Secretary of State, Cordell Hull, warning them against entering

---

7 For a definitive history of the Anglo-American air attacks on Switzerland during World War II, see chapter 5, 'Neutralitätsverletzungen durch angelsächsische Flugzeuge', in Bonjour, vol. V, pp. 106–35.

8 For the complete text, see Bonjour, vol. V, p. 350.

into any new trade deals with the Nazis, deals which the Americans said would only help extend the war. During that same month of July 1944, a conference designed to establish the postwar international financial framework was taking place at Bretton Woods, a New Hampshire resort, and one of the main items on the agenda was the fate of the Swiss-based Bank for International Settlements. Thanks to the activities of the Basel cell of the Soviet Rote Kapelle, the whole financial world now knew of the games which the BIS had been playing in cahoots with the Reichsbank and the Swiss National. On 10 July a resolution was introduced by a Norwegian economist named Wilhelm Keilhau calling for the dissolution of the Bank for International Settlements 'at the earliest possible moment'. He was fully backed by Henry Morgenthau, the American secretary of the Treasury.[9] However, after initial support, one of the key figures at this conference, and the preeminent economist of the century, John Maynard Keynes, now Lord Keynes, backed away from this proposal and called for a postponement of any action, suggesting that the BIS be kept going until a new world bank and international monetary fund was set up, and then closed down. Dean Acheson, representing the American State Department, sided with him, and a resolution was passed to this effect at the close of the conference on 20 July 1944. There could now be no doubt that the continuing existence of the BIS was hanging by a very thin thread.

Then there was a dramatic hardening of the British stance vis-à-vis Switzerland. On 27 July Anthony Eden, the British foreign secretary, warned the Swiss ambassador in London that unless Switzerland stopped exporting war materials to the Nazis, the Allies would cut that country off from any further supplies of raw materials and, yes, even foodstuffs.[10] That this was hardly an empty threat soon became obvious. For on 29 August of that

---

9 Morgenthau, for whom the BIS had become a bête noire, felt the bank 'should be disbanded because to disband it would be good propaganda for the United States'. See Higham, *Trading with the Enemy*, p. 13.

10 Reported in a cable sent by the Swiss ambassador in London, Ruegger, to the Swiss foreign minister, Pilet, on 29 June 1944. Bonjour, vol. V, p. 351.

year, the Allies landed in the south of France — three months after their invasion of Normandy — and within fourteen days had captured not only the entire Mediterranean coast from Marseilles to Nice, but had spearheaded all the way north to Grenoble, just a hundred kilometres south of Geneva and the Swiss border. This meant that the Americans had now cut off all communications and transportation routes between the German troops in France and those German divisions still fighting the Americans in northern Italy. It also meant that maintaining a direct line of supply between Germany proper and Italy, through Basel and the Gotthard tunnel under the Swiss Alps, had now become absolutely imperative for the Nazis if the war in Italy was to be continued. Yet the Swiss government insisted that it remain open, invoking an international treaty signed by both the Germans and the Swiss in 1907 (!) which, the Swiss said, precluded its closing.[11] Needless to say, the Allies were not impressed.

The penultimate blow in the dark days of September 1944, dark at least for the Swiss, came with the capture of Bordeaux by the Americans. Now all of southern France was in their hands, meaning that all rail and road routes between Switzerland and the Iberian peninsula were now controlled by Allied troops and not the Nazis who, during the entire war, had allowed the Swiss free transit through Vichy France to Spain and Portugal.

This cut to the quick where the Swiss were concerned. For those routes represented their very lifeline — the one they had almost exclusively relied upon during 1944 to get enough food to keep the five million inhabitants of Switzerland alive. During the initial years of World War II it had been the port of Genoa in Italy through which Switzerland had imported grain and meat from Argentina, oranges from Algeria, cotton from the United States. Even after the Allies had blockaded all shipping headed for the Mediterranean, except where neutrals were concerned, the Swiss had found a way around it. They had leased fifteen Greek freighters which, now flying the neutral flag of, yes, the

---

11 The treaty, the Haager Landkriegsordnung, excluded all war materials, however. Ibid., p. 351.

338

Swiss navy, had shuttled across the Atlantic between North and South America and Portugal unloading their cargoes in 'neutral' Lisbon. There the cargoes had been reloaded onto 'neutral' Spanish ships, which were allowed to pass through the British navy's blockade at Gibraltar, and proceeded to Genoa, where the Fascist regime in Italy allowed the cargo to be once again unloaded, this time onto neutral Swiss trucks. The tortuous journey had finally ended at the Swiss border at Chiasso. However, the invasion of Italy by the Allies had led to the port of Genoa being closed entirely. So the Swiss had been forced to find a new solution.

It had come in the form of a new deal which they cut with the Germans. The Nazis allowed them to use the port of Marseilles to offload their cargo from their leased Spanish ships onto Swiss trucks, which then ferried the cargo north along the Route Napoléon to Geneva. In addition, in early 1944 the Swiss had also established a direct rail route from the Atlantic. They purchased 200 wrecked Spanish railroad cars which ran on a gauge size unique to Spain and Portugal, one totally incompatible with the tracks used in all other European countries, and completely refurbished them. These 'Swiss' trains would then pick up cargo in Portugal and haul it to the French border, where it would be loaded onto French railroad cars, which moved it to Switzerland. Also a fleet of 100 huge Swiss trucks began an endless shuttle between Lisbon and Switzerland – again traversing the German-controlled southern part of France.[12]

All of this – the use of the port of Marseilles by 'Swiss' ships; the use of the French rail system between the Pyrenees and the Swiss border; the use of French roads by Swiss trucks along the same route – now came to an abrupt and total halt. The Allies had finally made it clear: unless the Swiss cut their economic ties with the Nazis, they were going to starve them. The Swiss, however, continued to stonewall.

---

12 Erdman, *Swiss–American Economic Relations*, pp. 90–1. See also André Egg, *Die volkswirtschaftliche Bedeutung des Hafens Genua für die Schweiz* (Bern, 1949).

Still worse was then threatened. In the late evening of 16 October 1944, the Political Department of the Swiss government – their equivalent of the Foreign Office – received a most urgent and highly secret message from the Swiss ambassador in London. It dealt with a conversation that had taken place in Yalta on 14 October 1944 between the Prime Minister of Great Britain, Winston Churchill, the President of the United States, Franklin Delano Roosevelt, and Joseph Stalin. Stalin had brought up the subject of Switzerland, and according to an impeccable source within the British Foreign Office, one still friendly to Switzerland, later that evening Churchill, in briefing the Foreign Office personnel who had accompanied him to the Yalta conference, had said, verbatim, the following: 'I was astonished at Uncle Joe's savageness against Switzerland. He called them "swine" and he does not use that sort of language without meaning it.'[13]

Then Stalin had made an astonishing proposal to Roosevelt and Churchill, one that he insisted would greatly shorten the war and save innumerable Russian lives, although it was also potentially lethal where Switzerland was concerned. His logic was impeccable. Stalin pointed out that after the Allied landing in Normandy in early June and the subsequent capture of Paris, the progress of the Allies in their eastward march on Germany had slowed to a stop. Ahead of them still lay the 'Siegfried Line', the 'impenetrable last line of defence' according to Hitler, which would stop them short of Geman territory. What Stalin proposed in the face of this was simple: to outflank the Siegfried Line to the south by invading Switzerland from France, and then sweeping through into south Germany – into Baden and Württemberg – across the Swiss border. Stalin was further quoted as saying that 'the Swiss had played a false role in the war and should be made to cooperate'.[14]

*

---

13 Winston S. Churchill, *The Second World War*, vol. VI (London, 1954), p. 616.

14 This was first revealed on 16 March 1954, with the publication by the US State Department of the secret Yalta conference documents. See Bonjour, vol. V, p. 408.

Needless to say, all this put an increasing strain on American diplomatic personnel representing their country in Switzerland, adding to their sense of isolation. It especially affected Nancy Reichman. For while she was in complete agreement with the harsh measures now being imposed on her host country by the Allies, she, better than most Americans, knew that the majority of the Swiss people were in full sympathy with the cause of the Allies and were violently anti-German; that they were at the mercy of a Swiss government which was stubbornly clinging to policies which had been totally overtaken by events, and for which they were now being forced to pay the price. The Swiss citizenry saw their allotment of gas for heating and cooking now cut to one-quarter of normal peacetime usage. Meat and sugar became rare items. They even saw their daily ration of bread cut from 250 to 225 grams, and, now that all food and grain imports had been sealed off by the Allies, their bread contained as much 'potato additive' as it did flour. Nancy Reichman was also aware, like almost no other American, of the many examples of assistance which Swiss Intelligence had given her and the American Office of Strategic Services so far during this war. Not all had led necessarily to success, and one in particular had ended in tragedy: the disastrous failure of the Kreisau Circle to assassinate Hitler.

On 20 July 1944, the bomb that one of its members, Colonel Count Schenk von Stauffenberg, had smuggled in his briefcase into Hitler's secret headquarters in East Prussia, the 'Wolf-schanze', had exploded just two metres to the right of the Führer, but, miraculously, the Nazi leader, seriously but not critically wounded, had walked away. Almost immediately thereafter the members of the Kreisau Circle were rounded up and executed, including the young man with whom Nancy had spent an evening in the company of Karl Barth the previous autumn, Adam von Trott zu Solz. Hitler thought even the rope too good for them. Most were strangled with piano wire.[15]

When news of this gradually trickled through to Nancy Reichman in the late summer and autumn of 1944, she knew that the

15 See Allen Dulles, *Germany's Underground*, p. 87.

United States was not blameless in this matter. Following that evening in Basel, von Trott had gone on to meet Allen Dulles under the clock tower in Bern as she had arranged. They had got on famously, and a second meeting, which included another emissary from the Kreisau Circle, took place in January of 1944, also in Bern. Dulles now became convinced that they were deadly serious, and reported back to OSS headquarters in Washington enthusiastically recommending that they be given full American support. The head of the OSS, Major-General William Donovan, was just as enthusiastic. He assigned the OSS codename Breakers to this group's plan, and when Dulles later forwarded their request that the OSS go beyond providing help where communications were concerned (via the Bally network), and should cooperate in supplying arms and arrange for American forces to come to their assistance, Donovan went personally to President Roosevelt to recommend that his organization be allowed to do so.

He was stunned when Roosevelt refused to permit him to help the German plotters. 'If we start assassinating chiefs of state,' Roosevelt told him, 'God knows where it all would end. If the Germans dispose of Hitler, that is their prerogative, but the OSS must have nothing whatsoever to do with it.'[16]

So Hitler was alive. And Adam von Trott zu Solz was dead.

All this added frustration to Nancy Reichman's increasing sense of isolation. She could hardly wait for this dreary war to be finally over. About the only thing that kept her going was the steady relationship which Peter Burckhardt maintained with her. But even there, the spark, though still alive, was increasingly in danger of going out, suffocated by the growing boredom which prevailed in a Switzerland cut off from the world and where, as the old year ended and the new began, the lights were growing dimmer, the food scarcer, and the future more and more uncertain.

That boredom was totally shattered by a phone call from Allen Dulles on 9 January 1945.

---

16 Dunlop, *Donovan: America's Master Spy*, pp. 450–1.

Chapter 27

The phone call came into the American consulate in Basel on Nancy Reichman's 'safe' phone at 9.15 am.

'I have to leave for a quick trip to Paris within the hour,' Dulles began, 'and so I will have to be brief. Now listen very carefully, Nancy. You can expect a call from Peter Burckhardt. He will alert you as to the time he expects his boss at the Bank for International Settlements, Per Jacobsson, to arrive at the Badische railway station. He's returning from a trip to Berlin. This was all prearranged, and originally I had planned to come over to Basel to meet Jacobsson. Now I want you to fill in for me.'

'Yes, sir.'

'You will need to know a few more facts. This trip to Berlin by Jacobsson was instigated by me. The reason goes back to the matter we last discussed in the restaurant at the zoo with the young Burckhardt woman: the state of the development of nuclear weapons in Germany. We have reason to believe that they are getting very close to manufacturing an atomic bomb. If you recall, for a while we mistakenly believed that this was taking place at Peenemünde and proceeded to bomb that island. Then we found out that their nuclear research and development has always been going on exclusively at the Kaiser Wilhelm Institute in Berlin under a team headed by Professor Werner Heisenberg and made up of some of the world's leading atomic scientists, including Otto Hahn, Carl von Weizsäcker and Max von Laue. A week ago we received some extremely disconcerting news. They have all disappeared from Berlin. So I asked Jacobsson to go to Berlin and make inquiries. I told him that we very urgently needed answers to two questions. How close are they? And where have they gone?'

'I understand.'

'I will be back in Switzerland late tonight. If Jacobsson turns up, I will expect to hear from you first thing tomorrow.'

One hour later, another call came in for Nancy, this time on the regular consulate line. It was Peter Burckhardt and he was all business.

'I talked to a mutual friend early this morning who told me that he has had a change in plans. I expect that you have also heard from him in the meantime.'

'I have.'

'Regarding that other party, here at the BIS we just received a telex from the Reichsbank in Berlin informing us that we can expect his arrival back in Basel at 9.55 this evening. I was told that you will now want to meet him there.'

'Yes.'

'Then I will pick you up at your apartment at nine-thirty.'

'I'll be waiting downstairs.'

She then hung up, and so did the man who monitored her phone calls at his post in the headquarters of Basel's political police, the unit in charge of counter-espionage in that region of Switzerland. He duly reported what he had heard to Dr Wilhelm Lützelschwab.

At shortly after ten that evening, Per Jacobsson walked out of the Badische Bahnhof and, spotting Peter Burckhardt and Nancy Reichman waiting across the street in front of the 'Kleinbasler Weinstube' restaurant, hurried to join them.

Once inside, after they had sat down at a table and ordered a carafe of Dôle, the heavy Swiss red wine which was fully appropriate on this icy winter night, the American woman was the first to speak. 'Mr Dulles was unable to come over from Bern this evening. His presence was urgently required in Paris. So he asked me to come instead.'

The Swede just nodded. He knew that the American woman worked with Dulles. In fact, the three of them had even dined together in Basel on one occasion.

'Were you able to find out where Heisenberg is?'

'No,' answered the Swede. 'Mr Dulles' information was correct. Heisenberg, Hahn, von Weizsäcker, they have all disappeared from Berlin. And all the equipment they were using at the Kaiser Wilhelm Institute has likewise disappeared.'

'Did you get any indication of how close they were before they disappeared?'

'Yes,' Jacobsson paused, and then went on. 'Close. Very close. I don't quite understand exactly what it means, but I was told that it was no longer a matter of design but just lack of heavy water and uranium. That final problem was expected to be corrected shortly.'[17]

'Mr Dulles will want to hear about this immediately.'

Peter Burckhardt then dropped her off back at her apartment before taking Jacobsson to the Three Kings Hotel where he now lived. At eight the next morning she telephoned Dulles on the 'safe' line from the consulate. He told her to make no plans for the next few days that could not be easily cancelled. He might have to call upon her for help in this matter 'one last time'.

After he hung up, he wished that he had not used that phrase.

Dulles immediately put all of his intelligence resources inside Germany to work on the search for the missing nuclear scientists.

---

17 The problem with heavy water stemmed from the effects of British commando raids and bombing attacks on the Norsk-Hydro facility in Norway, Germany's principal source of heavy water. However, none of these raids was totally successful, and all they did was periodically diminish the output to about 50 per cent of what it would have been otherwise. See the chapter titled 'The German Atom Bomb' in William Casey, *The Secret War Against Hitler* (Washington, DC, 1988), pp. 48ff.

In addition, he personally met with the head of the 'D' (for Deutschland) Section of Swiss Intelligence, Captain Hans Waibel, Lieutenant Peter Burckhardt's immediate superior, to enlist his help in the search.[18] Waibel did two things. First, he activated the 'Viking Line', Switzerland's highly secret intelligence link which led to a man in the innermost circle around Hitler. And on a much more mundane level, on a hunch he put out the word among the Swiss community living in southern Germany, which numbered in the thousands and which included hundreds of housewives, doctors, carpenters and cooks who remained loyal to their true 'Heimat' and who, despite the risk, acted as informants for Swiss Intelligence throughout the war. He asked them to report on any strange construction projects and/or any unexpected influx of scientists. Within forty-eight hours Waibel had the answer. It came from a Baumeister, an architect/builder, who lived in the Black Forest. In the autumn of last year he had been involved in a very strange project: the construction of a concrete pit with walls whose specifications required thicknesses of a magnitude he had never encountered or even heard of before. Not only that, but the pit was built in a cave in the side of a cliff! Then, a month ago, they had started to arrive: the Herr Professors. A dozen of them at least! And this in a sleepy little town in the Black Forest.

Waibel knew at once that this must be it. The name of the town was Haigerloch. It was situated exactly 120 kilometres northeast of Basel: just 75 miles. He immediately reported these facts to Dulles. The next day, Sunday, 14 January 1945, Dulles began the implementation of a plan which he hoped would meet two objectives: to ascertain how far they had progressed, and then, if it was determined that they had made a breakthrough (which the

---

18 Dulles had developed a close working relationship with Waibel, one which bore enormous fruit. For it was Waibel who later set up the negotiations in Switzerland (in Zurich, Lucerne and Ascona) in March and April of 1945 between Allen Dulles and SS General Wolff which led to the surrender of the German army in Italy on 2 May 1945. This was done without the knowledge of either the Swiss government or General Guisan. See Gautschi, pp. 645ff, and especially Allen Dulles, *The Secret Surrender*.

Americans still had not), to convince them to come out of Germany into Switzerland (and then, it was to be hoped, on to America) before it was too late, allowing them a last-ditch opportunity to build a new life and to continue their scientific research almost without interruption.[19]

They must surely realize that the Russian army was rapidly approaching from the East, and that if they got to Haigerloch first, the consequences for them personally, and for *both* Germany and the West, would be unthinkable. Whoever approached these scientists would have to appeal to their sense of solidarity with their former colleagues at Göttingen in the Twenties and Thirties, almost all of whom were now in the West — in Britain, in the United States, in Switzerland. Not one had headed East.

The first step, however, was to get them into Switzerland. Which would require that they be officially offered asylum there and that this offer be given on the spot . . . by a Swiss. It would also mean convincing them that the United States would not seek retribution, but was willing to help them out in any way they requested, including money and travel documents which would allow them to settle permanently in the United States now or at any time they might choose. They would also have to be convinced of this on the spot . . . by an American carrying the proper credentials. But a prerequisite to all of this was determining how close they were to developing an atomic bomb . . . which would call for the judgement of a Western scientist, one that could only be rendered on the basis of an on-the-spot inspection.

All of these considerations flatly ruled out any commando raid by the Americans or the British, as had been advocated by the men who were officially in charge of intelligence and countermeasures aimed at German nuclear projects, General Leslie R. Groves and his right-hand man, Colonel Boris Pash. They were the reason that Dulles had gone to Paris: to meet with them and specifically discuss this matter. A year ago, he had been warned off from any interference in their field of intelligence. But now

---

19 For the complete history of the resettlement of German scientists in the United States, see Tom Bower, *The Paperclip Conspiracy* (New York, 1987).

they were asking him back in. The reason: after having been stunned by the first attack on London by V-2 rockets on 8 September 1944, and then the appearance in the skies of Germany of the Messerschmitt 262, the world's first jet fighter, which could fly at a speed of 540 mph, as compared to a top speed of 358 mph for the American B29 bomber, and 302 mph for the Flying Fortress (B17G), they were now increasingly concerned that German science was about to spring another surprise on them. When the German army mounted its fierce counterattack in the Ardennes forest before Christmas of 1944, their concern had turned into acute worry that this might be a coldly calculated attempt to buy enough time for the final manufacture and deployment of a German atomic bomb. They had grown even more nervous when they received word just after Christmas that the German nuclear scientists had disappeared from Berlin. That was when they had appealed to Dulles for help, and when Dulles had, in turn, recruited the aid of Per Jacobsson. In return for his renewed cooperation, Dulles had asked that he be granted a free hand for a few weeks before they came down on the problem with a sledge-hammer, and General Groves had reluctantly agreed.

Now that both Jacobsson and Waibel had come through, Dulles was therefore at liberty to implement the plan he had had in mind all along: to send in a three-man team composed of Peter Burckhardt, his sister, and Nancy Reichman. Together they met all the requirements. If his plan were to succeed, however, it was imperative that he gain the full, unqualified support of Swiss Intelligence. For who could better get them in and out of Germany? Who could better take care of them while they were on the ground in the Black Forest than the web of agents which Swiss Intelligence maintained there? And what might get them more smoothly through the front door once they had arrived in Haigerloch than a letter from a former colleague of Heisenberg's, Swiss Professor Wolfgang Pauli of the Eidgenössische Technische Hochschule in Zurich, borne by one of his star students, Felicitas Burckhardt? He was sure that Swiss Intelligence could also arrange that.

So he requested a second meeting with Captain Waibel for the next day. Waibel promised him the full cooperation of his entire organization both in Switzerland and on the ground in Germany, but with the qualification that the two Burckhardts volunteer for the mission. Allen Dulles had to make a similar reservation where the participation of Nancy Reichman was concerned.

These caveats proved unnecessary.

At eight o'clock on the night of 17 January 1945, the Swiss tugboat *Corviglia* left the Rhine harbour in Basel. It was pushing three barges containing 6,000 bags of Swiss cement and bound for the Ruhr. It was also carrying three passengers: two Swiss and one American. During the cursory search of the vessels by the German authorities which had taken place in the harbour, they had hidden in a cache which the crew that loaded the barge had rigged under the cement bags on one of them. An hour and a half later, when they were ten kilometres downstream and approaching the village of Weil am Rhein, the tugboat and the barges it was pushing drifted toward the right bank and slowed almost to a halt. The three passengers boarded a small dinghy, and were quickly rowed to shore — barely fifty metres away — by two deckhands from the tug. The banks of the Rhine were not guarded, since at this point the river ran through territory which was under German control on both sides.

The three passengers wore heavy boots and overcoats, all well worn. In fact, the overcoats bordered on the shabby. They also bore small backpacks containing the minimum necessary for what was designed to be a forty-eight-hour trip. After they had scrambled ashore, they walked no more than a hundred metres through a pasture which was lightly dusted with snow to the main road which ran through the tiny German village. In the middle of that village was a small inn, and in front of it stood a man in peasant clothing. As they approached him, without saying a word he turned and disappeared into the darkness on the far side of the inn. The three followed him. There, leaning against the building, were three bicycles, two of which were designed for women. Again without anyone saying a word, the three wheeled the bicycles onto the road, mounted them, and then rode off into the darkness.

They moved fast during the next hour, taking narrow, completely deserted rural roads, but moving steadily in an easterly direction. Shortly before eleven they approached the village of Fahrnau. After they had passed through it, Peter Burckhardt, who had the lead, looked back at the two young women who were trailing him, and signalled that they were approaching their initial destination. It was a Bauernhaus on the northern outskirts. Burckhardt suddenly veered right off the road into a very narrow lane which ended in a barnyard behind the house. After all three had dismounted, he motioned to the two women to stay behind, then walked to the back door and knocked.

After only a few seconds the door was opened and the head of a man in his mid-sixties peered out at him. 'Peter,' he said, 'Gott sei Dank du bisch heil ako.' He stepped outside and embraced the young man. The Swiss 'network' had got word to him to expect his nephew.

Then he spotted Burckhardt's sister. 'Felicitas! Du bish au do!' He now went to her and caught her up in a bear-hug. He was a big man, and he also had a loud voice.

'Uncle Ernst,' Peter Burckhardt warned, 'I think it best we go inside.'

The four, with Nancy Reichman trailing, now entered the kitchen of the Bauernhaus, which dated back to the fifteenth century. The scene outside was repeated, only this time it was Tante Emily who embraced her nephew and niece; the difference was that now a few tears were shed. For it was the first time that the young Burckhardts from Basel had seen their mother's sister since the summer of 1939. To be sure, Fahrnau was no more than fifteen kilometres distant from Basel, but, after the war began and the border was sealed, it could just as well have been light-years away.

Then, all of a sudden, everybody seemed to take notice of the outsider in their midst. It was Felicitas Burckhardt who immediately stepped in to bridge the awkward moment.

'Onkel Ernst and Tante Emily,' she said, 'this is a very good 'friend of ours – of both Peter and myself – and her name is Nancy Reichman. She's an American.'

'En Amerkanere!' Tante Emily repeated. 'Do in Fahrnau!' She took the hand of this exotic visitor, shook it vigorously, and said: 'Wilkommen in unserem Heim, Fräulein Reichman.' Her husband, looking equally astounded, then did the same.

Tante Emily now insisted that the visitors immediately take off their backpacks, overcoats and boots and come into the living room, where she placed them all in a row on the bench which circled the 'Kacheloffen' in order to warm them up. The stove, which was clad in blue-glazed Dutch tiling, dated back to the seventeenth century. It was ceiling-high and built into the thick wall which separated the living-room from the kitchen. The heat came from the burning wood inside, wood which was fed in through an open fireplace situated on the kitchen side of the Kacheloffen where for centuries the week's bread, Bauernbrot, had been baked each Monday morning.

Tante Emily, who had gone back into the kitchen, now reappeared bearing a tray with three steaming bowls of hot soup – potato and leek soup. It was, of course, first offered to Nancy Reichman. As soon as the soup had disappeared, which was almost immediately, Tante Emily went back into the kitchen and reappeared this time with two huge pies – apple and cherry. She insisted that everybody try both. Then came the coffee, and with the coffee the Kirschwasser which Onkel Ernst had personally distilled from their own cherries for more than forty years.

Then it turned serious. What was going to happen to Germany, Onkel Ernst wanted to know from his nephew, when this war was finally over? He added that everyone now knew that it was only a matter of months before Germany would have to surrender . . . everyone but the madman Hitler.

Peter Burckhardt replied that this was still very unclear. There were some, like the American secretary of the Treasury, Henry Morgenthau, who wanted to reduce Germany to an agrarian state. He doubted that a reasonable man like President Roosevelt would go along with this. The Russians, no doubt, wanted to convert it to a Socialist state. But he was sure that the British, especially Churchill, would not stand for that. There could be no doubt, however, that Germany would never be allowed to threaten the world again.

Onkel Ernst just nodded silently until Peter Burckhardt had finished expressing his views. Then he gave his. 'It all started to go bad in Germany when Hindenburg forced the Kaiser into exile. That was the mistake which led to everything that followed. First the Treaty of Versailles and the reparations we could never afford to pay. Then the disastrous inflation. And finally the equally disastrous unemployment. These were all things we Germans had never experienced before. Then there was the so-called democracy of the Weimar Republic. We Germans neither understood nor wanted it, so it was bound to fail. All this made a Hitler inevitable sooner or later. Ach, Peter, if only they had let our Kaiser be. Then this calamity would never have happened.'

Tante Emily, who had no doubt heard this a thousand times, now broke in and wanted to know all about her relatives in Basel, how they had spent the war, and what they planned on doing when it was finally over. It was Felicitas Burckhardt who responded, and soon the mood shifted back to one of joyful anticipation of the time which was now not far off when they could all once again plan Sunday trips across the border in order to visit each other.

At midnight Peter Burckhardt brought the evening to a close. They had to get going early the next morning, he explained. As he understood it, he said to Uncle Ernst, the Postbus which followed the northeasterly route through the Black Forest left Lörrach every morning at seven, and came through Fahrnau a half-hour later. Was it still running on that schedule?

It was. But it did not stop in Fahrnau. You had to wave it down. Where? Anywhere. On the road right in front of the house would be as good a place as any. In fact, it would be a better place than further back in the centre of the village. The Gestapo informant who owned the butcher's shop there watched everything. In fact, everybody now watched everybody else. It would be best if the three of them stayed in the house until he had

flagged down the bus. Then they should board quickly. Uncle
Ernst did not ask where they were going or why. His nephew
Peter Burckhardt was obviously operating under higher Swiss
authority, and, as a good German who yearned for the return of
legitimate authority in his own country, he was not about to
question that.

Onkel Ernst then escorted his nephew to one of the two spare
bedrooms on the second floor of the ancient Bauernhaus, while
Tante Emily took the two 'girls' to the other one further down the
hall, stopping at a huge wooden cabinet from which she extracted
two heavy woollen nightgowns which looked almost as ancient as
the Bauernhaus. Then she bade them good-night, kissing and
hugging both of them as she did so. It was icy cold in the
bedroom, and so it took Felicitas Burckhardt and Nancy Reichman but seconds to don their nightgowns, turn out the lights, and
dive under the huge Federbett.

At first neither girl said a word, but then Felicitas broke the
silence. 'Do you mind if I ask you something really silly?'

'Of course not,' Nancy Reichman replied.

'Do Jewish people say a prayer before they go to sleep?'

'Yes. We call it "Shamah".'

'Do you pray?'

'Sometimes.'

'Same here. Do you mind if I include you in my prayer
tonight?'

'Of course not.'

Then silence, which again was broken by Felicitas.

'Are you scared?'

'I was until I got here. Now I feel completely safe. It must be
the nightgown.'

This produced a giggle from both of them.

'How would you like Peter to see you in *that* outfit?'

'Onkel Ernst probably has him in one too.'

Another giggle.

'Are you serious about Peter?'

'Sometimes. But lately I'm not too sure about him.'

'But I know he likes you an awful lot, Nancy,' his sister replied.

'He doesn't have any other girlfriend, you know.'

'Still.' Then: 'Don't tell him now, Felicitas, but I'm planning on going back home. I've already talked it over with Mr Dulles, and he said that he can arrange it with the State Department when this is over.'

'You mean when the war's over.'

'No. When this trip is over.'

'Well, I hope you change your mind. In fact, I'm going to include that in my prayer too.'

'We'd better go to sleep now, Felicitas. Sleep well.'

'You too, Nancy.'

At six-thirty the next morning, Tante Emily knocked on their door and then entered bearing yet another tray, this time with two cups of steaming coffee, Bauernbrot, butter and cherry jam. She insisted on serving them in bed, chattering away the whole time. Then she disappeared, and fifteen minutes later returned with two bowls, a huge pitcher of hot water, and towels. By shortly before seven the girls were dressed.

When they came down the stairs, the two men were waiting for them. In contrast to the evening before, their faces were serious, and the atmosphere tense. The radio was on, and it was tuned to Beromünster, Switzerland's German-language national transmitter.[20] The seven o'clock news was just coming on, and the lead story dealt with the latest events on the Eastern front. The Red Army offensive in Poland which had begun just five days earlier had already produced its first huge success: the surrender and occupation of Warsaw.

'They're coming much faster than any of us thought,' Onkel Ernst said, upon hearing this.

Then events on the Western front were summarized. The Americans had begun to turn the tide in the Battle of the Bulge, and had just recaptured Houffalize in the heart of Belgium.

---

20 The French-language transmitter is located at Sottens; the Italian-language one atop Monte Ceneri.

'Let's hope they get here first,' Peter Burckhardt commented. By 'here' he did not just mean this village of Fahrnau on the edge of the Black Forest, but also that other village sixty kilometres further into the forest, Haigerloch.

At the end of the news broadcast, as always, came the weather forecast: 'Kalt, mit zunehmender Bewölkung. Heute Nacht und Morgen Schneefall, teils schwer, bis in die Niederungen.' – 'Cold, with cloud increasing. Tonight and tomorrow snow, at times heavy even at lower elevations.'

'Not good,' said Onkel Ernst. Peter Burckhardt said nothing, but the two girls could not help exchanging glances.

Five minutes later Onkel Ernst put on his overcoat and left the house through the front door. Peter Burckhardt likewise put on his coat, but instead of leaving the house he stood behind the living-room window next to the front door, the one facing the road. Five minutes thereafter he looked at his watch and suggested that the two young women likewise put on their boots and coats. Tante Emily's chatter had now ceased. She just sat there, in front of the Kacheloffen, trying to look brave and unconcerned, but not succeeding.

Then it happened very fast. Peter Burckhardt could see his uncle starting to wave, and seconds later the bus, yellow with the insignia of the postal service on its side, the 'Posthorn', came to a halt in front of the house. Peter signalled to the girls, then opened the front door and strode towards the gate that led to the road and the waiting bus. The young women stopped to wave back at Tante Emily, who stood silently weeping at the front door, and then boarded the bus. Peter Burckhardt, after shaking hands with his uncle, did the same.

'Hechingen, dreimal, retour,' Peter Burckhardt said to the bus driver, adapting his Basel patois as best he could to the local 'Badische', which was not that difficult to do, since both were very closely related 'cousins' in the family of Alemannic dialects. Hechingen was the jumping-off point on the bus route for Haigerloch.

'Acht Mark, fünf und siebzig Pfennig,' the bus driver told him, after consulting his fare book.

355

Burckhardt fished the exact amount from his wallet (one of Waibel's men in Section 5 had told him what it would be) and then motioned to the two women who had been waiting in the aisle to proceed toward the back of the bus where most of the seats were empty. They stopped at the second-last row, stuffed their backpacks under their seats, and took the two seats on the left. Peter, keeping his backpack at his side, took the window seat across the aisle, and, as the bus began to move, once more waved farewell to his uncle and aunt who were now both standing in the doorway of their Bauernhaus waving back. It was a typical scene in the Black Forest as relatives from different villages took leave of each other after a short family visit.

The bus, a diesel Mercedes, belched smoke as it gradually picked up speed, and within minutes was up to a respectable 45 kilometres an hour. This soon proved to be its top speed for a while, however, since the road became increasingly narrow and winding and uphill the further into the Schwarzwald they went. Furthermore, although there was no snow on the road, there were frequent patches of ice, causing the driver to become increasingly cautious lest his bus skid on one of them and end up in the snow banks which now lined the road on both sides. The first stop after ten kilometres was the small town of Schönau. Two people got out, one in. Then came a brief stop at Todnau, and after laboriously climbing another fifteen kilometres they reached their first major destination, Feldberg, the village on the Feldsee which was situated in the shadow of the mountain of the same name, the highest point in the Black Forest, with an altitude of 1,493 metres, as was indicated on the information board in the middle of town where the bus stopped and waited for at least fifteen minutes. This wait was apparently part of the normal schedule, and intended to give the passengers enough time to load and unload their skiing equipment, since the Feldberg was the centre for that sport in this region of southwest Germany. However, in this January of 1945 there were no skiers to be seen. The young German men who would normally have been there, either alone or with their girlfriends and wives, were dying in such diverse places as Belgium, Poland, Italy and Yugoslavia. There had been, in fact, no young or even middle-aged men to be seen so far that day. The average age of the bus passengers, apart from Peter's group, must have been getting on for seventy.

They left Feldberg at 9 am and soon were alongside the Titisee, an Alpine-like lake. Here most of the passengers got out, carrying their rather pathetic looking suitcases. And after these seventy-year-old men and women had alighted, an almost like number of elderly Germans got into the bus. The reason for their comings and goings: the town of Titisee offered them the facilities and therapy of a centuries-old spa, one famed for its curative powers, especially good for rheumatism. It was there that the three young passengers in the rear of the bus saw their first German policeman. He seemed totally uninterested in the bus. But suddenly realizing that such a heretofore overlooked factor as his age could raise suspicions in this nation where everybody but the old people seemed to have disappeared, and especially the men, Peter Burckhardt now hunched down in his seat so as to become as inconspicuous as possible.

Chapter 28

The bus arrived at Hechingen at precisely 11.30. Peter Burckhardt, his sister Felicitas, and Nancy Reichman were the only
passengers who got out there. The bus-stop was in the middle of
the small town, right in front of the post office. Peter spotted
what he was looking for almost immediately. Parked directly
across the street from the post office was a van, and on its door it
bore the sign:

Häberlein Tiefbau
Donaustrasse II
Haigerloch.

There was a man in his mid-fifties sitting behind the steering
wheel, and as soon as he noticed Burckhardt staring in his
direction he put his left arm out of the window and waved. This
surprised Burckhardt, but then he immediately realized that the
safest way to establish contact in this country full of suspicion and
fear of the unknown was to be blatantly obvious. So he immediately waved back, and taking both women by the arm
headed directly across the street to the van. The man now sprang
out, and as Peter Burckhardt approached him moved forward to
grasp his outstretched hand and shake it vigorously. Next he
embraced Peter's sister, and then Nancy Reichman. Although
there were a lot of people in the streets, many of them on their
way to and from the post office where they made their payments
and settled their bills via the postal giro banking system, no one
paid the slightest attention to them.

Nor did anyone find it strange to see four people climb into the rather small van, since transportation in Germany in this January of 1945 was now reduced to the barest minimum. Peter took the seat next to the driver, while the two young women huddled on the van floor behind. It was only after they had pulled away from the kerb that the driver spoke his first words to Peter Burckhardt, and he spoke them in the Basel dialect.

'Es freut mi dass Sie do sin, Herr Doktor.' Then: 'You are right on time. I was starting to get worried, since the radio this morning said that the weather is going to be changing.'

'No problem,' Burckhardt replied. 'The sun was even shining on the Feldberg. How far is it to Haigerloch?'

'Eighteen kilometres. In fact, we turn off the main road right here.' Which he then proceeded to do. It was a much narrower road, and in bad repair.

'Are there any control points?' Burckhardt asked.

'No. Nobody around here has the slightest idea that anything unusual is going on in Haigerloch, and obviously the authorities want to do nothing to change that by setting up unusual security arrangements which might draw attention to the village. But still, one never knows. What is your story if we are stopped?'

'I'm with the Grenzwache, the border guard, stationed in Lörrach. I'm on a forty-eight-hour compassionate leave to attend my grandmother's funeral in Trilltingen, which I'm told is a tiny farming village just outside Haigerloch. My two sisters are with me. We are staying with you since you are a friend of the family, and have room and transportation for us.'

'And your documents are in what name?'

'Sempach. Peter, Felicitas, and Ursula Sempach.'

'Good. In fact, very good.'

'Our people in both Basel and Lucerne greatly appreciate what you are doing, Herr Häberlein, and have asked me to tell you that. We know the risk you are running.'

'When I grew up in Basel, our family lived right next door to the Waibels on the Gempenstrasse in the Gundeldingerquartier. You must know where that is.'

'Of course.'

'Although Hans is much younger than I, somehow we've stayed in contact over the years, even after I moved here. I was going to come home when the war started, but you know how difficult it is to just leave everything behind that you have built up over the years. But I still try to do my bit.' He now swerved abruptly to avoid a pothole, and immediately turned to the women in the back to apologize.

'Sorry about that. But if you just hold on, we should be there in about twenty minutes.' Then he once again addressed Peter Burckhardt. 'What is your plan once we get there?'

'One of us is going to try to contact Professor Heisenberg right away. Your friend Captain Waibel told me that you know him.'

'Yes. As you must know, my little company did the basic underground construction for the project he is working on. When it requires minor repairs or modifications, they call on me. So I see Professor Heisenberg regularly.'

'At work.'

'Yes. But just last week I also went over some plans for a major new project with him at the house he lives in. It is just down the street from our home in Haigerloch.'

'He lives alone?'

'No. His wife and children stayed in Berlin, as I understand it. But he has a full-time housekeeper.'

'Does she know you?'

'Yes. She's a local woman, and Haigerloch is a small town. We go to the same church.'

'Does Heisenberg come home for lunch?'

'Normally, yes. The place where they work is very uncomfortable. We almost always see his car – one of the few now operating – in front of the house between noon and two o'clock.'

'Herr Häberlein, I think you missed your calling. Your friend Captain Waibel could have used you in Section 5.'

Burckhardt could see that the expatriate Swiss was very pleased to receive the compliment.

It was exactly five minutes before twelve when the van crossed a bridge over a river, the Eyach River, after which they came to a

360

'Y' in the road. They kept to the right, taking what Häberlein explained was the 'low' road, one which now followed the river's course into a wide ravine where the small Black Forest town of Haigerloch was located.

'I see where it got its name,' Burckhardt said. 'Loch' in German means 'hole', 'gap' or 'opening' and it was into just such an opening between cliffs on both sides that they had entered.

Herr Häberlein now slowed the van almost to a halt, and pointed the finger of his right hand up to the left. 'See the church on top of the cliff?'

Burckhardt had to crane his neck to see it. 'Yes.'

'That's where it is. In a cave, under the church.'

'Amazing!'

'Ingenious, actually. There is no way that you can spot anything from the air, and even if you could, the cave is absolutely bomb-proof.'

'How big is it?'

'The main chamber is thirty metres long, fifteen wide, and twelve high.'

'How do you get to it?'

'Through a concrete tunnel we built. The entrance to the tunnel is just behind the church.'

Häberlein now turned the van into a side-street and almost immediately drew up in front of a rather large and handsome stucco house. As soon as the van had stopped, the door to the house had opened. The woman who emerged was obviously Frau Häberlein. She did not appear pleased. In fact, after the four had hurried from the van into the house and her husband introduced the new arrivals to her one by one, she acknowledged them with only a few curt words − in high German, not the Swiss dialect. Herr Häberlein also switched over to Hochdeutsch.

'Maria stammt aus Mannheim,' he said, explaining that she was originally a native of that German city. 'We met while I was studying engineering there. After we were married, we lived in Basel for a while. Then I got a big job here in the early 1930s − as a member of the construction team building a dam on the Eyach River about five kilometres upstream from here. We liked it so much here that we decided to settle in Haigerloch, and eventually I started my own firm.'

To some extent this sounded more like an apology than an explanation to his listeners from Basel, as was confirmed by Herr Häberlein's next words, which were addressed to his wife: 'But when this is all over, we will probably return to Switzerland, won't we, Maria?'

'We shall see.'

An uncomfortable Herr Häberlein then suggested that she prepare some coffee while he showed the visitors their rooms. As soon as she had disappeared, Peter Burckhardt said: 'The rooms can wait. I sense the concern of your wife and it is fully understandable. We also want to get this over as quickly as possible. You said that Professor Heisenberg usually comes home for lunch.'

'Yes,' Häberlein replied.

'Would you mind taking one of us over to his house? She has a letter of introduction to Heisenberg from one of his colleagues who now teaches at the Federal Institute of Technology in Zurich, Professor Wolfgang Pauli.'

The nodding of the Swiss engineer's head indicated that of course he knew the name.

'You mean right now?' he asked.

'Right now,' Burckhardt replied.

This appeared to come as something of a shock to Häberlein. But he immediately agreed. 'Fine, Herr Burckhardt. If you're ready . . .'

'I think you misunderstood. My sister will be going alone, at least on this initial visit. We have thought this over very carefully. A young woman is bound to attract the least attention. Especially if she is in the company of a local man who is well known in this town. That you are personally acquainted with the Professor's housekeeper makes it all the better. We must depend on you, Herr Häberlein, to get my sister past the front door without creating any suspicion in that woman's mind which might prompt her to do something foolish.'

Like alarming the local police, was the thought Burckhardt left unspoken. If Häberlein's wife acted the way she did, who could know how Heisenberg's housekeeper might react to the sudden appearance of a stranger at her front door?

'I will do my best, Herr Burckhardt,' Häberlein answered, but one could now detect a tightness in his voice.

Peter Burckhardt then reached into his backpack and lifted out a leather pouch. A red string could be seen protruding from it. One firm tug on the string would have set off a chemical reaction that would result in the immediate incineration of the contents of that pouch (this gadget had been given to Burckhardt by one of Dulles' men), which included the American diplomatic passport of Nancy Reichman, as well as papers which identified Peter Burckhardt as an officer attached to Section 5 of the General Staff of the High Command of the Swiss army, the credentials it would be necessary for them to produce when they reached Stage Two of this operation. But it was a third document which Burckhardt now withdrew from the pouch after he had unzipped it, an envelope bearing the insignia of the Eidgenössische Technische Hochschule in Zurich.

'Here, Felicitas,' he said as he handed it to his sister. Then he gave her a hug and a quick kiss on the cheek. Nancy Reichman stepped forward, and without saying anything, did the same.

'Let's get it over with,' Häberlein said to Felicitas. Then to her brother: 'We'll be going out the back door, as we always do. The front door is for visitors. I'll tell my wife that the two of you will be staying here in the living-room. I'm sure she will have your coffee ready in a few minutes.'

As Häberlein had mentioned in the van, Professor Heisenberg's house was just down the Donaustrasse from his own home. As Felicitas Burckhardt walked at his side, she could not help but think that this was probably *the* street in Haigerloch where the rich folk lived − all two blocks of it, which ran between the main road and the bank of the Eyach River. It was the last house on the street, overlooking the river, where they stopped. A large BMW was parked there.

'He's home,' Häberlein said. He took a deep breath, proceeded up the walk to the front door with Felicitas Burckhardt somewhat trailing behind, and pressed the buzzer.

A woman in her fifties, dressed in black, opened the door almost immediately. She smiled when she saw who was there.

'Ach, Herr Häberlein, what an unexpected pleasure! Is the Herr Professor expecting you?'

'Not really, Fräulein Schmidt. And I do hope that we are not intruding. But my niece here,' and he now nodded his head in the direction of Felicitas Burckhardt, who was standing behind him, 'is visiting us just for the day. She studies physics at the university, and when I told her that the famous Professor Heisenberg lived just down the street from us, she asked if she might be able to meet him.' In these parts, when one talked about 'the university' it was naturally assumed that one was referring to the ancient university in Tübingen, which was located just twenty kilometres to the northeast of Haigerloch.

These words of Häberlein's produced, if anything, an even broader smile on the face of Fräulein Schmidt. 'Oh, I'm *sure* that the Herr Professor will have time to see her. You know, he really misses his students. I hear him say that all the time. Because as you and I know, Herr Häberlein, as much as we love our Haigerloch, it is hardly Berlin, is it? So both of you come in. The Herr Professor is eating his lunch, and of course we cannot disturb him until he is done.'

Once they were inside she then said: 'Now let me take your coats and you both can make yourselves at home in the living-room. I'll bring you some coffee. It's awful stuff these days, but I hear it's getting very cold out there today so you need something to keep you warm, especially you, young lady,' adding after Felicitas had taken off her coat: 'My, how slender you are! What is your name, dear?'

'Felicitas Burckhardt.' Häberlein looked surprised when he heard her give her real name, but the housekeeper was so busy chattering away that she noticed nothing.

Ten minutes later Herr Professor Werner Heisenberg entered the living-room, causing the two visitors to immediately rise.

Felicitas Burckhardt was surprised by his appearance. First, he was much younger than she had anticipated – barely into his forties. And he was quite the opposite of the ascetic she had expected to meet. Heisenberg more resembled an athlete than a professor. And as he moved forward to greet Herr Häberlein, he moved with energy and grace. The fact that he had red hair added to his aura.

'Herr Häberlein,' he said, 'what a coincidence. I was actually going to telephone you this afternoon to suggest that we get together once more to finalize the plans for the new construction. Now that won't be necessary. If you have the time, we can go directly from here to the site. The blueprints are there, and anyway I think it would be a good idea to examine them on the spot, just to make absolutely sure that it will fit. I still have the feeling that it will be a very tight squeeze.'

Then he turned to Felicitas Burckhardt, and was obviously pleased with what he saw. She was a very attractive young woman, and Heisenberg was a vigorous man in his prime. So as he now greeted her, he kept her hand in his just that slight bit longer than was necessary. And it caused Felicitas Burckhardt to blush, which added to her allure.

'Fräulein Schmidt tells me that you are studying physics, young lady,' he said to her.

'Yes. And my Doktor Vater is an old colleague of yours from Göttingen.'

'Really! Who?'

'Professor Wolfgang Pauli.'

She could see his eyes flicker as the import of this sank in, but he said nothing. Then she reached into the pocket of her jacket and withdrew the envelope.

'Professor Pauli asked me to give this to you.'

Still not responding, Heisenberg accepted the envelope, carefully opened it, and after extracting the two-page letter that was inside, stood and read it in its totality as his two visitors stood there watching him. Then he folded the letter, tucked it back into the envelope, and put the envelope into the breast pocket of his jacket.

'Interessant, aber nicht praktisch.' — 'Interesting, but not practical.'

Then: 'Would you mind repeating those words to Wolfgang when you next see him, Fräulein Burckhardt.' When she nodded her agreement to do so, he continued: 'Good. And tell him not to worry about me. I'll manage. By the way, he writes quite highly of you. Which should please you, because Wolfgang has always had very high standards.' Then: 'Burckhardt. You are not by any chance related to the historian Jacob Burckhardt?'

'He was my great-uncle.'

'How interesting. In fact, this began as a very uninteresting day and your visit has suddenly changed that. You said Wolfgang is your thesis supervisor. What is the subject of your dissertation?'

'The measurement of the critical mass of uranium.'

Again she could see that speculative flicker in his eyes.

'Rudolph Peierls' specialty. I knew him well. Before he left Berlin for Cambridge. I assume that one of your starting points must be that paper he published in 1939 in the *Proceedings* of the Cambridge Philosophical Society.'

'Yes, sir.'

'Did Wolfgang suggest this thesis?'

'Yes, sir.'

'I assume that he has you concentrating on the difference, the potentially radical difference, between U-238 and U-235 where critical mass is concerned.'

'Yes, sir. Tons versus pounds.' The tons and pounds she referred to were the amounts of fissionable material necessary for the manufacture of an atomic bomb.

That answer seemed to have satisfied whatever lingering doubts Heisenberg might have been harbouring as a result of this very strange encounter in his living-room.

'Would you like to see my little factory — for making U-235?'

'I'd love to, Herr Professor!' And the spontaneous enthusiasm his offer had generated was written all over her now smiling face.

'Good. Then, Herr Häberlein, we'll take her with us. She can look around while we go over those blueprints one more time.'

It was a highly relieved Herr Häberlein who now nodded his unqualified agreement with that suggestion.

'Now you two just wait here, while I tend to a few matters in my study. I won't be long.'

It was a half-hour later when Werner Heisenberg returned to the living-room, this time wearing an overcoat and scarf. Fräulein Schmidt was with him, and she went to the closet to retrieve the overcoats of the two visitors. The Herr Professor took one of the coats from her, insisting that he help Felicitas into it. He also insisted that she sit beside him in the front of his BMW. He made a U-turn on the Donaustrasse and went back two blocks to the main road leading through town, where he took a left, heading back in the direction of Hechingen. When he reached the Y in the road on the outskirts of town, he swung the BMW almost 180 degrees, totally reversing course, but this time on the road which formed the other side of that Y. The road began to climb steeply almost immediately, and Heisenberg had to shift back to second gear. Five minutes later, the road began to level out and a few minutes after that Heisenberg drew the car to a halt in front of the church – the Schlosskirche, he explained to Felicitas.

When they got out of the car and began walking toward the castle church, she could see why it had been built there: the location was absolutely breathtaking. For as they continued to walk, skirting around the church through the graveyard, one could see that less than fifty metres behind the church the ground fell away almost perpendicularly. When they reached the edge of the cliff, they were greeted by a spectacular view of the lower part of the town of Haigerloch and the river it straddled, a hundred metres below the rim of the cliff where they now stood. The moment was made even more dramatic by the fact that just then a light snow began to fall.

'You see, Fräulein Burckhardt,' Heisenberg said, 'you Swiss do not have a monopoly on spectacular scenery. And this is nothing in comparison to what we have to offer in the village where I grew up in Bavaria.' There was an unmistakable note of pride in the voice of the German scientist.

Then he turned abruptly and began to walk toward a small box-like structure located in the middle of the graveyard, and which had the appearance of the place where the caretaker kept his gardening equipment. But this was soon belied by the fact that the door which blocked their entrance was made of heavy steel. The padlock on it hung loose, however. Heisenberg managed to swing open the door with great ease, and, gallantly bowing to his comely visitor from Switzerland, said: 'Welcome to my humble place of work.'

They found themselves at the top of a concrete stairwell, very wide and well lit. With Heisenberg leading the way, they now descended about twenty metres. At the bottom of the stairwell there was another steel door, and beside it a buzzer, which Heisenberg now pressed. The door was opened by a man in uniform bearing the insignia of the Waffen SS. A submachine gun was slung carelessly over his right shoulder. Upon seeing Heisenberg, he drew himself to attention.

Heisenberg addressed him immediately. 'Hans, you know Herr Häberlein, of course. And this young lady is one of my students who is going to be visiting us for an hour or so.'

And then he took the arm of Felicitas and stepped into the huge cavern which for centuries had served as a wine cellar where priests from the castle church laid down their sacramental wines. Situated in the middle of it was a concrete pit about ten feet in diameter. Within the pit hung a heavy metal shield covering the top of a thick metal cylinder. The latter contained a pot-shaped vessel, also of heavy metal, about four feet below the floor level. Atop the vessel was a metal frame.[21]

'Here it is,' Heisenberg said to Felicitas, as they now stood

---

21 This description is identical with that found in Boris T. Pash, *The Alsos Mission* (New York, 1969), pp. 206ff. Pash was the man General Groves, the ranking military officer in charge of the Manhattan Project (the codename of the American project aimed at developing an atomic bomb), had put in charge of intelligence in that area. Pash and his men discovered the Haigerloch cave containing the German reactor on 23 April 1945. See also Rhodes, *The Making of the Atomic Bomb*, pp. 609–10; Malcolm C. MacPherson, *Time Bomb: Fermi, Heisenberg, and the Race for the Atomic Bomb* (New York, 1986), pp. 275–6.

beside it. 'My uranium machine.' This was the phrase that German scientists used at that time to describe an atomic pile. Then Heisenberg went on to explain at length the details of his 'machine', pointing out the key components as he went along.

'The liquid in the vessel is, of course, the moderator, heavy water. One and a half tons of it. The fuel consists of 664 cubes of metallic uranium. They are attached to seventy-eight chains which are suspended from the metal shield which you see there on top of the pile, and then hang down into the water. Simple yet elegant, wouldn't you agree, Fräulein Burckhardt?'

The young Swiss scientist stood absolutely mesmerized by what stood in front of her. 'Oh, yes Herr Professor.'

Then she asked the question: 'What level of neutron multiplication does it achieve?'

Heisenberg hesitated. But then, finally, he answered: 'Just seven-fold, I am afraid.'

'What level is necessary to produce a sustained chain reaction?' Felicitas was referring here to the process she had described a year earlier over dinner at her parents' place, where the bombardment of a uranium atom by neutrons could release energy in a geometric progression − 1, 2, 4, 8, 16, 32, 64 . . . 67108864, 134217728 and so forth, in the form of an atomic 'explosion'.

Heisenberg hesitated again before answering, but again he did respond. 'One that is substantially higher. But we now know we can achieve that by simply increasing the size of the reactor by 50 per cent.' Then: 'That's why we are here today, to go over the blueprints for the construction of the much larger concrete pit to house the new reactor. In fact, Herr Häberlein and I must get to work. While we do, perhaps you might like to go to my little office in the back and read an article I just wrote on fission cross-sections for fast neutrons. It's not published yet, and the way things look now, it probably won't be for a while. But it might give you some ideas for your dissertation.'

The audience was over.

For the next hour Felicitas Burckhardt sat in Professor Heisenberg's office while he and Herr Häberlein, now joined by two technicians in white coats who had stayed in the background until now, huddled over various sets of blueprints which they laid out on a long wooden table beside the reactor. The typescript of Heisenberg's article lay in her lap. But it lay there unread. For Felicitas Burckhardt sat there totally stunned by the import of what she had just seen and heard.

The Germans were not even close to developing an atomic bomb!

She would of course ask Herr Häberlein how long he estimated it would take to construct that new reactor that had to be 50 per cent larger than the existing one. But she knew that in any case, it would be a matter not of weeks, or even a few months, but most probably many months. Now, all she had to do was get back to Peter with this information. And after that, they all had to get back home. Quickly. Before their luck began to run out.

It was just after three o'clock on that afternoon of 18 January 1945 when Professor Heisenberg came back into his office to fetch her. She was shivering from a combination of excitement, mounting apprehension, and the penetrating cold of the cavern. Heisenberg noticed this. 'Girl,' he said, 'I think we must get you home. I'm sure once you are there Herr Häberlein can provide you with some hot coffee, and perhaps even a cognac.'

When they emerged from the cavern into the graveyard of the Schlosskirche, the weather that greeted them added to her increasing discomfort. For now it was snowing, and snowing heavily. Ten minutes later Werner Heisenberg pulled his BMW to a stop in front of the Häberleins' house on the Donaustrasse. For a moment Felicitas was afraid that he might invite her to his home further down the street for that coffee and cognac he had mentioned, but Heisenberg's mind seemed to have shifted to other things. As they now stood beside his car, Heisenberg's farewell was still friendly, but curt, and cautionary.

'I understand from Wolfgang's letter that you are travelling in the company of two others. I am afraid they have made the trip in vain. I wish all of you a safe return. I trust that once you are back you will do or say nothing that might lead to trouble for those of us who will remain here in Haigerloch. Don't you agree, Herr Häberlein?'

'Totally, Herr Professor You can count on it.'

'Give my very best to Wolfgang Pauli, Fräulein Burckhardt. And tell him that I look forward to seeing him soon, under happier circumstances. Perhaps back where we nuclear physicists all got our start. Here in Germany. In Göttingen.'

Then the proud German professor got back into his BMW and drove off. Felicitas Burckhardt and Herr Häberlein hurried through the falling snow to the front door of his house. His wife was waiting inside, and immediately addressed him. 'Walter,' she said, 'come with me. I must talk to you.' When he seemed to hesitate, she added: 'Now!'

As they disappeared down the hall and into the kitchen, Peter Burckhardt came out from the adjacent living-room. He saw that she was pale and shivering, and was immediately alarmed. 'What happened, Felicitas? Is something wrong?'

'No, no. It's just . . .' And she could not continue.

'You look frozen. Come into the living-room. I'll get you something hot to drink, and then you can tell us what happened. Are you sure everything's all right?'

'I'm sure. It was just all of a sudden too much. And now that I think of it, Peter, I haven't had anything to eat all day.'

'I'll fix that.'

Her brother headed for the kitchen, and Felicitas went into the living-room to join Nancy Reichman, who was anxiously waiting for her. Minutes later the three of them sat huddled together on the sofa in the living-room while Felicitas Burckhardt told them what had happened. And she concluded with the words: 'So es war alles für die Katz!'

This prompted an immediate response from Nancy Reichman. 'How can you say that it has all been just a waste of time? We now know that we don't need Heisenberg. From what you have just explained, if I understand it correctly, they are hopelessly behind. The Germans have now finally and irrevocably lost the war. I can't even begin to imagine how Mr Dulles will react when he hears this.'

'If he hears it. Did you see what is happening to the weather? We could get stuck here for days.'

'Now Felicitas, you're just over-excited. And you need something to eat. You've done your job remarkably well. Leave our getting home to me.'

Just then Herr Häberlein reappeared in the living-room, went straight to Peter Burckhardt and drew him aside. 'My wife has asked me to talk to you, Herr Doktor. She is very upset. She says that because of you we are all going to end up either in a concentration camp or before a firing squad. She wants you out of here.'

'How? There's no bus back until tomorrow morning.'

'That's one of the problems. Forget about the bus. We know the Schwarzwald. With snow like this, there is no way that the bus will run tomorrow. By dawn there will be a metre of snow on the road up by the Feldberg. It will take them days before they can remove it. I'm not sure there are enough men and machines available now to even manage that. You must realize that this country is on the edge of chaos.'

'So what are we supposed to do?'

'There's a train that still runs once a day between Stuttgart and Freiburg im Breisgau, where it connects with the main line between Frankfurt and the Badische Bahnhof in Basel. It stops at Horb, which is exactly sixteen kilometres north of here. It leaves at seven-ten in the morning. I will take you there in the van in time to make tomorrow's train.'

'What about the snow?'

'I've got chains. And the problem is not the snow *here*. We'll get enough, but nothing like they will get in the high country to the south. Don't worry. I'll get you to Horb. And then you are on your own, Herr Doktor. There are limits to what any of us can do. And I tell you, no I warn you: my wife has reached her limit. In fact, she just told me that she does not want to have anything more to do with you. You told us your sister needs food, so I will be bringing you supper here in the living-room as soon as I can. It will be just soup and bread. You can stay down here as long as you want, but I suggest you go to bed early. I will show you where your rooms are now. I want you all ready to leave by six tomorrow morning.'

He took Peter upstairs, showed him the two spare bedrooms, brought him back to the living-room, and then disappeared back into the kitchen. As Peter explained the new situation to his sister and Nancy Reichman, they could periodically hear the sound of Frau Häberlein's voice — loud, shrill, hysterical — as she continued to work on him back in the kitchen.

Once Peter had finished, his sister immediately asked: 'You don't really think that we can simply go to Freiburg and then take the train to Basel, do you?'

'Of course not.'

'Then what do you think?'

'We will get off in Lörrach.'

'And then what?'

'I'm not sure. The original plan is out, of course.' That original plan had called for them to follow the same route out of Germany that they had taken in, getting off the bus in Fahrnau where they would wait in his uncle's house until darkness fell, after which all four of them would have cycled to the Rhine to meet up with a Swiss barge headed upstream towards safe haven in the port of Basel at the pre-appointed hour of 10 pm. The fourth cyclist would have been Heisenberg, and his bicycle, one borrowed from Onkel Ernst. Now all of this had been turned topsy-turvy: no Heisenberg, no bus to Fahrnau, and even if there had been a bus, there was no way that they could have cycled to Weil am Rhein through this amount of snow, either tomorrow or even most probably for the rest of the week.

Peter Burckhardt had arranged for a back-up plan. But, he now concluded, this was hardly the time or place to discuss it.

The soup and bread arrived a half-hour later, and even though it was getting dark outside and in, Herr Häberlein insisted that there be no lights on in the living-room lest they attract attention. In Haigerloch the use of living-rooms was usually reserved for entertaining guests, now a very unusual event, and thus one which could arouse the curiosity of neighbours. So they ate in the dark. Häberlein did turn on the radio, however, and tuned in to the German national sender, which at least provided classical music for the next two hours. Then it started to get very cold in the living-room, which was obviously not heated except for special occasions, and it seemed sure now that Frau Häberlein considered this occasion anything but special. At seven o'clock Peter Burckhardt suggested that they go to bed, no matter what the hour, simply to keep warm. And the sooner they got some sleep the better. Tomorrow would start very early, and might end very late.

It started at 5.15 when Peter Burckhardt knocked on the door of the girls' bedroom. At six, they sat assembled in the Häberlein kitchen, sipping the coffee that Herr Häberlein had prepared. His wife was nowhere to be either seen or heard. Shortly after six they emerged from the house. It was barely dawn. In the early light they could see that there was at least half a metre of new snow on the ground, and it was still coming down. The engine in Häberlein's van was already running. He let out the clutch a split second after Peter Burckhardt had closed the door on his side of the van, and after sliding around a U-turn, headed out to the main road, where he turned right, driving slowly through the lower town of Haigerloch. It was still completely deserted. On the northern outskirts of town the road rose rather sharply as they emerged from the valley floor. Twice the wheels of the van began to spin out of control, but then the chains caught, and they were off again, soon on level terrain, a condition which Herr Häberlein assured them would now continue all the way into Horb. Six kilometres later they went through the village of Weildorf, and five kilometres after that, Emfinger.

'How much further?' Peter Burckhardt asked. His watch indicated that it was 6.25.

'Another five kilometres. We should reach the train station in twenty minutes. Unless we get stuck.'

They were again completely surrounded by the countryside, proceeding at a careful 30 kilometres an hour. There were no tyre tracks whatsoever on the road, meaning that theirs was the first vehicle through the snow, which was growing deeper by the

minute. Häberlein kept the van in the middle of the road as best
he could, which was not easy: it was becoming increasingly
difficult to see out, since the wipers were no longer able to
completely clear the snow from the windscreen.

'Do you see that little bridge up ahead? It must take us over a
small stream. Would you mind stopping on it for just a brief
moment?' Peter Burckhardt now asked.

'That would not be a good idea,' Häberlein replied. 'In snow
like this the idea is to keep the vehicle moving. Once you stop,
you might not be able to get going again. Especially on a bridge
where the surface is normally icy.'

'Nevertheless it is very important that you stop, Herr Häberlein.' The tone of his voice left no room for further argument.

As the van gradually slowed, Peter Burckhardt opened his
backpack and withdrew the leather pouch from it. The moment
the van had stopped, he quickly left the van and moved to the
railing on the side of the bridge. He put the pouch on the railing,
and, while holding it with one hand, yanked on the red string
which protruded from it with the other. There was a hiss, and
then the pouch began to disintegrate in a burst of blue flame.
Peter Burckhardt involuntarily flinched backwards toward the
car. It was all over within seconds. Burckhardt then took one of
his leather gloves and flicked at the remnants of the pouch until
they had all fallen into the stream below, one which was still
flowing, though barely. All that was left to see was a black scar on
the bridge railing. When he got back into the car nobody said a
word. They all knew that what they had just witnessed was a
signal that they were getting near the danger zone of the German
railroad system, where suspicious eyes at checkpoints were
ever-present, on the lookout for deserters or potential saboteurs
in the employ of the approaching Allied armies. Häberlein soon
had the van moving again, and at 6.50 pulled up in front of the
station in the centre of the town of Horb. No one took even the
slightest notice of the town's romantic half-timbered houses, so
typical of the Black Forest. The two Burckhardts and Nancy
Reichman now scrambled out of the van, while Häberlein
remained behind the wheel with the motor running. There were

no handshakes this time. Once they were out, Häberlein just waved goodbye, once, and immediately pulled away.

Inside the small station, Peter Burckhardt approached the ticket window. He had decided to just purchase tickets to Freiburg. That was no doubt the destination of most passengers along this feeder line, and thus one that would not arouse any particular attention. The train arrived twenty minutes late, no doubt due to the snow, but no one even looked at them while they were waiting in the station, nor after they had boarded the train. They found a second-class compartment that was only occupied by two older women, both dressed in black, sisters as their conversation soon revealed. After greeting them with the usual 'Guete Tag', the three who had boarded the train in Horb kept their silence. Peter read the Stuttgart morning newspaper which he had bought at the kiosk in the station. He had bought two magazines for the girls, but for the most part during the next three hours they just sat and looked out of the window. The train pulled into the Bahnhof in Freiburg at 12.20. After climbing out of their compartment, they immediately hurried down the Bahnsteig to the main hall of the station. The huge 'Zeittaffel' that hung there indicated that the next train south, coming from Frankfurt am Main and bound for Lörrach, left in twenty minutes, and that it was on time. The one after that left five hours later.

There was a queue in front of the ticket counter, and it was 12.27 before Peter Burckhardt reached the front of it. 'Dreimal Lörrach, Zweite Klasse, einfach,' he said, and pushed a fifty-Mark note under the window.

'Bahnsteig seven. And you'd better hurry,' the woman behind it advised as she pushed three tickets and his change back to him.

They ran towards platform seven, and as they approached it they could see why they had been advised to hurry. There was another queue, this one caused by two armed men in uniform who stood on both sides of a gate leading onto the platform. They were checking documents.

The train from Frankfurt was just pulling in when it was Peter Burckhardt's turn.

He handed the guard on the right his military papers which identified him as a sergeant in the border guard stationed in Lörrach. He also gave him his travel papers, indicating that he was on a forty-eight-hour compassionate leave to attend a relative's funeral in Trilltingen, and was allowed to travel in civilian clothes. He also handed over the three tickets he had just bought.

'Where's Trilltingen, Sergeant?'

'Just outside Haigerloch.'

The guard then looked at the tickets.

'Who are the other two?'

Burckhardt pointed to the two women standing behind him. 'My two sisters.' They now stepped forward and handed him their ID cards.

'I don't understand something,' the guard now said. 'Why are these tickets issued here, and why are they one-way?'

'Because we came up to Haigerloch from Lörrach by bus yesterday, through Titisee and Feldberg, and had planned to take it back today. But . . .'

The guard interrupted him. 'The snowstorm.' Then: 'In Ordnung.' He handed them back their papers and turned his attention to the next person in line saying: 'Ausweis, bitte.'

The train was packed; it was standing room only. In contrast to the bus they had taken into the Black Forest, the majority of the passengers were not old and they were not civilians. They were mostly men in uniform, and they were either very young – some looked barely sixteen – or very old for soldiers – men with grey hair and stooped shoulders. Germany was scraping the very bottom of the barrel.

And this time, they were not ignored, especially the two girls. Twice young soldiers swaying next to them in the corridor tried to strike up a conversation, and when rebuffed did not look at all pleased. But the trip to Lörrach was mercifully short: fifty-nine minutes. This train did not go on to the Badische Bahnhof in Basel, so when it stopped at Lörrach-Stetten it was the end of the line, and everybody got out. There was just one platform and it was outside. What greeted them outside was nothing short of a howling winter blizzard. It had brought everything to a halt; there was no traffic whatsoever on the streets.

The two Burckhardts and their American companion, like most of the passengers who had disembarked, now began to trudge through the snow towards the centre of town. Nancy Reichman waited until she was sure they were finally out of earshot of potentially dangerous eavesdroppers − for the first time that day − before finally asking the question: 'How are we going to get home, Peter?'

'We can't get back by water. Getting from here to Weil am Rhein on foot today is out. Even if we could get to Fahrnau somehow, and go into hiding there until the storm clears and a new rendezvous could be arranged, I wouldn't do it. We've already exposed Onkel Ernst and Tante Emily to enough potential risk. So we are going to go back into Switzerland by land.'

'Where?' his sister now asked. 'That border is sealed by barbed wire and land-mines. Everybody knows that, Peter.'

'One place is not. I'll show you.'

They were soon on the Basler Strasse, the main street of the frontier town of Lörrach, with streetcar tracks running down the middle. Until the end of August 1939, the tram that ran down these tracks, the No. 6, had been part of the city of Basel's transport system and took passengers from Lörrach to the centre of Basel. You barely noticed that you were going from one country into another except for a cursory border check. You got off the tram, showed your ID, and then got right back on the same tram a few minutes later, which then continued down the middle of the same street, except that the street was now called the Aussere Baselstrasse and it was on Swiss territory. That border crossing was the only one in the region that had remained open during the entire war. To be sure, the tram had stopped running. Barriers like those at railroad crossings had been erected on both sides of the line that marked the border, with a narrow no-man's-land of about twenty metres in between. And there were guardhouses beside these barriers, but no barbed wire and no land-mines. This was, of course, the same border crossing that General Walter Schellenberg had used almost two years earlier.

At Basler Strasse 90, about 100 metres from that border crossing, there was a café and restaurant 'Zum Kranz'. It was about 2.45 when the three of them entered it. They ordered not only coffee, but also Wurst and bread. Peter Burckhardt also ordered a beer. They wanted to see his ration coupons before taking the order, and fortunately Section 5 had also thought of that and supplied him with some.

At exactly 2.55 Peter Burckhardt excused himself, telling his companions not to worry, that he would be back almost immediately. At precisely three o'clock on the second, he walked across the Basler Strasse and upon reaching the other side, turned, and walked straight back. Then, standing once again in front of the restaurant, he looked intently down the street. It was still snowing, although it seemed to be letting up. Even so, at precisely 3.05, again on the second, he saw the light blink three times. It came from a window on the third floor of the first building on the left on the other side of the Swiss border, an apartment building. Upon seeing it, Burckhardt immediately went back into the restaurant, where he ordered another beer and a half carafe of the local Badische white wine for his sister and his American friend. He also paid the bill.

Then it happened very quickly. At two minutes to four, he told the two young women that they were going to leave immediately. They were to leave behind both their backpacks and the overcoats which they had hung on the rack just inside the door.

'When we get onto the street, I want you both at my side. All right?'

They nodded.

'We're going to walk briskly toward the border. You're going to hear an explosion. It will be on the left side, behind the German guardhouse. There's a parking lot where the border guards inspect the trucks coming into Germany from Switzerland. It will go off when we are about twenty metres this side of the crossing. When you hear it, run straight ahead, keeping to this side of the street, duck under the barrier, and then keep running until you are on the Swiss side. That barrier will be open.'

When they stepped out of the restaurant onto the street, dusk was falling, and, with the snow still coming down, visibility was becoming more limited by the minute. Yet it was too early for the lights which illuminated the border crossing at night to come on. The moment had been carefully chosen, though nobody had even thought of factoring in the possibility of snow.

There were just two German guards standing outside the guardhouse in the falling snow. When the explosion went off it sounded like mortar fire. They turned in the direction of the blast and went into a crouch, their submachine guns at the ready. That was when Peter Burckhardt grasped the arms of his companions and said 'Go!' All three accelerated immediately from a walk to a dash. They had almost reached the barrier on the German side when the second explosion went off. Now the border guards dived forward for better cover in front of the grey cinder-block guardhouse. That was when the three ducked under the first barrier. The third blast came while they were sprinting across the no-man's-land in front of the second barrier, which now opened.

A man stood there waiting on the other side. It was Wilhelm Lützelschwab. As soon as they were beside him he bellowed: 'Down!' Then again: 'Down!' As they dropped to the snow-covered street, so did he. He later told them that he expected that they might be the target of a hail of machine-gun fire from the other side of the border, but it never came. Confused shouts were heard from over there, but no gunfire. Soon they were surrounded by a half-dozen uniformed Swiss soldiers, plus four of Lützelschwab's men in plain clothes, and in the middle of that massive protection the four of them walked to the two black Citroëns which were waiting 100 metres further down the Aussere Baselstrasse. Two men emerged to greet them: Captain Max Waibel of Section 5 of the General Staff of the Swiss High Command, and Mr Allen Dulles of America's Office of Strategic Services.

There were handshakes, pats on the back, and kisses exchanged, while the policeman Lützelschwab looked on proudly. Finally he stepped forward to say a word to Peter Burckhardt. 'We really showed them how these things are done, didn't we?' It was not clear whether he meant just the Germans or also the

Americans in their midst. But it did evoke a spontaneous answer from Burckhardt. 'I never thought I'd ever be pleased to see you, Wilhelm, but let me tell you, I shall never forget seeing your face and then hearing you shout "Down" for the rest of my days. I knew then that we were home for sure. Thank you, sir.' And he gave him a military salute.

Then they all got into the cars and drove off, Lützelschwab and his men in one car and Waibel and Dulles squeezed beside the driver in the front seat of the second, with the three 'returnees' in the back.

'Where's Heisenberg?' was the first question put by Dulles.

'He decided not to come,' Peter Burckhardt answered. 'But it doesn't matter. My sister will explain why.'

That evening all of the principals whose wartime espionage activities had been assigned the codename 'Swiss Account' by OSS headquarters in Washington gathered for dinner in the Schützenhaus restaurant: Allen Dulles and Captain Waibel; Per Jacobsson and Peter Burckhardt; Felicitas Burckhardt and Nancy Reichman. The final toast of the evening was given at eleven o'clock by the master spy, Allen Dulles: 'To the Swiss Account, and your remarkable achievement of developing at enormous personal risk what is undoubtedly the most significant single piece of intelligence of the war. My country extends to you all our eternal gratitude.'

Peter Burckhardt drove Allen Dulles back to his hotel, and then took Nancy Reichman home to her apartment on the Augustinergasse. When they arrived, Nancy turned to kiss him goodnight. He stopped her, and then took her hand in his and said: 'Would you mind if I came up for just a few minutes? I know you are exhausted, Nancy, but . . .'

'Of course, Peter.'

Once they were inside and had taken off their coats, Peter Burckhardt again took her hand in his and said: 'Felicitas told me that you are going home.'

'Yes.'

'Please don't.'

She said nothing.

'I want you to stay, Nancy, because I want to marry you. Will you?'

'But Peter, you know I'm Jewish,' she blurted out, now on the edge of tears. 'What would your family think?'

'You know what Felicitas thinks. And where my parents are concerned, I have fully discussed this matter with them. Their position is very simple. They are as Christian as you are Jewish. But they love you so much that they will welcome you as you are. They told me to tell you that they would be proud if you would now also bear the Burckhardt name.'

'Oh, Peter!' And now she could not hold back the tears.

Taking her into his arms, Peter continued: 'They also want us to be married in the family chapel in Benken, Nancy. Will you?'

'Oh, yes, Peter, but with one provision. That when the war is over we take a second honeymoon in America, and have a second wedding by a rabbi in my parents' home. Then they can share our joy, and can also welcome you into our family.'

They were married one month later in the small chapel in the grounds of the Benkener Schloss, ensuring that this account of the Swiss Account should have a happy ending.

Epilogue

The activities of all those figures associated with the Swiss Account continued of course until the end of the war, and during this period two episodes in particular stand out.

The first involved Allen Dulles and Captain Max Waibel. Through the intermediary of the Swiss intelligence officer, Dulles established contact with the commander of the German armed forces fighting the Allies in Italy, Field Marshal Albert Kesselring, as well as the chief of the SS units there, General Karl Wolff. The operation was given the codename 'Sunrise'. Meetings arranged by Waibel at various places in Switzerland culminated in the German surrender of all their forces in Italy, one million men, on 2 May 1945. Of Waibel's role in this, Dulles later wrote: 'As we proceeded to develop our secret and precarious relations with the German generals early in 1945, we would have been thwarted at every step if we had not had the help of Waibel in facilitating contacts and communications and in arranging the delicate frontier crossings which had to be carried out under conditions of complete secrecy. In all his actions Waibel was serving the interest of peace.'[22] After the war ended, Waibel remained in the Swiss army, served for a while as a military attaché at the Swiss legation in Washington, and eventually became Chief of Infantry. He retired with the highest military rank available in Switzerland in peacetime, that of

---

22 Allen Dulles, *The Secret Surrender*, p. 27.

Oberstdivisionär. But then his luck ran out. Jozef Garlinski, an expert on the subject of espionage in Europe during World War II, describes Waibel's latter days as follows: 'After leaving the service he gave himself over to his beloved horse riding, organizing and running clubs for children. He also went on the board of directors of a private bank, unaware that this bank was engaged in illegal and dishonest transactions. When this became common kn wledge Max Waibel, after trying to repay the shareholders, took his own life on 21 January, 1971.'[23] In fact, this decent and brave soldier was hounded to death by the local press and the ungrateful citizenry of Lucerne. Against the background of such behaviour, sometimes − even with the best will in the world − it is difficult to develop a real liking for the Swiss.

The second episode also involved Allen Dulles, and was also related to the desire of one of the warring parties to negotiate a surrender in the spring of 1945. But this time it was the Japanese who sought negotiations with Washington through Dulles. And in this instance the intermediary was not Waibel, but rather the Swedish economist and banker who was attached to the Bank for International Settlements in Basel, Per Jacobsson. Describing the origins of this incident, Jacobsson's biographer (his daughter) writes: 'Per Jacobsson was approached by two Japanese bankers, Kojiro Kitamura, a Board member of the BIS, and Kan Yoshimura, Head of the Exchange Section of the BIS. Would PJ be prepared, as a neutral with good connections, to try to arrange peace for Japan? They were talking on behalf of Lieutenant-General Seigo Okamoto, military attaché in Bern who (through an intermediary) could go directly to Emperor Hirohito. PJ suggested that the right person to approach was Allen Dulles, then head of the European branch of the American OSS, and a close personal friend.'[24]

Dulles picks up the story from there:

In April, 1945, while the battle of Okinawa was at its peak,

23 Jozef Garlinski, *The Swiss Corridor* (London, 1981), pp. 193−4.

24 Erin E. Jacobsson, *A Life for Sound Money, Per Jacobsson, His Biography* (Oxford, 1979), p. 170.

[I was] approached in Switzerland by Japanese army and navy spokesmen there and also by some Japanese officials at the Bank for International Settlements in Basel. They wished to determine whether they could not also take advantage of the secret channels to Washington established for 'Sunrise' to secure peace for Japan. Per Jacobsson, the able Swedish economic advisor at the Basel bank, was brought into these talks, and there was an active exchange of communications between Washington and Bern.

On July 20, 1945, under instruction from Washington, I went to the Potsdam Conference and reported there to Secretary Stimson on what I had learned from Tokyo – they desired to surrender if they could retain the Emperor and the constitution. By this time the news of the Italian surrender and the story of how it had been brought about had been widely publicized in the press: its effect was contagious. Unfortunately, in the case of Japan time ran out on us.[25]

Of course, the Japanese ultimately did surrender in August of 1945, after the US had dropped atomic bombs on Hiroshima and Nagasaki.

Against that historical background, another chronicler of this episode concluded his account of these Swiss negotiations as follows: 'When the fateful day of capitulation came at last Commander Yoshiro Fujimura recalled with chagrin the blindness which had contributed towards his government failure to follow to good advantage the Swiss path of negotiation; and in Zurich Lieutenant General Seigo Okamoto indelibly inscribed his name upon the sacred registers of the samurai by taking his life with his own hand. Both of these men had been involved in the Swiss talks. If there had been a little more time to develop this channel of negotiation, the story of the Japanese surrender might have had a different ending.'[26]

---

25 Allen Dulles, *The Secret Surrender*, pp. 255–6.

26 Robert J.C. Butow, *Japan's Decision to Surrender* (Stanford, 1954), p. 111.

After the war Allen Dulles returned to the United States and remained in private life until 1950, when he once again took up his career as a spy with the newly created Central Intelligence Agency. He became its head in 1953, and remained in that post until 1961. Per Jacobsson remained with the BIS in Basel until 1956 (during which time I got to know him), when he was made managing director of the International Monetary Fund, the world's most prestigious financial post, which he held for the next six years. He wanted to return to Basel upon retirement, but died in 1963 before this final dream could become reality. One final note on Jacobsson: although he travelled extensively in Germany during the war, and had contacts in Berlin at the highest level until the very end of that conflict, my description of his final trip there in January of 1945 is fictitious. Also, although he undoubtedly was fully aware of the dubious role which the BIS was playing during World War II, he never became personally involved in such matters as the secret transfers of looted gold from Germany to Switzerland. He used his post at the BIS exclusively in the cause of peace, and not for the pursuit of either profit or power.

The two generals in this novel, General Henri Guisan and General Walter Schellenberg, could hardly have been cut from more different cloth, so logically they spent their postwar years quite differently. Guisan, upon retirement as commander-in-chief of the Swiss armed forces on 20 August 1945, became a national monument who remained by far and away the most admired man in Switzerland until the day of his death in 1960 at the age of eighty-six. His biographer, in the last sentence of his exhaustive study of this man and his career, summed up why he received such adoration: 'The General's ultimate contribution to his nation was that under his command the army played a decisive role in maintaining the political and cultural independence of Switzerland.'[27]

By contrast, SS General Walter Schellenberg remained the slippery, elusive character until the end. He managed to travel to

27   Gautschi, *General Henri Guisan*, p. 765.

Stockholm, purportedly on a peace mission, just forty-eight hours before the German unconditional surrender on 7 May 1945. He subsequently asked for asylum in Sweden, and was given it thanks to the intervention of Count Bernadotte, whom he had helped to get a certain number of Scandinavian political prisoners out of German hands. His stay in Sweden was short, since the Allies demanded his extradition, so by June 1945 he found himself back in Germany. In January 1948 he came up before an American military tribunal, and was sentenced to six years' imprisonment, including his confinement since June 1945. It was one of the lightest sentences given to a leading figure in the Third Reich. By this time, Schellenberg was a sick man, and was released from prison as early as June 1951, by an act of mercy. Jozef Garlinski picks up from there: 'He then got in contact with his wartime associate, Roger Masson, and appealed to his generosity. Masson . . . facilitated a secret entry into Switzerland and introduced him to a friend, Dr Lang, who hid him not far from Romont. However the Swiss police very soon found him and ordered him to leave the country, so he crossed the Italian frontier and settled in the small town of Pallanza, on Lake Maggiore. There, with the help of a German journalist, he began to write his memoirs, but the work was constantly interrupted by a liver complaint, from which he had suffered since childhood. He died in Turin on 31 March 1952, aged barely forty-one.'[28] Schellenberg's SS associate, Rittmeister Hans Wilhelm Eggen, managed to sneak into Switzerland in an ambulance in the confusion of the final days of the war. He was picked up by the Swiss police almost immediately, and held in custody until 1 October 1945. On that day the Swiss authorities shoved him across the border into Italy. Then he simply disappeared.[29]

Roger Masson, the head of Swiss Intelligence in World War II, who fondly referred to Schellenberg as 'Schelli', paid dearly for that friendship. In September of 1945 he gave an interview to a reporter from the *Chicago Daily News* and told him about his

---

28 Garlinski, *The Swiss Corridor*, p. 196.

29 Braunschweig, *Geheimer Draht nach Berlin*, p. 322.

meetings with the SS general. Thanks to this, what had previously been a top secret, known only to the highest-ranking political and military authorities in Switzerland, was no longer such. Two members of the Swiss parliament now attacked Masson, demanding an inquiry. The investigation was carried out by Judge Couchepin, who rendered his opinion in January of 1946, completely clearing Roger Masson of all suspicions and wrongful acts. Nevertheless, he was now a marked man, and, as in the later case of his former associate Max Waibel, Masson was now subject to constant harassment from the Swiss press and citizenry. He could not defend himself, for he was bound by the secrecy of his service even after he had left the army and gone into retirement. He died in 1967 an embittered man.[30]

Wilhelm Lützelschwab was a real-life person, although I must confess that I have taken some liberties with him. There is no evidence that he ever resorted to beating confessions out of prisoners and a few other things that Swiss policemen aren't supposed to do. The real-life Lützelschwab actually left his post as head of Basel's political police in 1943, and was promoted to the position of Erster Staatsanwalt, or chief prosecuting attorney for the half-canton of Baselstadt, although he did not give up his counterespionage activities and was often called in to help in special cases. In 1945, at the age of forty, he resigned from government service, deciding that it was time to have a go at the private sector. He joined the management of a Swiss life insurance firm, 'Pax'. Predictably, he ended up as head of the company. He died a very successful and respected man in May 1981.[31]

The two professors, Karl Barth and Walter Heisenberg, like the two generals, could hardly have been more dissimilar, although they did have one thing in common: both, in their early years, had taught at the ancient university in Göttingen. Heisenberg was captured by the Americans at a lake cottage in Bavaria to which he had fled shortly before the advance team of Amer-

---

30 Garlinski, *The Swiss Corridor*, p. 192.

31 Braunschweig, *Geheimer Draht nach Berlin*, p. 36.

ican army specialists reached Haigerloch on 23 April 1945.[32] There they found the now abandoned atomic pile in the cave in the cliff behind the church; construction on the larger pile had barely begun, confirming the on-the-spot analysis which had been made by Felicitas Burckhardt three months earlier. After being transported to England, where he was held for a brief time, Heisenberg was allowed to return to his old university, where he resumed his nuclear research under British supervision. In February 1947 he was interviewed in Göttingen by a reporter from the *Washington Post*, where it was reported that he had received an offer from the Russians. According to Tom Bower, in his book *The Paperclip Conspiracy: The Hunt for the Nazi Scientists*, upon hearing this 'the Pentagon now feared that he and eleven other German nuclear scientists, including Otto Hahn, would be recruited by Moscow. To protect American security, the Joint Intelligence Committee (of the Joint Chiefs of Staff) recommended that the nuclear scientists be brought to America, but not employed. The British, annoyed that Truman would not share America's atomic secrets, rejected the proposal.' So Heisenberg was allowed to remain at Göttingen. For his version of some of the events described in this novel, see his article in the June 1968 *Bulletin of Atomic Scientists*, 'The Third Reich and the Atomic Bomb'.

Karl Barth died on 10 December 1968, and the twentieth century lost one of its towering intellectual figures. But it also lost a man who had an enormous zest for life, and enjoyed it to the hilt. His biographer, Eberhard Busch, in his superb book on the life and theology of Barth,[33] relates that he spent one of the final evenings with his family, listening to Mozart, smoking his pipe, and drinking some wine. At the end they all sang Advent chorales and some children's songs, including one of Karl Barth's

---

32 See Rhodes, *The Making of the Atomic Bomb*, pp. 609–10; General Leslie M. Groves, *Now It Can Be Told: The Story of the Manhattan Project* (New York, 1962), pp. 240–4; Malcolm G. MacPherson, *Time Bomb: Fermi, Heisenberg, and the Race for the Atomic Bomb* (New York, 1986), pp. 275–90.

33 Busch, *Karl Barth*, p. 497.

favourites which contains the words:

> *Now I gladly go to sleep,*
> *I've enjoyed the day*
> *God has truly cared for me.*

In what contrast this stands to the bitter ends suffered by some of the other 'real' characters in this book, especially those who had chosen to spend their life, not in the service of God, but in the shadowy, amoral underworld of state intelligence.

Which brings me finally to the fictional characters in this story. There were really only three major ones: Peter Burckhardt, Felicitas Burckhardt and Nancy Reichman. Felicitas Burckhardt, the lovely and refreshing Felicitas, never married. She stuck to her academic career and ended up as the most ravishing professor ever to grace the halls of the ancient university of Basel.

A year after the war ended, Peter Burckhardt resigned from the Bank for International Settlements, and accepted an offer from his father (also a fictional character) to join the management of the New York branch of the Swiss Bank Corporation. He eventually became head of that operation (showing once again that nepotism is not all bad). He retired in 1980 and moved to California with his dear wife, Nancy, where they bought a vineyard in the Dry Creek Valley of Sonoma County. They produce both an excellent Cabernet Sauvignon and a Chardonnay (very similar to those of the Jordan winery) and bottle it under the label 'Domaine Burckhardt' — a label which, if you examine it carefully, carries both the Swiss and American flags in the upper left-hand corner.